The House of Clementine

The House of Clementine

by Gill James

The Red Telephone

British Library Cataloguing in Publication Data

A Record of this Publication is available from the British Library

ISBN 978-1-914199-48-6

This edition published 2024 by *The Red Telephone*
Manchester, England

Contents

CHAPTER ONE

"It's definitely a miracle," said Rozia. "I really hadn't dared to hope for this much."

Kaleem had to agree. Petri was sitting in the shade. Full sunshine might be a bit much for her, yet, even with the magic of the medicine on Zandra. She was weaving a daisy chain. Seven months ago, when they'd first come to Zandra, she could hardly stand the gentle light of a low-level electric bulb.

"She's doing well," said Kaleem. "It's nice to see her looking happy." He remembered the first time he met her. The poor child had been in constant pain. Now she seemed like almost any other child.

Rozia touched his arm. "I really am grateful. You know that, don't you? To you. And the Zandrians."

Kaleem shrugged. "There have to be some perks about being the Peace Child." He cringed inwardly at his own words. He never liked to admit to this role. He wasn't really doing much at the moment in any case. He felt a bit guilty that he had such a generous allowance from both Zandra and Terrestra and that even Zenoto invited him back frequently. He wasn't actually doing any work for anyone at the moment. Sure, he had to keep his languages and his knowledge of other cultures up but this was so much of his nature now that he would do this even if he wasn't paid.

"This has been lovely," said Rozia. "But we shouldn't push our luck." She turned to her stepdaughter. "Come on little missy. Time to go."

Petri grimaced. "Oh. Do we have to?"

It looked as if there was going to be an argument. It was good to see Petri behaving like any other kid.

"Yes, we do," said Rozia. She shook her head and glanced up at Kaleem. "I don't want to take any risks. This is the longest she's been out in daylight."

"I'm sure she'll be fine."

Rozia bit her lip and frowned.

Kaleem touched her arm. "They are good, you know, the medics here."

"I know. I can't help worrying, though." Rozia started gathering up her things. "Come on then, Petri."

"Oh." The little girl began to pout. "I like it out here with Kaleem."

"Kaleem has to go as well. He's got work to do."

He didn't want to go. He just wanted to stay here forever and stare at her. The woman who would be the love of his life forever, no matter what happened. Even if she eventually found herself another man. She was some sort of angel or saint. He remembered how good she'd been with the Adulkis. She'd been so patient with these difficult, both physically strong and strong-willed adults who'd behaved like children and they'd loved her. She'd forgiven him for the really horrid way he'd treated her and she'd understood that he'd only left her because he thought he was a danger to her. Now she was taking so much care of a child that wasn't her own. On top of all that she was as beautiful as ever. The accident hadn't left any permanent scars – not any that showed, in any case. It was a surprise – and a relief – to him that she was on her own.

"Come on then," said Rozia, grabbing Petri's hand.

"I'll walk with you to the transporter station."

Rozia nodded. "That will be nice."

Petri took Kaleem's hand. "Now you two are joined together, through me."

If only.

Rozia blushed deep red and looked away. "Don't be silly, Petri."

As they walked Kaleem couldn't swallow. He couldn't think what to say to Rozia either. Whatever he said would be a lie; there was only one thing on his mind – how much he still loved her. He ought to get that out of the way first but suppose she totally rejected him? If he didn't confront her with this he could remain hopeful in his ignorance. Rozia just seemed embarrassed. He hated as well that he'd made her feel awkward. Perhaps he should keep his distance from her, pretend to be busy, put the whole problem on hold.

Petri had seemed oblivious to it all and had skipped along the pleasant pathway that was surrounded by artificial trees and bathed in late spring-light. She was singing to herself despite the brightness. Bringing her to Zandra had been the right thing to do. That was something at least. She would never have made this much progress on Terrestra.

A transporter came very quickly and Rozia and Petri clambered aboard. Something sank in him as they waved goodbye. Petri was enthusiastic. Rozia just looked sad. Was that a good sign? Was she sad that they were parting again? Or was it because she regretted seeing him today?

Oh, it was all too difficult.

He decided not to wait for a transporter himself. He'd do what he often did when he felt stressed. He began to jog, though he couldn't help chanting to himself as he ran, "She loves me, she loves me not." Well, whatever. Of one fact he was sure: he loved her and always would.

It would have been three stops on the transporter, so a fair distance in fact. Yet it would only take him about twenty minutes to jog there. He began to pound along the pavements. They were crowded today and even the newly introduced channelling was not keeping people apart. At one point he almost bumped into a Zandrian droid.

"Oy, watch it snazzy boy," commented the machine.

Odd. That went against the normal robot code, didn't it? Though perhaps calling a Terrestran a "snazzy boy" was harmless enough. The machine was actually not hurting human life. But why would it bother? There must be some wrong programming there.

It didn't improve his temper. Nor did the jog have the normal mood-enhancing effect. It just made him feel tired, drained and aware that he wasn't quite as fit as he used to be.

He carried on pushing himself, even though his legs were beginning to ache and he was getting so out of breath that his lungs hurt. At least when he finally got home he could be pleased that he'd kept going. So he arrived at his apartment block out of breath, sweating and with hardly the strength to command the door to open.

He leant against the wall whilst he tried to recover. A few

seconds later his breathing and heart rate slowed to something more normal. He still felt a bit weak. He decided to leave it a little while longer before attempting to get into the building.

One of the campaign holoposters caught his eye. His iris activated it. He watched with a mixture of disbelief and nausea as a fair-skinned, blond-haired Zandrian, who was so perfectly Zandrian that he was sure she was really a droid, described how Zandrians should stop offering so much medical help to people from other One World Community planets.

"We must put other Zandrians first," she said. "Whilst we feel duty-bound to offer help to the needy from elsewhere, are we actually helping them if all they do is drain our resources? Wouldn't it be better if we educated them to look after themselves more efficiently? Zandra's resources are not infinite."

"Stop," said Kaleem quietly. He should get the holoposter reported.

Now the strength returned to his limbs and his heart rate quickened again. He ran up to the apartment block door.

The monitor recognised his iris before he'd even said his name. The door opened immediately. He felt a level of fitness returning. The poster had fired him up.

He remembered living in the old cave system on Terrestra. He could still see the Z Zone there as well. That place where people lived outside of the system because of their sincere beliefs. Everything was improving now and that was down to people working together. How dare anyone try to stop that?

He decided to walk up the twenty flights. Half way up he started running again.

CHAPTER TWO

It was the autumnal part of the Zandrian day. Kaleem always rather enjoyed this – it provided a good bridge between the intense heat of summer and the bitter cold of winter. He thought of Rozia and Petri. This was actually the time that suited the little girl best. She was getting good, though, at tolerating all times of day. The Zandrian medics really had done wonders.

Kaleem sighed. Rozia and Petri. What he wouldn't give now to be going for a walk through the woods with them.

The communicator buzzed.

"Show me," he commanded.

The screen lit up. His heart jumped in his chest when saw Rozia and Petri standing at the entrance. Just when he'd been thinking about them. Rozia was frowning, though. She had dark circles under her eyes and she was quite pale. Petri, by contrast, looked full of life and her cheeks were pink.

He buzzed them in. What could they want? Was there something wrong?

"Have you seen the polls?" Rozia blinked as if she was about to cry.

Kaleem shook his head. He never bothered looking at the polls. They were rarely right for one thing and today's referendum was just a routine one.

"Well, you should take a look. Activate the dataserve."

"Report polls," said Kaleem.

Immediately the dataserve sprang into life. Kaleem was astonished to see a human reporter. Referenda like this one were normally so routine that they relied on the droids to analyse the polls about them and hardly anyone watched the reports. Did Rozia have good reason then for getting so paranoid?

She gripped his arm. "Do you see?"

He did see. Only 70% of people living on Zandra wished for Zandra to remain in the One World Community. This was extraordinary, but with 70% wanting to remain there was no chance that they would have to leave. Who were these 30% unhappy people, though? What was making them so unhappy? And why now, all of a sudden?

Rozia bit her lip. "Do you think the polls are right?"

Kaleem shrugged. They rarely were. People often said they were against something but voted for it in the end as they were afraid of the status quo changing. They were just making a point. "Even if they are, does it matter? Even if the vote matches the poll: 70% of us want to stay. So, we'll be staying."

"But when I walk along the street, I think that 30% of the people are staring at us and wishing we weren't there."

"Well, they probably think the same about me. You can't think like that."

"At least you're half Zandrian. You look a bit Zandrian."

Yeah. Global citizen. Citizen of nowhere. Hadn't some famous 21st century politician said something like that once? She'd been right in a way but not the way he suspected she'd meant. "Yes, and I look half Terrestran. It's of no use either here or on Terrestra."

"I know. I know. But…"

She didn't finish. Petri wailed.

"What is it?" Rozia scooped her up.

"My eyes are stinging."

Petri was going red and it looked as if her face was swelling up.

Rozia looked at Kaleem. "She's had her meds. I don't understand."

Kaleem's mouth went dry. This just wasn't right. "Come on," he said. "Let's get her to a medi-centre."

By the time they got to the medi-centre, Petri was covered in blisters and was shying away from the light. The droid nurse triaged her straight away. "A human doctor is on her way. She will be here in approximately five minutes ten seconds," said the droid.

Good old Zandra. As efficient as ever. Thank goodness.

"I just don't get it," said Rozia. "She's almost as bad as she was before we came here."

The five minutes seemed to last forever, but when the door swished open Kaleem noticed that in fact only four minutes thirty seconds had gone by.

"Doctor Joahnsa Brooken," said the young woman, stretching her hand out to Rozia.

Rozia returned a Terrestran handshake and blushed deeply when she realised her mistake.

"Ah. I know who you are. The Terrestrans and the Peace Child. Your little girl has this nasty skin disease."

On cue, Petri wailed again. "Rozia it hurts. I want to go back to the dark."

"Come on then. Follow me to an exam room." Dr Brooken smiled at Petri. "We'll soon get you right."

Rozia put her arm gently round the child.

"Let me carry her," said Kaleem.

"Best not. There's a trick to it."

Petri continued to whimper. She was being so brave. It must really hurt. But why hadn't the medication worked?

Within a few minutes of getting into the examination room Doctor Brooken had given Petri a sedative and the child was dozing. She examined her with a medi-wand.

She shook her head. "This child has had no medication for thirty-six hours."

"But I used the wand on her this morning and last night. I did. Really I did." Rozia looked as if she was going to cry.

Kaleem put an arm around her shoulders but she tensed up. He took his arm away.

Doctor Brooken looked up at Rozia and smiled. "Don't worry. I believe you." She took a medi-wand out of a drawer and plugged it into the dataserve. "I'll give her an extra strong dose now and I'll give you a month's supply charged on to a wand. Get rid of the others."

"But why didn't they work?"

Doctor Brooken shrugged. "It's unusual for anything like this to happen. But…" She sighed and bit her lip. Then she looked straight into Kaleem's eyes. "It's happened a few times recently.

And always with patients from other planets. One for you, Peace Child, perhaps?" She raised one eye brow.

What? Someone had interfered with the wands? Who would do that?

The dataserve bleeped. Joahnsa Brooken removed the wand and placed another into the fast charge drawer. "This will take about twenty minutes. Then she should begin to recover. The spare wand should be ready as well – I'm putting thirty days' worth on and I'd like to see her again just before they're up. You'll be free to go soon. I suggest you come to me for future supplies and don't rely on the couriers or even the fast drawers."

She started applying the wand to Petri. "And come precisely to me. To be on the safe side."

This was getting unbelievable. What was going on?

After about ten minutes, Petri held out her hand. "Rozia, Kaleem," she said softly.

"Look," said Doctor Brooken.

The blisters were fading and Petri's skin was returning to normal. "That feels better," said Petri.

"It's good that she wants to hold your hands," said Doctor Brooken. "It's a sign that the pain's gone."

"Is she all right?"

Rozia had just come back into the lounge from Petri's bedroom. She'd been in there almost an hour and a half. Kaleem had thought about slipping out quietly. Perhaps she was staying with Petri so long to avoid him. On the other hand, though, wouldn't it look a bit crass if he'd gone without waiting to see how Petri was? So he'd stayed. He would rather she were cross with him for being too concerned than because he seemed as if he didn't care.

She looked so pale. All he wanted to do was take her in his arms, hug her, make her feel safe. He daren't though. That might spoil everything.

Rozia shook her head and pursed her lips.

"Does she have a fever? Have the blisters come back?"

"No. Nothing like that. Her temperature's normal and the spots have almost completely disappeared. She's not complaining of any pain. She's just scared it will all come back again and that the wand won't work properly."

"Did you use the wand? Did it work?"

"Of course I did. But there's no way of knowing for sure, is there? Can we trust this Joahnsa Brooken?"

What could he say? She'd seemed trustworthy. He always found it better to trust people anyway. Trusting people tended to make them trustworthy. Most of the time. There were always some exceptions. "Would you like me to stay?" There. He'd said it now. Would she realise, though that he genuinely meant it to be helpful.

Rozia shook her head. "No. No. It's all right. I think you're going to be busy, aren't you?"

About time he had something concrete to do really. "You're sure? They can find me here if they need me."

She shook her head. "You go home. We'll be all right."

"And you'll contact me or Joahnsa Brooken if anything else goes wrong?"

She nodded. "I'll contact you first."

That was something. Yet it was clear she didn't want him there. He smiled and nodded. "I'll be off then. I'll call you tomorrow anyway."

Kaleem arrived back just before it started getting bitterly cold. As he went to let himself into his apartment he could feel the heat coming up through the pavements. Really, the technology was superb on this planet. And cost effective. There was a lot that others could learn here.

Something nagged at him as walked into his unit, though. He found himself thinking about the polls. The actual results would start to come in soon. He should look to set his mind at ease.

He started to activate his dataserve but even before he'd finished commanding it there was a news override. Humanoid reporters again. Something big then. His tiredness vanished. He became alert.

"We have been subject to cyber-attacks," said the woman who was being interviewed. Kaleem recognised her but couldn't quite work out where from. “The earlier polls had been manipulated. Currently, they’re saying a more normal 95% in favour of the status quo, 5% wanting change.”

“That’s still 2% different from normal. Is that of any concern?”

“We’re not sure, but we think it might just be an effect of the polls themselves. You know: I will if you will. It’s only a small effect anyway. Nothing to worry about.”

“And have we any idea of where these attacks are coming from? Word on social media is that they’re from Zenoto.”

What? That was madness. The woman laughed as well. “Improbable. It’s more likely to be some Zandrian kids messing around. We’re pulling together all of our resources to track down who is doing this and they will be severely punished. Even if they are just kids.”

“Thank you.” The presenter turned to the camera. “We’ll bring more news overrides as we get more information. In the meantime we’ll pass you back to the polls and the early results.”

The news override finished. Kaleem went to the kitchen and commanded a simple pasta and seafood dish and a bottle of beer. He returned to the lounge and carried on watching the results as they came in. Section after section reported between 95% and 100% wanting to remain in the One World Community. It was clear Zandra wasn’t going to change soon. Nothing to worry about.

He cleared up and then listened to a music channel while he read some French Wordtext documents. He began to feel sleepy again. At least now he could rest peacefully knowing that all was well on Zandra. He’d heard nothing from Rozia either so he guessed she and Petri were fine. At least now he had an excuse for calling her tomorrow.

Almost as soon as he pulled the duvet over him and commanded all of the apartment’s systems to go into sleep mode he fell asleep himself.

He woke late the next morning. The spring part of the day had already begun and natural light filled the room. There was still no message from Rozia so presumably all was well.

He got up, prepared breakfast and idly activated the news channel on his dataserve whilst he settled down to eat it. It was a normal droid newsreader. He blinked though when he saw the results of the latest referendum. A mere 52% of the population had voted that Zandra should remain in the One World Community. How had that happened? How could it have?

CHAPTER THREE

Rozia's Ulog

Hi all,

Time has just gone by so quickly since I was last in touch. I'm afraid, though it's not such good news at the moment.

As you know I've been made so welcome here on Zandra and it hadn't ever occurred to me to question whether I belonged at all. But that has all changed in just one day. That routine referendum. Why do so many people want to leave the One World Community all of a sudden? What does that mean for Petri and me? Will they not want us anymore? Will they see us a drain on their resources?

It's all right for Kaleem. At least he looks a bit Zandrian. He is partly Zandrian.

Petri had been doing so well. But then she became ill quite suddenly. It was terrifying. She was obviously in so much pain – worse, I think, than ever before. Although Kaleem was with me when it happened, I really felt alone. We're away from home.

The wands didn't work. How could the wands not have worked? Had someone interfered with them? I'm really scared that somebody is trying to get at us. The doctor admitted that this kind of thing has happened a few times now.

I was glad Kaleem was there and that he took us to the medi-centre.

Doctor Joahnsa Brooken was brilliant. I'm not sure that she believed me, though, when I said that I had applied the wands to Petri. But she soon sorted her out, anyway. It was really kind of her to give Petri something to make her calmer before she started applying the meds.

It was all still very worrying, though. The doctor admitted that this kind of thing had happened a few times now. And she doesn't even trust all of her colleagues. What is happening here?

I'm really grateful to her, anyway. I'm going to go to her for the wands in future – not rely on a courier to bring them, just as she suggested. And I'll only take them from her, not from one of her colleagues.

It took Petri a while to recover, even after we'd got her home. Kaleem stayed with me. He was so kind and I was glad he was there. I hope he hasn't got the wrong impression, though. I do care for him and I know he cares for me and Petri. But I don't think we can ever be together again the way we were. Not after the way he left me. Not with me having to care for Petri.

CHAPTER FOUR

Obek looked up through the leaves. The blue sky framed them perfectly. Now, the trees were covered in the orange fruit. Their experiment had been a success. Would the taste be right, though? Other small oranges were bitter. Was it the sunshine they lacked? The big juicy ones needed more warmth than they got here. Today was exceptional.

Well, just looking at them wouldn't get him a long way. He didn't want to go back and fetch a ladder. That might alert people to what he was doing. He would just have to climb the tree.

It wasn't that easy. The places where he could put his feet or get something to hold were few and far apart. The branches were thin and might not take his weight. A gentle breeze had sprung up. It was refreshingly cool but it made it difficult to balance.

At last though he could touch one of the fruits and even found a place to perch. The fruit fell easily into his hand. That was a good sign. It meant that it was ripe. He lifted it to his nose. Oh, yes. It smelt of oranges and there was something else as well. A hint of spiciness. Just a hint.

He started to peel the clementine. It peeled easily and the skin was so thin that pith came off with it. That would normally be a good thing but sometimes the flesh came off with the pith as well. Would they be able to make the skins a little sturdier?

He took a segment and put it into his mouth.

It was exquisite – sweet, juicy, orangey.

Yes, this is what they'd been aiming for.

He threw a dozen or so more clementines to the floor, scrambled down the tree, gathered up the fruits and rushed back to the mansion. His father must know of this as soon as possible.

"Well," said his father. "You have done extremely well. We'll need to expand the orchards now."

They had just returned from taking the first harvest to the

market. Every single piece of fruit had sold at a good price and they'd secured orders for the following year.

Obek nodded. "I think we can even stagger the crop. So that we can produce them most times of the year."

"Good. Good. And you think you can manage that?"

Obek looked into his father's eyes. "I'm sure I can."

His father nodded. "So, tell me. How will you go about it?"

"Stagger the planting so that the fruit appears between early summer and late autumn."

"Will that produce enough?"

"Can we buy more acreage?"

His father stood up and wandered over to the window. He looked out across his field. "Do you think you can persuade old Tunkin to sell us some of his land?"

"I'm sure I can. And there's something else as well."

"Oh?"

"The extra income we'd gain from being able to produce for more of the year would more than justify buying some greenhouses."

Obek's father turned back towards him. "Get all of this done, son, and you will be rewarded."

The year passed quickly. Tunkin had agreed at once to sell all of his 150 acres. Obek had offered him a good price and a share of the profits associated with the new land for five years. He had managed to build the greenhouses in time to use them for a winter crop and despite all of the money he had had to find and despite having to pay extra workers to help with the perpetual harvest, they had made three times as much profit this year.

Obek's father had decided to arrange a ball to celebrate. Obek found himself dancing with one of the most beautiful girls in the neighbourhood. He was annoyed when his father tapped him on the back. "We need to talk." He bowed to Penni. "Please excuse us. My son will rejoin you presently."

"Couldn't this have waited?" demanded Obek once they were inside his father's study.

"No. Business must always come before pleasure." He laughed. "Don't look so glum. That's only because then the pleasure is even greater."

Obek shrugged. Could it really be that important? He'd worked so hard, hadn't he? Didn't he deserve some relaxation? Besides, he was really making progress with Penni. He was sure they would become lovers very soon, and perhaps even more. He sighed. "Well what is it?"

"I want you to take over the clementine business completely. I wanted to discuss it with you now so that if you agree I can make an announcement tonight."

"You mean be totally in control? Make all the decisions on my own?"

His father nodded. "Even how to spend the profits. A word to the wise, there, though. Yes, you should pay yourself well and in the future you may have a family to consider as well, but at the rate this is all going, the clementine orchards will make so much money that you won't know what to do with it. Some, of course, will be invested back into the enterprise, but you must think how to use the rest responsibly. We'll discuss this again in a year's time. Well, are you up for it?"

Obek nodded enthusiastically.

"Good. Now I suggest also you just get on with it." He grinned at Obek. "And go on. Ask the girl."

Two announcements were made later that evening: that Obek was to take over completely the running of the clementine orchards and that he was engaged to the lovely Penni Mendat.

"Why are you looking so worried? I'm fine. The baby's fine. Do you want to feel him kick?" Penni took Obek's hand and placed it on her belly.

The baby obliged. Yes, it did seem like a boy. He was certainly very strong. Obek smiled at his wife and then drew her into an embrace.

"There that's better," she whispered.

Oh, he wanted her so much. The huge belly did not put him off at all. If anything he found it arousing. Then he remembered. He pulled away from her. Yes, he was so lucky to have her in his life and soon there would be a child as well. Might he soon lose all means of supporting them? Would his father take the clementine project away if he couldn't find an answer to that question he'd asked a year ago?

"Oh, come on tell me." She rubbed his arm.

Obek sighed. "I've got to find a good use for all of the profit we're making."

"I take it we are still making a good profit?"

"Oh yes." It was good. It was unbelievably good. The project was just growing and growing.

"Well then. Stop worrying. You'll think of something. Maybe take on a new enterprise. One that is good for everyone." She stepped forward and kissed him. She stroked his cheek. "You look so tired sweetheart. You should go and get some rest."

Obek nodded. That wasn't a bad idea.

He found a pleasant spot in one of the orchards that wasn't being worked today. There was already a hammock strung between two of the trees. He climbed into it and shut his eyes. The sun was making the almost ripe clementines release their scent. The bees buzzed and a gentle breeze cooled him pleasantly. It was all very soothing and gradually his eyes closed.

Something stirred Obek from his nap. There was a crick in his neck and he couldn't work out where he was at first. Then he gradually remembered going to the orchard. Some half-formed dreams came back to him. There were people in fine clothes, grand buildings and more and more clementines. Everyone was going about their business so purposefully. There was excellence and perfection here.

He was aware of a voice calling him. "Master Obek, Master Obek. Come quickly." It was his former nanny, Silvana. They'd reengaged her to help look after the new child.

He jumped from the hammock and ran towards the old lady. "What is it?"

"It's the baby. The baby's on its way."

Nothing else mattered now. Please let this baby be all right. He was arriving three weeks early.

They both hurried back to the house.

"I don't think he is premature, you know," said the doctor. "If anything, I think he's a month overdue. Look at his hair and fingernails."

Penni smiled at Obek. He understood exactly what she meant. Young Tomik must have been conceived the very first time they'd made love, when the pressure of the wedding arrangements had become too much and they could contain themselves no longer. Not during the honeymoon as everyone had assumed.

"Anyway, there is no need for you to be transferred to the hospital. Everything is fine."

"Just as well," said Silvana, sniffing. "We always managed without hospitals in my day. Nasty places. Full of germs." She frowned and stared at Penni. "That was very quick for a first time. Are you sure you're not hiding anything young lady?"

Penni blushed.

"Silvana!" Obek tried to sound cross but he really wanted to laugh.

"Now then," said the doctor. "There's no reason why a healthy young woman shouldn't give birth easily. It's more natural really." He patted Penni's shoulder. "Well done, you."

Obek gazed at his son and wife. They were perfect. Then it became clear to him what he must do. He would set up an institution, an order, perhaps, that would enable others to gain this sort of excellence.

Penni touched his arm lightly. "What are you thinking?"

"That I know exactly what to do with the clementine profits."

"Tell me."

So he started to outline his plans whilst she fed the baby. He realised after a while that his son had stopped sucking and that Penni was snoring gently. He stroked her hair. Poor love. The birth may have only take four hours but it must have been exhausting: Tomik was a big boy.

CHAPTER FIVE

Kaleem felt sick as he watched the continuing news. Had he woken up in a different world? This was a major event. Yet it was a droid presenter speaking quite calmly as if nothing in particular had happened. Surely something like this merited a news override and a human presenter. Could this be just a bad dream?

Why had this happened? How had it all changed in just a matter of hours? This position was really unheard of. How could it all work now with 48% of the people wanting to leave the One World Community and only 52% wanting to stay? Nearly half of the people would be extremely, unhappy wouldn't they? Why were they unhappy?

Or could this be a trick? Was it some sort of extended cyber-attack?

He'd better get in touch with Rozia. She would be worried as well. He called her up on the dataserve but nothing happened. The machine searched for a long time until at last it uttered, "Addressee not found." What the heck? What was it talking about? This must just be a malfunction, surely?

He had to find out.

Immediately he called up the Executive Palace. He was normally allowed an open link with a secure connection but this time he was waiting and waiting just as he had been with Rozia. At last, though, a robotic voice answered, "All of our portals are occupied. Please try later." So, there was some worry then? The executives were probably having some heated discussions right now. Using the droid presenters was just a ploy to keep everyone calm? Suddenly he longed for Terrestra where in a situation like this he would be summoned to the Citadel of Elders even before he'd realised there was a problem.

The dataserve buzzed. His father's face appeared on the screen. "Do you know what's going on?" asked Nazaret.

Kaleem shook his head. "I can't get through to anyone. I'm worried about Rozia."

"Why especially?"

"Petri's been very sick again. And Rozia was terrified about the way the referendum went. She's not responding to my calls. Something's happened."

"Shall we go over to her place? I'll meet you there if you like."

That would be good. His mother and father lived a little nearer to Rozia. They could be there in minutes.

"What about Mum?"

"We might get her to wait in. In case Rozia and Petri had been on their way over to us."

Kaleem nodded. Yes, it would be a good idea.

He finished the conversation and got ready to go out.

The streets were crowded. It was difficult to move. People had gathered on the corners and were talking excitedly. The cafés and bars were full. It was clear that personal communicators weren't working properly. The few people still trying to use them were giving up in frustration after a few seconds. Kaleem had not seen anything like this for a long time. This was usually a sign of major news breaking and the networks being overloaded. Something really big was going on. And it had never been quite this bad before.

He wanted to get to Rozia's apartment as quickly as possible but he couldn't resist going into a crowded news café. There were so many people there he couldn't see the screen properly.

"Anything new?" he asked the tall man standing next to him.

"Currency's dipping. The inter-planetary exchanges have gone mad. Our imports will cost."

Kaleem pushed forward so he could see the screen. The charts showed the full horror story. Of course after major news like this it was bound to happen. "Nothing about why the vote came out as it did?"

The man shook his head. "I can't work it out either. There must be some very unhappy people around. Nobody saw that one coming. Well, I didn't."

Kaleem nodded his agreement. He couldn't think of a single person he knew who would have voted to leave the One World

Community. Looking around this room now you had to assume that just under half of the people here wanted out. Was it that old man over there with the crooked back? Or that young woman holding a baby in a kangaroo carrier? Or even the teenager there who looked as if he may have voted for the first time this week? It was impossible to tell.

Well, he hadn't really found out anything new except that it was bad. He needed to get on now. He made his way out of the café and started jogging towards where Rozia lived. He really had to find her. If this was scaring him, just how might it be scaring her?

He ought not to arrive empty-handed, though. Was Nazaret already there and had he thought up an excuse for popping by? They ought to make it look like a visit to someone who had been ill and was now on the mend. That was precisely Petri, wasn't it? It shouldn't look as if they were checking up on Rozia. She liked to be so independent. What should he take? Flowers for Rozia, maybe, a toy for Petri and something nice to eat for all of them? Would that be right?

There was a merchandise hall just one block from where Rozia lived. That would do the trick. Even if they hadn't got the items in stock they would normally be able to get them to the apartment within the hour though that might be difficult if the systems were struggling.

He was pleased to see when he got there that they did in fact have some Terrestran flowers – presumably produced here – a fluffy toy that looked a bit like a Terrestran dog and some fresh fruit juice. That would do. They could dial up the rest of their breakfast through Rozia's kitchen.

He took the items to the shop droid and offered his iris to the scanner.

"Insufficient funds," said the droid.

"What?" He usually had so much credit on his account that he didn't know what to do with it. He'd always thought that was sign of being content. This now didn't make any sense. The systems must be really playing up. Perhaps it would clear the second time. "That can't be right. Can you try again?"

The droid obliged. "I regret sir. Prices have been raised in anticipation."

What a cheek.

"You could take either the flowers, or the toy or the fruit juice," the machine offered unhelpfully.

"Best not," mumbled Kaleem. They would have to sort this out and presumably the executives would soon. He might even be summoned to help.

He now thought it best to get to Rozia as quickly as possible.

When he arrived at Rozia's a few minutes later his father actually came down to entrance of the apartment block. "The systems are being so slow, this was quicker. Anyway I wanted a word first."

"They're all right aren't they?"

Nazaret shrugged. "Petri's okay now. But Rozia's in a bad way."

"Oh?" What had happened to her?

"Don't look so scared. There's nothing wrong, physically." He sighed and shook his head. He took a deep breath. "All of her credits have been wiped. Nothing works in the apartment now."

"So how did…?"

"I've put everything on to our account. It's working again but it's all so sluggish at the moment."

Kaleem didn't stop to ask for more detail. He didn't even bother summoning the lift. He just started to run up the stairs.

CHAPTER SIX

"You'll listen carefully won't you? You'll do what your teacher says?" Penni stroked her son's hair.

"Of course I will, Mummy. I want to grow up to be clever like Daddy. How much do you think I'll learn today?"

Obek laughed. "Lots and lots I should think. Especially if you do listen well like you promised."

Obek was proud of his little son. He looked so smart in his orange and brown uniform. Clementine money had set up the new primary school for all the orchard workers' children. They employed the very best teachers they could find and Obek knew that Tomik would be in good hands with Miss Silverton. She was patient, kind, energetic and set high standards. Yes, she would certainly do for his son.

They were almost there now. More and more children in the orange and brown were converging on the pleasant single-storey white-washed building that housed the school. Obek spotted half a dozen or so other children carrying the big cones of sweets that all were given on their first day. These youngsters would no doubt become Tomik's friends.

The children gathered with their parents in the pleasant garden in front of the school.

"Miss Silverton or one of the other teachers will come outside and ring a bell," Penni explained. "Then you'll have to line up with your class and Miss Silverton will take you to your classroom."

Tomik slipped his hand out of his mother's. Penni exchanged a glance with Obek. He could see there were tears in her eyes. "He'll be fine," he whispered.

She nodded.

It was Miss Silverton who came out with the bell. As she rang it, the children carrying the cones of sweets, Tomik included, scurried over towards her. She smiled at them. Tomik looked happy.

"I told you so." Obek took Penni's hand as they made their way out of the school grounds.

She sighed. "Yes. It's a great thing that you're doing."

He nodded. “And now I must hurry. The meeting starts in twenty minutes.”

The other members of the committee were already there when Obek arrived at the board room of the grand lodge.

“How did it go?” asked his father. “Was he all right?”

“Yes. He seemed to love it. It was Penni who found it difficult.”

His father nodded. “Your mother was exactly the same when you went to school for the first time. She’ll be fine. She’ll soon have the new baby to worry about.”

Just like his mother had? Hopefully not. Neither his mother nor his baby brother had survived the birth. At least things were different now. Very few women died in childbirth these days and there were very few still born babies. Hopefully, too, precisely what they were going to discuss today would ensure even better standards in the future.

Suddenly the room went quiet. It was like a signal for him to start the meeting. “All right everyone. Let’s begin. As you know we are here today to establish the rules and regulations for our new order, the House of Clementine. The school is hopefully a good example. Let’s now extend those standards to other schools, hospitals and means of transport.”

“And sports?” suggested one committee member.

“What about banks?” said another.

“Retail outlets?” suggested a third.

“Are we talking inclusivity or exclusivity?”

Obek recognised the speaker as a friend of Penni’s, an intelligent young woman to whom he was keen to give a role within the Order. Penni had shown no interest at all. She was much too focussed on providing a good home for him, Tomik and the new baby. Thank goodness for that, though. With all the responsibility he carried he needed it.

“Inclusivity, I should think,” he replied slowly. What would they do, though, if someone failed to conform? Would there be an outside? Should they keep everyone, no matter the cost? Or should being a member of the Order be a privilege that you had to earn?

"All would initially be welcome." This was something they would have to think about later.

They debated for a couple of hours and by the end they had a set of 100 rules.

"The bottom line is that the good of the Order is put before the good of its members," said Obek. "That good, of course, is the pursuit and attainment of perfection."

There was a general consensus, then one man raised his hand. Obek nodded that he should speak.

"Is this to be our constitution, then?"

Well he supposed they should have a constitution. But was this enough? He looked at his father.

"It's a step towards it," said the older man. "But we probably need to fine-tune it. These are really more like guidelines. We need some fundamental principles. Maybe five. Perhaps we should all think about that for the next meeting."

There were murmurs of agreement. The meeting ended.

Five weeks later they stood in the garden of the grand lodge.

"We bury this for posterity," said Obek's father. "But before I put the box containing our constitution and our guidelines into the ground, I will ask my son, the founder of the House of Clementine, to read out our five fundamental principles." He handed the document to Obek.

Obek took deep breath and started reading. "The needs of the Order are greater than the needs of the individuals in it.

"The Order has a duty of care to its members.

"Members of the Order will always pursue excellence and perfection, each according to his / her abilities.

"No one member will judge any other member but will trust that he / she is doing all that they can.

"The Order is bigger than the sum of its parts."

The crowd cheered.

"All workers on our clementine orchards are already considered as members of the Order. You will all receive copies of this. Welcome to the House of Clementine."

They cheered again.

Obek handed the documents to his father who placed them in the small chest and lowered it into the ground. The two other men shoveled earth on top of it. The House of Clementine was established.

"So what will happen the minute somebody starts acting up?" Silvana was dangling baby Harissa over her shoulder, trying to get her to burp. She was just three days old and Penni was asleep. The birth had been much more difficult this time and no one had been sure why. Penni had been as healthy as before and Harissa was quite small. It ought to have been easy. Silvana tapped the baby's back. "See, this wasn't exactly perfect was it? Yet it was nobody's fault."

"Well, that's one of the principles anyway. No judgement"

"You mean, if someone doesn't go for perfection or doesn't put the needs of the Order above their own you'll just ignore it?"

"No, we'd re-educate."

"I see. Easier said than done I'd imagine."

Harissa let out an enormous burp.

"Good girl." Silvana looked sternly at Obek again. "So, are you going to let just anybody into the Order? What about those people who can't be perfect or even excellent? Even your little one, see."

"What do you mean?"

"Look at her face." She handed him the baby. "Look at her eyes and her nose. There's something not quite right."

She was beautiful, his daughter. But yes, her eyes were a little odd. More like slits than almonds. And her nose was a bit squashed. Oh, why worry? It didn't matter all that much and she would probably change as she grew.

Her eyes closed. Silvana took her back. "There, my little lovely. Time for a nap." She got up and went to take the child back to her mother. She turned to Obek again when she reached the doorway. "So, you'll have anybody will you? Even if they've got two heads, and three legs or are so dumb they'll just use up resources without giving anything back? Hmm. It's all right to have fine ideas."

"We're going to be inclusive, no matter what." Oh, this woman was a tyrant. Maybe he should consider excluding her. He immediately felt bad about having that thought.

Later that evening Obek sat on the veranda with his father. It was mild but raining softly. It was good to be able to sit and look out on to the garden and to trees, waving gently in the breeze, in the orchards beyond. The damp air didn't bother him. They were sipping one of the orchard master's favourite malt whiskies.

"You should take no notice of Silvana," said the orchard master. "Yes, she's wise and she's old enough to have seen a lot of life but she's very opinionated. Set in her ways too. She's clinging on to the old way of life. We must look forward to the new."

Obek nodded. He took a sip of his drink. It was rich and invigorating.

He felt a rush of sharp warmth through his sinuses and his mind relaxed. "Let's hope it all works."

"It will," said his father. "It will. But you'll have to old tight to the dream. There'll be obstacles much trickier than your old nanny." He raised his glass. "To the House of Clementine."

Obek grinned. He held up his glass. "To the House of Clementine."

As the two glasses clinked Obek promised himself he would succeed.

CHAPTER SEVEN

"You're all right now? You really are a brave girl you know. I can't think of many Terrestrans or Zandrians who would put up with what you have to suffer day in and day out." Marijam stroked Petri's hair. The little girl pulled away.

Rozia couldn't help smiling. It was obvious that Marijam thought the world of Petri. Was it her imagination or could Rozia see some sadness in her eyes? She would probably like grandchildren. It didn't look as if it would happen, though. Kaleem was showing no sign of getting attached. She didn't know how she felt about that. Glad that he wasn't looking at anyone else or sad that it couldn't be her.

"Should I make some tea?" Marijam asked.

It was so warm and cosy here even if a little old-fashioned with the home-made throws over the comfisessels. It was kind of Nazaret and Marijam to have invited her and Petri to stay indefinitely while they sorted out what had happened to her credits. Tea just made it even better.

"That would be nice."

"Some juice for you?" Marijam asked Petri.

"Actually, could I have tea as well?"

"Of course, sweetheart." Marijam made her way towards the kitchen.

"Why does she fuss so much?" Petri was frowning. "Doesn't she realise I'm not a child anymore? Why doesn't she get the house droid to make the drinks anyway?"

"She's just being kind. She must think she's being more of a hostess if she makes it herself."

Petri sighed. "I know. It's just that it's so awkward."

Rozia nodded. It was difficult living in someone else's space all of the time.

The door to the lounge slid open and Nazaret walked in. A comfisessel glided over to him and he sat down. "Good morning you two. How are you doing?"

"We're fine," Rozia replied. She wanted to ask him if he'd found out any more about her credits and why everything had been shut down.

He seemed to read her mind. He shook his head. "I've spoken to everyone I can get hold of. They have no idea why everything's been frozen."

Rozia swallowed hard.

Nazaret hovered nearer to her and touched her lightly on the arm. "Don't worry. You are most welcome to stay here as long as you like."

Rozia just about managed to smile. She knew that she was welcome. Of course she did. But it didn't make her feel any better. She couldn't go out and give them some privacy. The flat was pleasant enough but it was clearly really only meant for two people. She and Petri were sharing the small guest room that clearly wasn't meant for extended stays. But it was getting more and more uncomfortable out there. She really didn't want to walk about outside. And she hated being so dependent on other people.

Marijam came in with the tea. She grinned. "Of course you are welcome. You mustn't worry at all. We'll take good care of the two of you. Any friend of Kaleem's is a friend of ours."

Petri grinned. "See, Rozia. Kaleem's mum thinks so too."

Rozia felt her cheeks burning. She looked down at the floor.

Nazaret laughed. "You would be welcome, my dear, even if you weren't a special friend of our son."

Rozia wasn't sure if that made it better or worse. She smiled and sipped her tea. Oh she felt so useless and pathetic.

Kaleem called round that evening. He was doing that a lot and was staying over quite often as well. "I can't expect you to do everything for Rozia and Petri," he'd told his parents. "It's only fair that I should come and help." He had to sleep in his father's study and that made Rozia feel even more awkward.

Were they such a burden? He barely spoke to her. Clearly they were a nuisance then.

Most of the time she didn't know what to say to him. Every now and then, though, they would have animated conversations just like in the old days. Just after that he would go all silent and moody.

"Can we talk?" she asked him that evening.

He shrugged. "What is there to talk about? We're doing our best to find out what's actually going on. We'll get it sorted. Don't you trust me?"

"Of course I do."

"Well then." He yawned. "I'm shattered. I'm going to bed."

And so he went. Was he trying to avoid her? Why would he never stop and talk to her? Was it so bad being in a room with her?

"What's the matter?" asked Petri after Rozia had got up for the seventh time that night. "Do you want Kaleem to be your boyfriend?"

"Of course not." Drat the girl. She was too good at figuring things out. "I'm just wondering whether we shouldn't go back to Terrestra."

"Why do you want to do that?"

"Because there are too many people who don't like us here."

"But there are a lot of people who like us."

Rozia nodded. "I know. It makes it difficult. At least we would be at home on Terrestra."

"You should be more like Kaleem. Your home should be where you are. I like it on Zandra. Even though there are some silly people here. I want to stay." She turned over and went back to sleep.

Rozia was awake for a while longer. Should they go or should they stay? If they went back, they would be free from all of the hate, the plots against them, and Kaleem's mood swings. But if they went she might be giving up all chance of being with Kaleem again. Besides, oughtn't she stay and fight this thing?

Eventually, weary and still undecided, she fell asleep.

CHAPTER EIGHT

"I don't know why you don't move in permanently here," said Marijam looking pointedly at Kaleem. "Then you two could see each other more of the time. You could even share a room then Petri could have her own"

Rozia blushed bright red.

Petri squawked. "Go on Kaleem. Move into Rozia's room. I'd like to have my own bedroom."

Yes, yes. That would be very nice. It just wasn't going to happen. Kaleem shook his head. "Stop it, Mother."

Rozia got up from the breakfast table and started clearing the dishes. "I really wish I could go back to my own apartment. I hate having to rely on you all. You've been so kind…"

Marijam put her hand on Rozia's shoulder. "Sweetheart, there is no question. You are to stay here as long as you like. Even after this mess is sorted out. And leave all of that to the droid."

"Cool!" Petri was grinning.

"Well, thank goodness it's all got back to normal for most of us. Do you know why it hasn't for Rozia?" Marijam looked meaningfully at Kaleem.

Why did they always think he had the answer to everything? Kaleem shrugged. "Maybe I'll find out later." He ought to get going. Especially as he intended to jog. Though maybe that was quite a good option. The public transporters were running slowly and they'd been asked not to use private ones. It would give him a chance as well to get a feel for what people were thinking.

It wasn't that easy running along the pavements. It seemed that every man and his droid were out there today. Since the cyber-crash and the shocking referendum result people had felt a lot more need to meet others face to face. Kaleem didn't quite get that, actually. Didn't they all feel as uncomfortable as he did? Just under half of the people you met didn't want Zandra to belong to the One World Community any longer. Yet he didn't know a single person who thought that way. Who were these people? Why did they want to break away? Why did they want to live in isolation from the rest of the universe?

The crowd thinned a little as he came to the first suburban ring. It was warming up. Spring was almost here. He had plenty of time. He would be able to shower and change when he got to the Executive Council building. He still had an hour before the meeting.

A couple of men came running towards him. What the heck were they doing? They were on the wrong side of the road. Joggers and hoverers had to follow the same rules as transporters. Everyone knew that. It made sense, didn't it? It prevented accidents and kept everyone safe. They made no sign of giving way to him, though, so he jumped off the path.

"Watch it, snazzy boy!" cried one of the men.

Snazzy boy. That again. What was it? There was something familiar about it but he couldn't quite place it. Was that just because he'd heard it so recently? And why had those two been so defiant about running the wrong way?

"Snazzy boy?" he whispered to his communicator.

The device whirred and spluttered for a few seconds. "Networks overloaded." Again. Still. Ah well, he'd have to save it for later.

He turned to watch the men move away. They were running quite slowly and seemed to be arguing. One on each side of the divide, then? And why were they being so difficult? He guessed he wouldn't get an answer soon.

He turned as well and started to jog again.

The Executive Council building was as overwhelming as Kaleem remembered. It lacked the homely atmosphere of the Citadel of Elders he was more used to on Terrestra. Here it was all clear veriglass and faux-steel. Tiled floors gleamed. Hoversessels glided effortlessly towards visitors, picked them up and transported them to their meetings. Insipid music played in the corridors. It was clearly supposed to have a calming effect. It only irritated him, though.

Kaleem's sessel took him to a small board room where a catering droid was setting out coffee and pastries.

"Executive Tyler will be here presently," the droid informed him. "Please help yourself to some refreshment." It bowed and left the room.

This would be the first time he'd met Tyler, the executive of Home Affairs. He never usually made any public appearances. He was normally represented by his personal droid. Kaleem's business was anyway more often with outward-looking executives. Well goodness knows how long the man would be.

The jog had made Kaleem hungry. Why not? He took a pastry and poured himself a cup of coffee.

He was just taking his second bite of the pastry when the door swished open and a sessel carrying Executive Tyler glided in.

Kaleem almost choked. It wasn't a man. Besides which he knew her.

"I guess you're surprised, Kaleem. Yes, I'm attached now and I took my attachment's name because I wanted not to be dependent upon my father's reputation. How are you, Kaleem?"

"Very well. You?" He felt his cheeks burning as he looked at his former lover.

"Very well indeed. I won't bother shaking hands with you. We know each other much too well for that. And we should not kiss or hug as that might be dangerous, given our past history. Best get down to business." Her pupils were wide open and her eyes were sparkling, though. Was she flirting with him?

He looked away. "Half of the population, more or less, want to break away from the One World Community. The other half want to stay. There is no easy solution," he mumbled.

Ella sighed. "Stating the obvious, Kaleem. We expect more of you than that."

He looked at her again. Her eyes were cold now. Thank goodness.

"There has to be a third way."

"Oh, who's the Buddhist now?"

"It's always the way." He knew that so well now. The solution was always an alternative to both opposing ideas. Compromise never worked.

"And you will execute that how?"

"I suspect there is some dissatisfaction with the One World Community. We need to find out what it is and see if we can address the concerns. Make the One World Community attractive again to those who are disillusioned."

"And who are these people?"

"We don't know – apart from the fact that they're just under half of the population."

Ella nodded. "Will you be able to find them?"

"I'll need some help. I expect I'll have to do some sort of infiltration."

Her face softened and she half smiled. "We'll provide you with whatever help you need."

"Well, I'll come up with a plan and contact you again."

"Do that. Thank you, Kaleem." She came over to him and rubbed his arm. "You know we could have been so good together, you and I. Still could be. It's not working out all that well with Tyler. My thoughts are elsewhere. You of all people must understand that."

Oh yes, he did. It didn't stop her being very attractive and desirable, though. What was she suggesting? It was tempting… Then he remembered the conversation they'd had at breakfast. Rozia needed him now, even if only as a friend and not as a lover.

He shook his head. "Sorry… I can't."

Ella sighed. "I guess not. Better get cracking, then Peace Child boy. You're going to be busy."

Kaleem hardly noticed most of the journey home. It had been such a shock meeting Ella again. It had stirred up some old feelings but he really didn't want to go there again.

And what about Rozia? Was there really any hope there? Or had he really scuppered that one forever? It had been right to leave her at the time. He'd been a danger to her. The timing hadn't been great, though, and he'd had a lot of criticism for that. It had taken her a long time to recover from the injuries she'd suffered because of him. She of all people, though, had really understood why he'd done what he thought he had to. Oh, it was this wretched job of his again. And now there was something else new for him to deal with.

He didn't jog this time. He just walked quickly.

He was almost back at his parents' apartment and hadn't really much idea of how he'd got that far when something grabbed his attention.

A lot of noise was coming from one of the big news screens. He stopped to look up and saw masses of people were marching along the streets in another part of the town. A protest march. That was something you didn't see much on Zandra.

A droid announcer spoke: "Thousands of people who voted to leave the One World Community have taken to the streets, making use of their democratic right to protest. This is the first time this has happened on Zandra in 200 years. These protesters are worried that their opinions are being ignored and that a 48% minority is highly significant."

Well. So that was them then. Kaleem watched the screen for several minutes. The camera zoomed into some of the crowd and he looked carefully for anyone he knew. There was no one. That was a relief. They looked ordinary enough Zandrians and there were clearly also one or two foreigners in the crowd. The usual sort of mix, then. What was eating them?

He guessed he would find out soon enough. He was going to get to know these people one way or another. He had to.

He turned away from the screen and carried on back towards his parents' apartment.

He jogged the last half kilometre, reached the apartment block, and lined his iris up with the scanner. A few seconds later he was in the apartment. It seemed oddly quiet. No one was talking. Petri was not playing with her toys. She would usually mumble to herself, making up stories about the little figures she liked to play with. Had something happened? Was she ill again?

Marijam came into the lounge, carrying a cup of tea.

"They've gone home."

"Home? How can they?"

"Your father's gone with them. He's hooking up everything to our credits. Rozia didn't want him to at first. Then he persuaded her by saying of course he knew she would pay us back as soon as she could. You haven't found out any more, have you, about why her credits have been stopped?"

Kaleem shook his head. That remained a real mystery but one he couldn't get to just yet. There were other, bigger matters to deal with first.

"So how was your meeting? Have you got an action plan yet?"

"A very vague one." He hesitated. Should he tell his mother about meeting Ella?

"Go on. Spit it out."

Yes, she always had this knack of knowing. "Executive Tyler is actually Ella Raymond. Tyler is her attachment's name."

"Oh!" Marijam's eyes grew round and she almost spilled her tea.

Kaleem sighed. "If Rozia's gone home, I may as well do the same."

Marijam nodded. She held up her cup. "Look at it as being a cup half full," she said. "Petri wants you and Rozia back together. And if that doesn't work out… there's always the other one."

"Mother, she's attached."

Marijam shrugged. "Few attachments are permanent these days."

What was she saying?

She grinned and shook her head. "No, your father and I are rock solid." She looked at her cup and held it up again. "Half full, remember."

It was high time he was going. "I'm going to pack," he said as he left the room.

CHAPTER NINE

Rozia's Ulog

Dear all,

I'm afraid it's all been going wrong recently.

All of our credits were frozen. I can't get at anything. Kaleem thinks it's just some sort of bug in the system. I think it's much worse than that. I really think that someone is targeting us. First the corrupt wands and now this. Everything in the apartment stopped working. We even had to open the door manually. I didn't know what to do. Kaleem wasn't available, of course. He's always so busy these days, now that such bizarre things are happening. I did manage to contact Nazaret and Marijam. Nazaret put everything on to his and Marijam's credits. I hate that. And in fact everything became very sluggish and in the end they invited me to stay with them. I hated being so dependent on others but I was touched by their kindness.

"You must stay with us," said Marijam.

"Yes, you should stay as long as you like. And you certainly shouldn't go home until we've sorted all of this out."

Marijam loved having Petri to stay. "It's like having a grandchild," she said. She had quite a wicked gleam in her eye. I think she would like Kaleem and me to get back together. Well, I'm sorry, Marijam; I don't think it's going to happen.

The bizarre thing is Kaleem decided to stay there as well a lot of the time. Marijam and Nazaret's apartment is quite big but it did become a bit crowded with all of us there. Then Marijam suggested that Kaleem and I might share a room. Really!

It was torture, actually, seeing him every day. I

longed to be with him again, like we were when we lived in the Z Zone on Terrestra. I just don't think I can trust him though.

Nazaret totally got it. He could see that it had become too much for me in the end. I just had to go back to our own apartment. It was awkward though. My credits still hadn't been sorted out.

I think he knew I'd been crying that day. He didn't say anything about that though.

"I'm sorry Marijam makes such a fuss. It comes from having had to bring Kaleem up on her own. She really values family now. If you want a bit of space, we can pay for your apartment instead."

It was a good solution, though I feel terrible about them paying for me.

Nazaret took us back home while Kaleem was out. It was a relief to get away from the continuous tension.

I do wish they would sort out my credits, though. I can't go on taking from Marijam and Nazaret like this.

Rozia

CHAPTER TEN

So, the young prospective attachment for the Peace Child had it all sorted out. Good for her. Clever young woman.

CHAPTER ELEVEN

Snazzy. Of course he'd got a sense of what it meant. Slightly flamboyant. A bit eccentric. Sparkly. Maybe. But he wasn't like that, was he? If anything he was just plain old, slightly ugly Kaleem. And why would a droid bother with any subtle message like that? Droids weren't supposed to be subtle.

He decided to do a dictionary search. The dataserve whirred and clicked away but gave him hardly anything. The New World records got him nowhere. There was nothing for it but to look at some Wordtext. Even that took an age.

"Stylish", "well-dressed", "flashy", he read. No, that certainly wasn't him. It wasn't really anybody on any of the One World planets. You didn't need to show off how you were different.

Was that what the droid and the man meant then? That he was making a show of himself?

He needed more examples. "Give me stories," he commanded the dataserve.

Silence.

The dataserve clearly was doing something but not fast enough for his liking. He helped himself to a frega and decided to use the exercise machine for a while. Soon he was pounding away and was lost in thoughts about what it would be like to lose the One World status, whether he and Rozia could ever get back together and what would happen if Petri's meds failed completely.

He was startled when the dataserve suddenly announced that it had something for him.

He stopped and watched as the screen loaded. A square still picture of three young men appeared. The word "Snazzy" in Wordtext was printed across the top of the picture. Those men did look strange. They were wearing uncomfortable looking leggings and tunics that were too short, one tucked into the leggings and the other not really fitting over the top. Around their necks they wore knotted pieces of pink cloth. Their hair was very short. Suddenly they came to life and started singing and dancing. It was a bit of racket, actually.

"Next clip?" asked the dataserve.

"Yes please."

The noise faded and the picture disappeared.

Next came a strange two dimensional figure, wearing a similar combination of odd leggings and an ill-fitting tunic. The tunic was a little longer this time as was the young man's hair. His outfit was covered in brightly coloured flowers, many of them different shades of pink. Did snazziness have to have the colour pink in it then? Again the figure sprang to life and started dancing this time to some slightly more palatable music. As the figure gyrated, it legs and arms stretched and shortened and his eyes bulged. Kaleem caught himself smiling. Then the clip stopped abruptly.

"Load third example?" he asked the dataserve.

"Yes."

This one seemed to be in the present day. Two young people were getting ready to go to a party.

"What do you think?" asked the girl.

"Snazzy," said her boyfriend or brother or whoever the young man was.

The girl became angry. "Snazzy? Snazzy? That's my grandmother when she puts on her holohead to go out for lunch."

So "snazzy" was these days a bit lame as an expression? Interesting…

"Other stories?"

"No others currently found. Continue search?"

Kaleem sighed. "Yes please." He didn't have much hope, though.

The search had got him hardly anywhere. It would be better to continue with his exercise and think about it a bit. He opted for the exercise machine again rather than going for a jog; it would be a bit cold by now and he wanted to be near his main dataserve in case it came up with any more ideas. Soon the treadmill was putting him through his paces again.

Running wasn't clearing his mind. Better run harder. He increased the speed and the incline.

Yes he always had to fit right in. He had to blend with others despite not quite being any one thing. He couldn't ever be completely Terrestran or Zandrian as he was a mixture of both. Anyway, over and above that he'd acquired so much understanding of other cultures that little bits of all of them had rubbed off on him. Could he ever really be snazzy, then? Was snazzy normal to him?

He increased the incline again. Now he was working really hard, becoming breathless. Good. His exercise would be effective.

He couldn't think so much now as he had to concentrate on his breathing. An image suddenly came to him. Plants like the ones his father grew. Only this time they weren't laid out like they would be in the growing fields and veriglass units. They were set out decoratively over a few steps. So "snazzy" could apply to objects as well, could it? Could this be defined as simply arranging things differently? Using something for an unusual purpose?

He slowed the machine and gradually stopped running. He was delightfully out of breath now.

At that precise moment his communicator sounded. Nazaret. Coincidence or what?

"Send via dataserve," he commanded.

Nazaret grinned at him. "Hi. How's it going?"

"Just trying to work out the meaning of something."

"Can I help in any way?"

"Would you ever arrange plants to be purely decorative?"

Nazaret shrugged. "If I had some to spare."

"And what would you call it if you did?"

"Extravagant."

That was a good point. "Hmm."

"Well you know, on ancient Terrestra, they had a tribe that kept lettuces in pots to decorate their tables and rooms. They also used to talk about weeds. These were really just plants growing in the wrong place. We don't have that problem on Zandra. It's difficult enough to get the right amount to feed us."

"But if you did have any spare… maybe if you arranged them over a series of steps. Say on a ladder or a staircase in a house?"

"That would be delightful. Very snazzy."

"Aha. That is the word I'm trying to define."

“Snazzy?”

“Yes. What do you understand by it?”

Nazaret shrugged again. “Flamboyant? Fun?”

“Yes, I still don’t get, though, why they call me ‘snazzy boy’.”

Nazaret smirked. “Neither do I. You’re much too serious.”

Kaleem tried to look offended. “So, anyway, was there anything specific you wanted to talk about?”

“I just wanted to invite you for dinner tomorrow. If you come you ought to talk to your mother about ‘snazzy’. I think you’ll find she has plenty of ideas about that. She used to use the word a lot when we first got together.”

She did? Well, that would be interesting. “Okay I’ll see you then. Usual time?”

Nazaret nodded. “We are creatures of habit.”

Nazaret’s head appeared as the door to the kitchen slid open. “Estimated eating time, ten minutes.”

He’d better get on with it then. “So, Dad said you might be able to help me understand the meaning of ‘snazzy’.”

Marijam blushed and cleared her throat. “I haven’t really got much to say. But they did use it a lot, you know. When they brought us from the Z Zone to the cave apartment. There we were in one of the poorest places that was allowed to exist in the Normal Zones and they thought it was the height of luxury.”

“Well, what did you think?”

Marijam shrugged. “It was coming home for me, in some ways. It was what I’d known before I’d gone to the Z Zone. But I was terrified. I would actually have preferred to stay with the Z Zoners. I was going to be on my own with a small baby. Even though everything seemed familiar I just didn’t want to be there. But you should have heard them: “Have you seen the way this cupboard works? And look at that light-well going up to the surface. Goodness, this dataserve’s dead snazzy. It’s all so snazzy.”

Kaleem nodded. He knew only too well about the contrast between what had been the Z Zone and the Normal Zones on Terrestra. Even though he’d been brought up in a cave apartment, the Z Zone had seemed really desolate when he and Rozia had lived there. Rozia had brightened it up for him of course.

"I began to understand what they meant," Marijam continued, "when I eventually got out and about a bit. What they'd done up on the surface on Terrestra after the poison cloud had shifted was like some sort of miracle. Everything worked so much better."

"So it's not just flamboyant and fun?"

"That definitely, but also extremely clever... and a bit sophisticated."

Nazaret came back into the room. "You know back on Terrestra, long before the colonisation and also before the poison cloud arrived there had been two terrible wars. Lots of different factions, Terrestrans fighting against other Terrestrans. It took a long time to get over it but then suddenly everything was fun and people starting dressing in very bright and unusual clothes. Despite another terrible war going on. Perhaps because of it. Young people had had enough. And those who approved of what they wore and what they did would definitely have described them as snazzy. But once that third war was over and the planet really began to function properly again all that fun and those bright and colourful clothes looked silly. Especially considering the glories that came afterwards."

"So it's about contrast as well?"

Nazaret nodded.

"Oh well." Kaleem wasn't sure he was going to get to the bottom of it. But the food looked and smelt good even though it was machine-made. That was snazzy, wasn't it? It still didn't explain why he been picked out as being snazzy, though. "I guess I'll figure it all out eventually."

The meal had as usual been filling and the conversation had gone on for a long time. The topic of snazz had been well and truly exhausted. Nazaret also told him about all of the new experiments at the plantations. Marijam talked a little about her work and had constantly tried to find out about how he and Rozia were getting on. Then of course they had to talk about the current political situation.

"Will they be using you again?" Marijam asked.

He'd shrugged. "I expect so. It's what I do. It's my job, Mother."

She'd frowned.

Definitely time to go now. Besides it was late and the table was covered with dirty dishes. The house droid was already starting to pack away.

Kaleem sighed. "I'd best get going."

"Well keep us informed about everything, won't you?" said Marijam.

Nazaret gave him a knowing look and inclined his head slightly. "Shall I call up a transporter?"

"No, I'll run."

Marijam frowned. "But it's so cold now."

"Jogging will keep me warm enough. I'm so full anyway. I need the exercise."

And without another word he'd left.

He wanted to think.

As he pounded along the frosted streets he half expected another droid to jump out and accuse him of being snazzy. It didn't happen though. No one else, not even a machine, was out in this cold. Was it difference that did it? But it had it be a marked difference didn't it? And that droid had seemed accusatory, hadn't it? Fun, but frivolous, perhaps? Oh he didn't know. One thing though, being so preoccupied made the journey go quickly. Before he knew it, he was home.

He woke up suddenly in the middle of the night. It was so clear now. Snazzy. Flamboyant and extravagant, yes. Quirky and different too. Cleverly different. Often extremely clever. But it was the effective difference that was the most important. And oh yes; he was different all right. Was he effective?

CHAPTER TWELVE

How was this happening? What had got into people? He'd never seen anything like this – neither here nor on Terrestra. There must be thousands of them. They were running now towards the area of town where Rozia and Petri lived. The streets were unusually dusty and the air hurt his lungs. It was rare to have so many people in the same place. There was a loud murmurring from the crowd and the faint smell of sweat. Kaleem desperately wanted to call Rozia and check that they were both all right, but he daren't; somebody might be listening in and that would blow his cover. That could put them all in danger. Besides, he needed to keep his channel with the Executive Council open.

Well, he was certainly amongst them now but he still couldn't figure out who they actually were and why they had become the way they were. Nor for that matter why they were running like this. It seemed some sort of madness. Hysteria. Almost as if they were programmed droids. Was that it? Had some sort of brainwashing happened? Well, his mission now was to get close to one and for the moment that meant following the crowd until he could make contact with someone who would believe he was on their side.

They were now making their way into the second urban band. Wasn't that where most of businesses owned by people from other planets were? It was almost mid-afternoon and it was getting very hot. Why must they charge about in these temperatures? No time to ponder on that. He had to keep up.

The people in front stopped suddenly.

"Snazzers!" someone shouted. There was the sound of something breaking.

More cries of "Snazzers" and "Scum!" followed, and more sounds of things smashing. The crowd edged slowly forward. Kaleem was amazed to see broken veriglass. Veriglass just did not break. What was this new technology? Where had they got it from?

"Snazz" was at least becoming clearer. It was obviously being used in a new way for something that people didn't like. Probably people from other planets like Rozia and himself. Ah well. They'd never guess at the moment. The Executive Council's disguise department had done wonders.

The group was getting away from him a little. Another was coming up behind now. He mustn't dawdle or he'd draw attention to himself. He rushed forward, shouting, "Snazzers."

The crowd now stormed one of the warehouses. It wasn't just a matter of breaking veriglass anymore; they were bypassing all of the electronic locks on the doors without apparently doing anything. He would have to find out more about that.

The warehouse contained catering equipment. The crowd rushed forward, ripping open containers and strewing plates, dishes and mugs all over the floor. Much of the crockery smashed as it hit the tiles. Kaleem watched in horror as many of the rioters picked up the big chefs' knives and stashed them into their rucksacks. He had to do the same. At least that would be a few more knives that couldn't be used for some sort of bad purpose.

He watched one man rummaging through a cutlery drawer. It was full of innocent-looking knives, forks and spoons.

"Man, what are you looking for?" he asked. "Shouldn't we be concentrating on the big stuff?"

The man stared at him and shook his head. Had his Terrestran accent come through? There was something a little bit strange about this man anyway. He didn't look completely Zandrian himself.

"Come, on man," Kaleem continued. "We don't want to get left behind."

"We won't. But these are important. House of Clementine." The Zandrian showed Kaleem the spoon he was holding. It had a tiny embossed pattern on the handle. It looked a little like a branch from an orange tree: leaves and tiny oranges.

"What does that mean?"

"The House of Clementine has suppressed Zandra for centuries. Now it's time to break away."

"But I thought we were rebelling against the One World Community."

The Zandrian nodded. “That’s what most people think. But it’s really the House of Clementine that’s caused the trouble. They control the One World Community anyway. “The Zandrian stared at Kaleem for a few more seconds. Then he nodded. “You seem a bit different from the others.” He took a handful of spoons and thrust them into Kaleem’s hands.

A new wave of rioters rushed past. The Zandrian touched Kaleem’s arm. “Meet me at the Refreshment Park pavilion at autumn-winter interface. He got up on to his feet. “Snazzers!” he called and hurtled after the others.

Kaleem started running after him.

It was freezing at the Refreshment Park pavilion. There was no sign of any life there. That didn’t surprise Kaleem. It usually closed half an hour before the summer-autumn interface. He was surprised, though, that the door was open.

As he walked in, the lights came on. Would that mean that he could be seen from the outside? Probably not. It wasn’t quite dark outside yet and anyway nobody would be near the Refreshment Park at this time of day. People would be making their way indoors if they weren’t there already.

Something rustled behind him.

Kaleem turned to find himself facing the Zandrian. “You came then?” the man said.

Kaleem nodded. The man puzzled him. There was just something not completely Zandrian about him but he couldn’t decide quite what.

“Let’s not tell each other too much about ourselves. Just call me Clemens. Clem for short.”

“All right. I’ll be Kay.”

“Follow me, then.”

Clemens led Kaleem into the kitchen. He opened a cupboard door and pulled a handle that was inserted into the side of the cupboard. A trap-door opened in the floor and a staircase led down to some sort of basement. He gestured that Kaleem should follow him.

They made their way for about eight hundred metres along a stone-tiled corridor. Lights snapped on as they approached them and then switched off again as they passed. The corridor then opened out into a wide room. About twenty people sat in front of dataserve screens.

"Welcome to operation Take Down Clementine."

Kaleem nodded. "What do I need to know?"

"It's a long story. Best start straight away." Clem pointed to an empty dataserve terminal.

Kaleem sat down at the work station.

"Go on," said Clem. "Command it on."

"Serve," said Kaleem.

Images started flashing across the screen. An icon of a stylised clementine appeared in the corner of each picture.

CHAPTER THIRTEEN

Despite the freezing temperature Kaleem decided to jog home. It was the middle of the night and he was returning from his tenth session with Take Down Clementine. This way he had time to think. What he'd found out this evening had totally shocked him. He'd spent a couple of hours talking it through with Clem and some of the others.

It had all been disturbing enough. The House of Clementine had operated on Terrestra, Zandra and Zenoto for centuries. It had controlled the banks and of course, whoever controlled the money pretty well controlled everything else. It hadn't been the politicians in the end. All they could do was work with what was in front of them and pretend they were achieving something so that they could massage their own egos. The House of Clementine was directed by just a small group of determined individuals in the beginning. Not all descendants were admitted to the House. They had to prove they had the right attitude first.

Now Clem's group wanted to find all of the people involved and take them out. Not kill them but keep them imprisoned. Take Down Clementine would also need to prove themselves to all the other people and those in charge. And some of those in charge might well be members of the House.

Then tonight he'd had the greatest shock of all: the One World Community bureaucrats were entirely controlled by the House of Clementine.

Kaleem paused for breath. He had a slight stitch. He stretched his side to relieve it. The cold now bit in sharply. He would have to get going again or he might just freeze to death. The One World Community, though. It was actually corrupt as well. His idea had been to find out what people didn't like and rectify it. Now it looked as if the whole organisation needed to be dismantled and something new must take its place.

He longed to talk to Rozia. She would have something sensible to say, he was sure. He'd have to be careful exactly how much he told her and it was much too late to call round now. Perhaps he could offer her and Petri breakfast tomorrow. Yes, that's what he would do. He jogged on. He'd get up early despite getting to bed so late.

The thought of seeing Rozia lifted his spirits somewhat. He found some more energy and doubled his pace.

The Cherry Bowl on the fifth urban ring was quiet today. It had been a good choice. The cherry-coloured furnishings and the large veriglass windows made it pretty and light. The food was good, he knew. This was a place used more in the holidays and today was a normal working day. Life was settling down again on Zandra.

Kaleem toyed with his napkin nervously. Would they come? He hadn't actually spoken to Rozia. He'd left a message in the middle of the night. She hadn't replied.

The waiting droid hovered near his table. "Would sir like some coffee whilst he's waiting for his guests?" said the machine.

Kaleem waved the droid away. He was much too nervous to eat or drink yet.

The doors swished open at last and in they came. My, they both looked so well. Kaleem stood up as they made their way over to the table.

"Can we have pancakes, Kaleem? I want pancakes." Petri jogged his hand up and down.

"You can have whatever you like. Of course you can."

Petri beamed.

"So what's this all in aid of?" asked Rozia as she studied her menu screen.

"Oh just celebrating the fact that we're making some breakthroughs."

"Really?" She looked away from the screen. "Can you tell me anything?"

"Not a lot. But I just wanted your opinion; just how important is it that we keep the One World Community intact?"

Rozia frowned and her eyes grew round. "Really important. Naturally. How can we not have the One World Community?"

"But suppose we found out that it was corrupt?"

"Is it?"

Kaleem shrugged.

"Well, if we had to get rid of it because it was corrupt, we'd better replace it with something else similar but without the corruption. Pretty quickly."

So ordinary people were still mainly in favour of the One World Community. He decided to change the subject. At that precise moment the droid arrived.

"Just toast with honey and tea for me," said Rozia.

"Have more, if you want."

"Pancakes," cried Petri.

Rozia shook her head. "We can't stay all that long. I'm doing some work for Nazaret today."

"No news about your credits?"

"No. And your parents are being so kind. It's only fair that I should do something to pay them back. I'm editing one of your father's reports."

Kaleem turned to the droid. "Yes pancakes for the young lady and toast and honey for me as well. With coffee."

The droid trundled back to the kitchen and just a few moments later reappeared with the order. They talked as they ate mainly about Petri's progress. She was steaming ahead on her dataserve course.

"No more problems with her drugs?"

"No, that was a complete mystery. Everything's fine." Her communicator bleeped. "Look, I'm sorry. We must go. Is it okay if I leave you to settle the bill?"

Petri pulled a face.

"Of course. Let Petri stay and finish her pancakes. I'll bring her along later."

Petri clapped her hands. "Thank you, Kaleem."

Rozia smiled and nodded then got up from the table. "See you later."

Kaleem waved to the serving droid which then trundled over to him. It took just seconds for him to align his iris to the scanner. He held his breath as he waited for his payment to go through. He was now slightly nervous every time he accessed his credits because of what had happened to Rozia.

He needn't have worried. The transaction went through smoothly.

They were just about to stand up and leave when a couple came in. Goodness what a nice surprise. He hadn't seen them for months. Petro and Tulla. He hadn't even realised they were back on Zandra.

"Don't rush off, mate," said Petro. "Stay for a catch up?"

Kaleem quickly introduced Petri. She stared at Tulla with her mouth open. Hardly surprising: Tulla looked so much like Rozia. He hoped she wouldn't say anything.

Fortunately Petro rescued them. He grinned at Petri. "My name's like yours a bit, isn't it?"

She giggled and nodded her head. "Oh yes, it is."

Kaleem nodded and soon they were enjoying some good Zandrian hazelnut chofas. It almost felt like the old days when he had first come to Zandra in disguise.

"But why have you come back? I thought you really liked your work out there."

Tulla sighed. "We do. Of course we do. But there's obviously something going awry here and we thought we might be able to help. We're also not sure how much longer we'd be welcome there, anyway, given Zandra's current attitude to the One World Community. We decided to quit while we're ahead." She looked down into her lap.

Kaleem noticed she had gone very pale.

Petro rubbed her arm. "It'll be fine," he murmured. He turned to Kaleem. "We've put ourselves forward for special home intelligence and we've been accepted. We might even be working with you."

Kaleem smiled. "That would be cool." Though actually he doubted whether they would be allowed into the Take Down Clementine project. "Talking of work, I'd better get going." He stood up.

Tulla and Petro also got out of their seats. Petro grinned. "No good asking you what you're up to, I suppose?"

Kaleem smiled and shook his head.

Petri was now wobbling his arm.

"I know," he said. "Grown-up talk. And yes. It's high time I got you back. Rozia will wonder where we've got to."

It had been good seeing Tulla and Petro again. It was always the same problem, though, wasn't it? He always knew too much and couldn't tell. Oh well. Best not to dwell on it. He had another meeting with Clem again in less than an hour. He dropped off Petri and started to make his way to where he'd arranged to meet Clem.

A huge crowd had gathered around one of the public information screens. Kaleem recognised at once the face of one of the most loved Zandrian actors, Karlo Dunston. Of course he knew him well: Karlo had played Kaleem in the film they'd made about his first trip to Zandra.

"I do this with a good deal of sadness," said Karlo. "But I feel I can't risk losing contact with the One World Community. For me, it's bigger than Zandra. Therefore, I have applied for Terrestran citizenship. My mother is half Terrestran and I think I'm in with a very good chance. That way I can continue to be a citizen of the One World Community."

This was intriguing. How did the actor come to have a mother who was half Terrestran? Even before the poison cloud, Terrestra had been a lone planet, barely connecting with others. It was rather ironic as well that Terrestra of all planets was now one of the most enthusiastic members of the One World Community.

He looked at Karlo's face. Did he look Terrestran? Maybe a little. Of course, they'd done an excellent job of making him look just like Kaleem for the film but he'd always put that down to clever use of make-up and CGI. Maybe there was a Terrestran element to him after all.

"You can't be persuaded to change your mind?" asked the droid presenter.

Karlo shook his head. "Zandra no longer feels like home. I'll be leaving as soon as possible."

"Even though Zandra has no plans to leave the One World Community?"

"It's too risky. I have to be where I can feel at home."

The screen went black. The crowd dispersed. No one said a word.

CHAPTER FOURTEEN

Clem had not turned up for the meeting they'd arranged. This wasn't the first time and Kaleem was sure it wouldn't be the last. It would now just be a matter of waiting until Clem contacted him again. He most surely would.

He was quite pleased to relax in front of the dataserve. He contemplated calling Rozia but decided against it. It was always a delicate balance between letting her know that he cared, that he would always be available if she needed some help, and smothering her. He hoped, though, that she would contact him.

He could find out nothing about Karlo Dunston. This was only the actor's pseudonym and strict protocols prevented his real name being revealed. In fact it had been quite brave of the actor to admit that he was one quarter Terrestran. Given enough time, Kaleem would be able to hack into the systems. In fact, he could probably quite easily access Hidden Information or even Golden Knowledge if he went on to the Terrestran servers but even he might get into quite a bit of trouble for this: he didn't actually need to find out about Karlo. He had been tasked with something bigger. Hacking into systems to which he sometimes had access anyway was a bit of waste of time although it helped to keep his skills fine-tuned.

But even the Executives, even Tyler herself, had no idea about the House of Clementine. He would have to find out more before he could disclose anything and anyway his role wasn't to disclose but to reconcile or find a third way.

Would finding out more about the poison cloud and the cave system help? Would his parents know more? His father had come secretly to Terrestra, hadn't he?

Nazaret apparently was in a meeting. That too was a puzzle. What was so urgent about crop control that they had to meet in the evening?

"He didn't say why it was so important," said Marijam. "But he is worried. Can I help?"

"I was just wondering what it was like in the caves on Terrestra – and before. And if any other Zandrians had ever been to Terrestra."

"Goodness. What do you want to know about all of that for? Best forgotten, isn't it?"

"Perhaps. But why was Terrestra so reluctant to communicate with others? They might have got more help with the poison cloud."

"Well, they did eventually, didn't they? Hence: your father."

"Okay, but why be so secretive?"

There was a brief silence, then Marijam sighed. "We were so proud of our disease-free society. We wanted to keep it that way." There was another pause. "Then you came along."

"Sorry about that." He never had quite got over being the one to bring disease back to Terrestra. "What was it like, living in the caves all of the time?" He knew a little about it; he had lived in a cave when he was younger and then again when he'd lived in the Z Zone with Rozia, but he had been able to go out of the cave into the fresh air. He couldn't imagine what it was like never leaving the cave system.

"Well, we didn't know any other way. The caves were all we knew. Your grandparents spent half of their lives down there. Why don't you talk to them?"

That would be a good idea. He could make a long-distance call.

"Thanks. I might just do that."

"Just one more thing before you go. I have heard that some Terrestrans went to Zandra just before the poison cloud became so bad that we all had to go underground. So, there may be some more Terrestran blood on Zandra apart from ours. Were you thinking of Karlo Dunston?"

"Yeah."

"Well, let me know if you find out. I'm curious too."

The caves felt familiar and yet they were not how he remembered them. The dampness and gloom that contrasted with the fresh air and the light. The long way down to the apartment from the surface. And the even poorer caves in the Z Zone where he and

Rozia had been so happy. He didn't remember this though. This was somebody else's story.

There was no way out. One cave just led into another. There were mirror systems that allowed light from the surface into the caves. It was a dull light though. The sky when you looked up at it here was overcast by a greyish-green cloud. Terrestran light, he remembered had always been bright. Zandrian, too. Where was this place?

The air was stale and a little musty. The back of his throat was choking. He was walking with the others. He didn't know these people but they seemed to know him. They smiled and nodded. He smiled politely back. Nobody spoke and they were all hurrying. Their pupils were huge. They seemed to look right into you, as if they could read your very thoughts.

He had to get out. He knew that. He didn't know how or why.

"This way," said a voice. It sounded as if the speaker was standing right behind him and was whispering into his left ear. He turned, but there was no one there. A hand grabbed his arm. "Come on. Follow me," said the same voice.

He found himself in a darkened passage. The ground was rougher underfoot. "The shuttle is almost ready. Just keep on following. Don't say anything."

His adjusted to the dark and he could make out the outline of his companion who kept his back to him.

"We'll soon be there," said the man. He sounded older, maybe like an Elder. It wasn't one he recognised though and he certainly wasn't dressed like an Elder. In fact, Kaleem had never seen such an extraordinary costume. Yes it was still a tunic and trousers but the tunic was longer than normal and the trousers much baggier.

The passage opened in to a flood-lit area. A rush of fresh air greeted Kaleem. He realised that he was now outside of the cave system. The man turned to him. Now he recognised him but still he couldn't think where from.

"You're ready?" the man asked.

He wasn't sure. He didn't know what this was all about. He had the feeling though that he ought to. He nodded.

"No regrets?"

Kaleem shook his head.

"Right then. We'll proceed to the interplanetary craft."

A shuttle craft with a droid driver stopped in front of them. They both stepped in.

The shuttle sped off across the concourse, rounded a corner, crossed another huge open space and then slowed so that it could make its way through a narrow archway. A new space opened in front of them and there she was: a rather old-fashioned looking space craft but nevertheless gleaming white and looking full of hope.

"She's all programmed ready for your crossing to Zandra. They're all waiting for you and your expertise." The man bowed slightly and invited Kaleem to walk towards the entrance of the space craft.

CHAPTER FIFTEEN

Kaleem was still feeling groggy from the strange dream. He'd woken late and felt exhausted. Clem had now rearranged the meeting but he would be late if he didn't get a move on. Yet he couldn't help revisiting that dream over and over. He must have been dreaming he was somebody else, mustn't he? That was another person's story, wasn't it? Although he hadn't known what was actually going on he'd had the very strong feeling that the person whose body he'd taken over did.

Or was it simply that he was still trying to work out how Karlo Dunston's mother could be half Terrestran? Certainly the man he'd dreamt he was could have been her father. That was possibly the explanation. It had all been so vivid though. It had actually seemed more than a dream and the emotions he'd gone through had left him exhausted. And now he had to muster some energy for Clem.

As he turned the corner, he was confronted by a sight that made him wake up straight away. A gang of Zandrians was marching towards him. Their eyes were glazed and they were all wearing brown tunics. He'd never seen people march like that before on Zandra or even on Terrestra though it did remind him a little of what he'd seen in the Z Zone when Kevik had produced his army.

Were these people real?

One turned to face him as they marched past. His deep blue eyes looked into Kaleem's.

He counted them as they went past. Thirty in total. It had seemed like more. They were marching with such force.

They stopped, clicked their heels and saluted, then started to disperse. What were they trying to do? Several made their way into a nearby café. He followed them.

He quickly counted again. Just eight of them here? The others had marched on. The ones who had stayed behind hardly seemed to speak to one another. They were using their personal communicators frenetically, however. Occasionally one would look up at one of the others.

They were working together. Like bees or ants. But why like this out in the open?

He kept his own head down, but was glad actually when the droid waiter appeared, giving him a chance to look up. This was so bizarre. They were clearly colluding, but why were they doing it in the open? And why did the need to be together physically?

Kaleem watched the behaviour of the other people in the café. They seemed fascinated. Were they afraid? Maybe a little. Then just as suddenly as the brown tunics had decided to stop, they all started to leave. One by one they got up and made their way to the door. It seemed random but as soon as they were out of the door, they fell into line and started marching again.

Just one stayed behind. He nodded at Kaleem and indicated that he should join him. Kaleem hovered the sessel over to the table.

"Peace Child, eh?" The man was sneering slightly. His dark eyes looked at nothing in particular.

"You recognise me?" Kaleem went hot and began to sweat. This should not be happening.

The man laughed. "We have our spies as well. Someone will always find out. You should know that."

Well he was right to some extent. There were spies, counter spies and double agents everywhere. But why "as well"? Kaleem never had been nor never would be a spy though he'd had to do his fair share of spying.

"You need to listen to what I've got to say. It's important."

"Go on then."

The man looked around, probably checking to see whether anyone was watching him. Then he tapped his personal communicator. "Come on, let me link to you."

Kaleem nodded and held his communicator near to the man's. The download only took seconds. It was in Wordtext. So this guy had some form of special education.

"Read it," said the man. "I guess you can."

Kaleem nodded. Not only could he read it but he recognized it quite clearly. The Universal Declaration of Human Rights. All interplanetary law was based on this. It had been important to civilisation since the middle of the twentieth century and had survived until now despite some attempted interference in the twenty-first century by one of the richest nations on Terrestra, the very planet where these rights had been established. Why was this man looking at it in Wordtext, though? Why was he concerned about it?

"Article 1 is incorrect," whispered the man. "We are not all equal. Some of us are superior."

Kaleem shivered. He'd heard that somewhere else before and it hadn't been good.

"Articles 14:2 and 29:2 don't protect us enough."

Kaleem quickly reread the two articles. Yes, these were the ones that allowed them to deal with anti-social behaviour effectively. "Surely they do?"

"We're challenging this. We want Zandra to be great again."

"Zandra is great."

The man shook his head. "There are too many foreigners. Sucking out the life-blood."

"Surely not. Surely more like making a positive contribution?"

"No, it's all getting diluted. Where is the purity now? Zandra is losing its essence." The man nodded and looked right into his eyes. "See, you and I read Wordtext. Not many others can. We need to build up that sort of superiority."

"I'm not pure Zandrian either."

The man laughed. "You'll probably be fine. You have many of the talents we admire. Be careful, though. All other things being equal we may choose to eliminate you as well."

What did he mean "eliminate"?

"You could make it easier for yourself. You can help us in our fight against impurity." The man got up from his chair and sneered at Kaleem. "Your choice." He laughed as he made his way out of the café.

What did this all mean for him and Rozia? Or for Marijam for that matter? And for thousands like them? He remembered a quote from somewhere: "Disdain for the Recognition of Human Rights – Because of fear of enemies and the need for security, the people in fascist regimes are persuaded that human rights can be ignored in certain cases because of 'need'." Where had that come from?

CHAPTER SIXTEEN

No, he couldn't let him get away with this. He must find out more and he must stop him. He glanced out of the window. Yes, he could still see him.

The waiter droid hovered over to him.

"Yes, settle," mumbled Kaleem, pointing his iris at the machine.

"Both covers?" the machine asked.

Drat the man. Not only had he rushed off but he hadn't even paid his bill.

"Yes. Please hurry."

The droid whirred and clicked for what seemed like ages but was he realised in fact only a few seconds. At last the transaction was complete.

"Confirmed," murmured the droid but still stood in Kaleem's way. Kaleem pushed it gently away. He could still see the brown tunic but he would get away soon. He had to hurry.

"Security," screeched the droid.

Too bad, thought Kaleem. He just had to get going. Brown tunic was just reaching the end of the street.

He rushed through the door. As he started to pound down the street Kaleem could hear a lot of fuss in the background. Hopefully they wouldn't catch him before he caught up with brown tunic. When they did, if they did, it could all be easily resolved. He just had to get this man and set him straight. How dare they mess with human rights? How dare they?

He was soon running faster. He was gaining on the man.

Luckily all of that running everywhere was paying off. Kaleem was soon at the corner and a brief glance in either direction confirmed that the man had turned to the left. This was quite a busy little street but was too minor to be divided into walking lanes. He had to concentrate really hard to be able keep the man in sight.

The man reached the end of the street and turned left again into a wider, more controlled road. And there they were again, all of them, marching on mass.

Kaleem watched as his man stepped into line with the others. It ought now to be reasonably easy to keep him in view as long as the crowds watching didn't get too dense and as long as he didn't let his eyes wander. If his eyes strayed away from the man he might not be able to pick him out in the crowd again. They all looked the same. It was some uniform, this brown tunic.

It was easy at first. He found that people stepped out of his way. He was sure the man couldn't see him. The brown tunic had his eyes fixed forward. He didn't look though as if he was just looking where he was going. He was looking at something much further afield. Something intangible most likely.

It was clear that the brown shirt really believed this was right. Incredibly.

Suddenly there was a kerfuffle in the crowd.

"Damn fascists," Kaleem heard someone shout.

He could see an elderly Zandrian shaking his fist at the parade. Others were turning away from the marchers to see what was going on in the crowd.

Kaleem looked back to the brown tunics. All he could see now was a mass of brown. He scooted forward to catch up. Was that him there, maybe? He fixed his eyes on the face of the man on the left of the third row away from him. Yes, he was sure that was him.

A shot rang out. Somebody in the crowd had fired some sort of gun. This time he chose not to be distracted. He kept his eyes firmly fixed on his man. The brown tunics dispersed. His man darted down a nearby alley.

Kaleem hurried after him down the alley. There was no way out. Was the man some sort of fool or was this a trick? At least he might get to talk to him again now.

The man turned to face him and grinned. "You didn't think it would be that easy did you?"

Kaleem heard two sets of running footsteps behind him. Someone punched him from behind. Someone else grabbed his arm.

"Get out of this one, then, Peace Child," one of them snarled.

How did they know? This was really worrying.

"Yes, hold him there. Perhaps we can make him negotiate a deal for us."

"On what grounds?" Could he stall them?

"Preservation of human purity, of course."

"It could be up for negotiation, I suppose," said Kaleem, "but only if you let me go."

The brown tunic signalled to the other two. Kaleem felt the pressure release from his arm. He could still hear the other two brown tunics breathing. They didn't move away.

"What can you offer, then?" asked the man.

"I can take you to someone who will listen."

"How would we know it wasn't a trick?"

Kaleem shrugged. "I always go for win win. It's just what I do."

"Boss, it sounds dodgy," one of the men behind him said. "Don't trust him."

"Who is this person?" asked the brown tunic.

"Ah, that I can't say. That would be the deal. We meet them without identities being revealed. I don't know who you are anyway. How do you know about me?"

The brown tunic grinned. "Let's just say I keep myself very well informed. Can my two companions come along as well?"

"Absolutely not."

"Boss, it's risky. We can't let you go alone."

"It isn't and you can." He nodded at Kaleem. "Turn round and start walking."

Kaleem felt something sticking in his back. Was it a gun? The brown shirt kept his hand on Kaleem's left shoulder.

"Let's chat as if we're the greatest of buddies," said the brown tunic. "All lies, of course."

Kaleem concentrated on not taking the most direct route and on talking about nothing more meaningful than the habits of the cyber red dog. That topic had saved him once before when the Zandrian prosecutors had tried to read his mind. Brown tunic kept to the latest sports and music news.

Kaleem zigzagged across town. He was a little puzzled that his companion didn't query this. Didn't they recognise that they were going past some of the same places twice? Was he not from this township then?

Eventually though he mumbled: "How much further?" and poked him hard with whatever he was holding to his back.

He would have to take him there now.

The back entrance of the building lacked the splendour that people usually saw at the front. Basic service droids were emptying rubbish into some large grinder-bins. Old technology. The windows here on the lower floors at the back were mere plastiglass. They needed cleaning but would never gleam like veriglass anyway.

Kaleem lined up his iris with the scanner.

"Special code?" asked an electronic voice?

Kaleem tapped the code on to an old-fashioned key pad. The door glided open and he and brown tunic stepped into a gloomy hallway.

"Where exactly are you taking us?" asked brown tunic.

"To someone who could talk to you about Human Rights."

"You're sure about that?"

Kaleem nodded.

"Well, let's get going, then."

The object that the brown tunic was holding against Kaleem's back seemed even bigger now. He called the lift and soon they were speeding up to the tenth floor.

The lift only took seconds to arrive. It seemed like forever as the brown tunic continued to hold him tightly and keep whatever he was holding up against his spine.

At last the door slid open. "Tenth floor," said an electronic voice.

"Now what?" Brown tunic jabbed him again.

Kaleem nodded and pressed the intercom on the door to the familiar suite of offices.

She answered straight away.

"I've code mauve," said Kaleem. "One of the brown tunics from the parade wants to talk to you about human rights."

"Give me two minutes."

"Why does she need two minutes?"

"You'll understand when you see her."

The two minutes passed eventually. The door to the office suite swung open. Executive Tyler was completely covered with a long tunic and veil. Only her eyes and her toes showed.

"This gentleman wants to talk to you about Human Rights."

Tyler nodded. She invited them to sit down.

Brown tunic released Kaleem and placed a plain metal canister on the coffee table. Not a gun then, after all.

Tyler blinked twice. "So, tell me about your concerns."

Brown tunic drew a large breath and started to speak. Kaleem couldn't concentrate on what he was saying. He could only stare fascinated as Tyler gave the brown tunic a run for his money with her words. She was as clever and as charming as ever. She was all the more intriguing because she was so mysteriously covered up.

CHAPTER SEVENTEEN

Kaleem decided to take a public transporter. His communicator was back on but he was ignoring the missed messages and missed calls. He now wanted to get back home, have a shower and change, then get down to some work. He hoped everyone he was ignoring would just assume he was on some sort of secret mission and he was incommunicado. There was a message from Rozia but he couldn't bring himself to answer even that one. Not after what had just happened. He now wanted to absorb himself in some demanding work.

How had that happened actually? What had he been thinking? It had been that mysterious clothing hadn't it? It had made her all the more desirable. She'd been wearing it apparently to try and understand better some ancient people who had worn similar garments. And it had changed her, making her even more attractive.

How was this going to affect his relationship with Rozia? Had he just thrown away months of careful work? For goodness sake, she was someone else's attachment. He had no right.

Wasn't she partly to blame, though? It had been just like the old days. That overwhelming desire and the ecstasy of climaxing at exactly the same time that she did and then as soon as it was finished starting all over again.

One touch on his bare arm had been enough to start it all off after they'd got rid of the brown tunic. It had added to the mystery when he'd had to fumble to find her under the shapeless robe. The second and third time they had both been naked. The fourth time had been the most intense ever but as soon as they'd finished the guilt flowed in. This should just not have happened. He now felt sick at the thought of it.

Something going on in the transporter awoke him from his daydreaming. He could hear raised voices.

"You'll have to go home soon," he heard a young voice say. "There are too many people on this planet."

Kaleem turned to get a closer look. He could see a young Zandrian standing up and cowering over a middle-aged man who was sitting on one of the seats reserved for disabled people. Kaleem guessed he was Terrestran or at least partly so.

The younger man now jabbed the older one in the shoulder. “You’re just a health tourist. You’ve just come here to get your gammy leg fixed.”

“Actually my leg is gammy because of an accident I had here working on maintaining the food-producing systems so that you and other Zandrians wouldn’t starve.”

“There are Zandrians who could have done that if they’d been given the chance.”

“Really? So why didn’t they?”

The young man looked puzzled for a moment.

The older man shook his head. “You see I’ve lived on this planet longer than you have. I came here before you were released from your growing cell. I’ve paid taxes for years and years. They’ve tried hard with my leg but this now is the best it will ever be. I can live with that. I’m still working for this planet.”

The rest of the people on the transporter were now silent. Everyone was staring at the two men. The younger one now lent forward and head-butted the older one. There was a loud crack and blood started pouring from the older man’s nose.

A young woman pushed forward and faced the younger man. “Is there really any need for that? Anyway, we haven’t actually voted to leave the One World Community and even if we had, it wouldn’t necessarily mean that valued people like this gentleman would need to leave.”

“It would,” hissed the younger man. “We just don’t like the look of his face.”

That again. It never went away.

The young man was now standing with his arms folded across his chest. “If we had another vote tomorrow, it would be to leave the One World Community. More and more people want this planet back for themselves.”

The transporter stopped.

"Code red security alert," said an electronic voice. "Please all remain calm until the security force arrives."

A middle-aged woman was now attending to the older man. She was clearly a medic and the wand she was using was being very effective. His nose had stopped bleeding and the swelling was already going down.

Another man stepped forward. Goodness, it was a Zenoton. This would be interesting. Zenotons were a different race altogether and didn't come from the original Terrestrans who colonised so many of the other planets. Plus they had a peculiar monetary system that even he'd found difficult to understand though he had been able to enjoy some of its benefits. What was a Zenoton actually doing on Zandra and riding on the public transporter systems at that? Normally only high-ranking officials visited and they never engaged with the general public.

"Son, what is actually troubling you?"

"What's it to you, snake head?"

Several of the Zenoton's snake-like curls twitched and he blushed. He cleared his throat and carried on. "There is abundance. There is enough for everyone. Leaving the One World Community won't increase the abundance – in fact it might make it harder to access."

The Zenoton was right but this would go above the young man's head. He wasn't ready for this.

The young man kicked the side of the transporter. "What the fuck snazz talk is this? Get home, snake-head."

There was a general murmuring. Several other people came forward now.

"There's no need for this sort of talk," said one woman. "You're being personal."

"It affects us all, you dick-heads." The young man kicked the side of the transporter again.

"Let's not get physical. We can talk it through calmly when they let us into the station, can't we?"

"Well somebody should do something." He kicked out again.

"You can't talk to people like that. Let the politicos sort it all out calmly."

"Wait for them and we'll wait forever." He now lashed out at one of doors.

"You need to calm down, sunshine."

"Why should I?"

"Because this isn't getting you anywhere."

Kaleem had the sudden thought that 48% of the people on this tram agreed with the young man's sentiments yet everyone was condemning his behaviour. That at least gave him some hope. Most people were good-hearted.

It was probably more than 48%, actually, given the type of people who would travel on a public transporter at this time in the morning. Oh, dear. What was he thinking?

A tall man grabbed the young man from behind. "You really need to calm down."

It was clear, though, that the younger man wasn't going to be happy about this. He began to fight back and it was obvious that not only would he get out of this man's grip quite easily, he would not hesitate to hurt other people.

Kaleem knew he would have to do something. He pulled himself up tall and abandoned the stance he took when he was trying not to be recognised. He probably would be recognised now. Well, so be it.

He went right up to the young man and stared straight into his eyes. He watched him flinch and try to look away. "What exactly are you afraid of? What do you think you might lose?"

The young man tried to look away again.

Kaleem nodded. "What is it then? Come on, what is it?"

"Room to breathe. We need room to breathe."

Kaleem took a big breath. He looked around the whole of the transporter. He shook his head. "Can't see that that's a problem. And here you are on a crowded tram, in the company of a Zenoton and a half-Terrestran. There's plenty of air for everyone."

The young man shrugged.

"Well, then, what else?" Kaleem deliberately folded his arms across his chest. He didn't want this young man to feel too comfortable.

"They're taking all of our jobs."

"Oh, you have no role at the moment?"

"Cheek. Are you saying I don't contribute?"

"But isn't that what you're saying?"

"Listen. I do my part. It's just that they're taking the better jobs."

"So you're fluent in over twenty languages and you have advanced negotiating skills?" He nodded over towards the Zenoton. "And you know the intricacies of Zandrian plant life? You can do what we can do?"

The young man frowned then shrugged. "Well, they're using up all of our medical facilities."

"You do know, don't you, that in fact that the immigrants from other planets give far more in taxes and insurance than they use up accessing our welfare systems?"

"That can't be right," mumbled the youth.

"I'm afraid it is." Kaleem unfolded his arms. "And even if it wasn't, is there really any need for you to be so nasty?"

The transporter suddenly started to move. "Approaching next station," its robotic voice said. "Please allow the security operatives on to close down this incident."

The young man had now gone pale. He was going to be detained, perhaps imprisoned. Kaleem touched him lightly on the shoulder. "Tell them who put you up to this. Explain your feelings. They'll be more lenient if you're honest."

The transporter stopped at the far end of the platform. The doors swished open and five security droids and one human stormed in.

"Thank you everyone. We'll take it from here," said the human. He grabbed the young man's left arm and held it behind his back. One of the droids used force-field cuffs to attach him to the human.

This was all a bit excessive, wasn't it? Why did they need six anyway?

They marched the racist out of the carriage. The doors swished to and the transporter pulled into the station properly.

People started to clap and cheer. There was no need for this, really there wasn't.

"You did well, really you did," said the Zenoton.

He hadn't though, had he? He hadn't really got him to see sense and that young man would remain resentful and possibly become even more so if he had to go to prison.

Kaleem bowed slightly and hopped off the transporter. He would run the rest of the way after all.

CHAPTER EIGHTEEN

Obek looked up at the high ceiling of the new Clementine Family Store. It was glorious. The tiles on the walls gleamed. The skylights let in air and light but an automatic system made blinds draw across when the sun shone too fiercely. The polished but slip-proof floors smelt faintly of orange and were orange in colour. The best quality goods were piled high. It was exciting and enticing.

The doors swished open. Tomik, Penni and Harissa came in. Tomik had not brought Flanda.

"It should be family only," he'd said to his father.

Obek thought it was a shame. Flanda would soon be part of the family and she would be a real asset. He was pleased that Harissa had been included, though, and that despite her problems she had been involved with the project: the orange and green theme in the window displays had been her idea and they did seem so right for the House of Clementine.

"Are we all ready?" asked Tomik as they rushed in.

Everyone nodded. If Harissa smiled any harder her face would split in two. Obek was continuously amazed at how well she understood the Order.

"Okay," said Tomik to the newly-appointed manager. "Let them in."

They looked almost frightened to walk on the sparkling floors at first. This was so different from the dusty little general store they'd been used to. Gradually though, the noise level went up as the sales assistants began to talk to the shoppers.

"We ought to play some background music," said Tomik. "It would stop it getting too noisy."

A good point. Obek nodded. Well this was Tomik's concern now. He could arrange it.

More and more people came into the store. Soon some were leaving, though, and they were carrying bags full of goods. Obek was pleased that there were such nice things for them to choose and that in fact they could afford them: they were able to pay their workers well. Now all of these sales assistants were going to enhance what was already a thriving economy.

A small lunch, accompanied by fresh clementine juice, had been set out for Obek and his party in the meeting room upstairs.

"We can't stay too long." Tomik touched Obek's arm as they sat down. "We have to get to the Elders' meeting."

Ah yes. That. He'd better enjoy this lunch while he could.

The board room in the lodge was getting too small. There were too many Elders now. Obek thought back to the time when it had been mainly he and his father who had dealt with the Order. It hadn't even been this crowded when his father had held meetings about all of his business interests. But the Order was getting very diverse now. It had been Tomik's idea to give the name of Elder to the representatives of each branch of House of Clementine activity.

"It's a bit of a romantic idea, isn't it?" he'd suggested to Tomik.

"I think it will command respect. Anyway, Elders should be elected for their wisdom and experience and you should be the first one."

So, ridiculous as it had sounded, he had become Elder Obek and was in charge of all the work in the clementine orchards. Soon there had been Elders to represent the health care system, the money system and a crude judicial system. Just recently Tomik, at the tender age of twenty-six, had become Elder of Retail. There was no one overruling Elder. That pleased Obek. They took it in turns to chair the sessions. It was Tomik's turn today. Had the boy been a little nervous? Was that why he'd been in such a hurry at lunch time? In the end they'd arrived much too early. Tomik always seemed so confident. Perhaps he wasn't though.

Tomik cleared his throat. "Everyone, will you please take your seats."

Well that seemed assertive enough.

They all sat down and the meeting began. Much of it was very routine. Obek resented a little how all this careful planning took away the excitement he'd felt when he first set up the Order but he supposed it was necessary.

"Any other business?" said Tomik at last.

Good. They would be able to get home soon.

"I have a proposal."

It was Janik Hanson, Elder of Law.

"Go ahead," said Tomik.

Was this about to become interesting?

"I think we should introduce a system of knights."

There was a general murmuring of what sounded mainly like disapproval.

"I don't mean men covered in armour who charge around on horseback. I rather mean a hierarchy of people, working towards being Elders, going through three stages: ordinary knight, knight of the second order, knight of the first order. They could apply or be nominated and they would have to work through a series of tasks. It could be very motivating."

Obek felt wide awake now as they began to debate the matter strenuously.

The documents that Hanson had supplied were spread out over the polished oak table in the larger meeting room of the grand lodge. There was so much paper that this was the only place where they could see them all at once.

"He's certainly put some work into this." Obek couldn't really fault any of the ideas the Elder of Law had put forward for how the knights on all three levels should be tested and trained. "I like the way the established knights will train and assess newcomers. But how are we going to test the first ones? And who is going to test them?" Tomik was frowning.

"I suppose it will have to be selected members of the committee. It would be only polite to include Hanson. I expect, though, we'll have to put it to a democratic vote." Always that. At times Obek thought he was beginning to lose control of his own order. His son was still frowning. "Do you want to be involved?"

"I don't think I should be."

Of course. Tomik would want to be a knight.

Tomik sighed. "It's important that the first knights are really special."

"Naturally. I'm sure you'll do a great job. There's no need to worry."

Tomik shook his head. "I was thinking of Flanda. She would be superb and she deserves this."

Flanda looked glorious. She had chosen a white, calf-length dress decorated with a red band which suggested the knights of old.

Tomik had been right. She made a splendid example as the first knight. It hadn't been that easy, even for her, though. Tomik had had to encourage her and even Penni had stepped in from time to time to reassure the young woman. Harissa had been the most helpful in the end. "You can do it, Flanda," she'd said. "You're not a poor empty head like me."

Then Flanda had laughed, stroked the younger girl's hair and said, "You're not an empty head. You are the kindest, the most generous person I know. We can all learn so much from you."

"I have a present for you," said Harissa. She handed Flanda a bulky parcel wrapped in brown paper and tied with string.

Flanda blushed as she struggled to untie the knots. Harissa was always so good at wrapping up parcels. At last it was open and out tumbled a glorious blue velvet cloak. It was beautifully soft and it would keep her lovely and warm on the colder days. She held it to her cheek. "This is lovely," she whispered. "Thank you so much." She hugged the younger girl.

Flanda had succeeded and here she was, ready to be knighted. She knelt down in front of Obek. Yes, a democratic process had taken place but the Elders had been unanimous in putting him and Hanson in charge of the Order's knights and everyone had also agreed that he should conduct the first ceremony. Maybe the Order did still belong to him after all. Naturally it had been Tomik's idea that this should still be done with a sword.

He smiled at the young woman. "Flanda Regan, you have proved yourself worthy of the title of Ordinary Knight of the House of Clementine. You have proved that you are worthy physically, mentally and spiritually of this title, so I hereby name you Ordinary Knight of the House of Clementine." He placed the sword on both of her shoulders in turn. "In bestowing this knighthood on you, I tie your loyalty to the House of Clementine for as long as you shall live. Arise, Madam Knight and take up your duties."

Everyone in the crowd clapped vigorously. Flanda blushed then turned to Tomik and grinned. He smiled slowly back but his arms remained crossed over his chest.

"For goodness sake, marry the girl before someone else snaps her up," Obek muttered. What sort of fool was his son exactly?

CHAPTER NINETEEN

"I really haven't ever seen anything quite like this," said Nazaret. "It's hard to take in. It's just not what happens on Zandra."

Kaleem and his parents were watching the news reports. He had gone round to their home half hoping he might get the courage to discuss, man to man with his father, his encounter with Ella Tyler. There was no chance, however. His mother was there as well. In any case the news reports were much too important.

It seemed that the transporter Kaleem had travelled on was not the only one to have had a nasty incident occur on it. Similar things had happened on several transporters, in a couple of the parks and in one or two cafés.

"Do you think there's any risk for me and Kaleem?" said Marijam. She was pale and frowning.

"I'll be all right. I can look after myself. I'm more worried about Rozia and Petri."

Marijam nodded. "I can't look at this anymore. I'm going to go and lie down."

Kaleem and Nazaret exchanged a glance. Kaleem knew his mother wouldn't cope with this. She'd protected him so well when he'd been a child, and had odd looks, on Terrestra. She couldn't look after herself so well.

Nazaret touched his arm. "Don't worry. I'll see that she's all right. I promise. You do know that, don't you?"

Kaleem nodded.

Then the screen grabbed his attention again. Six men were attacking a middle-aged woman whose skin colour showed that she was clearly not Zandrian.

Nazaret zoomed the picture in. "Are they anyone we know?"

No, Kaleem didn't recognise them. He did notice, though, that a couple of the men were wearing brown tunics. "Do you know what that's about?" he asked his father.

Nazaret shook his head. "I can only think that it looks a bit military. As if they're trying to look like soldiers."

Three of the men in the group were young, two were middle-aged and one was quite old.

"Definitely something odd," murmured Nazaret. "They just don't look right."

Kaleem could see what his father meant. There was something very strange about their eyes. Their pupils were very small as if they were trying to keep out the light.

"We are seeking the public's help in identifying these people," said the droid newscaster as pictures of thirty or more people began to load. "These individuals are refusing to give their names, their identity chips have been disabled and voice, iris and profile recognition are all coming up blank. They have covered their tracks very well. They are refusing to talk and are also refusing all nutrition."

Kaleem shivered. This was so bizarre. Were these people even human?

"I think I'd better get going," Kaleem murmured. "I need to get some work done."

"You wouldn't rather stay here?"

Kaleem shook his head. "No, I'd better not."

"Take care."

Kaleem nodded.

Just twenty minutes later Kaleem was sitting in front of his own dataserve screen. For once he had taken a private transporter home. Tonight it had become very cold very quickly so jogging was out of the question. Many of the public transporters had been suspended.

He actually hated going by private transporter and the luxury of it meant nothing. This time, though, it had been the only solution.

Now he stared at the faces again of the thirty people who had been arrested. Soon it was a lot more than thirty. More and more incidents were taking place. All of the people arrested had that same strange look about them. Had they been drugged or hypnotised or something?

He had access to some programmes that even some of the security people couldn't touch but these didn't help either.

He was about to give up when he suddenly recognised something in the face of one of the detainees. It was a mood or an emotion. He couldn't quite work out what it was. He was still trying to analyse what he was seeing when the dataserve pinged. "Would you like to access Hidden Information?" said the electronic voice.

Kaleem's mouth went dry and his skin prickled. Why would he want to access this forbidden intelligence from Terrestra? Was there anything he wouldn't know, in fact? The authorities on both Zandra and Terrestra gave him access regularly to material that was deliberately kept from ordinary people. He'd even been able to sample some Golden Knowledge that was normally the preserve of the Terrestran Elders. Because he was the Peace Child he'd even been able to scrutinise such information from other planets from time to time.

The very fact that someone was contacting him implied, though, that either the authorities were keeping something from him or that this problem was even bigger than he'd thought. Had someone got at his dataserve? It was quite new. These days he always got the best available. He was used to how good they were getting at anticipating what the client wanted to know. This was particularly uncanny, though. Should he accept?

Now he began to sweat as he remembered an earlier encounter with Hidden Information. It had been when his mother had been so ill. At the time he'd also felt very insecure about his Peace Child role. To his shame as well he'd rebelled at that time against the mentor he later grew to love and respect and whom he still tried to match. The world of the Hidden Information peddlers was not at all nice and there were severe punishments for people who were caught indulging in it. And yet. His encounter with it had made him stronger.

"Would you like to access Hidden Information?" the dataserve's electronic voice repeated.

"Proceed," said Kaleem.

The dataserve whirred and clicked for a few seconds. The

screen went black. Was it shutting down? Had he breached a security protocol? The machine was still ticking though.

Just as suddenly has it had appeared to stop it started up again, now loading file after file rapidly. He couldn't identify them. Chains of Figurescript flashed by. Then there came a loud ping and a face appeared on the screen. It had a mask covering it, though the wearer's nose, eyes and lips were visible. The hair was hidden under a scarf so Kaleem could not tell whether the person was male or female.

"You are aware of the consequences of accessing Hidden Information?" Female, then.

"Only too well. But I've done it before and survived. I have to now. Anyway, if there's any problem I'm sure I can find a diplomatic get out clause."

The woman laughed. "Oh don't rely too much on your role, Peace Child baby."

So, she knew who he was.

"I need the information, whatever the consequences."

"So, what do you need?"

"The identities of all of the racists and who's behind them."

"Okay. Here they come. You'll have to memorise them. You won't be able to record them. And hurry. They already have a trace on your machine."

Kaleem watched fascinated as the pictures and profiles of the racist attackers flashed by. All of the information was given verbally by voice-over. He did notice, however, that each profile picture was labelled in Wordtext. "Non-native Zandrian." This was bizarre. Why would non-native Zandrians want to get rid of other non-Zandrians? People had come to Zandra just to be disruptive? And if the authorities knew who they were why weren't they doing something about it?

He made a mental snapshot of each one. Thank goodness his memory worked well.

"Record complete," the dataserve announced. "Incoming message."

"Receive."

The dataserve spluttered a couple of times. Then Clem's face appeared. What? He was daring to appear over an ordinary data connection?

"Not exactly wise. But you've done it now so we may as well meet up and I can tell you more. Meeting place three. But get out now. They're coming to arrest you."

The screen went black. So, they'd shut him down. How could Clem know about all of this?

Arrest him? The world's ultimate peace-maker? Why would they do that?

Kaleem made his way out of the apartment as fast as he could. He took the back stairs, running down each flight and swinging himself across each landing. At last he was at the bottom of the building. He gently pushed open the emergency door. He made his way out and walked softly and cautiously around the side of the block, his feet making little impression on the ground. If anyone was around they would not notice him. He knew how to walk though crowds without people seeing him. He would avoid eye contact and he would dodge people before they needed to get out of his way. Just another Peace Child trick.

He saw them arrive. That was a bit heavy-handed, wasn't it? For goodness sake, they knew who he was surely? Or was that good old-fashioned Hidden Information too? But why the stun-guns and the paddle-shields? And by the looks of it the beefiest and burliest of the security personnel? They hadn't even bothered with droids. Was he that much of a threat?

Fortunately the air had turned a little milder. He set off in a well-controlled jog towards his meeting with Clem. He mustn't let his anger get the better of him. That would make him too conspicuous.

CHAPTER TWENTY

"How did you manage to get through to me? I thought I'd been totally closed down."

"They asked me to use my personal override."

"Your what?"

"Most parents have them. Didn't you know that?"

"No. And I would have thought that it might be appropriate for children but not for a grown man." This seemed ironic. Nazaret had never been there when Kaleem was a child. Now he was monitoring him as if he were a baby.

"Well it's just as well we have it. It's like the emergency channel. It works, no matter what."

"Okay. So what do you want?"

"You need to see what's been going on. Then you need to contact Executive Tyler."

Kaleem's stomach flipped at the mention of Ella's name. Another meeting with her was going to be extremely awkward. Maybe she would regret as much as he did what had happened last time they met. Or she'd be ravenous for more. Either way it would be really uncomfortable.

"Are you still there?"

"Yes, I'm listening."

"Take a look at the news channels and then contact Tyler."

"Okay."

"And of course let me and your mother know what's going on. Rozia as well."

He was about to ask if Nazaret had any news of Rozia but then realised that his father had ended the call.

"Well?" asked Clem.

"Can we access the news channels here?"

Clem nodded and pushed a button on a nearby dataserve.

The main news channel opened up. Chief Executive April Septimus was being interviewed by a human reporter. It must be important if they were using a human.

"So Ms Septimus, what are your main concerns at the moment? Would you agree that what is happening is unprecedented?"

"Certainly nothing like this has happened since centuries before the Terrestrans colonised. Never in living memory have the inhabitants of one planet been so divided. We need to root out what is causing this malaise and return to the normal Zandrian position of peace, strength and stability."

"Have you any idea what's causing this, as you put it, malaise?"

"Not yet."

"Is it really the will of the Zandrian people, as you so often say, or do you think there is something more sinister behind it?"

"The House of Clementine on the rise, I'd have thought," whispered Clem.

The Chief Executive tossed her silver curls back and smoothed down her tunic. She seemed vulnerable. "We can't be sure at this stage. But we need to take notice. In some ways we should welcome this. We suspect that the malaise was always there lurking below the surface. At least now it's out in the open and we can deal with it."

It was all just empty words. There was very little substance to what she was saying. Her normal style, unfortunately. How on Zandra she had managed to become Chief Executive Kaleem had no idea. She had as much charisma as a piece of tired lettuce.

The reporter turned and faced the camera. "That was Chief Executive April Septimus. Thank you so much Chief Executive. Now I'm going to talk to Jansen Poplar."

"Heaven help us," whispered Clem, "if there is such a place."

That buffoon. This was supposed to be a time of extreme crisis and they were interviewing two of the most inadequate executives. At least the junior executives like Ella had common sense and integrity.

Poplar, Executive of Foreign Affairs, gawped at the camera with a silly grin on his boyish face. He muzzed his hair before he started talking. That had become a trademark. Kaleem knew it was all an act. The man was actually dangerously clever and could well be a little devious. Up until now everything had been so ordered that he'd not really been able to do any damage. Things might be different now.

"I gather," said the reporter "that some measures have already been put in place."

"Indeed. We've now restricted migration, particularly immigration. We're only now accepting persons with Zandrian blood. And of those of mixed blood only the ones who have a secure work position on offer."

This was madness. Zandra always benefitted from the mixture of ideas that came from people from other planets.

"Is this because of the referendum result? Isn't it an odd thing to do if 52% of people are in favour of staying in the One World Community and allowing freedom of movement? Indeed, would we not be contravening a One World Community directive by not allowing this free movement?"

Poplar ran his fingers through his hair. For once he looked quite serious. "There will be riots if we don't do something. We have to respect the wishes of the 48%. We're bringing in the protocols for a state of emergency. The One World Community will have to respect that."

The buffoon did have a bit of a point for once.

The reporter turned to the camera again. "Thank you Jansen Poplar. Now let's take a closer look at the state of emergency the executive has alluded to."

A series of video clips followed. It was like what Kaleem had seen before: men – and a few women – marching in brown tunics, pure-looking Zandrians attacking non-Zandrians and mixed-bloods, and protest marches, some silent, some more vocal and tending towards violent. Both sides actually – those wishing to remain in the One World Community and those wishing to leave. Except now there was a lot more of it.

"Shocking," said Clem.

Kaleem nodded. What was going on here?

Clem sighed. "We've got our work cut out here all right."

Still Kaleem didn't recognise any of them. "I think it's an outside job," he whispered.

Clem nodded. "It has all the signs of being to do with the House of Clementine."

Then Kaleem saw something that horrified him even more. He recognised someone now. He saw a young Zandrian taunting Rozia and Petri. What were they doing out with the mobs? Did he recognise the people who were doing this? They looked familiar but maybe that was just because so much of this was going on now. "I have to go now," he murmured.

"Have you seen someone you know?"

Kaleem nodded.

"Well, get back in touch as soon as you can."

Kaleem made his way to the door. Just as he was about to leave, however, the video clips stopped and the presenter reappeared. "It's clear that we need the help of Peace Child Kaleem Malkendy. Kaleem, if you're watching this will you please make contact. Your recent illegal access to Hidden Information will be overlooked."

Yes, well. If they knew the identities of the troublemakers as his visit to Hidden Information had implied, why weren't they doing something about it?

"Will you give yourself up?" Clem was gripping the side of his desk. His knuckles were white. "Will you still be able to work with us?"

"Yes and yes. But there is something else I must do first."

He had to find Rozia. He just had to.

CHAPTER TWENTY-ONE

Flanda Regan paused as she made her way through the Great Hall. Everything seemed to be ready. It was to be the biggest ceremony yet. They were to confirm one thousand new ordinary knights, six hundred ordinary knights were to become knights of the second order and three hundred knights of the second order were to move on to the first order. One thing was going to be hard, though. Tamsin Lampeter, Tomik Lampeter's daughter was going to become the youngest knight ever.

Oh, Flanda knew she had a fantastic life as Head Knight. She loved her job. It didn't feel like work. Looking after all the other knights was a real privilege. She had to keep up standards and at the same time empower people to attain these highly set goals. It still hurt, though, fifteen years on, the way Tomik had broken off their engagement. He didn't love her any more, he'd said. She was sure really that it was because he'd never managed to become a knight himself. Then after just a few weeks he was engaged to Tamsin's mother and they were married two months later. Tamsin had been a honeymoon child. She was a sweet girl and Flanda had been pleased to oversee her training, yet those deep eyes of hers tortured her always; they were so like Tomik's.

Well, never mind all of that. It would soon get so busy here she would have no time to notice. Yes, the Hall was ready. The floor was polished. The windows shone. There were huge floral arrangements all around. The room was filled with the scent of the sweet-peas. The seats were numbered. The orchestra was warming up. Outside she could see the crowds beginning to arrive. The first ceremony would begin in forty-five minutes. Several of the knights were already robed up and looking splendid in their blue velvet cloaks. She was so glad that that had become part of the graduation uniform.

A noise from the ante-room caught her attention. Someone was in there. Maybe it was just her assistant. Why,though? She didn't need her. She was already robed and the lists were ready.

"Marita, is that you?" she called.

There was no reply. Should she call someone? She dug her nails into her palms and held her breath.

A young man appeared in the doorway. He looked harmless enough. He, too, was already robed up in the uniform of an ordinary knight, minus the bandanna that would be given to him during the ceremony. No threat, then, probably, but what was he doing here? All of the graduands had been told to wait outside until they were called in. Besides which that room was private. And how had he got through the door that was locked from the outside?

"Can I help you?"

"Maybe. It depends." He looked up at her through a curtain of hair. He couldn't quite let his eyes contact with hers. Why was he like this? Even an ordinary knight should have more personal confidence.

"Is there any way I can go straight into the second order?"

"Why do you think we should allow that?"

"Well I've been working on it for a while now. My instructor thinks I'm ready."

She wished they wouldn't do that. They really shouldn't start on the next level until the knight was established on the current level. Some were beginning to do it, though, and she hoped it wasn't just for the money. "You know you have to wait at least two years to graduate to the next level, don't you? You do need that time. Why are you in such a hurry?"

"It would help me to get a better job and it would impress my girlfriend."

Flanda laughed. "Fair enough. We all want to improve. You shouldn't need to impress your girlfriend, though. She should take you the way you are. But I'm wondering whether you should even be knighted at all if you're that impatient. Patience is a top quality for ordinary knights."

The young man went pale.

Flanda touched his arm. "I'm joking. Of course I won't stop you being a knight. I hope your ceremony goes well. Are many people coming to watch you?"

He now went red. "You do know, don't you, that some people buy their way up the ranks? That it's a matter of who you know and how much you can pay? You need to get that sorted." He stomped off towards the main entrance to the Great Hall. He turned towards her as he reached the door. "You do realise as well, don't you, how easy it was to get into that room? I should have done it sooner. Then I would have had time to change the records before you'd noticed I was there."

Then he was gone. She wanted to go after him but she couldn't move.

The six ceremonies proceeded without any other problems. Flanda couldn't enjoy them, though. Were people really buying their way to the top? Yes, she'd been concerned that some trainers were pushing people through a little too quickly. She'd been beginning to work on that anyway. But people actually paying to get a pass when they didn't deserve it? That was just not House of Clementine.

She looked out for the young man but it was impossible to recognise him: they all wore the same uniform, they all had the same floppy hair style that was fashionable at the moment and they were only in front of her for a few seconds. Well she hoped he'd be pleased to get his knighthood, even if it was only an ordinary one.

Processing that many knights was exhausting.

"Here, sit down," said Marita when they were back in the office at the end of the day." You look in need of a hot drink."

"I'd prefer just a cold clementine juice. You don't have to serve me. I can get it myself."

Marita shook her head. "You've been on your feet for hours and it looks as if you've got something on your mind. Even the Head Knight is supposed to rest from time to time."

Well yes, it was good to relax into the soft armchair. She shivered though when she thought about how easily that young man had got into their office and how he'd tried to amend the records. That sort of thing just shouldn't happen in the House of Clementine.

Marita came back a few seconds later with a large jug of clementine juice and some fruit segments. She placed the tray on the small table next to Flanda's chair. "This will raise your blood sugar. Eat and drink."

Flanda smiled at the older woman. Marita was a good sort. She always managed to do exactly the right thing.

"And now – tell me what's on your mind."

Flanda sighed. It's nothing. I just think we'll have to go for smaller ceremonies but more often. That was just too big today." Perhaps she shouldn't trust even Marita.

Marita nodded but something in her eyes suggested that she didn't quite believe what Flanda was saying.

Flanda stared at the document in front of her. This must be the millionth time she'd gone through the records and still she couldn't see anything that suggested there was any real bribery going on. Yes, what she did see here confirmed that some trainers were rushing some knights up the levels, and they were probably doing this for extra pay. That ought to be reasonably easy to fix though she was so tired now she couldn't think how.

"Nothing?" asked Marita.

Flanda shook her head.

"Well you need to stop now." She offered Flanda a fruit tea. "I've added some cold water so you can drink it straight away."

Flanda sipped the drink gratefully. Yes, Marita knew her so well. It was just the right temperature and just the right strength. She felt herself both relax and wake up as the tangy clementine-flavoured drink slipped smoothly down her throat.

"What about paying them more and giving them a bonus for producing the very best quality in the new knights and making sure that they really are worthy of the new levels?"

It was obvious really. Marita was always so pragmatic. It couldn't really be that simple, could it? She sighed. "I'm sure they'll still find a way of cheating."

"But it might make it easier to pinpoint."

Flanda nodded. "I suppose we could try it."

"I'll get some suggestions drawn up."

"Superb," said Flanda. "They are so nearly ready. Two more months, perhaps?"

The trainer grinned. “That’s what I thought.”

Flanda nodded. She looked around the sports studio with a sense of satisfaction. She was glad they’d introduced fencing for second order knights who wanted to progress to the first order. That couldn’t be learnt too quickly. Now that the trainers were being paid properly all of the knights were making a steadier progress. The studio had been another of Marita’s brilliant ideas. Flanda loved watching the trainees. This all now seemed to be working.

There was a soft knock at the door and then it opened.

“I think you’d better come and see this.” Marita’s face was flushed. She certainly wasn’t her normal calm self.

Flanda followed her as she walked briskly towards the office. She was frowning and her lips were pursed.

“What is it, Marita?”

The older woman shook her head. “Unbelievable.”

They arrived at the office. There were some papers spread out on the desk. Marika pointed to what appeared to be a letter.

Flanda read it quickly.

Dear Madam Regan,

You may remember me from my approach to you before my graduation as ordinary knight. I am pleased to inform you that I am now well into my training as a knight of the second order and am glad that I am doing this the right way. However, I also have to inform you that there is still one person accepting bribes. I have evidence of this. I would like to meet with you to discuss this in more detail. I look forward to meeting with you soon.

Arten Mitren

There was a knock at the door.

Marita nodded. “That’s probably him. I took the liberty of contacting him and asking him to come in.”

“Okay. Let’s see what he’s got to say.”

Flanda recognised him as soon as he got into the room. He was clearly a bit more mature now and his hair style was much more sensible. He had the proper bearing of a knight of the second order. He must be almost ready for graduation.

"Well," said Flanda, "what have you got to tell us?"

Arten Mitren took a deep breath. "Tomik Lampeter has been accepting bribes from knights who want to circumvent normal training."

Flanda clutched the sides of her desk in an attempt to stop the room from spinning. "You know this how?" she just about managed to ask. How could he anyway? He wasn't even a knight himself.

"Because he offered me a place as a knight of the second order. He said he could alter the records. I turned it down of course. I just thought you should know."

Flanda nodded and sat down quickly. How could he do this? How could Tomik threaten his own father's order?

Tomik still took her breath away. Tears pricked at her eyes when she remembered how they had first met. There was a lump in her throat that she couldn't swallow. She'd gone over it so many times before and here she was still trying to figure it out. Why had he suddenly turned against her?

He smiled. His dark eyes were looking straight into hers. He lent forward and stroked her cheek. He shook his head. "You just don't get it, do you sweetie?"

He pulled her towards him and she thought he was going to kiss her. He didn't. He whispered in her ear instead. "Just can't have you making better progress through the Order. It's not right. But oh my goodness, I still want you." Now he was going to kiss her.

And now she wasn't going to have it. She pushed him away. "Why are you accepting bribes from trainee knights? Why are you ruining your father's order?"

Tomik laughed. "If I can't get what I want I'll make the whole thing look like a sham. Besides it gives me great satisfaction to see young people graduate without having to go through all the nonsensical hoops you and my father have devised. And you have to admit: it keeps you well supplied with knights."

"Just how many are we talking about here?"

Tomik laughed again and looked up to the left as if calculating. "About one third of them."

Flanda thrust the fencing foil towards Tomik's face. She was appalled to hear him scream and to see blood pouring from his eye. She hadn't meant to hurt him that much.

"Bitch! You'll pay for this." He tried to stem the flow of blood. "Marita, send for the Guard," he called.

Marita appeared at the door. She went white and put her hand in front of her mouth. She turned and hurried away.

Flanda sank to the floor.

CHAPTER TWENTY-TWO

Kaleem had never been to this side of this town. He was astonished that anything like this could exist on Zandra. Zandra was the smart forward-thinking planet. There was not supposed to be any poverty or any class distinction. All were welcome. Normally.

It must be near a rubbish dump and a sewage farm. He could smell both at once. The road here had potholes in it and there were weeds coming through the cracks in the pavements. How could that happen? At least, he reflected, his father would be fascinated. Plants normally had to be forced on Zandra. Here they were growing freely.

The Shack, as Clem had described it, was made of some sort of metal. It had huge holes in the roof and the walls and looked as if its protective covering needed replacing. He'd never seen anything on Zandra be allowed to decay so much. He shivered as he remembered how Terrestra's Z Zone used to be. Well, it was much poorer than this even. But why was this even here? He just didn't understand.

He'd better go in, he supposed. It would be dark in there if there was no electricity and he suspected there wouldn't' be.

He pushed open the door and walked in.

"Glad you could make it." As soon as Clem spoke the lights came up and Kaleem found himself standing in a vast space full of dataserves and big screens. A lot of humans and droids were very busy processing information.

"How…?"

"Holoscenes."

Of course. The Zandrians were always so clever at that.

Clem laughed. "Fooled you, did it?"

Kaleem nodded. He ought to have realised.

"Well, Kaleem, we thought it was about time we were a bit straighter with you. We haven't really told you all that we know about the House of Clementine. Yes, we weren't lying when we said it has always tried to control Zandra and Terrestra before that. We just weren't honest about exactly how much."

"Kaleem. You called me Kaleem. How did you know?"

Clem smiled. "That's what happens if you go fooling around with Hidden Information. You get found out." Clem shook his head. "Anyway, I kind of recognised you. Not so much by the way you looked but by the way you acted."

"Really?"

Clem nodded.

Ah well. It was out in the open now. Perhaps it was better that way. "So are you saying that the House of Clementine is behind what's happening now?"

"We think so."

"The brown tunics? The racists? The questions about human rights?"

Clem nodded. "Yes, all of that and more."

"More?"

"Yes more. But let me introduce you to Sofia. She will take you through the history. We want you to know everything."

"Sofia? She doesn't have a code name?"

"We don't bother with those here."

"So what's your real name?"

Clem laughed. "It actually is Clem. Short for Clemens. Ah, here she is."

Kaleem gulped when the young women appeared in the doorway. She could have been Saratina when she was younger. Her face was distorted in a similar way though her body was a little straighter. She held her hand out to receive the Zandrian hand shake. Kaleem fumbled and shook her hand the Terrestran way. "I'm sorry," he mumbled. "It's just that…"

"You're wondering about this?" She pointed to her face.

That was different from Saratina for sure. She spoke clearly. Whatever had damaged her face had not affected the inside of her mouth.

Kaleem felt his cheeks burning. "It's just that I knew someone else…"

"Well mine was a birth defect."

That was unusual on Zandra.

Kaleem shook his head. “I’m sorry for staring.”

“Not a problem. Yes, unusually they didn’t detect it when I was in vitrio but they have managed to build me a bionic mouth.” She opened her mouth and pointed to a set of metal and plastic devices. “They offered me facial reconstruction but I turned it down. I kind of like this. It gives me some character. Much better than typical Zandrian good looks. Shall we?”

He followed her along the corridor and into a small windowless room. A hoversessel came over to him and Sofia nodded that he should sit down.

“In this little room we have all of the records that we could find of the House of Clementine. Sit back and enjoy the show.”

The holo presentation started. It was truly impressive. But if they were operating outside of normal society how did they get the money for this? And where was the hard evidence?

“You see,” said Sofia, “it started on Terrestra, centuries before we colonised.” A vehicle pulled by horses rumbled out of the screen. It was decorated with a branch bearing seven clementines. “It seemed quite benign in those days. In fact, they did a lot of good. They educated poorer children. Then it started going wrong.”

Kaleem did notice the subtle changes as they worked through the Terrestran centuries.

Sofia nodded. “You can see that they encouraged the poison cloud – they kept hidden the types of fuel available to Terrestrans and encouraged the use of the ones that would guarantee climate change. And by the time the colonies were formed they were influencing pretty well everything.”

“But they weren’t’ necessarily evil, were they?”

“No. But it is worrying just how much influence they had. We’re sure they’re connected to the brown tunics and the racist incidents that are happening now. That is bad and probably getting worse.”

Where was the evidence, though? “You know, this just looks like a pretty little story put together for tourists or college students. Is it all based on critical evidence?”

“Oh, it most certainly is.” Her jaw was tense and her lips were pursed.

Darn. He'd irritated her. He ought to be able to do better than this. Wasn't he supposed to be the ultimate in diplomats?

Sofia closed down the holo presentation.

"You read Figurescript and Wordtext, don't you?"

Kaleem nodded.

"Here's your critical data then."

Kaleem watched as file after file loaded on to the screen. Yes, it was all there. Goodness, they'd worked hard at this.

Someone cleared their throat. Kaleem turned to see Clem standing in the doorway. "So, you can see how widespread it is?"

"I most certainly can."

"Will you work with us more closely now?"

Why not? What else was he supposed to do? He shrugged. "I need to keep away from the normal channels for a while."

"You do, don't you?" Clem laughed. "Well, there's plenty of work needs doing. We need to find out what they have planned, where they're getting their people from, how they're maintaining their influence, how they're infiltrating into our society, why they're doing all of this. Most importantly as well: who is behind all of this."

"How are you going to do all of that?"

"Well it's already happening. We have agents in the field. Some people out there aren't quite what they seem."

"And you think there is just one person behind it all?"

Clem nodded. "Person. Or maybe entity."

Kaleem shivered. "What do you mean exactly?"

"This is something really huge. Maybe the biggest thing that has happened ever to humanity. Well, are you with us?"

"Yes, of course I'm with you. But what exactly do you see me doing?"

Clem laughed. "You don't get it?"

Kaleem shrugged, shook his head and raised his hands in the air.

"Well young man, we want you to find out exactly who or what is at the bottom of all of this. You're the best person for the task."

Kaleem's personal communicator buzzed. How could they reach him if he'd been cut off?

Clem nodded that he should answer.

Kaleem stared at the communicator. There was neither a face nor a symbol on the screen.

"Anonymous caller," said the tinny voice.

"Answer it," said Clem. "If they've found you it must be important."

Kaleem nodded. "Accept," he mumbled. Was he about to be called in and at best reprimanded though more likely to be incarcerated?

"You're needed. I know you've done something you shouldn't have. But have you seen what's been happening in the last few hours?"

Nazaret had managed to find him again.

CHAPTER TWENTY-THREE

There were no lights on in Rozia's apartment. He buzzed the intercom, just in case. Perhaps they were sleeping. No response. He buzzed again.

"Residents away. Please call again later."

Odd. Rozia didn't usually leave that message. She must be intending to be out for some time. That was also unusual.

Dare he key in the code? Perhaps they'd changed it. Best leave it a while; otherwise the surveillance system would become suspicious.

He looked up at Rozia's window. There was still no sign of life. Right. That did it. He would let himself in. He held his breath and mentally kept his fingers crossed as he typed in the code. He breathed out when the door opened and the lights came on in the foyer. Seconds later he was speeding up in the lift. He held his breath again as he tapped the code into the apartment door. That worked as well and the door slid open.

It looked as if Rozia and Petri had left in a hurry. The apartment was normally so tidy. Today, though, several of Petri's clothes were strewn over the furniture. Half a dozen or so medi-wands lay on the coffee table. There were two cups half full of what looked like tea that had gone cold.

Kaleem tried his communicator. No, it still wouldn't work. Could he use Rozia's dataserve?

He sat down at the console. "Serve!" he commanded. It booted up. So, they really had been in a hurry. He knew that Rozia was fastidious about shutting everything down properly and she changed her pass code at least once a month. This time, not however, apparently. Whatever had happened must be really bad. "Come on Rozia," he whispered. "Where are you?"

"Location not tracked," the dataserve informed him. Well at least they'd got that right.

Kaleem commanded up the news feed. He soon found the video clips where he'd seen Rozia and Petri. He froze the picture and zoomed right in. He couldn't recognise where they were but he could see that Petri was in pain. What on Zandra was going on?

He glanced back at the medi-wands. Was there something wrong with Petri's meds again?

Then he heard them. Petri was whimpering.

"Who's in there?" called Rozia. "I'm calling security."

Kaleem sprang up and rushed to the door. "It's only me."

"What are you doing here? How did you get in? Where have you been? We've all been so worried?"

"I could say the same about you. I saw you on the news video. Where was that?"

"It was near one of the old medi-centres. We were trying to find Joahnsa Brooken. The last three wands have been duds."

"But isn't she at the medi-centre just near here?"

Rozia shook her head. "She seems to have disappeared. They were all a bit cagey there. But one of the nurses told me that she thinks she's had to go into hiding. She's been threatened by some of the brown tunics because she's too keen to help non-Zandrians – like us."

"Did you find her? Did you get some good wands?"

Rozia shook her head and tears began to form in her eyes. Kaleem just wanted to hold her but he suspected she wouldn't let him.

Just at that moment Petri squawked.

"I need to get her into the dark," said Rozia, picking up the little girl and taking her towards her bedroom.

"Let me help."

"There's not a lot you can do. I'm used to this."

Rozia took an age. He could hear Petri crying.

"It'll be all right," he heard Rozia say. "When you've been in the dark a little longer it'll settle down."

He busied himself with Rozia's dataserve. It was useless, though. If Dr Brooken was in hiding, and it looked very much as if she was, there was no way he would find her without dragging Rozia into Hidden Information as well. He wouldn't dare do that.

Rozia at last came back into the lounge.

"She's really uncomfortable. The blisters don't seem to be subsiding. In fact, they seem to be getting worse. She's sent herself to sleep though. Let's hope she sleeps for a long time and that they sort themselves out by the time she wakes up."

"Should I stay for a while?"

"Yes, please. I'd like that."

Dare he put an arm around her? Perhaps not. She must have been exhausted though. Two comfisessel hovered over to them and they both sat down. The sessels styed so close together that after Rozia's head had nodded a few times it dropped on to his shoulder. Soon she was asleep and breathing evenly.

He dared it. He wriggled a little and managed to get his arm around her back. She hardly stirred. It felt so right. Her hair was soft against his cheek and smelt of roses. Oh, he still loved her so much. All that drama with Ella had just been nonsense.

"Dim lights," he commanded the apartment.

The lights did go down and some soft music began to play. This was exactly how it was meant to be. Would she be cross when she woke up?

He didn't have time to find out. Petri suddenly screamed. Rozia leapt to her feet and rushed to her bedroom. Kaleem followed her.

"What is it darling?" Rozia uncovered the girl. It was dark in her room but Petri protested at even the gentle light that shone from the hallway.

Kaleem's eyes adjusted quickly. He could make out the raw weeping sores that covered her skin.

Rozia touched her lightly. "She's really burning up."

"Make it go away," Petri whimpered. "I don't want this." Then she vomited over Rozia. She started shaking and convulsing. Foam came from her mouth.

"We've got to do something!" Rozia cried.

"Has she ever been this bad before?"

Rozia shook her head. "No, never, it's almost as if…" She bit her lip.

"As if what?"

“Not only are the wands not working but they’ve somehow poisoned her. Made her worse.”

That was it. Kaleem knew what he must do. “I’m going to get some help.”

“But how?”

Petri’s shaking became even more violent. Rozia tried to hold her down. “What can we do?”

Kaleem found it difficult to ignore them but he made his way to Rozia’s dataserve. “Contact Executive Tyler. Emergency protocol. Kaleem Malkendy Peace Child reporting back.”

Ella appeared in a holo. Her face gave nothing away. Decidedly frosty then. Well, they’d just have to work beyond that.

“I need your help,” Kaleem said.

“Really? And what do I get in exchange?”

“You know I’ll be back to help sort out the tensions. You know I only accessed Hidden Information in order to help me do that.” He wouldn’t say anything else. Not what she wanted to hear, most likely.

Ella just about nodded. Her lips remained pursed. She sighed. “So what’s the problem now?”

“Petri’s really ill. The medi-wands seem to have failed. In fact we even think…”

“You think what?” Ella drummed her fingers lightly on the table.

“Some attempt may have been made to harm her.”

Ella’s face softened slightly. “All right. I’ll get you some help straight away. You’re at their apartment now?”

“Yep.”

“There will be somebody there in less than ten minutes. I’ll link you up to the emergency medical line as well right now.”

“Thank you.” He could trust her, he knew that, even though she was a bit cross with him at the moment. He went to go back to Rozia.

“Kaleem?”

“Yes?”

“I’ve reinstated your communication system. Welcome back.”

The screen went black and Petri yelled again.

"At least she's stopped convulsing," said Rozia as Kaleem arrived back in Petri's room. "But I don't like the way she's swelling up."

Neither did Kaleem. At least though he could now use his personal communicator to talk to the medics.

"It sounds like anaphylactic shock," said the medic. "I presume you have no adrenalin wands?"

"No." They only had useless or perhaps even poisonous wands.

"Lie her as flat as you can and tilt her head backwards. My colleague will be there in two minutes."

Kaleem helped Rozia to lie Petri back and the girl's breathing eased a little but she was now swelling even more and there was a blue tinge to her lips.

"Hurry," whispered Rozia.

The intercom buzzed and Kaleem quickly verified the ID of the medic and let him in. Seconds later the medic was wanding Petri.

The swelling subsided and Petri began to return to a more normal colour.

"That's the allergy dealt with," said the medic. "Now to treat the blisters and give her the meds that will stop them forming."

He had to use six wands before Petri was completely back to normal. "I've also brought along a month's supply. In future Executive Taylor will personally authorise her meds. So, there shouldn't be any more problems."

"Do we have any idea how it all went wrong?" Kaleem asked.

The medic shrugged. "Who knows with everything that's been going on? The world's gone crazy, it seems. But she should be all right for a while now."

"Thank you so much," said Rozia as they let him out of the apartment.

Within ten minutes, Petri was sleeping peacefully.

"You should try and get some rest as well," said Kaleem. "I'll stay just in case. I'll get some work done, if you don't mind."

Rozia nodded. Her eyelids were drooping and she was very pale. "Go on then." She made her way slowly out of the room, her shoulders hunched up.

A few moments later Kaleem was engrossed in searching through some Wordtext files Ella had sent to him. There was nothing very exciting there. His own eyes began to close.

He decided to have a power nap and removed himself to the sofa. He lay on his back and felt himself relax deeply. He was just at that point where he was still awake and conscious that he was having surreal thoughts when he felt Rozia shaking him.

"I'm sorry," she said, "but I just had to tell you. I couldn't sleep. And I've made a decision. We're going back to Terrestra."

Kaleem was now wide awake. "You can't do that. Petri won't be able to get the treatment she needs there."

"We can control her condition. We did before and I expect Terrestra has moved on as well. At least nobody will try to poison us there."

She couldn't go. He mustn't let her. He would lose her all over again. Just as he was beginning to win her back. "Please don't go." He went to touch her but she folded her arms across her chest.

His communicator buzzed. No! Ella. He couldn't ignore her. It was marked urgent and this was his work now.

He reluctantly accepted the call.

Ella's face now filled the screen. "Get your butt over here. Have you seen the news?"

Rozia and Kaleem exchanged a glance.

"News," commanded Rozia.

A human reporter was speaking. "This is unprecedented news from Zenoto," he said.

CHAPTER TWENTY-FOUR

Rozia's Ulog

Hi everyone,

It's getting more and more complicated here and very frightening.

Kaleem asked me just after the Referendum what I thought about the One World Community and whether Terrestra, Zandra and Zenoto should be members. It seemed like a no-brainer to me at first. Obviously we all should. For sure it's better to have us all working together, isn't it?

But some things are beginning to happen now that are making we wonder.

Kaleem is being ambivalent as well. Not long ago he invited us to have breakfast with him. It was almost like old times and having Petri along almost made me feel as if we were a family. Actually, Petri is getting to be quite the little madam about that. She keeps on dropping hints that Kaleem and I should be together. But then I tried to contact Kaleem to get him to help me decide whether I should go back to Terrestra or not and he didn't reply. So we started getting all packed up, then we had all the trouble with Petri again and he just walks in as cool as you like. He was a great help, though. But I just don't know where I am with him.

They still haven't solved the problem of my credits. Nazaret and Marijam have been great but I can't go on taking from them forever.

There are some very strange things happening here on Zandra. We keep getting reports of riots and protest marches. And then there are all those people wearing brown tunics. What does that mean?

As far as I can tell, nothing like that is happening on

Terrestra. It will be a safe place for me and Petri. It may be that Terrestra becomes isolated again and that may be the safest place for us. So, clearly the One World Community isn't working any more.

It's horrible sometimes, out on the streets. I've heard people whisper and say things like "Go home, parasite." Oddly though I've never been able to see who's made the remark. I'm beginning to think I might actually be imagining it. I think I might only be able to get over this paranoia if I get away from this place.

Then when Petri became ill again it was terrifying. It was almost as if the wands were not just useless, but that they were actually making her even worse. We tried to get in contact with Doctor Joahnsa Brooken but totally failed. She seems to have disappeared. Petri was really ill – she kept vomitting and having fits. It was terrifying.

Then Kaleem turns up just at the right moment. It was so reassuring having him there. He also managed to get help from Ella Tyler, an executive he knows. She will guarantee that good wands will be supplied to us. The medic she sent was also able to help and eventually we got Petri calm and asleep. All good then in the end but I'm still worrying about Doctor Brooken.

Kaleem was such a support so it made it all the more difficult telling him that we were going to leave.I still care about him a lot but I'm having difficulty figuring out whether we mean anything to him.

I'll keep you all posted,

Rozia

CHAPTER TWENTY-FIVE

Tamsin and her classmates were now outside the House of Clementine High School. Those Clementiners. They were up themselves, weren't they? Poncy and posh. Just who did they think they were? Well, they were nothing. The Normalers were going to show them. Any minute now it would all kick off.

To think she used to be one of them. She'd felt uneasy at first and now she realised that had been the right instinct. That first day and that ridiculous uniform. She remembered the conversation with her mother.

"I hate it. I really do. Why do we have to wear this stupid orange? It's just not my colour." She'd tugged at the linen tunic that was part of the House of Clementine school uniform.

"Because that's what the uniform is. Everyone will be wearing it."

"The boys won't. And neither will Catty."

"The boys' trousers are made of the same cloth. Listen, I know you'll miss your friend but Catty just wasn't smart enough to get a place at the school."

"So what will happen to her?"

"Oh, I expect she'll be fine."

"Can I still see her?"

"Well, maybe that's not such a good idea. You won't be doing the same things at all. Come on. It's time to go. The walking bus will be here soon."

Tamsin grabbed she school bag and opened the front door. Yes, they were already making their way along the street.

"Go Tamsin!" cried one of the older boys.

Tamsin felt herself blush but soon she was talking to Rozzy Steeper a girl who had been in her class at her previous school.

"It's going to be really good, I think. So much more important and more interesting than the Ground School."

Tamsin shrugged. "Maybe." But she'd always found Catty so funny and they'd always played together so well. Catty had such a vivid imagination. Rozzy always seemed a bit dull.

The walking bus made its way past the orchards towards the shiny new school that had only been open a few months. A tiny girl, in the grey uniform of the Normal School, stood at the side of the road as they made their way past. It was Catty.

"I expect she'll have to get the real bus into town," said Rozzy."It was so worth making the effort to pass the entrance test not to have that hassle. Mind you, she might not have even been entered. She's so small. The Order wouldn't want her. We can't dilute the Order with misfits."

Catty was staring at Tamsin. Tamsin went to wave but Rozzy nudged her. "Best to ignore her, don't you think?"

Tamsin pulled her half-raised arm back down.

Catty shook her head.

Tamsin followed the others and wondered what had just happened.

Oh soon enough she'd go used to the posh school. And she'd got used to Rozzy. She'd found her good fun after all. What about the day when Catty had arrived?

Rozzy poked her in the ribs, making her giggle. Tranny was about to make one of her speeches and as usual, as she took in a deep breath, her breasts wiggled. The trouble was, Rozzy always managed to giggle quietly to herself. The teachers usually heard Tamsin. Rozzy was a laugh a minute these days. Why had she ever thought she was dull?

"As you know at this time of year we welcome new students who have passed the entrance test two years late. I urge you to make them as comfortable as possible. These late-developers often go on and do surprisingly well. And maybe the fact that they can enter our system will serve to remind us all that we can just as easily lose our own places in it." Miss Tranus banged her ruler down on the desk. "Tamsin Bokart and Rozzy Steeper, will you stop messing around and pay attention."

Tamsin felt herself blush. She wished that Rozzy wouldn't keep on getting her into trouble. They'd become good friends over the two years they'd been in the House of Clementine High School.

But it was all right for Rozzy. She got good marks even without trying very hard. Tamsin had to work harder. And Rozzy was continuously distracting her. “We’d better listen,” she whispered.

Rozzy shrugged. “If you must.”

“Girls. Enough.” Miss Tranus had gone red now.

There was a tap on the door.

“Enter.”

“Here they are,” said Mr Donelly, the school secretary. Three boys and two girls dressed in sparkling new House of Clementine uniforms followed him into the classroom.

Tamsin gasped when she saw the first of the girls. It was unmistakably Catty. She’d grown though, and filled out a bit. The orange uniform really suited her. She looked so confident, so different from the miserable little grey-clad girl they’d seen waiting for the bus two years ago.

Rozzy nudged her. “She won’t last. Just you see.”

Tamsin wasn’t so sure, though. She stared at Catty. Catty smirked back.

Of course, the inevitable had happened. Rozzy finally got her into such trouble.

Tamsin had known what was coming the day her parents were called in. They hadn’t. They’d been quite excited about being summoned to the school.

“It must be because you’re doing well,” her mother had said.

“Perhaps they want to recommend you for knight training,” her father had suggested.

But no. it was nothing like that. She knew. Her marks had been getting poorer all the time and then there had been the fight with Catty.

She’d tried not to care. Why would she want to stay here anyway? For some reason she couldn’t explain at all Rozzy had stopped talking to her and had chummed up with Catty. The two girls walked around the school arm in arm.

“Can you smell something funny?” Rozzy asked as they walked past her in the corridor.

Catty would giggle. "It must be something the cat's brought in."

"Well, I wish she wouldn't."

The two girls would then collapse in helpless laughter at their own pathetic little joke. Tears pricked at Tamsin's eyes. She tried to tell herself that this was for the best. Who would want to be around people like that? It didn't work, though. They'd both been her friend before and now she was on her own.

Now here they were, sitting outside the head teacher's office. That was bad enough. But what was the Normal School going to be like? It had certainly toughened Catty up. Perhaps Catty had always been stronger than her, though. Oh, and that awful grey uniform. Why had she complained so much about the orange one?

The door opened. Miss Frampton, who had always been so friendly and kind, looked very serious today.

"Good morning, Mr and Mrs Bokart. Tamsin, you wait outside a while. I want to speak to your parents in private first."

There was a lump in Tamsin's throat as she watched her parents go into the head's office.

"I'm afraid I have some bad news," said Miss Frampton as she closed the door.

Then she'd got used to the Normal school and she'd made friends with Kelvin. It seemed ages now since she'd first got together with him. Really got together with him that is.

She had missed the school bus again that day. There was nothing for it but to start walking and get the other one from the bus station. If she was lucky someone might pass her and offer her a lift. Perhaps Dad would be out delivering local orders. On the other hand, hopefully he wouldn't be. She'd only get a lecture about getting another detention. Looking on the brighter side, she might bump into Kelvin.

She smiled to herself when she thought how scared she'd been of him at first. He was the school's hard boy. Oh, yes, and he'd been hard in another way as well. She's noticed that when he'd kissed her the other week and pressed up against her. She wouldn't mind a bit more of that. She was ready for him. Well, which girl wouldn't be? He was the main source of the illegal contraceptive pills.

"Better stop," he'd said, and pulled away from her. He'd fumbled in his bag and pulled out a packet of pills. "You'll need to start taking these. Just follow the instructions." Then he'd kissed her gently on the head. "They take two weeks to become effective so best keep out of my way until then. You're so beautiful I can't control myself when I'm around you."

She wasn't daft. She knew he'd have more than one girl on the go and that she wouldn't be all that special to him. But she was ready for him now. The two weeks were up. If he wanted her he could have her. She wanted to know what doing "it" was like. Anything to get away from the boredom and the dreariness of the Normal School.

A motor-bike stopped beside her. Her heart skipped a beat. The rider got off and took off his helmet. Unmistakably Kelvin.

"Missed your bus again or were you deliberately waiting for me?"

She nodded.

"Well, which?"

"I, er..."

"You've been taking those pills like a good girl?"

"Yes!"

He laughed. "Good, good. Listen. I can't stop now. I have some business to attend to. I won't be long. Will you wait for me? Are you ready? Do you want to do it?"

"Yes."

"Good girl."

She watched him amble away. He went down the steps that lead to the back of the bus station. It was a popular spot for students from her school to hang out smoking or buying and exchanging drugs. A bus drew into the station. It was her bus. She'd have to miss this one as well if she was going to see Kelvin. Two girls in House of Clementine uniforms got off. Unbelievable, Catty and Rozzy. They made their way up the ramp to where Kelvin was now standing.

He took two packets out of his bag. They looked exactly like the one he'd given her. They were getting contraceptive pills as well? House of Clementine girls were doing something forbidden? Well, well.

She was even less special than she'd thought. She hurried down the steps and just managed to jump on the bus before it set off.

Of course, it had all gone wrong for Catty and Rozzy. Kelvin hadn't let her down after all.

"I've heard some shocking news," her mum said one day when she got in from school. "That old friend of yours. Catty Pulson? She's going to have a baby. And her best friend. Rozzy Steeper. Mrs Pulson tells me there are quite a few girls at the school in that position. So you see, House of Clementine High School girls aren't all they're cracked up to be."

Tamsin felt sick. Didn't those pills that Kelvin supplied work? What about if she became pregnant as well? She was meeting him now four or five times a week and they had sex every time, even when she had her period. He'd told her he was only seeing her but she didn't know whether she could believe him.

The next time she saw him she wanted to ask him first but before she could say a word his lips were on hers and his hand was up inside her bra. Oh, she wanted him now. She didn't care if this made her have a baby. Her hand found its way into his trousers. As she touched his hard penis she felt the first wave of an orgasm. Soon he was inside her and as he started moving faster and faster she found her excitement growing until, at the split second he cried out, something deep inside her own body exploded in ecstasy. Even better than before. This glorious sensation just got stronger and stronger each time.

"God, Tamsie," he murmured. "You ain't half good at this. Never known anyone better." He handed her a tissue, then took one out of the packet himself and wiped his now limp penis.

Might she be now going to have his baby? "You're sure those pills work, aren't you?" she asked.

"Of course. They have so far, haven't they?"

"Yes. But the girls at the Clementine school?"

Kelvin threw back his head and laughed. "Course they're screwed. The pills I sold them were fake. Not going to waste the real stuff on them. Their money's good though." He zipped up his trousers. He tapped the end of her nose. "You just keep on taking those pills."

Then he walked away without even looking back. Something sank in her. Still, it looked as if she was safe.

"Are we all ready then?"

Kelvin's voice woke her from her daydreaming. This was it.

She had never seen him looking so excited. Not even when she'd deliberately teased him and not let him get inside her straightaway. Now, his eyes were gleaming. His face was bright red and he was holding the fence post high above his head. His nose had never straightened properly after Catty's brother had broken it. It made him look evil. She liked that look. It suited him.

"You really need to go to the hospital," she'd said.

"Naw! Can't afford it."

He'd probably been right. The Clementine Clinic was way beyond the means of Normalers like him, even with all the money he was getting from the illegal contraceptive pills. There was no Normal hospital.

The crowd was now chanting.

He winked at her. "You take this." He threw the fence post to her and pulled a large kitchen knife out of his bag. "Come on. Let's get to them."

They all moved forward.

The bell rang, signalling the end of the school day for the House of Clementine High School.

The kids started ambling out totally unaware of what was waiting for them.

"Go!" shouted Kelvin.

The Normalers rushed forward. The Clementiners froze where they stood. Tamsin found herself face to face with Catty. Her former friend stared at her. She opened her mouth as if she was about to say something. Her face crumpled and she looked as if she was going to cry.

Tamsin was distracted by a scream to her right. She glanced quickly and saw Kelvin pulling his knife out of a boy's chest. Catty's brother.

"Go on. Do it." Kelvin hissed.

Tamsin raised the fence post and crashed it down on Catty's head. The Clementiner fell to the ground, unconscious.

That would show them. It made the Clementiners' raid on the Normal School last week look like a childish game.

She looked down at Catty. Was she dead? She didn't really care. It was a shame about the baby, though.

CHAPTER TWENTY-SIX

You see, none of them really know how to behave. Oranges go bad. It makes it all so easy for me.

CHAPTER TWENTY-SEVEN

It only took Kaleem ten minutes to get over to the Executive building. Ella had sent a transporter for him. Obviously this was urgent. In those ten minutes he'd been able to get the gist of it. Zenoto had a new president. The elections had been sudden because there'd been a massive argument in their parliament. The new president was Pangwit Exton. Kaleem had never heard of him before. He looked young – very young, maybe even younger than Kaleem himself. He seemed to have come from nowhere. And he didn't look completely Zenoton.

As soon as he stepped out of the transporter the door to the Executive building buzzed open. Seconds later he was in the lift and soon after that he was seated in Ella's office. She had six screens open.

"I'm trying to find out as much as I can about him. Look." She pointed to a screen where a Zenoton child was playing with a Zandrian mother. "I'm surprised they didn't want a pure blood."

What did she mean? That was an odd expression anyway. "Why wouldn't they like mixed race?"

Ella shrugged. "I don't see that they wouldn't particularly. It's just that they've never done it before."

"Have you found out anything else about him?"

She shook her head. "It's really difficult. He hasn't any record of being involved in politics before."

"Why are we so worried? Isn't it up to the Zenotons? If they want a new president why shouldn't they have one?"

"Fair enough. It's just that it happened so quickly. It makes you wonder. And we know so little about this man. We don't know what he might do."

She had a point.

A static picture of Exton appeared on the news screen. Yes, he was young. He was obviously very tall and there was something about the way he was standing that made him look arrogant. Was that a bit of a smirk on his face? A supercilious smile in his eyes?

"Panjit Exton, aged just twenty-three, is the youngest president of Zenoto ever. Indeed, he's the youngest president in the known universe. However, in terms of experience, President Exton is second to none. He completed his education at the age of eleven and is possibly the universe's greatest mathematician. Maybe we can trust this young man with the Zenoton economy. Indeed, he may be good for the whole universe. There are high hopes that he will be able to bring about financial stability universe-wide. We'll be going to a live interview with him soon."

"He seems like a bit of a nerd," said Ella.

"Quite probably." And there was definitely something in Exton's expression that Kaleem did not like. It may just have been the way the camera had caught him. But he definitely didn't like what he saw.

"Before we go over to Zenoto," said the reporter, "we're going to talk to our politics expert, Janice Wilton."

A woman about the same age as Marijam appeared on the screen. There was something about her that made Kaleem want to trust her. She wore a plain emerald green tunic and a pale blue scarf. Her hair was silver rather than grey. She looked smart rather than glamorous.

"So, Miss Wilton, how has this extraordinary situation come about on Zenoto?"

"Well there's actually been some unrest for quite a while over there. Particularly amongst the young. There's a lot of concern that because of the extraordinary economic set-up on Zenoto they are not able to trade easily with other planets."

"Are they not, really? They do trade, don't they? Do they need to in fact, though? Don't they have everything they need?"

"Well, they have a lot. Most certainly. But if they want to influence the universe, they need a bigger presence. And it's Exton's generation that wants that."

"Even so. How did he get through the democratic process so quickly?"

Janice Wilton laughed and ran her fingers through her hair. "I think he was waiting in the wings, ready to jump in as soon as the opportunity presented itself."

“Some people are suggesting that a full democratic process has not been followed.”

“Oh, I can assure you it has.” A chart appeared on the screen. As the cursor moved across, a voice-over read out the times and dates. The chart disappeared and the reporter and Janice Wilton reappeared.

“So, everything has taken hours, rather than days, and in some cases just minutes?”

Janice Wilton nodded. “So clearly this has been very well thought out. They’ve just been waiting to put this into place. A very clever mind is obviously behind this. I suspect Exton himself.”

“My god.” Ella shook her head and put her hand over her mouth. “This is worrying.”

“Worrying indeed,” the reporter continued. “Now perhaps quite appropriately we can go over to Zenoto where the new president is addressing the news channels there.”

The screen was now filled with Pangwit Exton’s face. He looked even more arrogant now that they had a live picture of him.

“It is imperative,” he said “that Zenoto has more contact with other systems, and I’m afraid that is going to mean that we have to trade using normal economic factors and not some grandiose idea about abundance for all.”

There was a loud outcry in the background.

Exton held up his arms. “I know, I know. Many of you think that this is putting back centuries of work that we Zenotons have done. Yes, we tried to convert the rest of the universe, but they just wouldn’t have it. There was a popular expression on Terrestra centuries ago: “If you can’t beat them join them.” We young Zenotons want to be part of the modern world, rather than live in some isolated idyll. If that actually means going back to older ways, then so be it.

“My immediate plans are to monetize our supply stores so that they operate the way others call ‘shops’. Then I shall audit working patterns. Zenotons will soon be enjoying earning an honest crust and then they can really appreciate what they gain for their efforts. Like any other creature in this universe.”

A close up of Exton showed eyes that stared without connecting and a smirk on his lips.

Kaleem shook his head. "There's something not at all right here," he said. "It all sounds reasonable but he doesn't look reasonable. And what he's planning is such a shame. He ought to be looking for a way of making the rest of us see sense."

"Zenoto will be great again. Zenoto will take its rightful place in the world. Zenoto will lead." He punched the air and now a cheer came from another side.

It seemed familiar to Kaleem. He couldn't quite work out why, though.

The screen suddenly went blank. He turned to see Ella smiling at him.

It was one of those looks again. Would he be able to get out of this easily? She stood up and walked over to him. She put her hands on his shoulders. "I'm sure we could do something that would make this all go away. For a while at least."

Her perfume made him feel dizzy. He closed his eyes and breathed in deeply. There was nothing he would rather do than sink into her arms and make love to her.

"Come with me." She shivered, taking his hand gently. "I can make this right for you. You know I can."

He shouldn't. He knew that. But he wanted to. Just to melt into her for a short while… what would be the harm? Who would know? Rozia wouldn't and anyway actually it was nothing to do with her. Ella wouldn't be stupid enough to let her attachment know.

"You know you want to." She pulled him towards her.

He wanted her now. He really did.

Suddenly though he remembered Razjosh. It was startling, almost as if his old mentor were suddenly with him in the room. He could feel his presence, even though he couldn't see him.

"It's your duty as Peace Child to secure the peace at whatever personal cost. Your reward comes as you guarantee the joyful lives of others. You must never pursue your own needs." It was almost as if Razjosh was whispering in his ear. He pulled away from Ella and turned to look. Was there some sort of technological trick going on?

“What’s the matter?” Ella was frowning and the corners of her mouth were turned down.

Kaleem shook his head. “I’m just thinking about Rozia and Petri.”

“They’re all right now aren’t they? Don’t forget I’m going to look after them personally.”

He nodded and turned away from her. Hadn’t what he’d just heard from Razjosh the exact argument he’d used to justify his abandoning Rozia?

It was just as well he did. The dataserve snapped back on. It was an executive override.

“Ella, Kaleem.” A young Zandrian nodded at them.

Ella blushed. “Kaleem, this is my attachment, Patrick Tyler. You’ve probably not met before. What do you want, Patrick?”

Patrick rolled his eyes. “This isn’t a social call or a domestic matter. God knows when they’ll give us any down time. Kaleem, I’m a junior executive for Outward Affairs. We need to talk to the two of you immediately. Please, both of you. Make your way up to the seventeenth floor.”

The screen went blank.

“That was close,” said Kaleem. “We really need to be more careful. In fact we shouldn’t take the risk at all.”

He turned his back on her and went towards the door but not before he’d seen her scowl at him.

CHAPTER TWENTY-EIGHT

The Outer Affairs offices were grander than anything Kaleem had seen anywhere before. Certainly the meeting room in the Citadel of Elders had been very plush in an old-fashioned way. But here was the most up-to-date luxury. From the veriglass walls he could see a vista of the whole town and beyond.

"It's actually a holoscene," Patrick explained. "We don't want to get distracted by what's going on outside."

"Can we do introductions quickly and then get down to business?" a shorter, blond-haired woman said as she used a dataserve to upload files to the screen.

Her name was Jadee Elliott and she was the special correspondent for Zenoto. A tall young man introduced himself as Rogery Mentis. He was a futurologist. The other young woman was Saleen Davisk, an economics expert.

"Right," said Jadee. "Let's get started then."

"I'm quite concerned about what's happening to my friend Rozia and her stepdaughter, Petri," said Kaleem.

Patrick frowned. "I don't think we can deal with personal matters in this meeting."

That wasn't what he meant. "They're just symptomatic of what else is going on."

"I don't get you." Jadee was looking at him with her eyebrows raised but her tone was warm and friendly.

"They're receiving some persecution from people who have become xenophobic. And people are making noises about them draining our health care systems."

"This happens when people become afraid," said Rogery. "Get rid of what's causing the fear and the fear will go away."

"That's rather obvious, isn't it!" Just how did they justify a futurologist's existence?

Rogery shrugged. "Xenophobia and fear are real. They make people behave in irrational ways."

How could this have happened? Zandra had always been a

peace-loving and welcoming planet, and Kaleem did know to his cost that it could be very severe with people who tried to be secretive. Now, though, it seemed it had its own secrets. "Have you got any idea what's behind all of this?"

"Something very manipulative and mysterious," said Rogery. "And we need to weed it out."

"It's a bit like what's been happening on Zenoto," said Saleen. "And look at this."

Some charts lit up on the wall. "The exchange rates have been going crazy over the last few weeks. Look at all of these dramatic spikes and drops." She pointed at some columns in red.

It didn't mean a lot to Kaleem. "How does this compare with what's normal?"

"Show prior twelve months," Saleen commanded the dataserve.

More charts appeared but this time without any red and no real spikes or dips.

"Has this been influenced by the situation on Zenoto?" asked Patrick.

"Possibly," replied Saleen.

"I think what goes on on Zenoto is the business of the Zenotons and not ours." Jadee's eyes were bright and her cheeks were red. "I don't think we like what they're doing but it has to be their decision."

"I agree," said Patrick. "But it might be useful to find out exactly what triggered that."

There was a general mumbling of agreement. Kaleem could predict what was coming next.

"Well, we need to send someone out there who can see what's happening. Someone who's been there before. Someone who they'll trust."

They were now all looking at him.

Jadee looked happier and was nodding now. "And someone who has the skills."

They were all still staring at him.

So, he was to go and spy on Zenoto. Inevitable, probably. But it would take him even further away from Rozia.

The meeting ended shortly afterwards. They only made very

vague plans. But it was going to happen quite soon. He would be going away on another diplomatic mission.

As he made his way home later he tried to work out what Razjosh would say about it all.

No doubt he would be optimistic. "Zenoto is a fine planet. You have good friends there. You should be able to enjoy your time there."

Annoyingly Razjosh would also have seen what had been happening to Rozia and Petri as a positive. "Of course it's not pleasant for them. But it's not their fault. And it's how they deal with it that counts. Anyway, you must uncover the hurt that is causing this to happen."

And how exactly was he supposed to do all of that. "Tut, tut, Kaleem. You know how. See both sides. Explain each to the other. Make them see that no harm is meant."

How, though. How?

"Open-minded discourse." Oh yes, that, just like the child's "why questions". Why is this an easier way for you? What do you gain from this? Why is that better than what you had before?

Not easy.

"No never easy. And it's crucial that you do this with your heart. You must absolutely respect the people with whom you are dealing."

Even if they don't deserve my respect.

"Come on now. You are the Peace Child. You know what you have to do."

Oh yes he knew all right. He'd arrived back at his apartment block. He rushed up to his flat and activated his dataserve.

CHAPTER TWENTY-NINE

Clem hadn't arrived yet. Kaleem was puzzled. He'd said something about getting to know an actual Clementiner. "There are some who are decent," he'd said. "Ordinary people leading ordinary lives. I'd like you to meet one."

So, here he was sitting in the café, waiting for Clem.

It was a dismal sort of place, right on the edge of the town. It had a sole droid waiter, an old model that hadn't been programmed with anything other than the very basic etiquette. It had already served Kaleem a mediocre coffee and was now occupying itself wiping already clean tables and rearranging the cutlery and the condiments. The insipid muzak didn't blot out the whirring and squeaking of the ancient machine.

Why were they meeting in such an out of the way place if this Clementiner was supposed to be normal? Where was Clem, anyway? How long should he give him?

Kaleem drained the last of his coffee. Should he order another one? He tried his communicator again. Clem just did not answer.

There was no point in having another coffee. If Clem and the Clementiner did arrive, no doubt he'd be forced to have another then. That would be soon enough. This stuff was gross.

He flicked through a few news channels. There was not a lot that was new. Yes, there were still arguments about all that was going on and there were a few protests still but this had all become normal now.

Kaleem sighed. This was such a bore. He'd just about made his mind to go when the door opened and in walked Clem. Alone. What had happened to the Clementiner?

Clem shook his head. "Sorry about this. He chickened out at the last minute."

"Why?"

Clem shrugged. "Loyalty to the Order, I guess."

"Oh, well. I'll just have to take your word for it."

"Or maybe not." Clem nodded towards the door.

A young man, about the same age as Kaleem, walked in.

Clem stood up. "You came after all, then. What made you change your mind?"

The Clementiner nodded towards Kaleem. "I've found out a lot about our esteemed Peace Child. I thought it couldn't hurt."

Clem nodded and sat down again. "Kaleem, Arboth. Let's just stick to first names for now."

Arboth held out his hand to Kaleem. Kaleem took it and shook it.

There was nothing about Arboth that immediately indicated that he was a Clementiner, though Kaleem did spot a tiny orange strip around the hem of his tunic. The man looked after his body: he was slender, muscular and impeccably dressed. His hair was neat and tidy. But he wasn't ostentatious in any way. He seemed confident and self-assured. Just an ordinary well-adjusted young man as far as Kaleem could tell. There was nothing that suggested he belonged to any sort of cult or order.

The ancient droid ambled over to them.

"Coffee?" asked Clem.

Kaleem pulled a face.

"We have a range of teas as well," said the droid. "The lemon and ginger is popular."

"Three lemon and gingers?"

Kaleem and Arboth nodded. The droid made its way slowly to the drinks machine.

"So," said Clem. "Will you tell Kaleem all that you know about the Order?"

Arboth shrugged. "I don't know where to start. It's just something I think is really good."

Kaleem was surprised that Arboth wasn't more evangelical about it. He'd expected Clementiners to be quite fanatical. Surely the more sensible people had left? "Well how come you're still a member of the Order?"

Arboth laughed. "Still? I've only been a member for three years"

"Oh." People were actually still willing to join cranky organisations like this?

"My uncle got a job at one of the orchards and…"

"There are still orchards growing actual clementines?" Kaleem made a note to himself to discuss the growing of this fruit crop with his father.

"Oh yes. They're still keen on growing excellent fruit. In fact…" Arboth frowned and looked up to his left. Then he lowered his eyes and looked straight at Kaleem. "All the other things they do so perfectly are still in support of the fruit. The Order aims to produce first-class workers."

"So how easy was it for an outsider to get in?"

"Not easy at all. But my uncle also has a very high standard and the Clementine Elders were impressed with him."

"Elders?" Odd that they used the same concept that they had on Terrestra.

"Oh yes. We have knights as well. I'm an ordinary knight and working towards becoming a knight of the second order."

It all sounded like a bit of a game to Kaleem. And Arboth still hadn't told him how and why he'd joined the Order. He was about to pursue this further when the droid arrived with the tea.

The machine placed the cups on the table. "I regret, gentlemen, that I could not offer you any Clementine Tea. The House is currently keeping all of its supplies just for members."

What? Kaleem and Clem exchanged a glance.

Arboth laughed. "Oh don't worry. This is a House of Clementine café. That's why I suggested coming here. Appropriate, don't you think?"

That couldn't be right. Kaleem shook his head. "But it's so shabby. Where's the excellence in that?"

Arboth smiled. "It's a great disguise, don't you agree?"

If the House of Clementine was so good, why were they disguising it? Kaleem was about to ask when Arboth started talking again. "My father died when I was very young and my uncle helped my mother to bring me up. I was in my late teens when he got the job with the House of Clementine. He got permission for me to help him occasionally if he did overtime at the weekend. One of his bosses saw me working and was impressed so suggested that I join the Order."

"So outsiders can get in?"

Arboth grinned. "Occasionally. It's not easy though."

"Do you think they'd offer me a place? Not that I want one, of course."

"Undoubtedly."

Kaleem laughed. "So would I be able to achieve enough excellence?"

The smile went from Arboth's eyes. He put his hand over his mouth and frowned slightly. "Actually, the excellence is something you learn. The Order has a very effective way of teaching it. It's willingness that you need."

Kaleem nodded. He remembered his own training. It had been hard. He'd had to be willing – more than willing in fact.

Clem had said nothing up until now. He had just sat there nodding his head and stroking his chin. "So how does Clementine define and maintain excellence?" he asked suddenly.

"Our shops sell the highest quality goods at affordable prices. Our workers are paid well. In return, they give 100%. The bosses are fair. Our hospitals have the highest standards – not that they're needed too much; Clementiners know how to keep themselves safe and well. Those who are fortunate enough to be educated in House of Clementine schools reach the highest standards in their learning. The knight system is challenging and rewarding."

Clem laughed. "You sound like an advert for a Clementine holiday camp. But not all Clementiners live in a Clementine settlement, do they? You don't do you?"

"No, and it's our mission to bring House of Clementine principles to the outside."

Clem nodded again and raised an eyebrow at Kaleem.

"What are the House of Clementine principles?" asked Kaleem.

"It's very simple. Bottom line: we only accept the very, very best." He grinned. "You understand that, surely?"

Of course he did. Only too well. "Indeed. I'd love to learn more, though."

"I just can't see what is so evil about the Order," said Kaleem, as he and Clem walked towards the public transporter station.

They'd finished their tea and Arboth had declared he'd work to do and he would have to leave. Kaleem had asked if they could meet up again and the Clementiner had been a little vague. "I've really got a lot on and I wouldn't want anyone to think you were spying on us," he'd said.

"I just don't get it," said Kaleem. "If they want to turn the whole world over to Clementine principles, wouldn't they welcome people finding out as much about them as possible. And why wouldn't the world want to turn to the Clementine way? It seems good to me"

"Yes, it's almost as if they've got something to hide."

They arrived at the transporter station. It was crowded. Kaleem laughed. "I wonder what the Clementiners would do about this."

"I wonder what they could do. And if the whole of the world belonged to the House of Clementine, what we'd do about people who didn't conform?"

Ah, yes. That.

Their transporter arrived. Kaleem found himself pushing forward with everybody else.

CHAPTER THIRTY

"Bakewell tart and builder's tea. That do you?"

Marijam placed the tray on the low coffee table. The tart, Kaleem noticed, was slightly oddly shaped. Why was she carrying the tray herself anyway? What did she think the kitchen droid was for after all? Oh yes. Right. It was obvious. "You made it yourself?"

Marijam nodded.

"Why?"

"Because I can and I wanted to."

"Why though? The droid would make it near perfect. And it would be more economical."

"Who knows how much longer we'll be able to have droids and all this fantastic technology? The world's going mad."

"You don't think it will get that bad do you? Surely not?"

"I hope not. We never seem to learn from history. We're repeating ourselves."

Kaleem shrugged. Well, maybe. He took a bite of his tart. Gosh it was good, even if it was a funny shape. Both the pastry and the cakey filling were extra light. You could really taste the almonds and the raspberry jam as well. "This is good, Mother."

Marijam laughed. "I always could make pastry. Don't you remember when we lived in the caves?"

Oh yes, he did. He nodded and took a sip of his tea. That was good too. It was unusual as well. Zandrian water did not usually make good Terrestran tea but this was really convincing. "How did you manage this then?"

"It cost a fair amount. I'm just making the most of it all while the communications are still open."

"You think it will get that bad?"

"It's best to be prepared for the worst. Anyway, now that you've enjoyed my afternoon tea, talk. I know you've come to tell me something. You've got that look about you."

"I'm going to Zenoto. I'm to find out what's really going on."

“What?” Marijam’s eyes flashed. She blushed. “You’re going to be a spy again?”

“Kind of.”

“It’s ridiculous.”

“It has to be done.”

“Why?”

“Because as you said, the world’s going mad.” Would they go as far as being without droids and all the new technology, though?

Marijam shook her head. “If we have to go back to living in caves would it really be so bad? Don’t you remember what it was like?”

He did. Only too well. They were dark and a little damp. They’d had some technology though it had been inferior compared with what had been up on the surface. The main problem, though, had been his isolation from other people. He looked different and he was different also because he had a poorer life physically. The life there hadn’t been unhappy in other ways.

Now, though, they were used to a much higher standard of living. He gestured round the room. “You’d miss all of this, wouldn’t you?” He knew his mother had adapted very well to luxury. Anyway, she’d been born into it in the first place.

She glanced at where he was pointing. “Maybe. A little.” Then she turned back to him. “But I’d miss you more.”

“Nothing’s going to happen to me.”

“Oh, you can be so sure of that, can you?”

Well, he had to be didn’t he, or he’d never do anything.

Marijam now looked straight into his eyes. “Look at what happened when you were in the Z Zone.”

Yes, that. He had mixed memories of that time. The conditions there had been really squalid compared even with the cave home he and Marijam had shared. But he had shared that time with Rozia and it had been wonderful until it became dangerous and Rozia had been hurt.

“Mother, I can take care of myself. I really can.” Even if he couldn’t take care of the person he loved most in the world.

“Let somebody else do it this time. You’ve done your share.”

“You know I can’t.”

"You won't have the protection of the Prophecy this time."

Kaleem sighed. "Mother, you know that there wasn't anything in that in the end. It was just a recording of Davina Patterson's therapy sessions."

"Yes. All right. But wasn't it odd how she sensed you?"

Yes, well that was a bit of a mystery, how a 20th century woman under hypnosis had described some of the things that happened to him. Might it, though, be a question of making the story fit? A bit like the way fortune-tellers could say something so general that it would actually suit anyone.

"Or it could have been Kevik."

Kevik had also been born in a cave in the Z Zone and his mother had thought he had been the one mentioned in the "prophecy" until Kaleem came along. Both of their names began with "K" after all.

Marijam shrugged. "Or it might not have been."

"Mother, you know that it was all the excellent training Razjosh gave me that protected me. Not some mumbo jumbo."

Marijam frowned. "All right then. We don't know what might happen if you go all that way and they're as hostile as they seem on the news here."

"Well Exton's an oddball, and it's puzzling how he got into office, but he's actually seeking connection with others. He doesn't want to be hostile. Just the opposite. He wants more connection with people." Kaleem wished he could actually believe himself. There was really something disturbing about the man. He had to reassure Marijam some way though.

"For goodness sake, Kaleem, isn't there enough to occupy you here? People wanting to leave the One World Community. Brown tunics marching on the streets. Nasty racist incidents."

"It's all part of the same thing isn't it?"

"Oh yes. So if you find out what's causing the trouble here, you could apply it to what's going on on Zenoto, surely."

"I guess it's bigger on Zenoto. They need me there. A Zandrian can sort it out here."

"Who would you suggest?"

"Ella Tyler, for example." He felt himself blush.

"Ah. There we have it."

"Mother, I'd be getting away from her, wouldn't I, if I went to Zenoto?"

Marijam sighed. "What is going on here, Kaleem? It's frightening."

Kaleem nodded. "And Zenoto, the old Zenoto, might have been able to save us. They need me to uncover it again." He wondered whether it all had something to do with the House of Clementine. He suspected it probably did. That was now becoming just as much a mystery as the Babel prophecy had been. Would that have a rational explanation in the end as well?

"Would it? And you're a bit arrogant if you think you'll be able to persuade them to go back to their old ways and help us. That you can do this better than anyone else."

Ah. There was his mother speaking.

He sighed. "Mother, you know I have to do it. That's all there is to it."

"What about Rozia and Petri? Are you going to abandon them?"

Oh, yes she'd got the measure of him, most certainly. Kaleem swallowed the huge lump that had formed in his throat. His mother was right. Of course he couldn't abandon Rozia a second time. Surely, anyway, he needed to stop her from going back to Terrestra. However bad it was getting on Zandra, there were still so many advantages for her and Petri if they stayed here.

"Well? You won't will you?"

He looked at his mother. "I don't think I can. You're quite right."

"Good. I'm glad we've got that settled. So you'll go and talk to them?"

Kaleem nodded.

"Today?"

"As soon as possible."

He got up from the table and started getting ready to leave. "The sooner the better, I guess."

This wasn't going to be an easy conversation. He knew that.

CHAPTER THIRTY-ONE

Kaleem made his way back to his own apartment and got into the shower. As the water flowed over his body he tried to think what he was going to say to the executives. How exactly was he going to talk his way out of this one? Now it felt cowardly to run away from his duty. But then there was Rozia. He had to look after her as well.

The water cascaded over his body and soothed him. Oh, yes life was good on Zandra. Even things as simple as hot water and toiletries were more effective than anything he had ever used on Terrestra. They were certainly having the desired effect here. He felt clean and he could also feel his body relaxing. They might not solve his immediate dilemma. They did make him care a little less.

Just as he began to think he'd had enough, the water stopped and the drier clicked on. The warm air was soothing as well.

It was maybe all a little too relaxing. He felt decidedly sleepy. He returned to his dressing room and selected a grey silky tunic and leggings to match from his closest and pulled them on. Yes, grey was a good choice. It was a solid neutral colour. The silky material suggested sophistication. These would certainly be right.

It was no good, though. He was just too sleepy. It was understandable, he supposed. He hadn't had a lot of sleep over the last few days. He staggered into the kitchen and commanded a coffee. Then whilst it was preparing he stretched out on the sofa in the lounge. His eyes closed.

He must have only slept for ten minutes. Maybe even fewer. He woke with a start. The machine was bleeping telling him the coffee was ready. That wasn't the only thing that had woken him, though. The main dataserve screen had opened and a familiar face was looking at him. Saratina. These days he just didn't see the distortion of her features and the ugly scars. She was just Saratina. She was one of his best friends. That was all.

She beamed at him. The smile came mainly from her eyes. Her lop-sided mouth couldn't make the right shape. It was so clear, though, that she was pleased to see him. Naturally he was pleased to see her.

But why was she contacting him from Terrestra? That was an expensive thing to do. Had something gone wrong there as well? He was wide awake now. He didn't really need the coffee anymore.

"Hello, Saratina," he said. "It's lovely to see you. There's nothing wrong, is there?"

She shook her head. "I just wanted to see how you were. It doesn't sound good there."

He could understand her perfectly these days. That was something that had actually only happened after they had both been prisoners on Zenoto during his earlier visit there. She did speak slowly but she always got there in the end.

"I'm fine. Though I have a bit of a dilemma."

"Oh?"

"They want me to go to Zenoto and find out what is really going on there. But I don't want to go."

"Why not?"

"Well, there's plenty to do here. And I want to keep an eye on Rozia and Petri."

"You should go to Zenoto. It's a good place."

"It was. I'm not so sure now."

Saratina shrugged. "It's a good place where something bad is happening. Bad things happen in good places. They need a Peace Child to bring the order back."

"Oh, I don't think I'm that good."

"You are, Kaleem. You are. Nobody could be better." She giggled. "Especially as you know so much about what they eat. Do you remember when we used to cook?"

Could he ever forget that? It was working alongside her in the kitchen for all of those hours and days on end that had made him finally understand her. She became great at cooking the Zenoton way as well.

The smile escaped from her eyes for a moment. "Seriously, Kaleem. You must go. You know them so well. It won't take you long to dig out what's really happening there."

She was right. His mother was right as well. This wasn't really helping. The dilemma remained.

"I wish you could come with me." Saratina was always so wise.

She laughed. "I'm too old for another big trip like that. But I could manage a shorter one."

"What do you mean?"

"I'll come to Zandra and look after Rozia and Petri."

"You would?"

"Of course. I like Rozia and I'm sure I'll get on well with Petri once she gets to know me."

This would be a good solution. Rozia did get on so well with Saratina. Saratina was very good with children anyway. Just look how she and Rozia had looked after the Adulkis.

"And if she insists on coming back to Terrestra, I'll look out for her here."

Of course she would. That was so much in Saratina's nature. Why hadn't he thought of that himself? Maybe she would even be able to talk some sense into Rozia about staying on Zandra.

Well, he probably hadn't considered it because she'd done so much for them all in the past. Last time he'd been with her she'd seemed tired. He hadn't wanted to impose. She glowed with health and energy today. This now seemed like an excellent solution.

"You have to be the Peace Child again, Kaleem. You're needed now more than ever."

"Yes, but really, why not here?"

"Lots of people can work with Zandrians. You have all of that experience with Zenotons."

"There are a few more who might be able to take them on."

"Yes, but not the people who have your diplomatic skills or your ability to blend in. This is about how you helped to get Terrestra and Zandra talking. How you reached out to us in the Z Zone and how you got rid of Switch-Off. How you appeased the Zenotons earlier. Just think as well of all the trouble Razjosh went to to train you."

A bolt of pain passed through Kaleem's chest at the mention of his former mentor. He still missed him. It seemed such a waste that they'd saved him from Switch-off only for him to die naturally a short time afterwards.

"You need to think of making Razjosh proud."

Kaleem nodded. He most certainly did. Staying on Zandra was no longer an option.

"You'll go then."

He nodded again.

Saratina jumped up and down and clapped her hands. "I knew you'd come through. One more thing though."

"Oh?"

"You must go and see Rozia. You must persuade her to stay on Zandra if you can. If she won't, well, yes, then she'll have to come back to Terrestra. If she stays on Zandra, I'll come to help her. I promise I will."

That would be a relief. If Saratina were with Rozia all would be well, he was sure of that. Then though he had a disturbing thought. What would these new Zandrian racists make of Saratina? Wouldn't they reject her because of her otherness? "I'm not sure you should come. It's not easy here now. Things have changed."

"I know. I know all about that. You don't think I'll let that put me off do you? It's not really new to me, is it?"

Well, she had a point. "I guess not."

"So, you'll go and see Rozia?"

Kaleem nodded.

"Right away, after we've finished this conversation?"

"Right away, after we've finished this conversation."

Saratina clapped her hands. "Good. Let me know what she says. I'll hear from you soon."

Kaleem smiled to himself. That wasn't a question.

The screen went to black. He started to call up Rozia. Then he thought better of it and left the apartment.

The lift deposited him on the street within seconds.

He started to jog towards Rozia's apartment.

CHAPTER THIRTY-TWO

"They look all right, don't they?"

Kaleem nodded. They certainly did. Just ordinary school kids who'd been called into a meet and who were now making their way home. There was the usual excitement, caused in part by whatever the subject of the meet had been and in part because so many of them were together which was something that happened only rarely.

"How do you know they're House of Clementine?"

"Just intelligence we've gathered. But I'd put money on there being some symbol on their clothing. It may only be tiny but it will be there. Besides, can't you see how confident they look?"

Kaleem watched a few of them closely as they walked past. Yes, every single one of them had either an orange stripe somewhere on their clothes or wore a small badge or brooch. Some of the girls had slides in their hair and some of the badges, brooches and slides were even shaped like very small clementines. All of this was hardly visible but, yes, if you looked carefully, you could see it. And Clem was right; they did all look very confident. Couldn't that, though, just be the effect of their teachers being good at their job?

He was glad, though, that he'd been invited to look at this. He was beginning to understand the House of Clementine a bit more now.

Kaleem shrugged. "They seem so normal, though."

"Part of the subtlety of the Order, I think. But these kids will have the edge on others, you'll see."

They watched the last of them make their way out of the building and towards the public transporters.

Clem nudged Kaleem. "It looks as if they're not going straight home." He pointed to the entrance of the transporter station. Most of them were making their way down a passage to the side. "Let's go and take a look. I think I know where they're going and it will all be visible from the transporter platform."

The platform was quite empty when they arrived. A transporter had just left.

"They'll be late home for lunch," Clem muttered. "Their mothers won't be too pleased. There they are, look. Just as I suspected." He pointed up to a pathway that ran above the platform.

The students were gathered there in small groups. The noise level was growing as they all shouted above each other, trying to make themselves heard. There were one or two play fights going on.

"That's all just normal, though isn't it?" asked Kaleem. He could still remember his own school days.

Clem nodded. "But House of Clementine kids are supposed to be a cut above the rest."

"Aren't we really pleased that they're not, after all?"

"I guess so. But I can't help feeling there's something extra going on. Oh, now look." Clem was pointing to the group at the far right of the walk way.

Two boys and a girl were pushing their communicators together as if the girl was collecting currency. She then took a packet out of her bag and took two smaller packets out of that and handed them to the two boys. Kaleem watched one of the boys sprinkle some white powder out of the packet and snort it up his nose.

Clem nudged him again. "Look at the guy with the red bandana."

The student, who was definitely taller and looked older than the others, took a medi-wand out of his bag and passed it to another student who handed him something tiny that Kaleem couldn't quite see.

"I'd imagine that that's some sort of expensive jewellery."

"But what's with the medi-wand?"

"Oh, it's not a medi-wand. It's a wand charged with some sort of mind-altering drug."

"Where would they get that sort of stuff?"

"There's probably a whole drug-trafficking ring set up."

"So they're not so squeaky clean as they'd like us to think?"

"It would seem not. And you have to ask who is behind all of this."

"You don't mean…?" Could it be an inside job?

"If it's House of Clementine it will be damned efficient."

The students started to disperse.

Clem nudged Kaleem again. "Here comes the cavalry."

Some adults were now making their way on to the walkway.

Clem nodded. "Knights."

They looked like ordinary Zandrians to Kaleem. "How do you know?"

"Well, look who's with them."

Of course. Arboth.

"How would they have known about this? And look at how effective they're being." It was clear that the adults commanded the respect of the youngsters straight away. Maybe this was a little different from what happened normally.

"Their spy network is at least as good as ours. Clementine excellence again."

Most of the students were now making their way down to the platform accompanied by the adults. They were talking quite seriously. Arboth and another knight had remained behind with the girl and the older student. They handed the wand and the packet of powder over to the two knights.

"Pretty good at clearing up, then," said Kaleem, "even if it is an inside job."

Clem nodded. "Let's see if we can find out more."

Arboth looked down at them suddenly and nodded.

The café was just as deserted as the first time and the ancient droid had not improved either.

"You're sure he'll come again?" asked Kaleem as the cranky machine trundled over.

"Gentlemen, I'm sorry for the delay," said the robotic voice. "The good news is, I do have Clementine tea in stock today. Would you care to try it?"

Anything would be better than the coffee.

"Yes please," said Kaleem and Clem together.

As the droid squeaked over towards his drinks machine the door slid open and Arboth walked in.

“Told you,” whispered Clem.

Arboth’s face was red. He pushed his dark hair back from his face. “Bring me a cool frega,” he called to the droid. He almost collapsed onto the comfisessel.

“That bad?” asked Clem.

Arboth nodded.

“Young people on drugs? Who’s selling to them? Outsiders or is it an inside job?” asked Kaleem.

“Actually both. And what’s more there’s other corruption.”

“Oh?”

Arboth nodded again.

“Some knight trainers are taking bribes.” He looked straight into Kaleem’s eyes. “You could buy yourself a Clementine knighthood. Very easily. Why don’t you?”

CHAPTER THIRTY-THREE

"So there you are," said Arboth. "That's all you need to do to become a knight of the second order." It was that simple? Kaleem had been reluctant at first to take on the knight training as Arboth had suggested. Then he'd realised with his trip to Zenoto coming up he'd better do it first if he was going to. It was important to understand about the House of Clementine, even if the problems on Zenoto were more urgent.

"You look puzzled," said Arboth.

"I can do this though I've not even become an ordinary knight?"

Arboth shrugged. "You have all of those qualities anyway. A Peace Child would, wouldn't they?"

"Maybe. And you say all. That's a lot actually." The video clip had gone on for what seemed an age.

"Yes but you can do most of those things already."

"I can, yes. But how can those knights who pay for their progression keep up their pretence?"

"Well we don't exactly flaunt our knight skills when we're in ordinary company. We just get the award and that's that."

"How can you keep up standards if your knights haven't been properly trained?"

"It's difficult, yes. It's a fundamental problem. But your standard will be all right. Are you ready to take the test? It would be good to get it done before you set off for Zenoto."

"I guess. Can we just go through the fencing one more time?"

"Oh I'm sure we can. Try with the epée."

Kaleem took the longer weapon. The two of them were soon engaged in a circular parry. Shortly after that Kaleem found himself able to touch Arboth's chest.

"Well done," said Arboth. "Now will you take the rest of the test?"

"Gladly." Kaleem sat himself down at the console and started answering the questions. Twenty minutes later the dataserve pinged.

Arboth nodded. "97%. Pretty good. You could graduate."

"I don't feel ready to be a knight, though. I don't really feel as if I could belong to Clementine. I still don't really understand it."

"What is it exactly that you don't understand?"

"Well, there seems to be so much about it that is good: very high standards in everything, happy workers and really good health care and education systems. Yet you have drug problems and there is corruption within your knight training system."

Arboth shrugged. "Doesn't that happen in most organisations?"

It did. Arboth was right. But there was something else he couldn't quite define. Then there was the suspicion that the House of Clementine might somehow be connected with all the strange things that were going on Zandra and Zenoto. Perhaps it would soon be Terrestra as well.

Arboth touched Kaleem's shoulder. "Once you become one of our knights you could find out more."

Well, it would be a sure way of getting to the bottom of everything. And it was very much the type of thing he'd done before. There was still a lot he didn't quite understand though.

"Well?" said Arboth.

Kaleem nodded. "All right. Let's go for it."

Kaleem adjusted his House of Clementine knight's graduation tunic. He looked at his reflection in the mirror. Yes, it certainly suited him. The blue cloak was especially stunning. These uniforms were very attractive. Perhaps that was one of the reasons so many people wanted to become knights.

"Thank goodness I made it," said the young woman who stood next to him.

"Which grade?"

"Oh, just an ordinary knight."

"Still an achievement."

She shrugged. "The first step on the ladder."

"But why is becoming a knight so important? Isn't being part of the Order enough?"

"It's easier to stay in the Order if you're on the knight ladder."

Kaleem nodded. He understood that. "You have a point. Were you born into the Order?"

"Yes, but I've seen some of my cousins being forced to leave. I don't want that. You're an incomer, aren't you?"

"Yes I am. I think sometimes it's easier for us."

"You're probably right. You have a better understanding of how dreadful the outside is."

"Oh, I don't know about that."

He would have liked to continue the conversation but they were now being marshalled into ceremonial hall.

The graduation ceremony was a bit of a bore. Two hundred young people were knighted. There were no swords on shoulders these days, nor did they have to kneel down in front of any important person. Quite simply, names were read out and they trooped in front of one of the senior trainers, who handed them the bandanna that completed their uniform. A holograph of a fencing foil hovered over the head of each graduand and an electronic voice confirmed their status as a graduated knight.

He thought about the conversation he'd started having in the robing room. Why was the fear of the outside so great? Was is just that being part of the Order was so good? How could you know if you'd not experienced anything else, as was the case with that young woman he'd spoken to? Was this simply fear of the unknown? How did people get expelled to the outside?

As soon as the last of the knights had moved past her the senior trainer stepped forward and began to make a speech.

"I won't keep you long, I promise," she said. "I know you are all anxious to celebrate with your friends and family. I would like to thank you for taking on this very important work. I hope that you will all consider your knighthoods not just as something symbolic but that you will go on to use your skills to champion the principles and ideals of the Order and keep the Order safe. That you will be proactive in identifying those who should be asked, or indeed, compelled to leave. We must keep the Order pure. Some of you will work on the outside but if you live according to House of

Clementine principles the Order will always be your sanctuary and we welcome also your efforts in identifying individuals who should be invited to join the Order."

A shiver ran down Kaleem's spine as everyone started clapping. It was those age-old issues of inclusion and exclusion. He knew too much about all of that by now to feel at all comfortable with it.

The clapping died down.

"Thank you," the chief trainer continued. "Now if you would all like to make your way into the banqueting suite, refreshments have been made available for you."

Kaleem mingled with the others. He had invited no friends or family to the ceremony: his involvement with the House of Clementine had to remain top secret. He helped himself to a glass of clementine juice and took one of the sweet pastries. He looked out for the young woman he'd been speaking to earlier but he couldn't see her anywhere. He knew exactly what he must do now. He must make himself disappear. He drew himself in, bowed his head slightly and kept his eyes looking down to the ground. He was in his invisibility mode and glided through the crowd without being seen. He kept his ears open.

"Well we're definitely insiders now," he heard one young man say.

"Yes, it's really hard to get rid of knights. Thank goodness. It's barbaric out there, I've heard."

"Not for me, thank you. Having to queue to see a medic. Sharing wands. Riff-raff in the classroom."

"Now we get to keep them in order."

Were they all like this?

Kaleem moved round the room.

"Will you go back outside now?" he heard another say.

"I hope not but I might have to," his companion answered. "I hope not, though. They're barbarians out there."

"Well at least we don't get any of the scum here."

Unbelievable. Surely this went against the code of conduct of knighthood anyway? Kaleem carried on walking across the room.

"I can't wait to get stuck in. To help other people to do their best. Help to promote the Clementine standards."

The girl must be one of the youngest knights ever. About twelve, perhaps? And her friend, also a knight of the second order, didn't look a lot older. The other girl was nodding vigorously. She caught Kaleem's eye as he walked past and he found himself dropping his invisibility and grinning at her. At least those two were being positive. But what would even they do if people didn't conform?

Kaleem decided it was time to go. There was work to be done here, he could tell. What, though? And would he have time with everything else? Could it be the House of Clementine that was interfering here and on Zenoto? Or was this just something else he would have to worry about?

He moved quietly across the room, then into the lift, down and out of the building. It was late spring / early summer by now. Pleasant time of day for jogging.

He glanced back up at the floor where the ceremony had taken place. No one would guess. No one would realise what Clementine was. It just looked like any other corporate event. Didn't that prove that they had something to hide? What though? His investigations so far had really got him nowhere.

He set off. By the time he'd reached the corner he had a steady pace. One foot in front of the other. Up and down. Breathing in and out.

After about twenty minutes he had to stop. He had a stitch. He bent down to relieve it. Then he remembered his time in Terrestra before the disease had taken hold. There had been fear then as well about letting outsiders in. Had that been the same? Had even that been to do with the House of Clementine?

His communicator buzzed. Rozia. He changed direction.

CHAPTER THIRTY-FOUR

I must take care now. The Peace Child is beginning to understand. Though of course he doesn't understand what he is understanding. I am real. He will have to learn that at some point.

CHAPTER THIRTY-FIVE

Petri was covered in spots and blisters again. Her eyes were running. She was worse than Kaleem had ever seen her before.

"Make it stop, Rozia. Stop it hurting."

Rozia frantically rummaged through a drawer. She found a flask of fluid and a wand. Kaleem held his breath as she passed the wand over the child's body. Petri continued to whimper.

"It will pass, sweetheart," Rozia murmured. "Try to sleep."

Petri pushed Rozia away and grunted. "Why isn't this stupid wand working?"

"Please try, Petri."

"I can't sleep. It hurts too much." Petri started screaming.

"I know. I know. Let's try some of this." Rozia looked up at Kaleem and frowned. "Good old Terrestran soothing gel."

She removed the cap, squeezed some on to her hands and started smoothing it on to Petri's body.

"Ow, ow," the little girl cried.

"It will start working in a few minutes. Hang on in there."

Rozia was right. Petri's screaming turned to a grizzle, then back to a whimper and as her eyes gently closed she stopped altogether and soon it was clear she was sleeping peacefully.

"That's something, at least."

Rozia shook her head. "It won't last. It'll wear off and then she'll wake in agony again."

They crept back out into the living area.

"I don't get it," said Kaleem. "That wand didn't work. But hadn't you given her her meds anyway?"

"Of course I had. Clearly that wand didn't work either."

"Well, was that a spare or something? I thought Ella had arranged to deliver them individually as and when you needed them?"

Rozia nodded. "Yes, so there'd be no chance for any interference. It clearly didn't work. That other was just a palliative one. They're sent every time just in case she's beginning to resist the meds."

"So you think there's been some interference?"

"I don't know. They could just be defective wands, I suppose."

"Goodness… if they're breaching that kind of security…"

"Or she might be getting worse."

He could see tears forming in Rozia's eyes again. Again he just wanted take her into his arms. He didn't dare though.

"Let me talk to Ella. See what she can find out."

It took a while for Ella to answer. At last she did, though, and her face lit up when she saw Kaleem.

"I'm at Rozia's apartment," Kaleem said quickly.

Ella's smile faded for a split second. Then it returned to her mouth but not to her eyes. "Well, Rozia, Kaleem, what can I do for you?"

"Two wands don't seem to have worked," said Kaleem.

Ella frowned. "That's terrible. Shall I send a medic over?"

Kaleem looked at Rozia. She shrugged. "It would be a shame to wake her now that she's asleep."

"Well, here's a plan." It was Executive Tyler speaking now, not Ella. "If she wakes again and is in pain, let me know straight away and I'll get someone over there. In the meanwhile, send the wands back and I'll get them analysed."

Kaleem nodded. He placed the wands in the return drawer and keyed in Ella's coordinates.

"Got them. I'll get back to you as quickly as I can." The screen went blank.

"You should go home," said Rozia. "You must still have a lot to do and a lot to think about."

"No, I'll wait until we find out. I'm not going anywhere until then."

They sat on the sofa. It was suddenly awkward knowing what to say.

"If she *is* getting worse…"

"Don't say that. Don't say that."

"But wouldn't it be better to stay here? Isn't medical research more advanced on Zandra?"

"Yes, but it feels so dangerous for us now."

He couldn't argue with that. Zandra was rapidly becoming a place he no longer recognised. He sighed.

Rozia frowned. "Yes, I know. It's lose, lose."

That was so unlike her. Normally she was so optimistic.

The dataserve bleeped and the screen came back into life.

"It's puzzling," said Ella. "Both wands were completely empty. But they were fully charged when they were dispatched. Two more are on their way. We've put extra tracking on them. Any further problems, get back to me."

The screen went blank.

"I knew it."

"At least it means that Petri hasn't deteriorated."

"So, we can return to Terrestra."

"But if Ella's going to monitor it even more closely?"

"I just don't feel safe."

The drawer edge illuminated to show that a delivery had arrived. Petri began to whimper.

Rozia grabbed the wands. "Let's see, shall we?"

"Shall I…?"

"No, come with me. I couldn't bear it if they don't work."

Kaleem followed Rozia into Petri's room.

"We've got some new wands," said Rozia. "These should do the trick."

"They'd better. It's all sore." Petri grimaced.

Rozia looked at Kaleem and nodded. He primed the palliative wand and handed it back to Rozia. As soon as Rozia started applying it the blisters and sores started disappearing from Petri's body.

"Better," murmured the little girl.

"At least that seems to be working," said Kaleem.

Rozia nodded. "We'd better give her the normal meds now."

Kaleem once again primed the wand.

"I want Kaleem to wand me," said Petri.

Kaleem looked at Rozia. She nodded. "It's good for her to get used to other people."

Using the wand wasn't as easy as Rozia had made it look. He kept going either too fast or too slow and the wand constantly bleeped in protest.

"Kaleem's useless." Petri giggled.

"Don't be such a cheeky little monkey." Rozia was frowning.

"She's right, though, I am. Just like with the kaartjes." Rozia had been so much better at driving those strange little vehicles than he had been when they lived together in the Z Zone.

"Oh, you weren't so bad really. That was a long time ago anyway."

There was now an awkward silence again. Kaleem got a little better control of the wand and it finally gave its double bleep to show that the treatment was complete.

"I'll get going," said Kaleem.

"Don't go just yet. Wait in the lounge while I tuck her in."

Kaleem made his way through to the lounge. Dare he hope? Maybe that conversation about the kaartjes and their time in the Z Zone meant something? And now that Petri's medication was sorted again?

She seemed to take an age. He had the impression that she was hesitating. At last she came through though.

"I know what you're thinking," she said as she came into the lounge. Her eyes were fixed on the ground and she wouldn't look up at him. "We're still going back though."

"Why? Now that Ella's really fixed the meds? She will take care of you. You know that."

"Yes, yes. She's been very good. You all have. But you'll be going away soon as well."

"My parents will look out for you and if Saratina comes?"

"They would. I know. But it isn't just that. We just don't feel wanted here. By too many other people. My mind's made up." Now she looked at him and he could see the tears in her eyes. That was something at least. It was as hard for her as it was for him.

"I'd best get going then."

Rozia nodded and pressed the buzzer that opened the main door to the apartment.

Kaleem left without another word. He ran down the fourteen flights of stairs and out into the cold night. He jogged home, despite the cold.

He decided he would go and see her again the next day.

The poor, poor child. I wish I didn't have to be so cruel. Yet on the other hand I'm glad. I so often have to suffer physically like that. What they all do hurts me. I am the physical manifestation of their rot.

CHAPTER THIRTY-SIX

The outside door to Rozia's apartment block opened almost as soon as Kaleem touched the buzzer. The screen was only on for a few seconds.

"Come on up," said Rozia. She was looking down and her voice was hoarse. He suspected she had been crying.

The lift transported him up in seconds and the door to her apartment was already open when he got there.

Rozia was not in the lounge. He could hear her talking to Petri. The house droid was busy packing things into crates.

"What's going on?" asked Kaleem.

"Mz Rozia and Mz Petri are preparing to leave for Terrestra."

"When exactly do they expect to leave?"

"I do not have that information, sir. Would you like me to ascertain the exact departure date from Mz Rozia?"

"No, it's all right. I'll ask her myself." Kaleem went towards the inner hallway that led to the bedrooms.

The droid stood in his way. "I'm afraid I can't allow you through there. Mz Rozia gave strict instructions that you were to wait in the lounge. I could go and tell her you're here, sir, if that would be helpful?"

"Yes, please do that."

"Very well, sir."

What was Rozia playing at? What was going on back there that she didn't want him to see? He could actually override the droid easily enough but he didn't really want to do that. That would be disrespectful towards Rozia.

A comfisessel hovered towards him and he sat down. Goodness, this place was beginning to look cold. Rozia had made it such a comfortable home for herself and Petri. Now it was beginning to look bleak.

Rozia appeared in the doorway. He'd been right. She'd been crying though she'd probably been trying to disguise it. Her make-up was immaculate and her hair was shining. She'd been tidying herself up and hadn't wanted him to see her looking miserable. But he could see the swollen cheeks and the red eyes beyond the make-up.

He just wanted to take her into his arms and hold her close. He didn't dare, though.

"You're going back to Terrestra then? Definitely?"

She nodded.

"I still don't understand. I thought Ella was guaranteeing the meds?"

"She is and I'm sure she would make sure the supplies came through regularly. But it isn't just that."

"Oh?"

She sighed. "We were out earlier and we were attacked."

Kaleem felt the blood thudding in his ears. "Attacked. Who by?"

"No idea who they were. But they had a real go at Petri. She still had a slight rash and, well, her colouring is a bit odd for Zandra anyway. Then they had a bit of a go at me as well. Told me to get back to Terrestra. So that's what we're going to do."

Kaleem wanted to punch a wall or do something equally violent. He kept his hands to himself though and dug his fingernails into his palms. "If I could only get hold of them. They didn't hurt you, did they?"

"No, it was just verbal. You would have to talk them round and you probably would. But that all takes time. Too much time."

"You know I'd look after you don't you?"

"How can you when you're going to Zenoto?"

"I won't go. I'll stay here."

"Do you really have that choice?"

"Someone else can do it. It sounds anyway as if things here are getting worse. Maybe I should be staying on Zandra after all."

Rozia shrugged. "It was only verbal."

"Then stay."

"No, enough is enough."

"You surely won't get the care on Terrestra that's offered here?"

"Probably not, but things are improving all the time. And at least they accept us there."

"Where are you going to live?"

Rozia smiled and blushed. "In what used to be the Z Zone. There are still some underground apartments there. They've made them really nice. They'll also be ideal for Petri. They don't let the sunlight in."

"If you stayed here, you wouldn't have to worry about that."

Rozia shook her head. "I'll be able to get more work more easily on Terrestra. Everyone has been so generous here but it's time I looked after myself. And Petri will be able to find more people like her to play with. There will be people who look like her and there'll probably even be some with the same condition."

"But the pain? Surely you don't want her to go through the pain?"

"We'll manage. They do have pain relief on Terrestra, you know. It's not that primitive."

"I wish you wouldn't go."

"And I wish you didn't have to go to Zenoto but you do and here's nothing we can do about it."

Neither of them had any more to say. Then she stepped towards him. She put her hands on his shoulders and kissed him on the lips. They both hesitated for a second. She pulled him into a proper embrace.

The months melted away. He was back where he should be, in her arms. What was she expecting, though and how far could this go? Whatever was happening now was surely only temporary. He had to go. She couldn't come with him. He could see that she was right as well. It would be safer for her to be on Terrestra and he would even feel happier with her there while he was away.

She pulled away from him, in fact. "We can't do this."

He nodded. Yet it had felt so right. They belonged together didn't they? Yet time and time again this demanding role of his would get in the way.

The tears were streaming down her face.

"Rozia," he whispered his voice hoarse. He was fighting back the tears himself.

"I love you," she said. "I've never stopped loving you. But you're unreachable."

"Rozia," he said again. He loved her too. Didn't she know that?

She shook her head. "We can't go back. It's too late."

The droid ambled into the room. "Reactivate? I have been on standby for twenty minutes."

Rozia turned to the droid. "Please complete packing."

Kaleem watched her as she continued to sort her belongings into piles. "Just how soon are you going?"

Rozia wouldn't look at him. "In three days' time."

At least he had three days. A lot could happen in that time, couldn't it?

"But you've packed pretty well everything."

"We're going to stay in a hotel at London Harbour. A supercraft can take us to Terrestra. We don't know the exact time of departure yet. It will be handy to be nearby." She wiped her hand across her face. "Please go now, Kaleem. It's too painful with you still here."

"Perhaps when I've finished on Zenoto..."

"If you get back. And then what will come next? There's always something."

"But we can keep in touch, can't we?"

"I don't know..."

"I'd like to know how Petri gets on."

Her face softened. She half smiled. She knew he cared at least.

She nodded. "Yes, of course. I'll let you know. Perhaps via your mother or your grandmother. But go now. Please."

Kaleem moved towards the apartment door.

Then Petri screamed.

Both he and Rozia ran towards her bedroom.

"It's all right sweetheart," said Rozia.

Petri nodded but looked as if she wanted to scream again. Her breath was coming is short, sharp pants.

Rozia turned to Kaleem. "Can you prime the palliative wand while I get her undressed?"

Kaleem located the charger and pressed it gently. The wand lit up and whirred softly. He handed it to Rozia as she gently pulled up Petri's clothing. "You are a brave girl," said Rozia. "I'm sorry if I'm hurting you."

Petri shook her head but Kaleem could see that her fists were clenched and her face was white. She was biting her lip. She must be trying not to scream.

Rozia worked with the wand gently but steadily. Gradually the blisters disappeared and Petri's skin took on a more normal colour. She relaxed and began to look sleepy. Rozia kissed her head. "You can't go back to sleep yet, monkey child. You've got to have your med wand as well."

Kaleem started preparing it.

"I want Kaleem to do the wand."

He looked at Rozia. She nodded. "I'm sure you'll do better than last time."

He moved nearer to Rozia and Petri and started waving the wand carefully above the child's body. It still kept warning him that he was going too fast or too slow.

Petri giggled as the wand constantly bleeped but perhaps not quite as often as the last time. "Kaleem still needs wanding lessons but he's better than he was."

"I do. You're quite right."

"Don't you be so cheeky. But I suppose it shows you must be feeling better if you can be naughty like that."

"I am better. Kaleem is magic with the wand – even if he can't drive it properly."

Rozia looked at Kaleem. "Let's hope this one has worked as well," she said.

"Would you like me to stay and see?"

"There's really no need. But there is something I'd like to talk to you about before you go. Wait while I put her back to bed. Come on Petri." She bundled the little girl off towards her bedroom.

It took Rozia quite a while. There were some arguments about whether Petri had cleaned her teeth and then she declared she wanted Kaleem to tuck her in.

"Kaleem's too busy. Come on now. Be good."

"He's still here though. You said you wanted to talk to him. Why is he still here?"

"Yes I do need to talk to him. But you would dilly and dally too much if he were here. Now into bed and not another word."

Petri grumbled but Kaleem couldn't hear exactly what she said. He busied himself disposing of the two used up wands. Obviously Rozia didn't want him to get too close to Petri. This showed she was still intent on returning to Terrestra? Oh how he'd hoped that she was about to tell him she had changed her mind and was going to stay on Zandra. Fat chance of that.

Then it went quiet.

A few seconds later Rozia came into the lounge.

"I just wanted to thank you for being so supportive," she said.

Kaleem shook his head and shrugged. Why wouldn't he be?

"You're still such a good friend, even if…"

Even if what? They were no longer lovers? "I try my best."

"I know that, but you have other work to do. And actually I don't think I can manage without you here. So…"

"So?"

She sighed. "That's why we definitely have to go back to Terrestra."

"But you've seen how good the medication is for her here. They'll monitor it even more closely now. And you have a hotline to Ella. Nothing else can go wrong. My parents would always help out as well."

Rozia shook her head. "It's not just that. It's because we're not wanted here. We have to go."

"There's nothing else I can say that will persuade you?"

She shook her head. "You'd better go now." She activated the apartment door which slid open. Her arms were folded across her chest and she was looking at the ground.

"This is goodbye, then?"

She nodded. She was still looking at the floor.

Kaleem left the flat, ignored the lift, ran down the stairs and then started hurrying towards his own apartment.

Kaleem sat in the dark in his own apartment. He tried to relive every single contact he'd had with Rozia. When they'd been schooled together and she'd been different from the others. Then they became lovers. He remembered the first time they made love.

How it had been when they'd lived together in the Terrestran Z Zone. How wonderful she'd been with the Adulkis, managing to let them play but making sure they were safe. He smiled when he thought of her skill with a kaartje compared with his own clumsy attempts. That had just all repeated itself with the wand. Then there was that awful day when she was so badly injured. And the worse one when he realised he had to let her go. The worst day of all came when he actually went to tell her this. Then she'd half come back into his life and he'd had the hope that they might get back together again and that they could now be a couple again. The danger was past, or perhaps it wasn't. Anyway she'd dashed that hope. Soon they would be further apart than ever. Darn their Peace Child role.

The dataserve lit up. Patrick Tyler's face appeared. "Hi Kaleem. We need to bring your mission forward. That young Zenoton is getting crazier by the minute. Can you be at the Executive building at first light tomorrow? We'll send a transporter."

"I guess I don't have a choice." Kaleem was surprised at how bright his voice sounded.

Tyler laughed. "See you then."

"Yep."

The screen went blank again. Well, at least it might take his mind off Rozia.

CHAPTER THIRTY-SEVEN

Kaleem's communicator buzzed as he entered the street of his apartment building. He was glad to stop running. He was almost out of breath. He'd been determined to keep going, even though he thought his chest was about to explode, but at least now he had an excuse to pause.

"Send," he said.

"Urgent… sooner… videos. Look." The signal kept coming and going. What was going on? This never happened these days. Particularly not on Zandra.

"Stupid signal," Kaleem muttered. "I'm only a few metres from my apartment. I'll look on the dataserve when I get in." He couldn't be sure that the person at the other end could hear him. In fact, he hadn't been able to identify who had been speaking to him. He couldn't even tell whether it was a man or a woman.

He carried on. There was a lift already on the ground floor, though, when he got in so he took it.

Seconds later he was in the apartment and could already see the red light on his dataserve that told him he had messages.

"Open," he commanded.

Ah. Jadee Elliott. She must have news from Zenoto.

"Connect."

She answered straight away. "It's getting worse," the correspondent said. "Exton is really making a mess of things. In fact, he's being quite dangerous. Look."

A video clip loaded. A Zenoton droid presenter was interviewing Exton. Even before the man opened his mouth Kaleem sensed something bad, perhaps even evil. His face. Those piercing eyes again and that supercilious smile. Only they'd become even more threatening.

"So, President Exton, what are your plans for continued connection with other communities?"

Exton now smirked. "We want to connect with as many other planets as possible but we're restricting movement into Zenoto.

We'll still allow Zandrians and Terrestrans in – for the time being."

"How can that help you connect with others? Surely that's going in the opposite direction?"

Now Exton really did smirk. "Oh we want connections. But they have to be the right sort. Everything must be carefully negotiated first."

"I see. And what about your plan to return to a monetary system on Zenoto?"

Exton's grin got bigger. "The Zenoton way is fraught with problems. We're getting greedy. We're going to have to learn to pay for what we want. To earn what we get. This lack of token representing labour and raw materials is too idealistic. Even if it's still working to some extent here on Zenoto it won't elsewhere. It will be open to abuse. We need to be more pragmatic."

"But what do the rest of the Zenotons think?"

Exton laughed. "They voted for me, didn't they? This was a campaign pledge."

The clip faded and Jadee came back on screen.

"I can't believe that most Zenotons really think that way," said Kaleem.

"No, it doesn't seem likely, does it? We think the Zenotons have been manipulated."

"Really? By whom?"

"We have no idea. We're rather hoping you'll be able to find out."

Something stirred at the back of Kaleem's mind. Something Clem had said about the House of Clementine. Could it be?

"There's more. It gets worse."

Another video clip loaded. It was another interview with Exton. This time, though, it was a Zenoton presenter.

"So what is the point of this barrier? Surely normal entry controls on the ground would be sufficient?"

Exton laughed. "No, not at all. By the time they've touched down on the planet it will be too late. There's too much danger that hostile visitors may storm onto the rest of the planet."

"But won't there be a high cost in terms of labour and raw materials? And then in labour to operate it?"

Exton sat back in his sessel, put his hands together and crossed over his fingers. He then shrugged and opened his hands. He grinned. "The ideal opportunity for introducing the new monetary system. The units of currency will be called Zens."

"This is a huge step."

"Isn't it? Just what the planet needs."

Kaleem shook his head. "I can't see Zenotons liking this."

"Not all of them do. In fact they're pretty divided. Look."

The video clip stopped and another started loading.

Kaleem was shocked to see two huge groups of Zenotons marching on the Zenoton streets. A few scuffles were breaking out and some of the Zenotons were throwing things at each other.

"Unbelievable," Kaleem muttered. The Zenotons he knew were peace-loving and always ready to negotiate. "What are they doing?"

"Listen closely to their chants."

"Zoom," Kaleem commanded the dataserve. Straightaway he could see the expression on some of the Zenotons' faces. Pure hatred. On both sides. "Keep Zenoto pure. Say no to money," he heard one of them shouting.

Kaleem gasped. "360 degrees."

The video panned round. Now he could hear the other side. He could now hear another. "Bring back sanity. Stop the shirkers."

A female Zenoton punched the face of the male he'd just heard. Blood streamed down his face and he crumpled to the ground.

Kaleem shook his head. "This can't be happening."

"Unbelievable, isn't it? They've definitely been got at, don't you think?"

"They must have been."

The dataserve buzzed indicating that there was another call coming in.

"Send," they both said at once.

It was April Septimus. The chief executive was pale and her forehead was pulled into a frown. "More bad news from Zenoto. We're going to bring the mission forward."

Kaleem felt as if someone had punched him in the gut. "So what's happened?"

Executive Septimus sighed. “He’s threatened to attack Lupino.”

Jadee frowned. “That’s that little independent planet isn’t it? Not too far from Zenoto?”

“Yes, that’s right. They’ve been trying out their total annihilation weapons. Without much success, I’m pleased to say, but that can change. The One World Community has tried to negotiate positively with them but Exton says that is taking too long. He’s threatening an attack. There is every danger that he could instigate a full scale war. It would be extremely destructive in all sorts of ways.”

“So how soon do you want me to go?” asked Kaleem.

CHAPTER THIRTY-EIGHT

After the conversation with Jadee Kaleem showered, drank a frega and went straight to bed. Despite the drink, which was normally so relaxing, his mind kept jumping. Zenoto was a long way away anyway. This was possibly the most sinister mission he'd had to date. There'd been danger and intrigue before. The whole way he'd got into this in the first place had been pretty scary; he'd been so ill when illness had not existed for centuries on Terrestra, the whole mystery of the Babel Prophecy had been complex and puzzling and at first Razjosh, his mentor, had seemed really strange. That was all solved now – more or less – and if anything seemed trivial compared with what was happening at the moment. Now he was facing this huge problem on Zenoto and one that was equally puzzling on Zandra. And then there was Rozia and Petri. They were now on their way to Terrestra.

Terrestra. He hadn't really checked out that much what was going on there. Nothing had come up in the news channels. Could it be, though, that something sinister was also happening there?

He leapt out of bed and darted into the living area. "Find news from Terrestra," he commanded the dataserve.

The machine whirred into life. A Terrestran news channel opened on the screen. A droid newsreader was reading out a report about health care. All seemed to be well. In fact they were making good progress. Perhaps Petri would be all right then. It didn't look as if anything sinister was happening there. No brown tunics. No sign of the House of Clementine. No one calling anyone else a snazzy boy. Maybe he could stop worrying.

He may as well go back to bed. He poured himself another frega, drank it quickly and made his way to the bedroom. He put on some music, so low that he could hardly hear it. This particular piece was supposed to soothe people who were having difficulty sleeping. It must have worked because he was soon fast asleep and dreaming.

There were thousands of brown shirts marching. He couldn't

work out where he was. It could have been Zandra or Zenoto. Or even Terrestra. It had indicators of all three. Thousands more Zenotons, Zandrians and Terrestrans looked on.

"The brown shirts are trying to take away Human Rights," said a voice behind him. He couldn't help shuddering when he heard the voice. It couldn't be, could it? It certainly sounded like him. But he'd died. How could he be talking to him now? "Disdain for the Recognition of Human Rights – Because of fear of enemies and the need for security, the people in fascist regimes are persuaded that human rights can be ignored in certain cases because of 'need'."

Kaleem tried to turn but he still couldn't. "So why are all these people here?"

"You know you're dreaming?"

"I think so."

"Well, these people are symbols. The Terrestrans are affected as well."

"But they didn't seem to be, in the news broadcast I just watched."

"It is yet to come."

"Why can't I turn round?"

"You can. You just don't want to."

"I do."

"Do it then. Go on. Make the effort."

Was he really stopping himself seeing Razjosh? Was he afraid? He made one last effort. Then he was facing his former mentor. He was there, solid and full of life. He wasn't a ghost and he wasn't a holograph. He was real and he was speaking to Kaleem now. But of course, this was a dream.

It still fazed him seeing Razjosh so close up. At last he managed to speak. "So why is this happening?"

"There is some underlying discontent. We need to flush it out and reassure the people."

"Why do so many of the Zandrians want to leave the One World Community?"

"It's the same problem. So many are afraid of something. They no longer trust the Community."

"But isn't it better to stay in and fight for any necessary changes from the inside?"

Razjosh nodded and chuckled. "We both know that. They don't. You have your work cut out, young man." He laughed again. "I'm glad it's you and not me."

"Huh."

"Seriously, though, the Community must stay whole and become pure."

"How can we make that happen?"

"You mean how you can make that happen. It's up to you, now. I'm not really here. The usual diplomacy. All those techniques I showed you."

Kaleem sighed. "Are they being got at?"

"What do you mean exactly?"

"Is somebody manipulating them?"

Razjosh turned away from Kaleem. He muttered something to himself.

"What's the matter?"

Razjosh turned back. "Have you heard of the House of Clementine?"

"Yes. You know about that as well?" Kaleem's ears began to thud and his mouth went dry.

Razjosh nodded. "It's been around for centuries. You do realise that we're dealing with Golden Knowledge here? This isn't even merely Hidden Information. The House of Clementine has connections with controlling organisations that go back for centuries and they made their mark even on Terrestra before the time of the poison cloud. There is something at the very core of it that represents pure evil. You need to get that core out."

Now Kaleem went hot and then cold. This mission was getting bigger by the minute.

"Find the core. Find the core. Get it out."

Razjosh faded and Kaleem found himself facing a Zenoton who was looking at him with a question in his eyes. Kaleem couldn't work out what he was trying to ask.

Suddenly a Terrestran in a brown tunic jumped out of the crowd.

"Hey, Snazzy Boy. Don't you meddle." He tweaked Kaleem's ear.

Kaleem woke up.

Only a dream then. Well, he'd known that, hadn't he? No wonder he'd dreamed about Razjosh, though. It had been useful to get his ideas about the Community and about what was happening on Zenoto. It was reassuring, too, to think that Razjosh may have known about the House of Clementine.

Meeting his former mentor made it clear to Kaleem that he needed to work out not so much what he had to do but what his attitude needed to be to his work. Yes, it was absolutely clear: he had to be enthusiastic. He didn't need Razjosh to tell him, either, that this was somehow connected with the House of Clementine. Yet because Razjosh had told him this it seemed more certain. Razjosh, was dead though. So it wasn't really Razjosh but a part of himself that had become like Razjosh.

This was the biggest challenge ever.

And now he was up for it.

CHAPTER THIRTY-NINE

He was hot and bothered and his sleep tunic was drowned in sweat. It was no good just lying there. It would be better to get up. Maybe even take a shower.

He got out of bed and stripped the sheets off. He didn't want to activate the droid. He would leave that until the morning. It was the middle of the night and he needed some more sleep.

He decided to have a drink of house water. It wasn't often he did that. There was so much more to choose from. The trouble was, he couldn't decide what. So water it was to be. At least it was filtered and purified. And tasted of absolutely nothing.

There was a delay before the water came out of the faucet. The plumbing whirred and clicked almost like a dataserve that was thinking. That must be its filtering process. He remembered what it had been like getting cave water in the cave apartment when he was younger. No such complex filtering process there though the diastics had been good. This was so snazzy compared with that though even so.

That word again. And it had been in his dream as well. This wasn't going away.

He finished the water, quickly stripped off his sleep tunic and ran a shower. Soon the warm water was cascading over his shoulders. That felt good.

Then he helped himself to a clean sleep tunic. Nothing snazzy in that drawer. Just a set of six identical tunics. Snazzy might have been good.

He pulled on the tunic. Well, at least he felt refreshed now.

He climbed back into bed and hoped he would sleep soundly until the morning.

It was a peculiar place he was in now. He recognised it. Or at least, he could define it. A good name for it would be Snazz Land. Everything was larger and more colourful than normal. Everything seemed like a stereotype of itself. He was in some sort of opening in woodland. He touched a nearby tree. It felt real enough. No, actually it felt more than real.

The colours were dazzling. The green of the leaves contrasted with the brown of the bark more than he'd ever seen before. It was almost like a child's painting. Was this a cartoon world he was in? No, it was three dimensional enough. But it didn't seem quite real. He touched a leaf again. Oh yes, it was real.

The air seemed fresher, cooler, and softer than normal as it brushed against his face.

The grass *smelt* green.

He looked down at the path beneath his feet. It was paved. Man-made. Or at least, made by some sort of conscious being. Could it have been built by a form of artificial intelligence? Had something tried too hard? He bent down to touch it. Yes. It was really solid. Then he touched the grass next to it. Very soft and slightly damp. A stark contrast.

So why was he so certain that this was Snazz Land? Was there actually such a place? He was dreaming again, surely? Was it a good name for this place?

Exaggeration was part of it wasn't it?

He started walking along the path. Hopefully he would soon come across some people and some buildings.

He hadn't gone very far before they all started arriving. It was if he wasn't there though. Nobody got eye contact with him. He tried greeting them but they just kept their eyes fixed on where they were going. Was he invisible?

Yes, these people all looked madly eccentric but actually this was the norm here. Nobody stood out. He looked down at what he was wearing. Just a plain old grey tunic. Did he stand out for being ordinary? Not that anybody was looking at him as far as he could tell.

Then he saw the woman with the weird dog. She seemed dramatic enough. She wore a high red turban and a vast coat to match. As she walked the coat swirled around her. The dog was a peculiar little thing. It had very short legs and a long body. It looked like a sausage on legs. Its coat was made of strips of material in really vibrant colours, as if his back was a paint pallet. The dog stopped and sniffed Kaleem's leg. So, he was visible, then? Or at least sniffable. The woman tugged on the dog's lead, though, and they were soon out of sight.

Next came a couple of buffoons. No one dared dress like that did they? Not in ordinary life, surely? The young man had a huge collar on his tunic. The girl had long spikes where the heels should be on her shoes. They both had painted faces. They giggled as they walked past him. Had they actually seen him? That would surely make them titter. He looked odd because he looked ordinary.

Then came a young girl all dressed in green. She wore no leggings and her tunic had layers of material under it, making it stand out. Her cloak, made of a crushed, furry material came down to the ground. On her head was a tall pointed hat. Her shoes sparkled. She carried a long stick with which she drew circles in the air. "A spell for me, a spell for you," she muttered as she hurried past Kaleem without apparently seeing him.

So they were all walking in the opposite direction from him. Yet he felt he was going the right way. There were others in front of him, a long way ahead. He looked behind. In the distance as well people were following him. Well, walking in the same direction at least.

And yes. He could see now that he was approaching something that looked like a village. A town even? Buildings definitely.

Were they snazzy? Dazzling coloured outfits here and there. Not ordinary tunics and leggings anywhere. Brightly painted faces. And shoes. So many different shoes. At least nobody seemed to see him. So perhaps he still didn't look extraordinary to them.

He came to what was obviously a café. There was the familiar sound of a coffee machine. Kaleem stared in through the window. The decor was bizarre. Huge over-stuffed, ludicrously-coloured comfisessels – which seemed to be remaining stationery. Thick cotton rags as carpeting and walls lined with what must be cork board. He had heard about this material and seen pictures but never seen it for real. This looked like the actual thing. He wanted to go in and touch it. The customers were drinking from tubes that swirled around the cups several times. It didn't look very comfortable.

Loud music was coming from the building next door. Was that jazz? He'd heard that before. He rather liked it, in fact. Worth investigating?

He ambled in.

At first glance it was just like any bar he'd been in before. Naturally that had included a lot of variety because his work took him all over the place. Here though there was even a fairly normal-looking droid serving. The music was superb. Like nothing he'd heard before.

"Can I serve you, sir?"

"A frega, please."

The droid didn't hesitate and soon Kaleem was sipping the familiar Zandrian drink. How did they know about that here? Where was he, in fact? How come the droid could hear and see him but the others didn't seem to? A couple even approached his table. They did turn away at the last moment but they still didn't seem to see him.

The music was astonishing. Perhaps that was what was so "snazzy". He'd never heard it played live like this before. It was mesmerising. The notes seemed to tumble over each other. It sounded like silk felt next to the skin. It was refreshing like water from a cool waterfall. The players were moving with it. He could feel it through his whole body. But then he started to feel uncomfortable.

Was he imagining it or was the frega a little stronger than usual? Was his vision becoming blurred? He hadn't even drunk half of it. He needed to get out of there.

He staggered out towards the door. The cool air hit him and suddenly he was wide awake and alert.

He noticed that opposite there was an entrance to what looked like a park. It seemed warm enough. Wherever he was had a more stable climate than Zandra, clearly. He set off along a path that led to a wooded area. Those trees looked just like Terrestran ones. But he'd never noticed any "snazziness" on Terrestra before.

He came to a clearing. Now there was a more formal garden. Four benches surrounded a fountain. He sat down. The tinkling of the water was soothing. But where were all the people now? That was odd as well. It wasn't water in the fountain after all but lots of tiny beads of some hard material.

He became almost memorised by the sound. Then, though, there was another sound over the top off it. Heeled shoes walking on a hard surface? Was someone else coming along the path? He tried to see but now a curious mist hung over the park. He looked in one direction and then another. Every time he turned his head the footsteps stopped for a few seconds and then started again. If there was really someone there, they must be watching him, wherever they were. But how could they see him if he couldn't see them? It didn't make sense.

The mist cleared suddenly. Coming towards him along the path opposite was – a man, he thought. He was bizarrely dressed. He wore no tunic but some sort of short jacket with another jacket over the top. His leggings were wide and flapped as if moved by a breeze. He wore a copper-coloured hat that had seven spikes sticking out from it.

He moved straight towards Kaleem. Then he was standing in front of him. He looked directly into Kaleem's eyes.

Kaleem felt odd. He had the disturbing impression that he was looking at himself. But this stranger was nothing like him. His hair was white – what there was of it. It had mainly been shaved off. He had the beginnings of a beard and moustache. His left cheek was decorated with a red patch that blended into a green one above on his forehead. His left eyelid was shaded red and his right one blue. His jacket, which from a distance had looked as if it was made from the same material as his trousers, was actually very silky and covered in a monochrome pattern of roses. His boots had a short heel, which explained the noise Kaleem had heard on the path.

"We've been expecting you. Good to meet you again."

Again? Well, yes, Kaleem did feel as if he knew him, but he couldn't think where from.

The stranger laughed. "You can't remember who I am, can you?"

Kaleem shrugged. “Sorry, no. But I’m sure I should.”

The man laughed again. “Oh, yes, you most certainly should.” He cocked his head on one side. “Would it help if I told you my name was Meelak?”

“Meelak?” Meelak? That was familiar too. Of course!

“Yes, my friend, I think you have it. Your own name backwards.” He chuckled. “Oh, but you don’t understand why.”

“No, I don’t. Are you going to explain?”

“Perhaps.” Meelak smirked. Then he started whistling. He finished his little tune and grinned at Kaleem. “It’s just that I am you and you are me.”

“I don’t understand.”

“I am another aspect of you. The snazzy one.”

He must be dreaming again.

“Oh, no doubt you are, my friend.”

What? He could read his mind as well?

Meelak nodded. “Yes, that too. But it’s not really mind-reading because we are one and the same person.” Suddenly Kaleem was wearing the odd clothes. He could feel the hat on his head and he was staring at himself. How boring and conventional he was. Then he was back in his own body, looking at Meelak. How crazy he was.

Meelak winked at him. “Yes, I can read your mind for sure. And yes this is a dream. Kind of. You’ll probably understand more when you wake up. But I’m here to help.”

“How can you help?”

Meelak smiled again. His eyes teased Kaleem. “You must always remember the fun side. The snazzy side. Stop being so serious all the time.” He waved his hand in the air.

The fountain disappeared and in its place stood a small bush. Silver-coloured fruits with blue pips on them hung from the branches. Meelak plucked two. He put one into his own mouth and handed the second one to Kaleem. “Eat and enjoy.”

Kaleem took the fruit and began to eat it. It was sweet and salty at the same time. The taste kept changing, however. In turn it tasted of all the fruits he’d ever eaten.

"Remember to call on me when you want help. Snazz is good – sometimes. But like with these fruits, too much can be harmful. We'll leave you now."

The mist returned. Kaleem's feet were no longer touching the ground. He felt dizzy and it seemed as if he was falling.

The dizziness got worse and soon he felt sick as well. Would this ever stop? Would he ever wake up? He was moving faster and faster and he thought his ears were going to burst. He tried to call for Meelak but he felt so nauseous he couldn't even form a proper thought.

Then came the jolt. Once more he was in his own bed.

Another dream, then. Yet this time he didn't feel as if he had been asleep. He was exhausted. There had been so much to take in in that snazzy land. Where was it though? If that had been a dream was it based on a place he already knew? He went through every place he could think of. Mm. There had been Terrestran trees and Zandrian frega. Jazz from early Terrestra. Meelak had been at once very familiar and very strange.

"Time," he commanded the dataserve. "Zandrian time: 09.00. Do you wish to commence morning routines?"

"Yes please." He didn't really want to. He would rather go back to sleep but he thought better of it. He needed to get this day started. "Deliver breakfast to the drawer, please. Fruit juice of the day, breads and spreads, coffee."

As he showered he thought of all he had learnt about snazz. Was it about being different, being brighter? Was Meelak real or just part of the dream? Could snazz be snazz if everybody was snazzy? If everybody was snazzy did ordinary become snazzy?

He felt a little more awake and actually quite hungry after he'd showered. He was pleased to see when he went into the kitchen that his draw delivery had arrived.

He opened it and there it all was. The coffee was steaming so was probably good and hot. But what was this? He took out a small blue stick. It felt silky to his touch and stained his fingers. What was it doing there? He knew what he must do, though.

He went back into his bathroom. His tongue stuck out as he concentrated but it didn't take him long to achieve what he was aiming at. He grinned at himself. Yes, the shading on his right eye was perfect.

CHAPTER FORTY

It had been five days now since Kaleem had boarded the supercraft. He was getting used to its routines and rhythms. Naturally he's been on a supercraft before but each one was different. They made improvements all the time. This was just about the very newest produced on Zandra.

He sat by one of the huge veriglass windows and stared into space. There were so many more colours and variances in the light than you saw from static pictures. Yes, he was used to travelling this way but he'd never quite got used to how breath-taking space could be. Zandra was well behind them now and they'd not passed too closely to any other planets. He wondered whether Rozia and Petri would enjoy the approach to Terrestra. That always looked so remarkable as you got nearer to it. It was the most beautiful planet he'd ever seen, like a marble with its blue and white swirls. The blueness came from its oceans.

The sessel on this particular supercraft were especially luxurious. The food and drink were better than ever. He'd managed to get plenty of work done. His Zenoton was in good form and he was beginning to get some insight into Exton's psycho. He'd even managed to communicate with Clem a couple of times without their connection being noticed. He was pleased with his work so far.

Yet there were worries and he shouldn't be complacent. What would happen when they got to Exton's barrier? Were they going to come clean about who Kaleem was and what his mission involved? Did they even actually understand, the people who were sending him there, that his must be a peaceful mission?

A young man about his own age approached him. "May I join you?"

Kaleem nodded. "Please do." It was always interesting and often useful speaking to other people.

"How are you finding the trip? Is everything satisfactory? I'm D-Ken-Maloney, by the way. I know that you are Peace Child Kaleem Malkendy."

D-Ken-Maloney? This was a droid? That was something else about this supercraft. It had the most sophisticated droids. They were impressive if a little disturbing. Kaleem had watched hundreds of old fictional videos of artificial intelligence clashing with and taking over from humans. It hadn't actually happened yet, though these specimens here looked as if they might.

"Is anything wrong?" asked the droid.

"No. I just find it's hard to believe you're a droid."

Ken Maloney chuckled. "Yes, the technology is impressive, isn't it? Don't worry, though, the ethics remain. We are programmed never to injure a human being or allow one to come to harm through our inaction. We will obey humans. We will protect our own existence – as long as that doesn't conflict with the other protocols. Asimov is still revered."

"But you reason? Do you have emotions as well? Are you ever afraid, or jealous, or do you ever want something?"

This was a little crazy. He was using Peace Child tactics on a droid.

"We simulate those actions to gain better communication with humans but we feel nothing. We are just machines. You can switch us off at any moment you choose."

The words "switch off" made Kaleem shudder. He'd fought compulsory euthanasia for older Terrestrans in the past. He'd won and the practice had been abandoned. It still bothered him that it had ever existed.

The droid back sat back in its sessel, crossed its legs and placed its fingers on its lips. "So, is there anything I can help you with?"

"Okay. So, this Pangwit Exton is about the same age as us. Why does he want to take the Zenotons back to a monetary system?"

Ken Maloney chuckled again. "Well, I'm actually just three months old, but yes, indeed, I've been programmed to act like a twenty-six year old humanoid. Don't we young people think we can rule the world? Aren't we fed up with what the older generation has done?"

"Well I certainly don't want to rule the world. Too much responsibility."

"Ah, you are wise beyond your years."

"Maybe. But shouldn't he perhaps think of being even more revolutionary with the Zenoton system? Couldn't he roll it out to other parts of the world? Wouldn't he make his name that way?"

"We're young. We want quick results. We want to be modern."

"And what about the barrier?"

"A sign of our inadequacy. We young people seek control."

Kaleem sighed. "Maybe you're right."

"Glad to have been of service." The droid stood up. Was there perhaps a little droid-like stiffness in his manner after all? He was certainly quite formal. "Do call me up if you need further assistance. My call sign has been programmed into your communicator."

So, a droid was talking a lot of sense.

Kaleem thought about Zenoto. He'd been very well treated when he was there – after an initial period of them testing him to see if he could be trusted. There was always the argument, wasn't there, that people wouldn't be motivated to work if they never had to pay for anything. This had never seemed a problem on Zenoto. People had enjoyed working and did it well. Of course they had a good supply of droids for the more menial tasks. That was sensible. Also he had been very well vetted before he was allowed on the planet. So, did Exton have a point with his barrier?

The Zandrians were worried, too, about their health care system that was open to anyone in the world and was usually free. Health tourists they called them, the people who came just to use the medical facilities. There was so much fear, now, that these facilities would run out for the Zandrians themselves. Terrestrans had handled the problem the other way. They'd tried to keep people healthy. They'd done that by keeping everybody out. Oh yes, he'd been the first person to be ill in centuries. Yet his very illness had put him and Terrestra in contact with the rest of the universe.

Zenoto was beautiful, though. In contrast to Terrestra's blueness, Zenoto was mainly a deep red with splashes of emerald green, lemony yellow and pale blue as you approached it in a supercraft. Zenoton technology was more advanced than Terrestran or Zandrian. Everything was more sophisticated. Household furnishings were more elegant and more comfortable. Odd, how Zenotons showed more respect to droids. They were almost friendly to them. He also remembered the dramatic view from Rogin's apartment. On one side were snow-capped mountains and below them was rich green meadowland. In the distance a green sea's waves caught the light of Zenoto's sun. Intriguing too how Rogin had explained that his work seemed more to him like he imagined a hobby would to a Terrestran. Well. This Peace Child business didn't seem much like a hobby to Kaleem though he took pride in his work and often enjoyed it. At times, though, it was terrifying.

He'd tried the Zenoton form of "shopping" and it worked. Shopping seemed more like a leisure activity on Zenoto. The Zenotons didn't get just what they needed. They looked for things that were beautiful and that gave them joy. The shops were inviting. Yet you were carefully questioned about your choices. Some really deep instinct seemed to be at work. It was almost as if the object wanted you as much as you wanted it. He remembered the exquisite brooch that had the black Tulpen and red roses in a holograph. Flowers of love and lust, Pendalon, the merchant had said. The work that had gone into that brooch was amazing. It was tragic, though, how Zarifi, the designer had died. He couldn't find a balance between work and relaxation and he'd worked towards perfection in creating this brooch. He'd actually imported the seeds for these flowers that didn't grow on Zenoto. He'd had to make several attempts at growing them before he found specimens good enough to photograph. A fault in the system, perhaps, but otherwise everything worked well on Zenoto. It was luxurious and everyone took pride in their work. Now, he couldn't understand why Exton wanted this all to stop, even if he now had some sympathy for the barrier.

Kaleem had not managed to give the brooch to Rozia. It was now safely tucked away in the luggage he had brought on board. He still hoped that one day it might lead somewhere.

He was woken from his day-dreaming by someone clearing their throat. He looked up. It was another young man, maybe a little older than himself. He was definitely not a droid, though, this time;

he wore the unmistakable taupe silky tunic of a supercraft's senior officer.

"We just wanted to check that everything was in order, sir," said the young man.

Sir? For goodness sake. "Well, yes of course it is. Why shouldn't it be?" Everything was absolutely fine on this supercraft. He totally trusted the people driving and managing it. There was a bonus, too this time – a level of luxury he'd never experienced before whilst travelling.

"We just like to be certain. Would you like a tour of the operational areas?"

Now that would be interesting. "Yes, please. But what should I call you?"

"My name is Kendrick Manton, sir."

"Drop the sir. It's just Kaleem."

"And then I am Kendrick."

"Lead on."

The tour was fascinating. Kendrick explained a lot to him about the technology. It was difficult to grasp it all. He understood things that Kendrick explained to him for a few moments and then when he went on to the next thing what he'd heard just before was gone.

Kaleem loved his enthusiasm, though. Kendrick was so excited about everything.

"And these pipes feed in the fuel that we recycle five times before sending it to waste. So, we use only a fifth of the fuel that used to be needed. You can imagine how much cheaper that makes a trip by supercraft."

Kaleem noticed that the engine room smelt almost like syrup and certainly didn't have the burning smell he'd experienced before when he'd been near a supercraft's engine. "It's a different sort of fuel, isn't it?"

"Yes. That's also a factor. It's actually sugar based."

"Goodness."

"Notice something else?"

Kaleem shook his head.

"It's much quieter than the older supercrafts."

Yes, it was. There was just a little buzz instead of the more normal loud chugga-chug.

"All so much cleaner and safer."

"It's all really good. I just hope I'll be as successful in what I have to do as you're being with this craft."

"I'm sure you will. Of course, we'll need your skills when we get nearer to Zenoto. To negotiate our way across the barrier."

Ah yes. That. "I'll do my best."

"Well, you'll have a very good communication system to help you with that. Here's our communication deck."

Kendrick showed him into another area of the operational floor. There was the normal array of screens and dataserves and twenty or so technicians busily operating them.

"The difference this time is that we always holo people up. And the definition is really convincing. Look." Kendrick pointed to where a young Zandrian woman was talking to a Terrestran. "Can you tell which is the real one?"

"No."

"It's actually the Zandrian. She's our crew member – in civvies. We always wear ordinary clothes to communicate."

It really was astounding. He could even smell two different perfumes. He wanted to touch the Terrestran.

"Come on," said Kendrick. "Let me introduce you." He walked over to where the two women were talking. "Excuse me. May I introduce our VIP, Kaleem Malkendy, Peace Child."

Kaleem stretched his hand out to offer the Terrestran handshake. The Terrestran smiled as she accepted it. "Amazing isn't it?" It certainly was. He could feel her hand warm in his own.

Kendrick showed him a few more items and then Kaleem returned to his cabin, quite exhausted after such an intense tour. It was good though, to see someone so committed about his work. He'd appreciated how joyful Kendrick had been about everything.

Something was stirring at the back of Kaleem's mind. A story he'd read. Yes, actually read. Old technology then, but it still had something to say. What was it called? There had been something about Kendrick that he had understood so well. The technology was mainly beyond him but Kaleem could understand his attitude. It reminded him of his father who never tired of working with plants – and they could be quite difficult on Zandra.

He'd recognised something in Kendrick. It was as if – what was that expression? Something about "walking"?

He commanded the dataserve to search for something about "walking" and "understanding others".

The machine responded faster than anything else he'd ever known. Another good feature of this craft. Fantastic technology. Much better than anything he'd seen before. "We'll probably need Wordtext. It's a very old story I'm looking for," he said.

The machine paused for a fraction of a second. The screen lit up. A picture of a young girl staring at the moon appeared. Some said "walk a mile". You couldn't really know someone unless you walked at least a mile in their shoes. A mile was an old Terrestran measurement. It was almost two kilometres. He remembered from somewhere that "moon" could sometimes mean "month" i.e. 30 / 31 Terrestran days. The "in another man's shoes" was understood this time.

Should he try to do that with Exton?

He started reading the story.

Just over two hours later he had finished. Goodness, there was a lot in this. It dealt with grief, death, loss, cultural identity, women as wives and mothers, the hardships of life and what the consequences were when there were misunderstandings. They really did learn to "walk two miles in another man's *moccasins*". The writer had found this saying in a biscuit she ate at the end of meal. Fortune cookies they were called, apparently.

Exton, then. Why was he being the way he was? Kaleem realised the Zenoton president was passionate and daring. He really believed that what he was proposing was right for his planet. Everyone thought they were right, didn't they? Kaleem realised he was going to have to use all of his Peace Child strategies to find out why Exton thought that way.

Peace Child! What was a Peace Child supposed to do?

"Search on 'Peace Child'," he commanded the dataserve.

"Still in Wordtext?"

"Yes." He knew the expression had originated in the 20th or 21st century on Terrestra. He'd often looked at this old material. Here it was again. Warring tribes exchanged a child when the peace was established. The child came from the culture of one tribe and lived with the other. So, then the child understood both cultures and could act as a diplomat for both sides. It prolonged the peace. Yes, that was what he had to do. He even had to establish it in the first place.

Not a lot then.

Someone buzzed at his door. The door screen showed a Zandrian droid standing there. Kaleem activated the lock. The droid entered his cabin.

"Your presence is required at a meeting with Janice Wilton, Patrick Tyler, Jadee Elliott and Rogery Mentis." What would that be about? Why did a politics expert, the outward affairs junior executive, the special correspondent for Zenoto and a futurologist want with him? And why had they sent a droid? "Why didn't they just use their communicators?"

"Because you have been known to ignore them, sir."

How true. He would certainly have ignored anyone who had tried to interrupt his studies that morning. His work was much more important than anything they had to say.

Ah.

"When and where?"

CHAPTER FORTY-ONE

They were all at the board room when he arrived. They were talking vigorously but he caught nothing of what they were saying. They stopped abruptly and all turned to look at him. Then Janice Wilton exchanged a glance with Rogery Mentis and Patrick Tyler did the same with Jadee Elliott.

Jadee Elliott smiled at him. "Don't worry, Kaleem. We forgive you for following Terrestran habits. I'm always too early for meetings on Zenoto. They have the same habit as the Terrestrans – always turning up exactly on time, not a minute too early or too late."

"I'm glad I'm not late. I gather you've started without me?"

"Not really," said Rogery. "I was just sharing some forecasts and worst-case and best-case scenarios. You know. Depending on whether you manage to persuade Exton to step down or to reverse his decision about the Zenoton monetary system. Or whether you're entirely unsuccessful."

"Ah, you've that much faith in me, have you?"

The four Zandrians stared at him blankly.

He ought to have remembered they didn't share the Terrestran sense of humour.

"Well, we do want him to give up this crazy idea one way or another," said Patrick Tyler. "If that means he steps down, so much the better, surely?"

"So what are you saying?" asked Kaleem. "The only solution is that he abandons his plan to revert to a normal monetary system?"

"We can't see it working any other way," said Patrick. His eyes were cold as he looked at Kaleem. Kaleem wondered whether he suspected about him and Ella.

"So you're all pro the Zenoton money-less society?" asked Kaleem.

Rogery nodded. "The predictions for the whole of the Community – and indeed systems that aren't in the community – switched over to this are extremely good. There will be a more stable economy and a more stable society. There are some hurdles to be got over first. But that's achievable. Unfortunately what Exton is proposing runs exactly contrary to this."

"You see, it's just like our health system," said Jadee. "So many Zenotons have told me how much they envy us that."

"Presumably we're the envy of everyone?" said Janice.

"Except that there's now quite a bit of xenophobia on Zandra." Kaleem shuddered inwardly as he remembered recent events. He thought of Rozia again and how she felt she had to return home.

"Are you saying you agree with Exton?" Patrick was frowning.

"No, not at all. I think the Zenoton monetary system – if you can call it a money system – is the best in the universe." He glanced at Rogery. "We would do well to adopt it everywhere." He looked at them all now one by one. "And maybe we should also all adopt the Zandrian health policy."

"So why don't you want to persuade Exton to revert or to get rid of him?" Patrick was frowning and he had folded his arms across his chest.

"That might be easy enough but I suspect someone similar would just take his place. We'd have to peel one after another off."

Janice nodded. "There are countless examples of that in the history of politics. You get rid of a leader because they have evil ideas only to replace them with another who is just as evil but has weaker leadership skills and also causes chaos on top of the other problems."

"Exton is certainly strong," Patrick added.

"It's difficult to understand why the Zenotons elected him," said Jadee.

"There must be something, don't you see? There is something causing them to be discontented." They were now all staring at him.

"So how would you approach Exton?" asked Janice.

"I would have to find out what motivated him."

"You'd befriend him?" Patrick's tone was cold.

"Maybe. We're both young. It might work."

No one said anything and everyone was looking down at their tablets.

"He's young, strong and really believes that he is right and that he is doing the best for his planet." Would they buy that? Kaleem held his breath.

"Well, I suppose it's your job to think the best of everyone." Patrick was frowning hard.

"It's a bit more than that," said Kaleem. "I have to find out why people behave as they do and offer them an alternative that doesn't compromise the other party. Something is really worrying these people."

"But what kind of thing can you mean?"

Kaleem was actually convinced that the problems on Zandra and on Zenoto had the same cause. He was also sure that it was something sinister and evil. Could it be to do with the House of Clementine? He knew so little about that really but he did know that it had constantly interfered in human activity. He shrugged. "I've no idea. Maybe we'll just have to find out." Now was probably not the time to introduce them to the concept of Clementine.

"Do you really think it so bad on Zandra?" asked Jadee.

"Well, nearly half of the people want to leave the Community. There are all these brown tunics marching and parading. There's a lot of tension between the Zandrians who want to carry on as normal and the ones who want to break away from the Community." Kaleem closed his eyes. "And I've got personal experience of a sudden dislike of strangers."

Patrick banged his fist on the table. "Oh come on. If it's Rozia and Petri you're talking about, that's hardly a good example. Look how well they've been treated by my attachment. Any attack on them may really have been an attack on you, perhaps from someone who wanted to sabotage this mission."

"You may be right." It was best not to argue, even though the first problems for Rozia and Petri had started before everything had gone strange on Zandra and Zenoto. "But please, give me the time to work properly with Pangwit Exton."

"I think we should do that," said Janice quietly. The others nodded.

Yes, he would certainly keep his ideas about the House of Clementine to himself for the moment at least. Well, this meeting didn't seem to have achieved a lot. Not to worry too much though. There was still a long journey ahead of them.

An alarm started ringing. A flashing light showed that it was a Level 2 Alert. This meant that they were not in immediate danger but that the crew had important work to do and that the passengers were to keep out of their way.

"All crew to the engine floor. All passengers please return to their cabins. Meals will be served in cabins until further notice. There is no cause for alarm. We will keep you updated."

"That seems to be that, then," said Patrick.

As they made their way back to their cabins Kaleem noticed several of the crew rushing towards the engine floor. They looked serious but not afraid.

His cabin seemed peaceful in contrast. Soft music was playing and the lights were dimmed.

"Please feel free to select an entertainment channel," the dataserve announced. But then a news flash loaded.

"We would like to update you on the current state of affairs. Supercraft Bellatunda II is now on mission to help Supercraft Camarada. She is on her way to Terrestra and has experienced a small fire and has lost power to all but two of her engines. We intend to bring the passengers on board Bellatunda II and we shall delay our further journey to Zenoto whilst we and the Camarada's engineers repair the Camarada. We apologise for any inconvenience."

Kaleem shivered. That was the supercraft that Rozia and Petri were travelling on, wasn't it? He hoped they would be all right. Transferring from one supercraft to another in space was not always that easy. He hoped they hadn't been hurt by the fire. Then, though, he might see her again.

The news flash ended. He wanted to find out as much as possible.

"I wish to speak to Kendrick Manton," he commanded his dataserve.

CHAPTER FORTY-TWO

Kendrick had not been pleased at first. "You'll get in the way. We have to have all areas clear. The priority is to allow the crew to do their work undeterred."

"I'm used to keeping a low profile," Kaleem had argued. "It's part of my job. Anyway, I believe there are two people who are very important to me on that craft."

Kendrick shook his head. "It will still seem as if I'm giving you some extra privilege. Other people might not like it."

Kaleem took a deep breath. "I can be very reassuring if anyone is scared. You could really benefit from me being here."

He hoped Kendrick would consent. It would be torture just sitting waiting in his cabin.

There was a flurry of activity. Droids and human personnel began to move swiftly in every direction.

Kaleem spoke to a couple of the people. He used an old mantra Razjosh had always been keen to repeat. "Easy now. One step at a time. Be mindful." He held his breath and hoped that it would work this time.

The people he'd spoken to directly slowed down. This seemed to have a calming effect on others.

Kendrick frowned. "All right. All right. But please, keep out of the way."

So, here he was now, on the communications deck. The screens had been lifted and he had a full view of the stricken supercraft. Its lights were low. The shuttle containing the engineers from the Bellatunda II had just docked and they seemed to be making their way now safely into the Camarada. At the same time a rigid covered causeway was projecting out from the Bellatunda II towards the Camarada.

"It will hook up in a few minutes and then it will light up. That will mean the Camarada's passengers are making their way across." Kendrick was now being generous with his information. His trick had worked, then?

A few moments later the causeway did light up. Now Kaleem held his breath. It seemed easy enough. The causeway was rigid and airtight. However, there had been a couple of disasters when supercraft had been linked like this and only in fact ten successful transfers. There wasn't a lot of need for this. It was a pity they couldn't use shuttles but generally they wouldn't evacuate travellers quickly enough.

"You should go down to the reception station. You should be able to spot your friends there." Kendrick rubbed his shoulder.

The reception station was already heaving. Kaleem watched the people emerging from the causeway tube. Most of them were Zandrian but there were a few Terrestrans too and just one or two from other planets. Their faces relaxed as they stepped on to the deck of Bellatunda II. Faces remained pale, however. A hospitality team offered them drinks. The beverages must have been drugged. Relaxation turned into euphoria and the ones who had already consumed their drink started chatting excitedly. They were being shown to some of the lounges that had been set aside for them. There was no way that they could all be offered cabins. There was a backlog anyway in getting them across. It was getting more and more crowded. Hopefully, though, the repairs would not take too long and then they could all be got back on board the Camarada. There would be some anxiety then but for now the spiked drink was taking the edge off.

Where were they though? Rozia and Petri?

Every aspect of society was represented in the people that Kaleem watched. Old people, business people, young people, babes in arms, children, rich and poor people. But where were the two he was waiting for?

At last he saw them. Of course, the lights had hurt Petri, despite her medication, but he could see that she was trying not to cry. She was such a brave little girl. All these other people should be ashamed if they considered what she had to put up with.

Rozia was frowning and her shoulders were stooped. It was so unusual for her to be defeated like this. Understandable though – it was such a responsibility looking after Petri. And now this. No wonder she was tired.

She didn't see him for several minutes and he had to push his way through the crowd to get to them. There were so many people here he had to watch very carefully so that he didn't lose sight of them.

At last, though, she looked straight at him and beamed.

"Kaleem!" called Petri.

A few seconds later he was right by them. Petri hung on to his tunic. He couldn't help but open his arms to Rozia.

To his great surprise she fell into his arms and began to cry. It felt so good to hold her. He held her tight until the tears stopped. Then he kissed the top of her head. "It's all right. You're safe now."

Petri wobbled his tunic. "Can we have one of those drinks?"

Rozia pulled away from him. "I suppose it can't hurt?"

Kaleem shook his head. "I think you might want to avoid those. I'm sure they've got something in them. Come back to my cabin and I'll order up something ordinary."

Rozia nodded. "That's a good idea. I can re-medicate madam there."

They made their way to his cabin. Although her skin was obviously still sore, Petri was amazed by the Bellatunda II. "It's so much nice than the Camarada. Why is Kaleem's supercraft better?" She kept touching the panels and feeling the furniture.

"Our supercraft is fine as well. This one's just a bit newer."

"Oh, it's so fine it caught fire and broke. I say Kaleem's is better. People who give up and go back to Terrestra don't get nice things."

Rozia looked at Kaleem, half smiling. Kaleem didn't know whether to laugh or tell Petri off. The girl was growing up. Just because she was little didn't mean she wasn't getting older. They would do well to remember that.

Once they arrived at Kaleem's cabin, Rozia flopped down into a comfisessel. "It's good to get away from all the panic," she said.

Kaleem nodded. "I'll order some tea."

"And a fruit juice for Petri."

While they waited for their drinks to appear, Rozia got on with wanding Petri. The girl seemed self-conscious, so Kaleem made a show of looking at his dataserve. Yes, Petri wasn't a very little girl any more. She really was growing up now.

"It's still all working all right?"

"Yes, everything works perfectly – at least when the supercraft is functioning correctly. The lights on the causeway made it a bit difficult but she's all right now."

They sipped their drinks in silence. Petri must be feeling better. She was watching a film on her communicator. He ought to find out where they were going to be accommodated, he supposed. He was enjoying their company, though. He didn't really want to broach the subject but he really had to.

"I wonder how comfortable it's going to be for you all," he said to Rozia. "You'll have to sleep in one of the lounges, I think."

Rozia nodded. "Yes, I was wondering about that." She looked around Kaleem's cabin. "Would there be room for us here?"

Well, he had a big enough cabin. That was for sure. There were two generous double beds in the bedroom and the sofa in the lounge would make a third.

"Of course. I just didn't think you'd want to."

Rozia shrugged. "It would be more restful here."

"I'm sure it will be fine." It would be nice having the two of them to himself for a few hours.

He contacted housekeeping and asked if it would be all right.

"No problem at all," said the droid operative. "One of my colleagues will make up the extra beds."

A few minutes later, two droids arrived with bedding and soon Kaleem's cabin was transformed.

There really was something different about Rozia. They chatted easily just like they used to. The hours sped by and soon it was time for dinner. They decided to order Terrestran food and were soon enjoying a chicken dish with rice and a fine French wine. There was sparkling mineral water for Petri but Kaleem persuaded Rozia to let her have a little wine with her water.

"Can we have ice-cream for dessert?" asked Petri.

"I don't see why not," said Kaleem.

The ice-creams arrived and Kaleem began to feel almost as if they were a little family. Better not go too far down that route, though.

"That was really yummy," said Petri. "But I'm tired now and I want to go to sleep."

"Then so you shall," said Kaleem. He exchanged a glance with Rozia.

Petri took herself off to the bathroom.

"That is one side effect of all this medication. She needs more sleep." She chuckled. "It's a bit of a relief, actually. She's getting really cheeky."

Petri emerged from the bathroom. Kaleem had lent her a spare tunic to sleep in. It was much too long for her and he and Rozia had to stop themselves from giggling as she tripped over the hem a few times. She climbed, with considerable difficulty, into what had been Kaleem's bed.

Kaleem and Rozia returned to the lounge area.

"I'm sorry I couldn't find anything a better fit," said Kaleem.

"Don't worry," said Rozia. "I think she was putting it on a bit. She enjoyed the attention."

"Stop whispering, you two," Petri called. "I know you're laughing at me. Anyway, I love this bed." She snuggled down.

"We'll be quiet so you can sleep," said Kaleem.

"No need. We really don't have to worry about making a noise, you know. She's a sound sleeper when her meds are working and they are working now." Rozia beamed at Kaleem.

He was sitting on the sofa, already made up as his bed. To his great surprise she came and sat down right next to him. Perhaps though, if they were going to talk, it was better like this, that they sat really close together. Despite Rozia's reassurances, he was still worried that they might disturb Petri.

She laid her head on his shoulder. "You know I was really scared when the fire broke out on the supercraft. I thought our lives might be over. I don't want to waste another moment."

"You're safe now, though, aren't you?"

"Yes, but you don't know when something else might happen."

"I suppose not."

She sat up and turned to face him. "I never stopped loving you; you know that, don't you? I was very fond of Julien but it was never the same as with you."

Something leapt inside Kaleem. He didn't know how to respond to her. He couldn't speak anyway even if he had known what to say.

Then she leant forward and kissed him. More gently than she had just before she and Petri had left. My goodness, how he'd missed that. Ella was all very fine but he realised that everything with her had only been lust. This was the woman he'd always loved and still loved. In fact, he couldn't see himself loving anyone else. He fell into her caresses and felt himself loving her back. Yes, loving her, not making love.

"Are you sure we won't wake her?" His voice was hoarse with emotion.

"Even if we did, I'm sure she'd be delighted to find us in bed together."

"But won't she be puzzled?"

Rozia laughed. "You were right. She is growing up. She knows all about everything. And besides, she keeps saying 'You should get back with Kaleem. You two are so right for each other'."

"Wise child."

Rozia kissed him again.

It was like the very first time all that time ago when he'd taken her to a very special hotel and then worried about whether he'd done the right thing. And yet it was a little bit different. They still knew each other's bodies so well though he winced a little when he felt the scar on her back from the injury that had really been his fault. They made love three times altogether and spent a good deal of the rest of the night talking. Petri didn't stir at all.

Now Kaleem was wide awake and both Rozia and Petri were sleeping peacefully.

He decided to get up. He went to the bathroom and took a

shower. When he got back, Petri was sitting on the sofa bed and grinning at him. She must have realized.

Rozia stirred. She blushed bright red. "I'll go and get ready," she muttered.

He thought of the brooch. He opened the drawer where he kept it and slid it out of its pouch. "What do you think?" Was he really asking a young girl for advice?

Petri just stared at the piece of jewellery.

"Where did you get it?" said Petri.

"From Zenoto."

Petri touched the brooch. "This is really special."

"Yes it is. Very special."

He told Petri all about how it had been made.

The bathroom door opened. Rozia came out. She looked more composed now. She smiled tentatively at him.

Petri dashed towards the door. "Just do it," she said to Kaleem as she pushed it open.

"What was that about?"

Rozia looked so gorgeous. Kaleem pulled her towards himself and kissed her. It would have been so easy just to make love again. Petri would be quite a while in the bathroom, wouldn't she? Then he must make an effort now to find out where they were at. He pushed her away again gently. "I have something for you." He handed her the brooch.

She examined it carefully. "It's beautiful."

"It was made on Zenoto. Perhaps it will remind you that that planet isn't all bad. So maybe you needn't worry too much about me." Was he being presumptuous? "If you care at all." Oh, why had he said that?

"Of course I care. You should know that."

"Then come with me. Stay with me. Both of you."

Rozia shook her head. "I can't. It might be too dangerous. Especially for Petri. I want to get her safely back to Terrestra. If we came with you and something happened you might give us both up for our own sakes, just like you did to me before." Ouch.

"But you'll keep the brooch?"

"Of course I will. I'll wear it every single day and I'll think of you. There will never be anyone else for me."

"For me neither." He kissed her on the lips.

She pulled away from him, looked into his eyes and stroked his hair. "Come and see me when your mission's complete. Let's see where things are then."

Kaleem nodded and pinned the brooch on to her tunic.

The bathroom door burst open. Petri ran in and hugged them both. "I knew it. You two will be together. You'll be attached when Kaleem gets back from Zenoto."

It was clear that the little monkey had been listening at the door.

Kaleem's communicator buzzed. "Send," he muttered.

"It's time for your guests to re-join their supercraft," said an electronic voice.

CHAPTER FORTY-THREE

It was a strange day. Kaleem had woken as usual and gone through his normal morning routine but today he just didn't feel like working even though he knew had a lot to do. There were mild flutterings in his stomach. It was as if he were nervous about something but he had nothing to be nervous about. Something was going to happen today, of that he was sure. This had happened before. He'd had this overwhelming feeling several times that drama was about to unfold and it always had. He didn't know why or how this happened but he was certain that it was more it do with some deeply seated awareness than any form of magic. He didn't really believe in magic.

He became aware as well of a faint throbbing in his forehead. Yes, a headache was developing. It would be easy enough to apply a Zandrian wand. That would cure it in no time. Yet he had the strangest feeling that this pain was actually useful. Was that to to do with the deep inexplicable understanding? The pain was increasing and he was beginning to feel nauseous as well. Something was pressing outward from behind his eyes. His field of vision was narrowing. It was as if he were looking through a tunnel.

He still wanted to resist the wand, though. More than anything he wanted some fresh air. Difficult to get on a supercraft but at least there were effective holoscenes that offered a good approximation. He would take advantage of one of those. He could return for a wand later. Maybe he could also then eat or drink something. Not just yet, though; he would probably throw up. Yes, it was a bit stupid he knew, not applying a wand, but there was something he wanted to find out here. This was madness but it seemed important.

He found a scene that represented a small park. He began a gentle jog. The nausea was becoming milder now but he could still only see a very narrow field in front of him. He could only go very slowly and had to look mostly at the ground. It was boring though, just looking at gravel and grass. He rarely did this. Normally he just felt the ground beneath his feet. Why was he so intent on looking down? Perhaps because he couldn't see that far in front of him? He usually looked at his surroundings, didn't he? He always knew what his feet were doing.

He stopped. He looked up. Goodness. It was spectacular. The trees were covered in jewels. What was that? Why had he never seen it before? One tree near him had some rather low branches. It too was covered in what looked like fine necklaces. He touched one gently and the chain broke. Now, though, even with his disturbed vision he could see exactly what it was. A spider's web was covered in dew and the droplets were catching the light of the early sun. Had he never seen that before? Well, yes he probably had. But had he noticed it? Was he seeing it more easily at the moment because his vision was a bit odd?

Another pain shot through his head. Maybe he should go to one of the medi-centres and get wanded. He took a deep breath and the pain eased a little. He closed his eyes. He wanted darkness but could still see light and orange and purple patches. Was the sun so bright already? Nonsense, it was just a holoscene. They were cheating a bit, making the sun rise high into the sky more quickly. He opened his eyes and could see nothing but the bright colours of the leaves on the trees. Some were still green but others seemed to hum and vibrate in their ethereal yellow, orange, red and pink.

It was too much. It was on overload on his senses. He retched and then the bile rose up through his gullet and he threw up. His vomit tasted vile. Thankfully no one saw him. Vomiting was rare these days. It was so easily prevented and if it happened it looked like a lack of control. He immediately felt a bit better but there was still some pressure behind his eyes and his vision had only improved a little. Time to find that medi-centre. He was relieved to see a Cleansing Department droid approaching. There would soon be no evidence of what had just happened.

It was too early. The nearest medi-centre was not open. He considered going back to his quarters instead. He was still curious, though, about something. He didn't know what and he wanted to stay out. Again it was if he was noticing everything for the first time. Or was it still that funny vision? The whiteness made his head hurt.

He found a pharmacy open.

Fortunately the pharmacist was a Zandrian and not a droid. It would no doubt be easier to explain to her.

"My goodness," she said after Kaleem had told her about his symptoms. "I've not heard of a case of that for a long time. You have a good old-fashioned migraine. It's been eradicated from the Zandrian race but you're not pure Zandrian are you?" She put her hand in front of her mouth. "Oh gosh, I didn't recognise you at first. You're so pale."

Kaleem nodded as she fumbled in a drawer. "It's not a problem."

She took out a wand and charged it. Then she held it to Kaleem's forehead. The pressure went away immediately and he could see properly. But the pure whiteness of the place had disappeared also.

"Better?" she asked.

Kaleem nodded. "But the colours don't seem so vivid either. That's a shame."

She frowned. "Mm. I think I've heard of something like that." She then spoke to her dataserve in words Kaleem did not understand. Neither did he understand its reply. She nodded. "Yes, it seems that that heightened awareness can be a warning of an eminent seizure. The wand will also have prevented that so there's no need to worry. You should book in for a thorough examination, though, so that we can get to the cause of it. Sometimes, you know, space travel can upset our systems and rhythms. And the good news is that once you have experienced this type of awareness you can bring it on at will."

"Thank you. I really feel much better now. Thank you for the information, too."

"My pleasure. Don't forget to get checked out."

Soon Kaleem was moving along the corridors of the supercraft as if nothing had happened. He decided to do an extensive circuit instead of going straight back to his cabin. He still noticed new things, though. It wasn't quite as intense as seeing the jewelled spider webs or the vibrant colours in the leaves as he had in the holoscene. Yet each deck and corridor was different from each other. Some windows sparkled more than others. Each new passage was quirkier than the one before it. Did this represent someone trying to be cleverer that the rest? Was this snazz? And why had he never noticed these things before?

There were now a few more people walking the decks. He started looking carefully at their appearance – the way they were dressed and the way they had applied any make-up. At first there was nothing too spectacular. Everyone was wearing a fairly normal combination of a plain coloured tunic and leggings.

But then he started seeing small differences. A few wore a tunic in a different colour from the leggings and in some cases the colours didn't go together at all well. In other cases the colours enhanced each other. Some people had a little decoration on their clothes or even on their skin. There was nothing as spectacular as Meelak and no sign of the House of Clementine. Kaleem was astonished that every outfit seemed exactly right for its wearer. Was that another possible definition of "snazzy"?

Did he look the same to other people?

He was getting hungry now. He would go back for breakfast and take a look at himself in the mirror.

He stared at himself while he waited for the drawer delivery.

Yes, his outfit was pretty plain. He knew that his overall appearance was strange to most people. He was neither Zandrian nor Terrestran. Was his outfit "snazzy" because its plainness contrasted effectively with his oddness? Or should he in fact go in completely the opposite direction and dress as Meelak did?

As he looked in the mirror he remembered the strange blue stick he'd found after he'd first met Meelak. He felt for it at the back of his drawer. Yes it was still there. He took it and carefully shaded above his right eye. Suddenly Meelak was looking back at him. Just for a fraction of a second. Then he was himself again. Then Meelak. Meelak grinned. "Go Kaleem," he said. "Welcome to my world."

The images in the mirror started to change faster and faster. A pain shot through Kaleem's head. He thought he was going to vomit again. Before he could though everything went black.

"Ah, you're back with us now."

It was white here. Very white. The light was bright. His head was no longer hurting though and he had the feeling that quite a lot of time had passed. His vision slowly cleared and he could see that he was in a medi-centre.

"How long have I been here?"

"48 universal hours. Two whole Zenoton days."

"Where am I exactly?"

"Medi-centre West 3."

"West 3?" That was the biggest medi-centre on the supercraft, wasn't it?

"Yes, you were transferred across from your local one."

"Why?" Kaleem's throat threatened to close and he started to choke. The medic handed his a tumbler of water.

"This has got the correct nutrients in it. Drink it slowly."

Kaleem felt himself calming down as he drank. Had it only got nutrients in it?

"You had a massive seizure."

"Really?"

"Yes a full-blown attack, very unusual these days."

"How did you know though?"

"Your dataserve alerted us and you were taken to the nearest medi-centre. Fortunately they managed to stabilise you very quickly."

"So why have I been brought here then?"

"My colleagues detected that your brain waves were not behaving either the way that those of a normal healthy humanoid's should or the way that those of someone prone to seizures would. So they put you into an induced coma, transported you here and we've now completed some investigations."

Kaleem became aware that his head was a little sore. He rubbed his scalp and was surprised to find that it was partly bald.

"That scar will heal in a few hours and your hair will grow back quickly."

"So it's not another headache starting?"

"No not at all."

"So what did you find out?"

The medic sighed. "Nothing really. By the time we'd got into your brain everything had completely normalized. You are a complete mystery. There is absolutely no indication that you'll ever have another seizure or indeed a migraine."

"So what caused it?"

The medic shrugged. "No idea. You've puzzled us all."

This was annoying. Yet another oddity about him.

The medic folded his arms across his chest. "We've installed a chip to further monitor your brain activity. It will alert us if anything untoward threatens to happen."

Kaleem nodded. "Won't the chip itself have some effect?"

"Unlikely, and you'll never know it was there."

"It can't be used for anything else?"

"Not at all. Are you feeling okay now?"

"Yes." He was actually. His head had stopped being sore and he was beginning to feel full of energy.

"Then you may go."

Kaleem stood up and made his way to the door.

"There's a transporter pod just outside."

Kaleem shook his head. "It's fine. I'll jog."

CHAPTER FORTY-FOUR

Rozia's Ulog

Hi everyone,

Oh, it is so confusing.

We're well on our way back to Terrestra now.

Life was getting even more curious just before we left: Zenoto has got a new president. He's very young. He wants to build a barrier around the planet so that all entrants can be fully checked before they land. Fair enough, I suppose, but this really goes against the One World Community. His other plans are even more disturbing. He wants to introduce normal currency to Zenoto. This seems such a shame to me. Shouldn't the rest of the universe actually be following the Zenoton way? The universe is going mad, for sure.

Saratina has been in contact. She tried to persuade me to stay on Zandra. She has this incredible belief that people will see sense soon and everything will return to how it was.

"It's sure to get better with Kaleem involved," she said. "And won't you and Petri be better off than on Zandra? Where the medical facilities are better?"

"I suppose we could come back."

"It's a long two-way journey."

"And I'm still worried not having any access to my credits. Nazaret and Marijam are being really kind. But I can't go on like this forever."

"You can. Let them be kind. They like being kind."

Saratina is such a lovely person and always so wise. She almost persuaded me in fact.

Then something really horrible happened. We were attacked as we just walked along the street. We weren't really hurt and lots of people came to help us. The people who did it soon ran away. I still can't stop thinking about it though. One of them – I think it was a man – pushed me over and I fell to the ground. I got a nasty graze on my face and I fell so hard that it's a miracle I didn't break something. Worst of all though was what they said to Petri. "Freaky snazzy girl," they called her. Bless her, though, she just stuck her tongue out at them and then helped me up.

So, we decided we would leave despite what Saratina had said. It wasn't easy telling Kaleem. I made out that we were really looking forward to living in one of the refurbished underground apartments. I couldn't help thinking how great it would be if he came along as well. But I couldn't let him know that and anyway I still can't quite trust him. Yet he was so tender – if a bit clumsy – when he volunteered to wand Petri.

I was already sure we'd made the right decision when it really was confirmed for us. The wands stopped working again, even after this promise of secure delivery. Had someone managed to interfere with them on the way? Oh, the medication is fantastic on Zandra but if the supply's not reliable… No, we had to go.

I was glad we'd decided that. I'm concerned that on Zandra and on Zenoto in fact we're beginning to ignore Human Rights. I say Human. What was invented on Terrestra before we started the colonies has now been extended to all intelligent life. But some people are trying to take it away.

So there we were, off on a supercraft. I'm relieved that I didn't have to ask Nazaret to pay. We managed to get a grant from Terrestra. They have a special scheme for returning Terrestrans. Petri is apparently of special scientific interest. Who'd have thought it?

The journey started off well enough. I'd forgotten how luxurious a supercraft could be. We were so comfortable. The medics gave Petri a lot of attention and the atmosphere suited her. I was a little sad as we watched Zandra slip away from us but was already looking forward to seeing Terrestra. It is such a beautiful blue planet. The star scape is magnificent. Much better when you're away from the artificial lights on a planet.

There's always plenty to do on a supercraft. Petri loved everything. The food was superb. It would have been so easy to eat too much of it. It's good that the sport facilities are so good and that you can go for really long walks around the decks.

But then one day an alarm started to sound, though, and it was really frightening. We didn't know what it was at first. We hoped it was just a false alarm. It wasn't. And soon we could smell the smoke. There were other unpleasant smells as well. Hot metal. Plastic burning. You could tell even the crew were worried.

Eventually they made that terrifying announcement. "We are going to transfer all lives to another supercraft. The droid fleet will be left to contain the fire and make repairs. This is a difficult manoeuvre and you must listen very carefully to instructions from the crew if this is to be successful."

It was so frightening. It really was. That was their optimistic message? You could hear the tension in their voices. This was them trying to be cool and collected?

It took them some time to hook the linkup between the two supercraft. The fire and the smoke seemed to be getting worse while we waited. Once the tunnel was ready, it was important that we were properly spread out, that we didn't disturb the air in the tunnel more than was necessary. We couldn't talk and I don't think we wanted to. It seemed to take forever to get through.

It was such a relief to walk at last on the more solid ground of the very supercraft on which Kaleem was travelling to Zenoto. I was so glad to see him. We could have died. We didn't though and here we still are. I have come that close to death before but I wasn't aware of it that time until it was all over.

No wonder Kaleem and I ended up making love. Petri would really like us to be a family. That is what my heart says, too. But my head says no, we shouldn't do this. Will Kaleem's role ever let us be together properly again? I think not. Yet it was good to be with him that way again. Just for a short while.

It would have been all right if he hadn't given me the brooch. In the end they fixed our supercraft quite quickly and we were able to do a more normal side dock which made the return journey easier. If only I could have stayed in that bubble a little longer. Yes, I do love him and it's clear he loves me. That's what the brooch means.

It was something he found on Zenoto. It is really beautiful. Black Tulpen and red roses. The flowers of lust and love. A piece of jewellery crafted with love. I couldn't throw that back at him. But Petri and I were going back to a new life on Terrestra. He was off to Zenoto, on the other side of the universe. When that mission was over he'd be back to Zandra until the next one happened and I couldn't see Petri and me ever leaving Terrestra again. How could this ever work?

Yet it seemed right to keep the brooch and it has become precious to me.

It was so hard leaving him again.

CHAPTER FORTY-FIVE

Ella kept trying to communicate with Kaleem. Yes Ella. Not Executive Tyler. He had turned down over forty calls from her. Sooner or later he was going to have to answer one of them. But not just yet. Not after what he and Rozia had gone through and not after his recent illness.

What had that been, though, with Rozia? It had been tenderness and love. The brooch belonged to her and she was going to look after it. But her determination to stay on Terrestra with Petri was devastating. How could they maintain a relationship over that distance? Could he go back to Terrestra? It might be possible. But not yet. Not while he had this mission. He had to take this slowly. And even if they worked something out there would always be missions. That was the problem with being the Peace Child.

Ella of course could no longer fit into his life. Sure, she was a beautiful woman and intelligent as well. But there was no way he could be with her that way now if he was to try to get back with Rozia. He could no longer consider himself a single man.

His communicator bleeped again. Ella. He sighed and accepted the call.

"Hi." She was pale and had dark rings around her eyes.

"So, how are you?"

Ella shrugged. "Tired. Missing you."

She mustn't. Best to ignore that idea. "They're keeping you busy then?"

She nodded. "With this crisis on they certainly are. Well, you know. You're involved too."

This was true enough. But he wasn't losing sleep over it even if he grumbled to himself about it often enough. If anything he felt a glow inside and he was sure it was making him look brighter. That's what being with Rozia had done to him. "You need to put your foot down. Tell them what's what. Isn't Patrick being supportive?"

Tears started flowing from Ella's eyes. "I think he knows about us."

This could be disastrous. Kaleem could hear a thudding in his ears. "What makes you think that?"

Ella took a deep breath. "He's avoiding me as much as possible. He's making sarcastic comments about you."

"Such as?"

"Why don't you ask the Peace Child? Surely he can do better than a mere junior executive? Why don't you get your precious Kaleem to explain?"

"But he hasn't actually accused you of… sleeping with me?"

"No, but." She bit her lip and looked down.

"But what?"

"We've not had sex for almost a month now. He's not made any effort and if I approach him he turns away."

"Might he be tired as well?"

Ella sighed and shook her head. "He actually asked me yesterday if we ought to detach."

Ah. "And do you want to?"

"That depends."

"On what?"

She looked straight at him. "On you?"

"On me?"

"On whether you would become my attachment."

"I thought we were just having some fun."

"It would be a problem if we were caught out. It would look really bad. But if we became attached it would be all right."

"Do you want to stay with Patrick? Do you still love him? Have you ever loved him?"

"I did. I could again if I can get him out of this moodiness. But I actually love you more." She looked away from him.

Oh dear. Was she going to cry again? Unfamiliar feelings stirred in Kaleem. He wanted to take her in his arms and comfort her. This would be a bit difficult over all the light years. This was so different too from the usual lustful feeling he had towards her. He bit his lip.

She looked at him again. "Don't you feel the same way?"

He couldn't. That brooch he'd given Rozia meant such a lot.

Now though the more familiar feelings came back. She was so beautiful and sexy. He felt an uncomfortable erection growing. He suspected it wouldn't go away on its own. Oh, he was such a bastard.

"I'm sorry, I don't."

Ella nodded. "I was afraid you would say that. Is there someone else?"

He managed to nod.

Ella pursed her lips. "I knew it." She sighed. "I guess I'll just have to work on Patrick."

"He's a good man."

Ella snorted. "You know, I only accepted his proposal to attach because I thought it might finally help me to get over you."

"I'm sorry."

"Are you? Are you really?" Her eyes flashed. "I was just a game to you, wasn't I?"

"No. Not really. I was besotted with you. Still am. But I can't call that love." What a stupid thing to say.

"Oh, you're a bastard. An absolute bastard."

Now she'd said it. Kaleem nodded. "You're right."

"Well it's finished now. Never come near me again. There is no way we can carry on the way we were. You bastard." The screen went black.

She was so right. He was not fit to be called human. But all he could think of was the countless times they'd made love and how glorious it had been. How addicted he'd been to her.

CHAPTER FORTY-SIX

Beast

So, our dear Peace Child, trapped by one of the oldest concerns in the history of the universals. Will you be able to give her up that easily? Will you? A brave try but what exactly are you doing in that shower?

CHAPTER FORTY-SEVEN

There it was. Exton's barrier. If you didn't know better, Zenoto now looked like any other ringed planet and in fact quite beautiful in its own way. Zenoto had always been beautiful. Kaleem remembered the first time he'd seen it. Its deep red was as impressive as Terrestra's blue. The splashes of lemony yellow and emerald green worked the same way as Terrestra's touches of white, green and brown. If anything Zenoto's colours were even more vibrant.

How he would love to show Rozia and Petri this. Petri would clap her hands and dance with delight. Rozia would nod and smile quietly and whisper. "It's so lovely."

Rozia. Petri. They had been back on Terrestra for weeks now. Petri was well. Rozia seemed content if not exactly happy. They'd communicated often but it was becoming awkward. He had little to report. Just day after day trundling through space. He'd not dared to talk too intimately. She seemed shy of it too. She was always wearing the brooch, at least, though. But she might have been removing it as soon as they'd finished talking.

Rozia and Petri were like this beautiful planet. His relationship with them was like this curious ring around it – cold, blue, metallic and yet beautiful and full of promise if you stopped fearing it.

"Soon be there," said Kendrick.

As he spoke the supercraft slowed and Kaleem could tell by the change in engine tone that they were about to dock. His stomach flipped. What would happen now? Would they just be allowed to carry on and land on Zenoto normally or would there now be a lot of questions and examinations?

One of the communication team stepped on to the observation deck. He nodded to Kaleem. "Sir. President Exton is on the barrier ring in person. He wishes you to board and speak to him."

"I'll have to consult with the rest of the team."

"Understood. But he says you are to come alone."

"Tell him we'll get back to him as soon as possible."

Kendrick was already summoning the others to the observation deck. They all arrived within a few moments.

"We should monitor you and pull you out the minute anything goes wrong," said Janice Wilton.

"He has a damn cheek," said Patrick Tyler.

"I think we have to conform." It was so obvious to Kaleem. "We have to meet his requests. He just wants to talk and I'm kind of good with that. It goes with the job title."

"I'm sure no one on Zenoto would harm Kaleem. Not even Exton." Jadee idly fiddled with her correspondent badge as she talked.

"I certainly can't see any problem with letting Kaleem go down to the barrier." Rogery Mentis grinned at him.

Patrick sighed. "Very well, then. But we monitor you very closely." He turned to the communicator. "Tell Exton Kaleem Malkendy will be with him shortly."

As Kaleem was about to leave the observation deck to make his way to the shuttle bay, the dataserve screen opened. Pangwit Exton appeared on the screen. The ever present smirk played on his lips. He bowed slightly. "I look forward to welcoming you, Kaleem Malkendy."

"I'll be with you soon," muttered Kaleem.

Barely twenty-five minutes later Bellatunda II's shuttle was docking with Zenoto's barrier. Close to the barrier looked bleak and unfriendly. The docking hangar had guards surrounding the inside walls. Kaleem had never seen a Zenoton guard so heavily armed. There had never been a need for them before. Only when he had been kept prisoner on a supercraft had he been guarded by Zenotons. These looked completely different from those. Colder – and completely bored.

There was no resistance, however, as he left the shuttle. The Zenotons who met him were at least polite and almost friendly. A little more distant, though, than Zenotons had been towards him before.

He was shown into a room that was lined with dark fakewood panels. The thick carpet gave a spring to his step. There was no one else in the room but it looked as if he was expected. A table covered in plates of rich canapés and jugs of fruit juice was laid for two.

A door at the far end of the room slid open.

Exton walked in. He indicated with a wave of the hand and a nod of the head that Kaleem should sit down.

"I've been looking forward to meeting you," the young president said. "I think we can have a very intelligent conversation."

Exton's deep blue eyes looked right into Kaleem's. All traces of the smirk had vanished.

Kaleem took his time looking at Exton. He would wait until he spoke again. This was a trick he'd used lots of times before. It made the person you were talking to feel uncomfortable.

Exton nodded. Was he trying to say that he knew what Kaleem was up to? "Well, Peace Child, what have you really come for?"

"To try to understand. It's always about that."

"You don't want me to try to change your mind?"

"I never do that. But I do try to make you understand the other point of view."

"How do you do that?

"Open questions."

"Question away, then." He was smirking again now.

Kaleem gave himself a few moments to think – or at least, appear to look as if he was thinking. "Okay. Why is it of benefit for Zenoto to go back to an older way of trading?"

"Well, it puts us in closer contact with other planets."

"How does it do that?"

"We're using the same currency, in a manner of speaking. We can negotiate more easily."

"How does it make it easier?"

"We don't have to negotiate for so long. The terms are clear."

"What is so wrong with the established Zenoton way?"

"It's often abused."

"So if it's so often abused, why has it lasted for so long?"

Exton paused for a few seconds. "People don't like change."

Exton seemed unsure of himself. Time to go in another direction. Kaleem nodded.

"So why did you use this for election campaign?"

"Because the way without money was getting too popular. We Zenotons were getting worried that we would lose something that was unique to us."

"And hence your building of this barrier ring?"

Exton actually blushed. "I think it's my turn to ask you some questions."

Kaleem sat back, held his hands up in the air and then placed them at his sides. "Go ahead."

Exton cleared his throat. "What do you expect to achieve by coming here?"

"I'd like to maintain the peace. And get down to the bottom of what is really going on in the universe."

"What do you mean, what is really going on?"

"There are strange things happening on Zandra and possibly on Terrestra too." A picture of Rozia and Petri flashed in front of him. They'd not said much about what was happening there. Had that been deliberate? Were they keeping something from him?

"Well, we need to bring some law and order now."

"Who are 'we'?"

"Those of us who are willing to take charge of the world."

"Willing? Isn't it more a matter of wanting to?"

Exton shrugged. "Either way. But I intend to do it."

Ah. That was it.

"And will you let me visit Zenoto?"

Exton didn't say anything for several minutes.

Kaleem raised his eyebrows.

Exton's eyes were steely. "All right then. But you come alone."

"Can I go back and debrief my colleagues?"

Exton stood up and adjusted his jacket. Kaleem wondered at the Zenoton's short hair. He'd had it cut in a Zandrian / Terrestran style. He seemed to be cutting himself off from the world but at the same time mimicking it. "Out of the question. I will arrange for some of my people to bring you down to the planet. We will supply you with everything you need. There is no need for you to return to your ship. I will be in contact again soon." He snapped his heels together and then he was gone.

What would happen next?

CHAPTER FORTY-EIGHT

Kaleem gazed thought the window of the apartment he'd been given. This was a real view, not a holoed one. The lemony sky reflected on the deep red rocks. The green water glistened in the strong sunlight. A gentle breeze made the long fronds of grass sway. Zenoto was still amazing, even if it was having problems at the moment.

He was reasonably comfortable here. The apartment was light and airy. The furnishings were smart. The food was very good. He couldn't really complain.

He needed air, today, though, but he'd been forbidden to go outside if not accompanied. At least they allowed droids to accompany him. They had not been intrusive. They'd just let him get on with his exercise. He wondered though, what they might do, if he tried something unorthodox. He just might today. He'd been getting nowhere.

Exton had been polite enough. He'd even shown him certain aspects of Zenoto that he'd changed. He'd answered Kaleem's questions calmly and fully but Kaleem was no nearer understanding why the president was behaving the way he was.

The barrier was now more solid. Many supercraft and other space vehicles were being turned away. Zenoto was becoming a closed planet. Yet President Exton was making trade deals with individual planets all over the place. None could have been fulfilled yet, surely, as the new monetary system was not yet in place. If it all happened, it would bring so many changes throughout the civilised universe. If it didn't, there would be so much anger directed at Zenoto. He shuddered to think what might happen.

The Zenotons were divided, just like the Zandrians. Did it all have the same cause?

He'd been here three months now. He was getting nowhere. He was in effect under house arrest. He'd not heard anything of Rozia and Petri for quite a while. He was only allowed access to local news channels.

He commanded the dataserve to show him the latest. There was another protest march against Exton. It was becoming violent as Exton's supporters started attacking them.

Then he noticed a woman in the crowd. That was surely Jadee Elliott. How had she got here? It made some sense, he supposed. She was a correspondent and it was her job to be here. Yet she wasn't acting like a correspondent this time. She was trying to hide. She was also talking to a Zenoton who had a large red scar across his face. How had that man got that? Zenotons usually didn't get into fights.

She disappeared from the screen.

That was it then. He'd decided. He was going to have to find out what was going on out there.

"Inform droids I'm going for a run," he commanded the dataserve. He would have to find a way of getting rid of them. Perhaps if he headed for where he'd seen those crowds they might get separated anyway.

He was soon out on the road that led towards town. He had gone a few hundred yards when the droids caught up with him.

"Sir, you must wait until we arrive," one tinny voice said.

"Well, you take too much time," Kaleem muttered. "I'm only going for a run."

"We are the latest spec," the other droid answered. "And you know our presence is required at all times when you are out of your apartment."

"So let's see if you can keep up with me." Kaleem started to speed up. He must try and find Jadee. What was she doing? He was pretty certain he knew exactly where she'd been when he saw her on the video clip. Not that he could guarantee she'd still be there.

He made his way down the hill towards the nearby town.

"Sir," said one of the droids. "You are going towards a built-up area. That is not desirable. May I suggest that we turn off unto the park?"

No, you may not.

He accelerated again and was soon at the centre of the town. As he slowed his pace and the droids actually stopped running –

their walking pace was the equivalent of Kaleem's slow jog – he found himself surrounded by crowds. He enjoyed for a few moments the sensation of being amongst ordinary people. It was busy here but relatively calm. People were just going about their normal business.

He noticed one of the droids was sending a message. Was it requesting reinforcements? Should he just comply and go back with them?

No, enough! He had to get something done.

He saw his opportunity. A man was negotiating with a market-stall holder who was displaying some fine textiles. At least money had not yet come back to Zenoto. He ran over to the stall and pushed the Zenoton out of the way. "I think my need is greater than yours." He pulled the roll of cloth off the stall and threw it over the droids.

The droids whirred and spluttered for a few seconds and then shut down.

He knew it wouldn't be too long until someone else found him. The chip in his right arm would help Exton's people to locate him. But he had a little time. He was now pretty near where he'd seen Jade.

Then he saw him – the man with the scarred face. That was a bit of luck. He might be able to take him to Jadee. He started to follow him.

The Zenoton walked briskly but with a bit of a limp. Every so often he looked over his shoulder as if he was expecting someone to be following him. Kaleem had long ago perfected the skill of making himself almost invisible and the man clearly had no idea he was being followed.

They took a zig-zag route through the town. It was clear that this man knew what he was doing. Kaleem recognised where they were. They could have got there in a third of the time. The Zenoton was certainly trying to confuse anyone who was watching.

At last the man made his way into a shop. Kaleem stood outside on the street, looking into the window. It appeared to be an antique shop. Some of the items on display were really old. A large musical instrument made out of real wood dominated the window. There was also a small table. It looked like real wood again. Its top was made of a very yellow metal. Then there was a small figure of a woman in the same metal. He had the feeling it was some sort of bell. His mother had talked about her grandmother owning something similar.

An elderly Zenoton appeared in the doorway. "Can I help you, young man?" Thank goodness he didn't recognise him.

Kaleem pointed to the metal figure. "Is that a bell?"

The expression on the Zenoton's face changed. His eyes narrowed and he frowned. "Come in quickly. The others are already down there."

The man ushered him across the shop and through a door hidden behind a curtain. He slammed the door behind Kaleem. A set of uncarpeted steps led down to another door. The light was dim in there but as soon as he started walking again the staircase lit up. The door at the bottom swung open and Kaleem found himself in room with about twenty other people. There sitting right in front of him were Jadee and the man with the scar.

Jadee sprang up out of her seat. "Kaleem, what are you doing here?"

"I followed him." He pointed to the scar-faced man who was now looking at Jadee, obviously expecting some sort of negative reaction to the fact that he'd been followed.

"Zabren. Kaleem." She waved her hand vaguely as an introduction. "But how did you get in?"

"I asked if that metal figure in the window was a bell."

Jadee chuckled. "Thereby showing that you understand about antiques. Yes, that would be enough for old Gentio to be convinced that you were one of us."

"Well, who are you?"

"We are the resistance. I'm working with the anti-monetary Zenotons to resist the change to monetarism. And you'd better sit down for the next bit of information."

Everybody in the room was staring at Kaleem. He sat on the comfisessel that Jadee had pushed towards him.

"Our founder was Pangwit Exton."

A few of the others nodded.

"What? So what happened?"

"Power went to his head. He was actually making some crazy suggestions and first of all he was replaced as leader and eventually asked to leave. So he then chose to do everything he could to undo what we were doing. Including becoming president and changing the regime."

"What made him so motivated?"

"His parents were high achievers. He always had to prove himself. Of course I'm no psychologist but that's my guess."

"So this resistance existed even before Exton got into power?"

Jadee nodded. "There was always some dissatisfaction amongst the Zenotons. Pangwit is just using that as a tool."

She'd called him by his first name. That was interesting. He would find out more about that later.

"How did you get through the barrier?"

Jadee tapped the side of her nose. "I'm not going to give away all of my secrets. Not even to you. But let me show you around."

The resistance centre was impressive. Kaleem found the people interesting and friendly. They were doing really good work and they were clearly using many of the diplomatic techniques he was familiar with. The most important though was that he now knew that Exton didn't really believe in what he was doing. That was useful. But he couldn't stay here for ever.

"I suppose I should get back. I'm surprised they haven't found me yet."

"They won't get a signal on your chip down here. The minute you step outside they'll probably pounce. But do come back here as often as you can now – if you're allowed out again after your escape." Jadee grinned. "Your expertise would be useful."

Kaleem braced himself to go outside. They would probably swoop on him as soon as his head was out of the doorway. At least now though he had something pretty powerful he could use against Exton. No, against wasn't the right word. He wasn't against the man. He wanted to understand him, persuade him that peace rather than conflict was the better option and that peace could mean everyone could win.

He was soon out in the open air. Nothing happened for several seconds. Then, though, much as he had expected, a police transporter drew up. Two droids and a Zenoton stepped out. Kaleem held his hands above his head. People stopped to stare.

"I'm glad that you're coming without a fuss," said the Zenoton.

"I was just curious about that antique shop," said Kaleem. Would this man know about Exton's former activities? "Your droids obviously can't cope with crowds very well."

The two droids in the transporter clicked and whirred.

"I'm sure police droids are finer-tuned."

The droids settled down.

"Well, you will be interviewed," said the Zenoton officer.

A blast suddenly shook the transporter. Kaleem and the Zenoton officer turned to see what was happening. A ball of fire was rushing towards them along the street. People were running and screaming. The air was hot and smelt of melting plastic.

One of the droids became very active. "The explosion seems to have originated in the antique shop, sir," it reported. "All occupants have been killed. There are no survivors.

CHAPTER FORTY-NINE

This must be the nearest the Zenoton had to the court rooms that were used on Zandra and Terrestra. It was a modern building, high-ceilinged. Light streamed through wide veriglass windows that looked out on the city. There were no holographs. It lacked the formality of a Terrestran court. There were no wigs and robes. Yet it was somewhat more formal than a Zandrian one. Zandrians conducted all of their legal business in normal meeting rooms. Today, here, there were quite a few Zenotons in smart business tunics. Those who made up the equivalent of the judge and jury wore a red band over their grey tunic. The woman with the green band and the man with the purple must be the equivalent of barristers. All in all, though, it felt more like a conference than a court hearing.

Exton was there as well. He sat on an elevated comfisessel, his elbow on his knee and his fist up against his mouth. He was frowning and staring at Kaleem.

The murmur in the room got louder and louder and soon everyone was shouting in order to make themselves heard.

The judge lifted up his hand. A bell sounded. This must be it, then. Kaleem's stomach lurched. Certainly not a conference, then.

"So, let's begin," said the red-banded man who sat a little apart from the others. "Kaleem Malkendy, Peace Child, you are accused of planting a bomb at the premises of Gentio Robizen, antiques dealer. You are also accused of deliberately absconding from your droid guards. How do you answer to these charges? Do you verify them or decline them?"

"I decline both."

"Very well. I will ask my colleague for the enforcement of the charge to question you."

The woman wearing the green band stood up. "So Kaleem Malkendy, let us start with the relatively minor charge that you deliberately absconded from your droid guards. What do you say to that?"

"Yes, all right, I did. They were getting annoying and very agitated.

I thought they might become a nuisance to the general public. So I switched them off the only way I could. I threw some cloth over them to confuse them. I wasn't trying to escape from the regime here. I was just trying to stop a pair of out of control droids harming the general public. If you hadn't picked me up I would have made my own way back to my apartment."

"Why were you down in the town anyway?"

"I'm forbidden from going into town, am I?"

The young man wearing the purple band stood up. "Can we confirm if indeed Malkendy is forbidden from entering our built-up areas?"

Exton cleared his throat. "Not specifically, though he is not allowed to fraternise with Zenotons. What was he doing talking to Robizen?"

"Well? What do you say, Malkendy? Why were you talking to the antique dealer?" The woman was now frowning at him.

"I was intrigued with a very old bell I saw in the window."

"You were a very long time in that shop. We lost your signal. Why was that?"

Kaleem shrugged. "I was down in the cellar. I think the layer between ground floor and the one below must be very thick."

"And Robizen must have had a lot of intriguing bells."

Everyone in the room laughed except the judge and Exton. A smile flickered across even their lips, though.

"Or were you wiring up a bomb?"

"Why would I want to do that? I'm here to negotiate the peace. Not to cause more friction. Besides, why would I want to harm an antiques dealer and the people who work with him?"

"Why indeed? Or why would anybody else for that matter? But someone did. Was it you?"

Kaleem shook his head. "No." If only they knew. They might be quite happy, in fact, that the resistance had been destroyed, depending on whether they were really behind Exton or not. Could they tell he was lying? He realised that he was digging his fingernails into his palms. He glanced quickly at the President, who was clutching the arms of his comfisessel.

"Right. Thank you Mz Stanton. What do you propose Mr Arquis?"

Arquis stood up. "I propose that Mr Malkendy had nothing to do with the bombing. Or at least, we do not have enough evidence to prove anything either way. He has however, been somewhat truculent in his misuse of his free time and that the charge that he deliberately absconded from his guards should be upheld."

Fair enough.

The judge stood up again. "Then we shall put it to the vote. Selected Zenotons, will you please make your choices."

Was that it?

There was absolute silence as the other red-banded Zenotons tapped away on their mini-dataserves. A screen showed their verdicts. They appeared to be unanimous. Kaleem was guilty of having deliberately got away from his droid watchers but not guilty of planting a bomb.

Everyone started clapping. Why? Were the congratulating the jury for being unanimous? Were they clapping Kaleem for admitting to one offence and being found not guilty of the other? Or were they just pleased that it had all been over in less than ten minutes?

The judge stood up again. "Well, that was short and simple. Now Mr Malkendy, we just have to find a punishment for you." He turned towards Exton. "President Exton. What do you suggest?"

Exton stood up. "More security. Less freedom. Malkendy's excursions will be limited to twice a week and he will be accompanied by one human and two droid police officers."

The judge nodded. "Somewhat restrictive for someone with the diplomatic role that Mr Malkendy enjoys. However not too punitive. May I ask you, Mr Malkendy, what we might offer you to make your stay with us less boring, so that you are no longer tempted to escape from your guards?"

"I'd like to research the history of Zenoto a little more."

The judge looked at Exton. "Well?"

"We can give him access to the people's files. That can't harm."

That would be something. Not a lot because they would be heavily censored for sure. But at least they might give him some insight into what motivated the Zenotons. He'd always taken their good nature for granted. There must also be something that made some of them somewhat dissatisfied. Maybe he would be able to find out what.

Soon Kaleem was speeding in an armed police transporter back towards his apartment. As Exton had commanded he was accompanied by two droids and one human officer. The droids said nothing and he was aware that they were also armed. Best probably not even to move. The human officer didn't appear to have a weapon but he wouldn't allow Kaleem to get eye contact with him, let alone make small talk.

Kaleem looked out of the window. The transporter was taking a strange route to his apartment. They were probably trying to keep him out of the public's sight.

Who could have planted that bomb there and why? How would whoever had done it have known about the resistance group operating in the cellar of the antique shop?

The transporter's communicator bleeped. Exton's face appeared on the screen.

"How can I help, sir?" said the human officer.

"Put Malkendy on. His personal communicator is still blocked. And this call is private by the way."

The officer moved so that Kaleem could get closer to the dataserve. He activated the internal barriers of the transporter so that Kaleem was in effect alone with Exton.

"Malkendy, there are things that you and I need to discuss. I'm inviting you to a private meet. It won't be for a few days yet but I'll send for you. There is something you need to know."

CHAPTER FIFTY

Kaleem hardly noticed his extra confinement. In fact, he wasn't going out nearly as often as he was allowed. Officer Marten had even contacted him a couple of times to see whether all was well. He was beginning to quite like this officer. Whenever he contacted Kaleem or Kaleem contacted him they chatted freely. It reminded him of the relationship he'd had with Charlek when he'd been imprisoned on Zandra.

Now Kaleem was becoming totally absorbed in the history of Zenoto. There was so much more to the planet than he had ever imagined. It was widely believed for instance that the Zenotons weren't native to the planet at all and that they had been transplanted from elsewhere. Not so different then from the theory that life on Terrestra had begun as alien dust. Fascinating anyway that the Zenotons had not originally come from Terrestra as had most of the inhabitants of other planets. This indicated at least two other species of intelligent life other than Terrestrans. Above all Kaleem was intrigued by how similar to Terrestran humans they were.

The history of their planets followed similar patterns, too. There had been wars, class systems and even some genocide but the turning point came when in order to create a classless society they had abandoned money. Everyone's basic needs were catered for. Extras were "bought" by negotiation. Everyone only did the work they loved and felt passionate about. Droids were sophisticated because all the work that the Zenotons didn't want to do was assigned to them.

He was just beginning to find out, though, that there was some discontent. Some Zenotons felt that their merit was not justly rewarded. That seemed to be a very human characteristic and possibly a reason why it might be difficult to bring in the Zenoton system elsewhere.

He was reading an old Wordtext article in Zenoton. It took a lot of concentration. It wasn't really Wordtext because the symbols that represented sounds were different from the Terrestran and Zandrian ones. But it was similar and it was totally fascinating as well. It detailed how droids had been prevented from becoming too sentient. When he did respond to his communicator he realised that it had been calling him for a good five minutes.

Ah. The President. He looked a little pale and tired. No doubt his job must carry a lot of responsibility. Exton cleared his throat. "I gather our history files must be fascinating. So glad you're interested. Well I have some more fabulous news for you. I want to give it to you in person. I'll send a transporter to fetch you."

Exton didn't wait for a reply. The screen darkened before even Kaleem had a chance to say anything.

He'd better get going, then. He closed down the applications on his computer. Was he dressed correctly for talking to the President? He went into his bedroom and glanced into the mirror. Was his grey old work tunic good enough? Well it was practical and inoffensive.

Even if he'd wanted to change, there was no opportunity. His apartment communicator buzzed.

"Transporter for Malkendy," said an electronic voice. "Please do not keep the President waiting."

He quickly climbed into the transporter. As soon as he was seated, the blinds slid down to cover the windows. So that's how it was going to be. Clearly Exton didn't want Kaleem to know where he was going. Why was it all so secretive?

"How long will the transit take?" he asked the machine's dataserve.

"Approximately seventy-five universal minutes. Would sir like some entertainment?"

"No thank you. Or maybe just some light music." He welcomed the thinking time. But seventy-five universal minutes? Almost two hours Terrestran time. This was really getting intriguing.

He sat back and relaxed. He started to assemble the knowledge he had of Exton. The man was a complete enigma.

Kaleem was surprised that the time passed relatively quickly. The transporter stopped and the door opened. "The door to the meeting place will open automatically," said the dataserve.

Kaleem stepped out of the transporter. He blinked. The light was extremely bright. One small solitary building stood surrounded by a huge formal garden and then wide open countryside.

The transporter departed. There was nothing for it but to go into the building. As he made his way towards it the door slid open.

"Come on up," Exton's voice said.

There was clearly no lift. Kaleem started making his way up a wide, stone staircase. It opened out at the top into a light and airy room. Exton was sitting behind an old-fashioned desk. He looked less sure of himself than he normally did.

"Sit," said Exton.

A comfisessel immediately floated towards Kaleem.

"I'll be frank, Malkendy. I want to know exactly why you planted that bomb." His eyes had grown icy again.

"I didn't. The trial proved that."

Exton shook his head. "The trial merely proved that there was not enough evidence."

"I still didn't do it. Why do you think I did? I have no interest in destroying anyone or anything on Zenoto. And if I were trying to fight you, maybe this sort of resistance group would be the last type of thing I would want to destroy."

"Are you telling me you were colluding with them?"

"No."

Exton nodded briefly. "Ever the neutral Peace Child. At some point you've got to take sides."

"No I don't."

"Why won't you confess to what you've done?"

Why was the man persisting? Kaleem shrugged.

Exton laughed. "You don't get it, do you?"

"Apparently not."

"I did it."

Was he saying that he had deliberately murdered people? Why would he want anyone to destroy something he really believed in?

"Why?"

"They're radicals."

"Okay. But taking life?"

"They wouldn't mind. They'd be dying for their cause."

Kaleem stared at Exton for several seconds. "But it used to be your cause as well."

Exton nodded. "So they told you."

"What made you change your mind?"

"I'm concerned about what is best for the Zenoton people."

"Why are your proposals better?"

"They will allow us to trade more freely. We'll be more in line with the systems of other planets. We'll be more acceptable to the rest of the universe."

"Even if these systems aren't as good as what you've been developing up until now? Even if it is really the case that the universe would be better off with the old Zenoton system than what they've got at the moment?"

"That was just abstract ideology. It couldn't really work on a large scale. Okay, so most Zenotons worked with it well, but there were always some who rebelled. There wouldn't have been a resistance if there hadn't been something to resist."

He was beginning to make some sort of sense now.

He stared into the middle distance. "I really used to believe in what they were doing. They were once my friends."

"Then it's all the more puzzling that you might want to kill them."

"I didn't. That explosive device was only meant to irritate and get them out in the open. Something went wrong."

"You mean someone may have interfered with it."

Exton nodded.

"Any idea who?"

Exton nodded again. Then he looked straight into Kaleem's eyes. "I need your help. I believe it has to do with the House of Clementine."

Kaleem shivered.

CHAPTER FIFTY-ONE

"So why do you stay here most of the time?" asked Kaleem. "Isn't it a long way for you to commute to the government buildings?"

Exton nodded. "It's more peaceful here. I can take the time to think."

Kaleem looked at the walls of the building. This was Exton's home. So he didn't live in the official president's home.

"I like it here," Exton continued. "I'm not so surrounded by people. I can please myself what I do."

"But why did you have to bring me out so far?"

Exton grinned. "I had the feeling you would like the peace and quiet as well."

Fair enough.

"So, how did you get involved with the House of Clementine?"

"It's more that it got involved with me. My father belonged to the House of Clementine but I didn't know anything about it when I was younger."

"Oh?"

"Yes, even when I was a child. Just nine years old. My father took me out hunting one day."

"Hunting?" Kaleem hadn't realised there were blood sports on Zenoto. That seemed contrary to the Zenotons' normal gentle nature but they'd been full of surprises recently.

"Oh, don't worry. We don't hunt real animals. Just holos. When I was nine I didn't see the point and I didn't try very hard. That made my father really angry. He said I would never be a man. That I was a total let-down. He left me out in the forest."

This was beginning to sound like an ancient fairy-tale.

"Well, you obviously didn't die."

"I don't think that was ever his intention. Later, I found out that he'd had droids watching, ready to intervene if anything untoward happened. But I was taken care of so he needn't have worried."

"So, what happened?"

“I found a cottage in the woods and knocked at the door.” Exton frowned and stared into the middle distance.

Goodness, this was really becoming like one of the old Wordtext stories he’d read. You couldn’t make this up, though, could you?

“Did they let you in?”

Exton nodded. “Oh yes. And I know what you’re thinking. You know about this stuff, don’t you? Yes, it was the brave woodcutter and his kind wife. And yes, they offered me food and a bed for the night. Just like in all of your good fairy tales.”

How did he know that Kaleem knew about that?

Exton laughed. “Except it wasn’t. They gave me some sort of drug. And they started reprogramming my mind. When I eventually got home my father laughed. “Well, well, well,” he said, “so the Clems have found you. Good. It saves me a lot of effort.”

“What about your mother? Wasn’t she kinder to you?”

Exton shook his head. “She was never around much. She was a very successful actor.” He sighed. “It’s hard having two parents who are successful.”

Kaleem thought of his own parents. Both were successful. His mother had survived and brought him up well despite some very difficult circumstances. His father enjoyed tremendous success with plant production on Zandra. The difference, though, was that his parents were totally unselfconscious about it. Goodness what would it be like if he had children? Was he successful? He had an important job, for sure. And was he going to succeed this time? Well, at least he was beginning to understand Exton a bit.

“Do you ever hunt now?”

“Occasionally. I’ve learnt to, just to show my father that I can. Would you like to try it?”

“Why not?”

“Is this cold for real or is it just part of the holoscene?” Kaleem’s fingers and feet were numb.

“You’re right. It’s all part of the holo.”

Kaleem was beginning to get the hang of finding the holoed animal in the site of the revolver and he’s even managed to hit a couple. He pulled the trigger again and the beast he was aiming at fell to the ground.

"Spot on. Hmm. Not bad for a beginner."

"I think I understand, though, why you found it a bit pointless."

"Yes. Though it wasn't just the pointlessness. It was also that my father thought it so important."

Kaleem bit his lip. When he'd been nine he'd have given anything to know who his father was and join in some activity with him. He got on well with Nazaret, now, on the whole, but he'd still never completely forgiven him for abandoning his mother even though he realised that Nazaret had not been able to help it. He's been whisked away before he'd found out that Marijam was pregnant and anyway that had been something that was not supposed to happen.

"Zenotons on Zenoto," Exton suddenly shouted.

Kaleem's heart rate quickened. Had something happened? Was Exton hurt? Had something gone wrong with the holoscene?

Exton had just gone into a copse. Kaleem hurried after him. He found the President staring toward the other edge of the group of trees. "It's there again, look." He pointed towards a small building. "Exactly like before."

"Should we go and look or keep well away?"

Exton shrugged. "What do you think?"

It could be dangerous. But they ought to go and look. Presumably Exton had taken some precautions. There would be a get-out plan. "Come on. Let's go."

A few moments later, Kaleem pushed open the door of the small house. There was a fire burning in the grate. It smelt of wood smoke. Something was cooking in a pot. The smell of beef stewing in red wine mixed with the woody smell. Fairy tales again.

A blinding light flashed across the room and he could no longer see anything. The light then started blinking on and off. A siren started wailing. "You are on House of Clementine property. Step outside. You are on House of Clementine property. Step outside." The message was repeated over and over.

Kaleem couldn't see Exton anymore. He walked backwards,

fumbling for the door pad. He found it eventually and then was once more outside. The building looked like a harmless fairy tale cottage again. He still couldn't see Exton, though.

Then the forest and the house disappeared. It became warmer instantly and Kaleem had to remove his hunting coat. Now he could see Exton again. They were in some sort of huge metal hangar. No doubt this was a Holocene studio, though he'd never seen one quite so big before. Yes, he could see the laser projectors around the room. A transporter had entered the building. Another Zenoton was talking to Exton. He looked up and saw Kaleem. He then started walking over to him.

"You are on House of Clementine property. You are trespassing."

"What do you mean, House of Clementine? What is House of Clementine?"

The Zenoton frowned. "Stop playing games. We know you have been investigating us. Desist now."

Kaleem shook his head. "How? How do you know?"

The Zenoton threw back and laughed. "We have our spies everywhere. Everywhere. Take care, Kaleem Malkendy Peace Child."

The Zenoton raised his arm as if to strike Kaleem. Kaleem raised his own arm in defence.

Exton shook his head. "Give in to them. Don't fight."

Give in? No, he wouldn't. He lent forward towards the Zenoton, reached round his neck and pushed on a nerve. The Zenoton collapsed to the floor. Good. So that nerve was in exactly the same spot on Zenotons as it was on humans.

What should he do next?

Before he could think, a droid stepped out of the transporter. "Red alert, red alert," an electronic voice from the transporter's dataserve said over and over. Before either Kaleem or Exton had time to react, the droid had pulled Exton's arms behind his back and was pushing him into the transporter.

Kaleem watched helplessly as the transporter sped away.

CHAPTER FIFTY-TWO

It was now five days since Exton had disappeared. Kaleem had somehow found his way back to the President's private residence. He was managing to live without it looking as if anyone was there. He'd found out how to make the windows dark all of the time. He wasn't using power from the main grid. There was a private generator that he could run long enough during the night to give him enough power for all day. He avoided using any of the communication systems. No one would guess he was there. That meant there was very little he could do, though. He didn't even dare use the dataserve. There may be some sort of trace on that, either by the House of Clementine or by the presidential team office or both. He knew that the next move would become apparent when he needed it to.

He spent plenty of time exploring the residence. It too had many aspects so like the old fairy tale castle. There were vast high-ceilinged rooms decorated with tapestries of hunting scenes. He'd even found a secret passage connecting a library to a bedroom. Each evening as it grew dark a holoed fire lit itself in the main room – yes, that happened even though he was using the minimum of power. And joy of joys, the library contained some old Wordtext books. That at least stopped him being bored. In fact, some of the stories were helping him to figure out what was going on. Wasn't that after all the purpose of stories?

It was a bright and sunny day. He had set the windows so that he could see out but nobody could see in. He had just finished reading a rather gruesome story about a girl who had been eaten by a wolf. What was that all about?

He didn't have too much time to think. The light at the window suddenly changed. A shadow crossed in front of it. He glanced out. There was someone in the garden. He or she was wearing a blue cloak rather like the ones the House of Clementine knights wore. Who was it? What were they doing there? He couldn't tell whether it was a woman or a man. Whoever it was actually seemed to be rooting around under some of the plants. Were they looking for something? Were they actually digging?

She or he suddenly stood up. There seemed to be something under their cloak.

Should he try and find out what was going on? Well, he did know how to follow people without being noticed and nobody suspected he was living there – probably.

He pulled on some outdoor clothes quickly. He made his way down into the garden. The mystery person was now leaving. Kaleem quickened his pace but kept in the shadow of the garden walls. He managed to keep the stranger in sight. He was certain he couldn't be seen.

There was something about the person's gait that made him think he was following a female. They were light on their feet and there was a slight sway in the hips. Yes, definitely female.

She started walking more quickly and was out of the grounds in no time. She stood at the edge of the road looking to her right as if waiting for someone.

After a few minutes a transporter drew up. There was no one else inside. She stepped into it and removed her hood – yes, it was definitely a woman – and was soon on her way. There was nothing more he could do.

He wandered back into the garden. He looked at where she'd been digging. The soil hardly looked disturbed. Maybe she'd put it all back. He dug down a little with his bare hands. Nothing. No sign, either, of much disturbance. What was that all about then? What exactly had she found?

Well this was going to have to remain a mystery for a time now. He looked around. No sign of anyone anywhere. He had blocked the signal from his communicator. Nobody could locate him. He was outside now, and rather enjoying it. Maybe he could venture a little further. It seemed quite safe.

He really ought, anyway, to find out what was going on. Could he get a signal on his communicator but keep it blocked? It might be worth a try. Even if he had to unblock it he might be able to move on quickly and then block it again.

He wandered a little way along the road. There were no transporters moving around here. It was pretty isolated. A pathway led off from the road and seemed to make its way into some woodland. He could see a small hill beyond the trees. Maybe that would be an ideal place, as long as he made sure he wasn't visible.

The path through the wood only took a few minutes and then he was out in the open. He would have to be careful now. He flattened himself against the hill-side and moved very slowly. He switched on his communicator but didn't unblock it. Good. It had some sort of signal.

He had a message from Rozia. His heart skipped a beat but he decided not to access it. That relationship had to stay on hold for a while.

"News," he commanded.

He was shocked as he found himself watching thousands of Zenotons rioting. It was difficult to work out which ones were on Exton's side and which ones were for the old regime. It was certainly very violent in any case. And so much against the normal nature of the Zenotons.

He skipped through various news channels and at last found some mention of Exton. No one seemed to realise he was missing. However, his own cover may be about to be blown. They were reporting Exton as holed up in his summer retreat and not answering messages. People were aware then that someone was living in the castle. Time for him to move on.

He pondered whether he should go back and kit himself out with a few supplies. Probably best not to. How he was going to get anywhere, though, he wasn't sure.

He started walking and was soon under the cover of the trees. He stayed parallel to the road but kept himself hidden by the woodland. He had a vague idea which way civilisation was. He decided he would stay in hiding even when he got back. He wouldn't go to his old apartment but would hide up somewhere until it seemed right to communicate with the authorities. He wanted to find out a lot more first.

He made good progress for a couple of hours but then his feet became sore and he was rather thirsty. This was going to take forever. Should he give himself up? He was going to have to at some point. It wasn't anyway as if he'd done anything wrong. Would it be useful to the Zenotons to know that their president was missing?

He could hear a stream not too far away. Fortunately he had a tester in his tunic pocket so there was no danger of him accidentally drinking acid. He found the stream and tested the fluid. Good. It was pure water. He cupped his hands and took several mouthfuls. He removed his socks and bathed his feet. That was better.

Yes, he was all right for now. But what should he do next? It was going to take him several days to get anywhere at this pace. The Zenotons needed to know what was going on. But he also relished the time this was giving him to find out a little more about what had been happening in the background.

He didn't have time to think for too long. The hum of a transporter was getting louder. Just at that particular moment he was unfortunately a little exposed. He stood as still as he could. It was clear, though, that the vehicle was slowing.

It stopped. Its windows were opaque and he couldn't see in. The door slid open. "You'd better come with me, don't you think?"

He recognised the voice but still couldn't see the woman's face. She had a mask over the lower half and the top was covered with a hijab that came down over her forehead.

CHAPTER FIFTY-THREE

As soon as Kaleem had sat down and fastened himself in, the woman removed her headdress. "Good to see you again," she said.

Jadee Elliott. But how could she be here?

"How did you manage that? The bomb…?"

She nodded. "Several of us got out. We quickly realised what was happening and there are several escape routes from the cellar. In fact we've only had a few injuries, none of them too serious. Not that we want Exton to know that."

"You know it was him that planted the bomb and they accused me?"

"I'd heard you'd been tried and found – well not exactly innocent. They didn't have enough evidence, did they? And he planted the bomb? Well, I guess I can sort of understand that."

It occurred to Kaleem that maybe Exton had just the tiniest bit of a conscience. He'd allowed the lack of evidence to stand. And although he'd made his house arrest stricter, he hadn't actually wished Kaleem any harm.

"You know the President's been taken?"

"No, but I'd guessed as much. Who do you think got him?"

"You have no idea?"

"Only one." She looked at him directly now, one eyebrow raised.

"And that is?"

She sighed. "You'd better take a look at this." She handed him a small package.

It was lightly covered in soil. So, she had been the mysterious woman digging in the garden. He didn't understand, though. That person had had the blue knight cloak on. And she had been hooded. He shook his head. "I don't understand… the blue cloak."

"Under your seat."

Kaleem felt underneath where he was sitting. Yes, there was something. He pulled it out. It was a blue cloak, made of a velvety material. Definitely the one he'd seen earlier. Definitely a Clementiner knight's cloak.

Jadee nodded. “The uniform of the Knights of the House of Clementine. In case I got caught in the act of stealing it. I could then argue I was working for the House.”

“I don’t understand.”

She nodded towards the packet. “Go on. Open it.”

Kaleem carefully unwrapped what turned out to be a small wooden box. Yes, it was real wood and had some suspicious-looking holes in it.

“I’m sorry about the woodworm,” said Jadee. “A problem with the old materials.”

The box came open easily. There were lots of papers inside, all covered in Wordtext. It wasn’t a language Kaleem recognised, however and even some of the characters were foreign to him.

“By the look on your face I’m guessing you can’t read it?”

“No. Sorry. I could probably decode it after a while, though. I need a lot of time and the help of a sophisticated dataserve.”

“That’s a shame.”

“But how did you know where to find it? How come it was on Exton’s land?” What exactly is it anyway?”

Jadee sighed. “It’s a long story. But the short version goes a bit like this. Pangwit Exton is one of the Super Knights of the Clementine Order. And I’m a second-rank knight. And what you’re holding there is the constitution of the House of Clementine.”

What? And what was a Super Knight? He’d not heard of that rank before. “How can you be involved with something like that?”

“It isn’t quite what it seems. I’ll explain in full later. But look.”

He looked to where she was pointing. They had arrived at the outskirts of a town. They now had a decision to make.

He lent forward towards her. “Should we go straight to the authorities?”

She nodded. “It’s best to, don’t you think?” She turned to the control panel. “Take us straight to the Zenoton council,” she commanded.

The transporter suddenly zoomed up a small incline.

“Is it far?” asked Kaleem.

Jadee shook her head. “No. And before you ask, no I don’t have enough time to tell you all about the House of Clementine and why Exton and I are involved in it. It's really complicated. It will all become clear eventually. Trust me."

The transporter drew to a halt in front of a tall white building.

"Are you ready for this" asked Jadee. "It's not going to be easy."

The Zenoton Council building was light and airy inside. The floors were covered in a polished grey material that resembled the old world marble. Kaleem and Jadee were shown into a room with high ceilings. It was obviously meant to hold a full council session but today there was just him and Jadee and three council officials.

The one who seemed to be of the highest rank and wore a red tunic braided with gold, spoke first.

"So you two say you have some information about the President? What might that be?"

"He's been abducted, sir." Kaleem held his breath as he awaited the older Zenoton's reply.

The senior Zenoton and the other two in grey talked excitedly but quietly together. They spoke too softly for Kaleem to be able to make out what they were saying.

The smallest of the junior Zenoton then spoke to him. "How do you know?"

"I was actually with him when it happened."

"Why didn't you report it straight away?" The Zenoton in the red tunic was now frowning at him.

"I couldn't. I was totally isolated. I had no means of communication or transport until Mz Elliott came along. We came as quickly as we could."

"Do you have any idea who might be responsible for this?"

It was looking more and more likely to Kaleem that this was all tied up with the House of Clementine. It was puzzling, though, that Exton was one of their Super Knights – whatever that actually meant – and yet was being harmed by them.

Jadee caught his eye. She shook her head slightly.

"No. No idea."

"And you didn't get a good look at them?"

"I'm afraid not."

Now Jadee nodded and smiled faintly.

Urgent running footsteps were heard outside. Everyone turned to the door. Two tall Zenoton guards rushed into the council chamber.

"Sir," said one of them addressing the Zenoton in the red tunic, "we have just heard from a group of people holding the President. They have asked for a ransom of five million bars of Terrestran gold."

The Zenoton in the red tunic went pale. "Who are they?"

"They claim to be the House of Clementine."

The senior Zenoton looked at the other Zenotons and at Kaleem and Jadee. "What on Zenoto is the House of Clementine?"

"No idea," said Jadee quickly.

CHAPTER FIFTY-FOUR

It was comfortable enough here. They'd even managed to grab a shower. They'd been given good food. They'd even been allowed limited use of their communicators: they could look up information but they couldn't make or receive calls. They'd been there hours and hours, though, and nothing much seemed to be happening.

"It's a heck of a lot of money," said Jadee.

"If you can really call it money. Most Zenotons wouldn't understand what that meant."

"Yes, and it's a little bit crazy for a society that is supposed to manage without money."

"Except isn't that what they're trying to change?"

Kaleem's head was beginning to throb. He hated being cooped up indoors like this without anything to do. He sighed. "It's a lot for anyone. Any planet would find it difficult finding that amount of money. It really makes you wonder who would be behind this. Is it down to the Zenotons who want to maintain the status quo? Is it someone from the outside? If so, why would they want to harm Zenotons?"

"I'm still not convinced that it's just the House of Clementine." Jadee had gone pale and she was looking down at the floor.

"You're part of it? Could they do something like this?"

"Was part of it."

"Was? And why would they hurt one of their own?"

"It's easy to fall out with the Clementine regime."

"So, tell me. Why do you think it's them?"

"Well, I haven't actually left. As far as they're concerned."

"Wait a minute. You're in a lot of places all at once: Resistance worker, House of Clementine and a bona fide extra-planetary correspondent. How do you keep all of that going?"

Jadee laughed. "Oh ironically, it's down to the good training that House of Clementine gives us. We're taught to survive, to influence and to turn everything to the House's advantage."

"So, you use other people?"

"Not as much as we help other people. The House of Clementine is very rich but it is also very generous with its money."

"Perhaps it has to be if it's always manipulating other people," Kaleem muttered. He was beginning to get the impression that this organisation was part way between some sort of secret religion and a type of vigilante group. People who took the law into their own hands.

"I was born into it."

"Oh, so you couldn't help it? You didn't choose it? And it didn't actually choose you? Does it ever choose people?"

"Yes, most certainly." She laughed. "I'm sure it would have you. You're brave. You're good at handling conflicts. You're good at establishing strategies."

He wasn't so sure. He might be able to do these things but he wasn't good at them; he didn't do them easily. As for being brave, that was only because most of the time he was scared. "And Exton? I suppose he was chosen?"

She looked down to the floor again. She shook her head. "No. He was born into it as well. In fact, he's my brother."

Her brother? This just got better and better.

"So you're Zenoton as well?" She didn't look Zenoton. He guessed though that modern Zandrian cosmetic techniques made it easy enough to change appearances.

She shook her head. "He's my half-brother. We share a father – one who wanted nothing much to do with either of us. But he insisted that our mothers should give us to the House. We didn't actually ever meet until recently. We knew of each other, though."

"So why are you trying to get away from the House of Clementine now?"

"It's become corrupt. It's all about power now. No one is allowed to think for themselves. That's why I stole the constitution."

"Surely they've got a more up-to-date one than that?"

"Naturally. But that is the original one. I wanted to help to bring them back to basics. If that's any better than the one they use now." She smiled at Kaleem. "I was rather hoping you would help me with that."

Kaleem shrugged. “Maybe. Sometime. But don’t you think there are more urgent matters now?”

She nodded. “What are we going to do?”

“What do you know about Exton? I thought his parents pushed him but you say your father wasn’t around much?

“Well, our father didn’t ignore us completely. He was interested enough in how our schooling went. He was very strict with us and our mothers. He was quite nasty to Pangwit. His mother was a high-flyer too; someone quite high up on the Board of Exchange.”

“I thought Exton said his mother was an actor. What is the Board of Exchange anyway?”

Jadee laughed. “They are the people who make sure that our exchange system works fairly. Anyway, Pangwit’s mother had a lot of influence whereas my mother was just a regular Zandrian banker. And her being an actor? Oh I think my brother was being ironic. She certainly had to be very diplomatic. And that included pretending to be something she wasn’t. Acting indeed.”

“So what was it like, belonging to Clementine?”

“There was a lot about it that was good. They made sure that we had somewhere really nice to live -over and above what our mothers should really have been able to afford. We were schooled by them and they had very high standards and fantastic equipment. We lived near other Clementine families. It was good to be near people like us.”

“But this had to be done secretly? How could they manage that?” Kaleem rapidly tried to remember anything he’d seen on Zandra, apart from what he’d seen with Clem, but there was nothing. Was she saying it was like some secret underground society?

“Yes. You’re right. You wouldn’t have known us from any other family. And if you’d looked in on one of our school meets you would never have noticed anything different. You’d have had to follow me very closely for at least six months to see anything unusual.”

“What do you want to do, then?”

“We need to find him and get him back.”

"But you were part of the resistance."

"Yes, and it's not just him that's involved in this. It's all part of something much bigger. Something we really do need to resist." She paused and looked down at the floor. "And after all. He is my brother."

"You say that, even though you had little to do with him."

"We still shared a father."

That was important, Kaleem knew. He remembered back to the time before he'd met Nazaret. When he hadn't known who his father was and how important it had seemed to find out. And how now, gradually over a few years, he'd begun to understand himself better as he'd got to know him.

"You know my position isn't so different from yours. You're supposed to negotiate with him and persuade him to do the best for everybody. You need to understand why he is the way he is. I do understand a bit already."

"And you still think it's the House of Clementine?"

Jadee nodded.

He still couldn't quite get this. "So why are they trying to harm one of their own?"

"Because he's turned against them as well."

It was possible perhaps.

Jadee sighed. "I want to get out there and look for him."

"Surely they'll be on to it already?"

"They won't understand how Clementine works as well as I do. Or even as well as you do. And they probably wouldn't believe us if we tried to tell them."

What was she saying?

"It would be better if we looked for him ourselves. We'll probably find him more quickly and we'll be able to negotiate more easily." Ah. That was what he was afraid she meant.

The door opened. A Zenoton official came in.

"Thank you, both of you, for all of your help. You are free to go."

"We'd better get on with it then," said Kaleem as they made their way outside.

CHAPTER FIFTY-FIVE

Of course, it wasn't all that simple getting away. The Zenotons may have told him he was free to go but in Kaleem's case that meant he was escorted back to his apartment and put under droid guard.

"I'll find a way of communicating with you," Jadee whispered as Kaleem was accompanied to a waiting transporter. "We'd both best get some rest first."

He hadn't realised how tired he'd become. He went straight to bed and was soon in a deep sleep.

A tap came on his bedroom door and woke him up suddenly. His heart started racing.

"It's only me." Jadee.

Kaleem grabbed his robe and pulled it on. "How have you managed this?" he asked as he opened the door.

"Oh, you know. Just disabled a droid or two and your entire security system. All routine stuff."

Goodness. There was more to this woman than he'd realised.

"So what now?"

"Well, I think you should get dressed for one thing." She wrinkled up her nose. "And maybe take a shower? If you don't mind, I'll talk to you while you get ready. I'll keep my eyes averted. I promise."

There was no point in arguing.

"I'm pretty certain I know where they're holding him," she said as Kaleem showered. "It will take us about four hours to get there by transporter."

"We can't take a flyer?"

"Best not. We'd be too easily seen. And it would be quite a job to get one."

"How can you be so certain that he's where you think he is?"

She laughed. "I just know the Clems so well. And I'm enough like my brother to know how he thinks."

Kaleem stepped out of the shower. Jadee hovered in the lounge while he got dressed.

"So where is the place?" He selected a plain grey tunic made of thick sturdy cloth. He guessed he was in for some dirty work.

"It's not so far from where you were before. But it's even more isolated. Difficult to get there, though. You have to use a specialised transporter for the last section."

"And how will we manage that?"

Jadee grinned. "Oh, I'm sure we'll find a way."

Kaleem thought it best not to ask how she'd managed to get the transporter. In fact, he wasn't sure even how she'd found the earlier one. This one was state of the art, though. It had a complex control panel and the furnishings were more luxurious than Kaleem had ever seen before. It seemed to go faster, too.

"It's a combination of correspondents' perks and a few House of Clementine skills. Always good to know your enemy."

Her whole relationship with the House of Clementine was so complex. She must know it well and she could exploit it. Usefully she would even know its weaknesses. But was there some part of her that still conformed with its ways?

She laughed. "I could see you were thinking about something. I guess you're finding this all very difficult to figure out. Don't worry so much. Even if I've got it wrong, I'm sure we can find out more once we're there. Just relax and enjoy the view."

He did as she suggested. Yes, he could see they were to some extent going back the way they'd come the day before. The built up area thinned out quickly and soon they were travelling through Zenoton countryside.

"We'll be back at the castle before you know it."

Sure enough it soon came into view. Then the roadway started climbing. The countryside became wilder. There were no more cultivated fields or gardens. Just rocks and a few scrawny trees. A wind howled outside and the transporter was buffeted from side to side.

"It's always like this up here," said Jadee. "Don't worry. Nothing bad will happen."

Kaleem wasn't so sure. This was not a comfortable ride despite the obvious superior competencies of the transporter.

Then without any warning at all they stopped in what looked like the middle of nowhere. Had the transporter broken down?

"Come on," said Jadee. "We're here now."

They stepped out. A cold, salty tasting air greeted them at once. Odd, they weren't near any sea. Or did salt exist in quantity elsewhere on Zenoto? Kaleem couldn't see any building, though.

"Up there!" Jadee pointed to a small house perched on the top of a very high cliff. "The special transporters go up inside the cliff."

"So how do we get one of those without being noticed?"

"We make ourselves invisible and steal one."

That easy?

"Come on. Let's get to it. Shh!" Jadee pointed to a transporter that was just coming out of an opening in the cliff. "Good. It's just a droid getting out. Watch and learn."

She marched confidently towards the machine. The droid looked as if it was about to start panicking. Yes in fact it did start marching backwards and forwards on the spot. Its head shot from side to side. How had she managed to make it do that? She swept her arm into the air and then made a chopping motion with it. The droid stopped moving immediately. Was this a Clementine trick? Then she pushed her finger under the machine's chin. It's head dropped at once. She turned to the others. "Come on. Let's get going."

Kaleem followed her to the special transporter.

"Will it work without the droid?"

"Of course it will. They only have droids or humans in them in case of problems. Oh of course they have humans who are going up to the Lair in them."

"And if there's a problem?"

"I know a few more Clementine tricks."

Kaleem followed her into the transporter. It was very crude compared with the one they'd just left. Once they were inside, the door closed automatically. The machine started whirring and soon they were going upwards through tunnels carved into the cliff. The transporter kept bumping into the walls of the tunnel.

"Is that normal?" Kaleem was gripping the edge of his comfisessel tightly.

“Absolutely. These transporters use the momentum of the crashes to propel themselves forward more quickly. Don’t worry. Nothing bad will happen to you. These machines are built to preserve sentient life.”

He wasn’t convinced. “And how long before we get there?”

“The journey is twenty universal minutes in total. So another fifteen.”

“And what happens when we get there?”

“We look confident and you let me do any talking.”

After a long fifteen minutes the transporter came out into the daylight and the door slid open.

“Come on,” said Jadee. “It actually looks deserted.”

It was true. There was no one to be seen.

The sun was bright on the landing platform which also served as a patio to the house. The smell of salt was even stronger up here and it was mixed with a smell of pine needles. They were high up but Kaleem could see that the Lair was surrounded by Zenoton pine trees. Bizarrely, it wasn’t as cold up here as it had been down below. The house was quite dilapidated. It looked as if no one had been there for years. But they’d seen a droid go up there.

Kaleem shivered. A gentle breeze had crossed the patio but that wasn’t it. He felt as if someone was watching him. “What now?”

“We go inside.”

Jadee nodded towards to a door that was partly open. “Let’s go.”

“Wait. Why would they leave a door open like that if they’re holding someone?”

“They wouldn’t expect anyone to come up here. Very, very few people know about this place. Not even all members of Clementine.”

“So how do you know?”

Jadee grimaced and sighed. “Because of my brother.” She was already making her way towards the open door.

Kaleem followed her.

It was dark inside and it took his eyes quite a while to adjust. Eventually he saw that they were in what must have once be a rather grand entrance hall. Now, though, some of the floor tiles were broken and it smelt damp. Wall coverings were peeling away.

Jadee was looking around the room. She put a finger to her lips. Yes, it would be sensible not to talk. He totally got that. It irritated him a little that she'd bothered to point it out.

Then she gestured to the opposite corner of the room. They tip-toed across the hallway. There was a staircase leading down. They followed it. It seemed just as damp and uncared for there as everything else they had seen so far at the Lair.

Jadee stopped suddenly. Kaleem could hear it too. There were people talking in the room below them. He could make out three different voices but he couldn't actually hear what they were saying. Then the voices got louder. Were they coming this way?

"We'll have to move him soon," he heard a male voice say.

"They're being too slow getting back to us."

"So what shall we do?"

Then the words faded again. They were moving in another direction. There must be more than one way to where they were holding him then.

Jadee touched Kaleem's arm and nodded. They carried on down the stairs. There was a small corridor at the end of the stairs and at the end of that a crude door.

Kaleem pushed the door open. Jadee gasped. There was Pangwit Exton, sitting comfortably in the middle of a room that almost matched the one Kaleem had had on the supercraft.

Kaleem could now almost understand why his captors were asking for so much. This was the height of luxury here. And there was Exton, looking as smug as ever, busily engaged with a very high spec dataserve. He didn't look at all as if he had been treated badly.

On a small table in front of a very comfortable looking comfisessel were the remains of a meal: a quarter bottle of Terrestran wine and a plate of half-eaten cheese and biscuits.

Exton turned to face them. "Well, well, well. If it isn't my little sister and the professional negotiator? Are you two an item then?"

"Don't be stupid Pangwit. We've come to rescue you."
"Who says I want rescuing, sis?"
"Who did this?"
"Who do you think?"
Jadee turned to look at Kaleem. "See. I told you. It's an inside job."
Something didn't sound quite right about this though. Exton seemed confident enough and even a little bit aggressive. But Kaleem thought he also saw something like fear in the President's eyes.
Exton laughed.
Jadee turned back to him. "It is the House of Clementine, isn't it?"
"Oh, my dear little sister. You are funny. Why would the Clementiners want to kidnap me?"
"Well, you're here at the Lair."
Exton held up his arms. "Ever thought they might have rescued me and hidden me here? Anyway, I'm enjoying a bit of peace and quiet. It's a shame you had to come and disturb it."
They heard voices in the corridor outside. Exton indicated with his head that they should hide in the bathroom. Kaleem thought he caught a flicker of alarm in Exton's eyes.
"Are you ready?" a female voice said.
Exton sighed. "I guess so. As ready as I'll ever be."
"I think they've gone," whispered Jadee.
Kaleem nodded. "I wonder where they're taking him and whether he really wants to go."
They made their way out of the bathroom.
"We'd better find out."
They managed to catch up with the Exton and the woman without being seen. Two more Zenotons had joined them. They were making their way towards the patio area and a transporter was waiting for them.
"Now where are they taking him?" Jadee muttered.
This was going to be tricky. If Exton and the two Zenotons got into that transporter and left, not only would he and Jadee have lost

Exton but they probably wouldn't be able to get down from the Lair.

Kaleem remembered something he'd used before. It was scary in any case and it would be really bad if it went wrong. It was their only chance though.

Without stopping to explain to Jadee he made his way quickly to the transporter.

"What are you doing?" whispered Jadee.

He shook his head and muttered, "You'll see."

"What?"

He ignored her and kept on staring at the woman who seemed to be in charge. He consciously pulled all of his forces together. Just as he'd been taught, he imagined the strength from all of his organs, from the blood pumping round his body and the electrical activity in his brain all concentrating on this one person. He could feel the energy draining from him but it was beginning to work. The woman was as still as a statue and staring into space, beyond where Kaleem was standing. He held on to the mantra. You are in my power. You are in my control.

"Ma'am?" said one of the other Zenoton.

The female shook her head.

"Release the prisoner. Stand your guard down," Kaleem commanded. The mantra continued on and on. You are in my power. You are in my control.

"Release the prisoner. Stand down," the female repeated.

Kaleem turned toward the other two Zenotons. He felt the energy gather up inside him again. He hoped he would still have the strength to do this. He felt slightly sick and he was very hot but couldn't sweat. Within seconds, though, the eyes of the two males glazed over. "Step away from the transporter. Let us get away," he just about had the energy to whisper.

He nodded to Jadee and Exton that they should get into the transporter.

"What just happened?" asked Jadee.

"Old Terrestran trick," Kaleem managed to reply.

The transporter started its bumpy journey to the bottom of the cliff. He shut his eyes, hoping he could fall asleep and that the nausea would go away before he threw up. Thankfully oblivion arrived.

Kaleem had no recollection of moving from the Lair's shuttle transporter into the one they'd come in. Sleep had brought some welcome oblivion. Now, though, his mouth was dry and he was thirsty. He helped himself to a drink from the transporter's water cooler.

He looked out of the window. They were clearly at least half way back.

He was aware that Exton and Jadee were talking quite heatedly. They didn't notice that he'd woken up. He shut his eyes again quickly. He might find something useful out this way.

It was hard to make out exactly what they were saying but his years of training in listening to foreign languages came in useful here.

"But had you had contact with them again before they came?"

"Of course. You know I always play the double agent."

"That's a dangerous game."

"You should always know the enemy."

"So, if you were pretending to be on their side, why did they take you prisoner?"

"They didn't really. I gave them the impression I was going along with them. That was just all for show back there."

"So what do they want?"

"To rule the universe."

"So do a lot of other people. But what were they trying to achieve exactly this time?"

Exton sighed. "It wasn't the gold. It was the control they wanted. Holding most of the Zenoton wealth would give them a lot of power."

"But how could you pretend to go along with that?"

Exton laughed. "That's what I'm good at. That's what I do."

"Oh, you're so annoying." Jadee's voice was becoming so loud that Kaleem couldn't pretend to still be asleep any longer. He opened his eyes and rubbed them.

"Where are we?" he asked.

"We'll be back in the city in about another twenty universal minutes," said Jadee. "Are you all right?"

"I'm fine. The mesmeriser trick always drains you, though. What about you two? Is everything in order? Are we sure that it's the House of Clementine?"

"Nothing's certain," muttered Exton.

"At least we've got you back."

Was that actually a good thing? It seemed to Kaleem that he could trust no one. He lent forward and helped himself to another cup of water.

CHAPTER FIFTY-SIX

The transporter drew up in front of the presidential building. The sun was quite low so it reflected off the shining white walls and dazzled Kaleem. Droid reporters and a few Zenoton ones swarmed around the vehicle.

"We're going to have to dash," said Exton. "Are you ready for this?"

Jadee nodded and Kaleem sighed. He hated this sort of attention though he had had his fair share and ought to be used to it.

Exton commanded the door open. Right, so he seemed to be in charge again. The noise was deafening as they moved between the vehicle and the door of the building. There were shrill voices, demanding questions and flashing cameras. This was all familiar territory to Kaleem but he never quite got used to it. He did know you just kept your head down and ran. So, he kept his head down and ran. They got through without any harm being done. The Zenoton officials were effective and unobtrusive. Within seconds they were in a lift making their way to Exton's office suite.

"So how did you manage to get away from your captors?" asked one of the officials.

Exton caught Kaleem's eye. "We can leave that for the formal debrief, can't we? For the moment my sister and her companion, and indeed I myself need a little time to recuperate. We can do this all later, can't we?"

"Of course, sir." The official bowed slightly.

The lift stopped and they stepped out on to the thick carpet. The veriglass in the windows was the sort that enhanced the light and the colours outside. The walls were covered in what looked like a silky cloth. Kaleem couldn't resist touching it.

Exton laughed. "Enjoy my friend. A sign of Zenoton excellence."

Just like House of Clementine?

Jadee went bright red. "So why are you so intent on making the

Zenotons so much like other people? What was wrong with the way you used to do things?"

"It's not as straight forward as you think, sister dear." He indicated that she should go into his office.

She rushed in. Kaleem, Exton and the officials followed. The comfisessels hovered over and all but the two officials sat down.

"Please organise some refreshments," said Exton.

The two officials exchanged a glance. The more senior one nodded and the junior one went out of the room.

Exton looked intently at the remaining official. "I do promise a full debrief can happen in a couple of hours. My two companions should be present. They have valuable information about how I was found."

"Very well. Can I be of assistance now sir?"

"No. I think we all need a little privacy for a while."

A few moments later a simple droid arrived with steaming cups of fruit tea and sweet snacks. No official in sight. They had taken notice of Exton, then. He clearly hadn't lost his charisma.

"Good," said Exton. "They're leaving us in peace. Now perhaps, I can explain a few things."

As soon as the droid left Exton started pouring the tea. "This is the best fruit tea. It will revive us and help us to think clearly. These sugary snacks are good too. Try one." He handed the plate first to Kaleem and then to Jadee.

Kaleem took one of the little squares and bit into it. It was, if anything, a little too sweet but yes, he guessed, it would wake him up. And it had quite a pleasant taste as well, something like vanilla and caramel. He was rather glad for the moment that there was no hint of orange. The tea, he noticed was bright red. Good. Not clementine, then. They'd probably had enough of that for the moment.

"Everything okay?" asked Exton. Kaleem nodded. "Good. Good. Well listen. We needed to do two things at once. We needed to trade with more people and then we needed to make sure it didn't get out of hand. You see that's why we needed to adopt a proper monetary system so that we can trade with other planets. But we might become very popular because of our excellent ways so that is why we created an off-planet barrier so that we could vet all those who wanted to come to the planet."

"But Pangwit," Jadee began.

Exton held up his hand to stop her. "Zenoto had to become a great planet again. This was the only way. That was why I had to do it."

Needed. Had to. Was. Why was he using the past tense? Had he changed his mind? He'd certainly now paused for breath. Jadee went to speak again but Exton waved his hand at her.

"Some Zenotons were getting lazy. Some were taking advantage. Not pulling their weight. You couldn't punish that so easily as you can with a normal monetary system. So we were going to have to change." He started pacing up and down. "But we still looked good. So we had to make sure not too many people came." He pushed his hair back from his forehead. He carried on walking to and fro, muttering to himself.

Was there something wrong with him? Was it something in the tea? He had drunk two cups of it rather rapidly.

Jadee touched her brother's arm. "Zenoto is great isn't it? Shouldn't you share it?"

Exton stopped and stared ahead. He shook his head and pursed his lips.

Kaleem cleared his throat. "Why are you talking about everything as if it were in the past?"

Exton was quite white now. He sat down. "There's a bigger problem."

Exton pushed his hand through his hair. "I… I had to do it. There is something rotten in the House of Clementine."

Well, yes. Kaleem had already realised that. "You mean about the corruption in the knights' training? Or the way outsiders are treated and created? Or all of that?"

"Yes, yes. All of that. But in the normal course of things we'd have been able to diffuse it. It's stubbornly there now. There is something big behind it."

Jadee frowned and looked at her brother. "What are you talking about, Pangwit? You're not making sense."

"What is this something?"

There was a long pause before Exton spoke. "A beast. A demon."

Jadee gasped. "What? You're going mad." She started thumping her brother. "President of Zenoto? Believing in superstitious nonsense?"

But Kaleem had come across this sort of thing before. What about all of that business about him and the Tower of Babel? Okay, so it had all been a misinterpretation about what had happened to Davina Patterson. As yet, though, there'd been no logical explanation about why she'd been so concerned with that old story.

Exton shrugged. "There is no other real explanation."

"You are definitely mad." Jadee turned away from him, folded her arms across her chest and turned to face the window.

"So, then. This beast. This demon. What makes you think that?" Kaleem tried to maintain eye contact with the young president.

Exton looked away and sighed. "When we pin people down they can give no real explanation. They tell us that they've felt some sort of presence. A voice sometimes."

"Okay, someone is manipulating them."

Exton shook his head. "I've actually seen him."

"Him?"

"Him. Her. It. But it seems male to me."

"What do you mean, you've seen him?"

"Out of the corner of my eye. In my dreams. I've heard his voice. I've felt his presence."

"Are you sure that's not just your imagination?"

"He smells like nothing I've ever smelt before. Nastier."

"What have others reported?"

Exton nodded. "The same."

Exton seemed to recover himself. He took a deep breath and drew himself up taller." Beast or no beast. The Order's problems are getting worse."

Jadee turned back to face them. "Oh? What do you mean?"

"We no longer produce the best clementines in the universe. Our competitors are doing better."

"Can't you learn from them? Can't you exchange ideas?" It always irritated Kaleem that people guarded the secrets of their success. Wouldn't the universe be a better place if everyone learnt from everyone else? Of course, money got in the way. But if everyone took on the Zenoton methods money would literally be no object. Darn. Exton was trying to make the Zenotons like everyone else as far as money was concerned.

"They won't let us near them."

"Who are they anyway?"

Exton laughed. "The Terrestrans."

No. Kaleem felt his cheeks burning.

"Well, Peace Baby. It's not all that surprising is it? The Order was born on Terrestra, after all. And your home planet has the best climate for growing clementines. Now that you've got rid of that awful cloud."

"Couldn't you try…?"

"What? Get Terrestrans to talk? Come on. I doubt whether even you could. And before you put it all down to money and commercialism, think on this; for some time now, even though we don't have currency as such, many Zenotons have started thinking in terms of commercial values. I had to formalise it. Something or somebody has got to them, I tell you."

Something changed in Kaleem. Suddenly he understood. He nodded.

"But do you know what the worst is? It's the infighting. The petty jealousies. The constant vying to be the best. It's destroying the Order. It's leaking out and destroying Zenoto. It will spread out further from there and destroy the planet. And other planets. In fact, it's already started. Look what happened on Zandra before you came away. We must bring it under control. We must find the beast and destroy it."

"You're still talking about an actual physical being?"

Exton shrugged. "Real or just in our imagination, it's powerful and it's doing a lot of damage. It has to be stopped."

The room's dataserve buzzed. The red light that indicated urgency flashed.

"Send," commanded Exton.

A young man who had a small House of Clementine badge on his tunic appeared on the screen. Exton seemed to know him.

"They're all dead, sir," he stammered.

"Who are?"

"The people in the Daschia community."

"All of them?"

"Every single one, sir."

"So what's happened? Has there been an accident?"

"It seems to have been a mass suicide."

"Why? How?"

"We don't know exactly why. But it seems to have been some sort of poisoning. There were several discarded wands at the scene. There are people looking for a reason right now. And the analysis of what killed them should be ready in three universal hours."

"Thank you for letting me know." He looked away from the screen and towards Kaleem and Jadee. "You see. It's just getting worse and worse."

"Just one more thing, sir."

Exton looked back towards the screen.

"There seems to have been a theft involved as well."

"A theft?"

"All of the furnishings and decorative goods have been stripped from every home."

Exton was now pale. "A theft? In an Order community? On Zenoto? So what makes us think it was a mass suicide? Wasn't it a robbery in fact?"

"Even we have looters it seems sir. There was just one note sir. A voice message on a dataserve. Listen."

Kaleem shivered as he heard the voice of the now deceased Zenoton. "We just couldn't go on. The dream is broken."

"Thank you. You'll let me know when there's more news?"

"Right away, sir."

The screen went black.

"That's so shocking." Jadee also now looked very pale. "How could they do that?"

Exton shrugged. "Just one more sign of the difficult times we live in, I suppose. But you're right. It is shocking. Nothing like this has ever happened on Zenoto. Nor at a House of Clementine community anywhere in the universe."

"Do you think it's some form of mass hysteria?" said Kaleem. "Might they have been hypnotised?" He knew a few tricks like that himself. And he'd been subject to them as well. It always seemed very clever and almost magical but it was of course very scientific.

"Undoubtedly." Exton tapped the table and pursed his lips. "But who – or what – and why?"

Yes, it was difficult to think who might want to do such a thing. Someone was probably just trying to cause havoc.

"You can see where this is pointing, can't you?" Exton was frowning now.

It has seemed so far-fetched but now Kaleem could see that he had a point. "The beast," he murmured. "I guess we should try and find out more."

"You two are joking aren't you? You're making it all sound like something out of a cheap horror video."

"Horror is correct. Story and entertainment isn't," muttered Exton. "This is real and tangible."

Jadee shook her head. "Unbelievable."

"Well, you need to start listening to me."

Kaleem stood up and turned to Exton. "Do you have any files on this?"

"A few."

"Send them over to me, then. Let me have a good look at them before we do anything else."

Exton nodded.

Kaleem turned to Jadee. "If he's right, we have a lot of work to do."

CHAPTER FIFTY-SEVEN

Kaleem's back ached. His eyes were sore. His legs were twitchy. He ought really to go and get some exercise but he felt too weary even for that. He sighed and pushed his sessel back. He was a bit hungry but felt too tired to eat. Maybe he should go and take a shower and ask for something light to be ready for when he'd finished.

"Which light snacks can you recommend?" he asked the dataserve.

The machine just blinked at him. What? Oh, maybe he'd used up all of its memory. That was quite hard to do here on Zenoto. Zenoton dataserves had huge powerful memories. Still, he'd searched archive after archive. He'd linked to other research. He'd looked at tons of video footage. He'd been attached to the dataserve all day.

There had been nothing. Not a trace of a beast.

"Close down all files and folders," he commanded the machine.

It carried on blinking at him. Then it started whirring and he could tell it was beginning to clear its memory. He wished he could do the same with his own, but thoughts were tumbling through his head. None made any sense. Could this beast just be in Exton's imagination? Was the man ill?

Something was niggling at him, as well, at the edge of his memory. It wouldn't leave him alone. He had the feeling that it wasn't something he'd seen recently but rather from earlier studies, from an experience he'd partly forgotten. What was it though?

A name came to him. Lucifer. Of course that was it. In the ancient religions there was a belief in the Devil but he had many names and many faces and he was, if he existed at all, probably several different entities.

Oh this was absurd. But worth looking into? "Find me Lucifer," he commanded.

The dataserve sprang back into life. Lucifer. The bright and morning star. Yes, that would go well with the House of Clementine. They liked the bright and shiny. Perhaps they liked it too much and there wasn't the opportunity for balance? He whispered the name.

An old Wordtext file appeared. It looked like the opening of a story. An introduction. He found it reasonably easy to read, but the actual ideas were a bit more difficult to follow. That people had free will. Well, of course they did – to an extent. They would be restricted, wouldn't they, by what was actually available to them? Wasn't there something as well about restrictions making people stronger and more creative? He carried on reading the text. The Devil, Satan. Other names for Lucifer. Actually on the same side as God, whatever that was. You can't have good if you don't have evil. You can't have white if you don't have black. You can't be brave if you're not afraid. That again.

"Okay. I get it. What else have you got?"

A video clip started. A group of young people were being shown around a factory where some sort of confection was being made. There were two men leading them. One was full of life and joy. The other kept having whispered conversations with the young people. There was no sound on the clip so Kaleem couldn't hear what they were saying. But it was clear that he was tempting them by offering them something from his pocket. One by one they succumbed. Was this man testing these kids? Was his dataserve trying to tell him that evil was working on the side of good?

The clip faded and another one appeared. The characters all wore long robes and held sticks which seemed to make miracles happen. Someone had clearly just died. This time there was some sound.

"He was on our side all the time," said one of the young people.

"It was almost like a test," said another.

The dataserve went quiet. What was it trying to tell him? What did he want to know now?

Another clip loaded. It was bizarre. It was a family watching a film. A clip within a clip then. In fact they seemed to be watching the previous film.

"I knew it," said the older, female child. "He was on their side all the time. He was only pretending to be on the dark one's side."

"You mean like a double agent?" said the boy.

"Kind of."

"Just seems like your typical chemistry teacher to me," said the male adult. "Reminds me of the idiot we had. He was always blowing things up."

The mother sighed. "Good against evil again. Good's winning. He was on the side of good."

The clip faded and the dataserve screen went blank. This machine was really clever. It was almost reading his mind.

Now, though, the machine sat idly blinking at him.

What should he do next? "Can't you show me traces of the beast in modern life?" he muttered to himself.

The machine sprang into action again. What was happening? It couldn't be that efficient, could it? Well, technology was good on Zenoto. Were they going to lose that if Exton got his way?

The machine chuntered and clicked away for several seconds and then a documentary film loaded. It appeared to be about banking systems throughout the universe.

"Not Zenoton, then," he said to the machine.

The clip paused. "Your beast isn't restricted to Zenoto," announced the machine.

What? There was real evidence of this entity? And not just here? Could this thing be behind all those other peculiar happenings on Zandra as well?

The clip continued. It was all about an exaggerated love of money and it was those people who looked after the exchange systems that were the most involved.

"Are you saying that there *is* an actual beast behind this?" he asked the machine. "Do you have real evidence of… Lucifer?"

The clip stopped and a man's face appeared on the screen. It was a normal shape but the skin was slightly orange. Not a Clementine orange but a burnt orange. In fact, his skin looked burnt in places as did his tunic. It was the eyes, though, that were the most disturbing. The pupils were small, like pin holes and the irises were bright orange. The man seemed to shine.

"Not just Lucifer," said the dataserve. "Not just the demon of bright things."

Kaleem shivered. What was going on? What was this machine doing? "What else?"

Video clip after video clip now loaded. Masses of people in uniform assembling on a giant parade ground. Windows being smashed and buildings being set alight. Then brown tunics on Terrestra. Exton's barrier. And then Petri and Rozia walking through the streets of Zandra. Petri's skin was not too bad but she didn't look normal. Some Zandrians were pointing and laughing. Kaleem felt sick.

"One of Satan's minions," said the machine. "The beast of xenophobia."

Another face appeared on the screen. It looked even more normal than the first one. Then, though, it distorted. It became fatter and turned bight orange. A hideous grin appeared, the ears grew large and the eyes shrank to almost nothing. There was a loud bang and the dataserve and the light switched off.

This was really odd. Outages of any sort were unusual these days, but especially here on Zenoto and particularly as he was in presidential accommodation. Could he be dreaming?

He didn't have long to dwell on it. The lights flickered and the dataserve stuttered. Then the lights came back up. The dataserve switched itself back on and immediately went into standby mode.

"So, where is it now? This beast?"

The machine chuntered to itself for a few seconds and then a still picture appeared on the screen. It was of a typical Zenoton village. Clean-lined glistening white buildings sat in neatly cultivated gardens. Mountains formed a backdrop. The picture zoomed in to one of the doors. He could see now that this wasn't in fact a village house but a cave. So there were people living in caves, were there? Now that seemed familiar.

This dwelling, though, wasn't quite as neat and tidy as Zenoton homes usually were. Rubbish covered the path up to the house. The cladding on the walls had faded.

"Is this because of the beast?"

The image changed. A short video followed. It was as if he was walking through the door and then along a dimly-lit passage way.

The noise of what sounded like an animal in pain gradually grew louder. A face loomed into the camera. It was the second demon again, though now its face was even more swollen. It looked kind of ill or at least tired.

"Save this video and the previous still." He'd acted just in time. The dataserve shut down again but this time the lights didn't even flicker.

Might that be a real place? This was all a bit odd and certainly very disturbing but maybe now it was time to summon the others. "Connect to President Exton and Jadee Elliott." He watched anxiously as the dataserve started labouring again.

So, will you find me now? Is that enough information, Peace Child? Not beyond you is it? Come now. Come now.

Jadee replied first. "Hi Kaleem. Have you found something?"

"Quite a lot. It's bizarre. What about you?"

She shook her head. "Nothing really. But then I can't read Wordtext or Figurescript like you can."

Had that helped? He wasn't sure. Yes, okay, he'd literally read a lot of files, but they hadn't lead anywhere much. Was there really something odd about his dataserve? Maybe just all of that reading had given the machine more clues about what he was looking for. "It may have helped. I have got something extraordinary to show you, though."

"Can you send it across?"

"I could but I think it's better if we meet up. It's just too peculiar." If he'd described it, they wouldn't believe him.

"Have you contacted Pangwit?"

"Yes, but he's not responded."

At that precise moment a bleary-eyed Exton appeared on the screen. "Sorry. I was asleep. A droid woke me in the end."

Kaleem nodded. It must be hard work being a president. "So, do I take it you've not found anything else out?" This was a bit of a pain: surely the President would have access to even more information than he had. A pity he'd not been working.

" 'Fraid not. What have you got?"

"Oh, just a picture of the beast and where he lives."

Exton was wide awake now. "Will you send it to us?"

"No. Both of you come over here. You need to look at it with me. It will be easier if we're all together."

"Right. Jadee, do you agree?"

Jadee nodded.

Exton grinned. "See you in a short while."

Whilst he waited for Exton and Jadee to turn up, Kaleem looked again at the videos and the still pictures he'd saved. There was no information at all about where it had come from. That might have finally convinced him that this was something real. It couldn't be genuine could it? Was somebody setting him up? Yet the more he looked at it the more it did seem authentic. It could be a single powerful entity making people behave this way.

It didn't take long in fact before first Jadee and then a very short time later Exton arrived.

Exton had brought no bodyguard. He shrugged when Jadee challenged him about that. "I just think I need to do this on my own."

Jadee bit her lip and shook her head. "It might be dangerous. What do you say, Kaleem?"

It was difficult to answer that one. Everything he did was dangerous when he was working as the Peace Child.

Exton ignored his sister. He nodded towards Kaleem. "Anyway, what have you got?"

"This is weird."

He commanded the dataserve to re-open the videos. Nothing happened.

Exton laughed. "Don't tell me you dreamt it all."

"No. Really. It was all there a few seconds ago. I was watching it all again just before you came."

Jadee was frowning and had her arms crossed in front of her chest. "I thought Zenoton dataserves were supposed to be the best in the universe."

Exton sighed. "So they say. But there's a fair bit of entropy happening now. Everywhere."

Kaleem shivered. Was he facing something a bit supernatural

again? Even though all that stuff about the Tower and Davina Patterson had been mainly explained there were one or two questions still. And here were now a heap more about something else, not least of all about why all of his saved material had disappeared on a planet where technology was normally faultless. "Reload recently viewed files," he commanded.

The dataserve spluttered for several seconds and then gradually started doing something. The picture of the abandoned village eventually appeared.

Exton gasped. "I know that place. It's the Daschia community."

Ah.

Exton's eyes were blazing. "We should get there straight away."

"Shouldn't we get some back-up?"

Exton shook his head. "We don't need masses of people. The danger isn't physical. In fact other minds and emotions might spoil our concentration."

Kaleem looked at Jadee. She nodded.

CHAPTER FIFTY-EIGHT

It was a reasonable enough transporter. Not the most modern but it looked adequate for the job. Exton had said they were in no immediate physical danger.

"Are you sure we shouldn't have someone else with us?" asked Jadee. Her face was pinched and very pale.

"Absolutely not. They'd never believe us anyway."

This was familiar territory to Kaleem. He realised that Exton was looking at him, expecting agreement. He sighed. "You're probably right. Let's see if we can solve this on our own. We can always call for back-up later if we need to."

"All right then. Let's get on with it." Jadee walked towards the transporter and the door slid open. Kaleem and Exton followed.

"Well, now what?" Kaleem asked.

Exton spoke to the control panel. "Daschia community," he commanded.

"Valley route or high road?" the machine asked.

"Valley route." Exton looked up at the other two. "We're less likely to be seen that way. It may take a little longer and it may be a bit rougher but it's ultimately safer."

The transporter started to glide along smoothly.

"How long will it take?" asked Kaleem. Why did they need two days' supplies?

Exton shrugged. "Two or three universal hours. No more I shouldn't think. But we don't know how long we'll need to be there to get this all sorted."

Jadee was staring out of the window. "Where on Zenoto are we going?"

Kaleem and Exton turned to look out of the window. It was getting darker and they seemed to be in a tunnel.

"I didn't quite mean that when I chose the valley route," said Exton. He turned towards the control panel. "Explain route."

"This unit is following the ancient, forgotten trails," the dataserve responded. "This is compatible with your need for secrecy."

Exton nodded. "Clever machine, after all. And yes, there was always something a bit odd about the Daschia community. They were hung up on some old ways."

The transporter slowed as it negotiated some bends in the tunnel. There was very little clearance between it and the sides. It was getting darker and darker. Were they going underground or up inside a mountain? Kaleem had no sense of whether they were going up or down or even staying on the level.

Then there was a terrible crunching noise as the transporter wedged itself into the wall. Was the tunnel too narrow for it? It whirred and clicked for a few seconds whilst the three of them remained silent and held their breath. Just as suddenly as it had stopped, it started moving again and even began to pick up speed. As it rounded another curve, they were flooded with light. The transporter charged forward and they were out of the tunnel.

"Goodness." Jadee pointed at the view from her window. They were now on a plateau. The land was uncultivated and peculiar rock formations rose up from the ground. They looked as if some intelligent life form had sculpted them.

Kaleem had never seen anything like it before. "What is it?"

"It's called a torcal," Exton explained. "One of the most famous ones was actually found on Terrestra."

"Oh?"

"There it was to do with erosion in mountains made from flat-lying limestone. Here though there is no such explanation."

Jade turned to her brother. "Do you think someone has created this artificially?"

Exton shrugged. "Maybe."

"You seem to know a lot about it though." Kaleem could at least credit him with that; Exton was well-informed.

Exton grinned. "You wouldn't expect less of a president, surely?"

"I suppose not."

"Oh, look, it's finished."

Kaleem looked where Jadee was pointing. Yes they were in more normal Zenoton terrain now. The transporter was following a conventional route. There was still very little sign of civilisation though. Perhaps that was nothing to worry about. Zenoto was a sparsely inhabited planet. You wouldn't expect to find the big conglomerations you found on Terrestra or Zandra.

"We'll soon be a little nearer civilisation," said Exton.

The transporter carried on its journey quite smoothly now. Beautiful as the scenery was it soon became monotonous. Jadee's eyes closed and soon she was snoring gently. Exton had his eyes closed as well but Kaleem didn't think he was asleep. He felt drowsy himself but something told him he should try to keep awake.

He remembered some of his earlier training. He didn't need sugary or caffeine-filled drinks to keep him alert. It was more a matter of pure will-power. He also found it useful to think of a time when he'd not been able to sleep.

It did the trick and soon he was wide awake again. He carried on observing the landscape. There were some signs of civilisation now. There was a dwelling here and there. This was odd. He had always thought that Zenotons were sociable creatures and lived in communities. He would ask Exton about it later.

Something made him look through the rear window. He wasn't sure what it was. There was a shadow or something. Yet when he looked closely there was nothing. Perhaps it was just a feeling. Or maybe not. Could he hear something as well? A faint rumble, perhaps?

Exton opened his eyes. "What's bothering you? You look worried."

Kaleem shrugged. "I thought I saw something. Or even heard something. We might be being followed."

Exton frowned as he looked back the way they had come. He shook his head. "I can't see anything. We've been so careful about this. Nobody can possibly know we've even left." He stared hard at Kaleem. "I think you're feeling the power of the beast. It will be watching."

Surely not? That sounded like a fairy tale.

Exton nodded towards the side window just as they passed one of the isolated dwellings. "Daschia hermitages. It means we shouldn't be too long now."

Jadee woke up and rubbed her eyes. "Are we nearly there yet?"

Exton laughed. "Impatient as ever."

Jadee glanced out of the window. "Daschia hermits," she whispered. "Do you think we might see one?"

"I think not. They all went in the mass suicide," said Exton.

Jadee sighed. "I've heard they're a bit weird. Very antisocial. And they have a very peculiar belief system."

"Were. Had."

Kaleem couldn't believe what he was hearing. "You're sure they're all dead now?"

Exton nodded. "Yes. It's confirmed. I actually think the hermits promoted the suicides. They used a form of mass hysteria."

"Awful. But actually what they believed was pretty grim. That they were the chosen ones and that they would be given eternal life on Zenoto."

This didn't quite make sense. If they believed they were entitled to immortality on Zenoto why would they kill themselves unless they thought they were going to come back to life after everyone else had died or left the planet?

Exton folded his arms across his chest. "I actually think the beast got to them."

More fairy tales.

"You really think that this beast is a tangible, living creature?" Kaleem asked.

Exton nodded. "Yes and no. It too might also be a result of some sort of mass hysteria. But to those who feel it it's real enough. Don't you feel him?" He was staring at Kaleem now. Kaleem could almost believe that Exton himself was the beast.

Jadee suddenly shivered and went pale. Kaleem felt a curling in his spine too and had the feeling that something terrible was going to happen. Everything was black inside. It was as if he was feeling the black mood of a hundred or so people.

"Oh yes," murmured Exton. "He's around all right. You sure can feel him now."

The sky was blackening and the first drops of rain were starting. Serious stuff on Zenoto. When rain came here it came thick and fast and if the liquid touched your bare skin it burnt.

Within seconds the rain was crashing down on to the roof of the transporter. A wind sprang up and they were buffeted violently from side to side. The vehicle was still moving forwards but only very slowly. They could barely see out of the windows. The noise was tremendous, like rocks hitting the roof, and even within the sealed unit they could smell the sickly Zenoton acid.

"Will it hold, do you think?" asked Jadee.

"Hope so," Exton mumbled.

Kaleem realised that the road ahead was rapidly turning into a river. "Do you think we should try and get out?" he asked.

"Definitely not," replied Exton. "That fluid hurts. We're safer here."

At that very second the transporter lost its connection with the ground. Jadee's arm crashed into the side of the vehicle. There was a loud crack. She screamed. Kaleem suspected she had broken something. He too was flung into the side and a pain shot up from his hip. He had to take deep breaths and count his way through it.

"Hopefully the storm will soon be over and we'll find a resting place," said Exton. "Give location," he commanded the control panel.

There was silence. It seemed that the transporter had lost its operating system. "Perhaps when everything's dried out we'll be able to get it working again," he said.

That certainly wasn't to be. The roof snapped off and Kaleem found himself catapulted away from the transporter.

"Don't let the fluid touch your skin," Jadee called.

"But don't worry if it does," shouted Exton. "It will smart but it won't kill you." It was too late. His hands were already sore. Just at that moment, though, he realised that he was quite close to the side of the road that had now become a river. A handy tree trunk allowed him to pull himself up. He turned to see what was happening to his companions.

Oh no. The transporter was beginning to disintegrate. He watched in horror as Jadee and Pangwit fell out into the water.

CHAPTER FIFTY-NINE

The river was rising rapidly. Jadee and Exton were drifting further and further away from Kaleem. There was nothing he could do. Exton just looked like a terrified boy rather than a president who had lots of responsibility and who had to make important decisions. Kaleem held his breath as he watched them drift towards the river bank. The transporter seats were at least acting like rafts and they looked as if they were going to hold.

Jadee flung herself forwards and grabbed on to the branch of an overhanging tree. He watched her wriggle until her feet were on dry ground. That was something at least. But what of Exton? He was still struggling for sure.

Another surge of water came. The seats drifted away from the bank. Jadee screamed. Then the two seats came apart. Exton was still strapped into his but it looked to Kaleem as if he was trying to get out of it.

"Don't be a fool," Kaleem shouted. It was clear though that he couldn't be heard. It was of no use anyway, for at that very second the seat came apart and Exton was flung into the river.

He started to swim. Kaleem could see he was quite a strong swimmer. Was this some House of Clementine training? He was actually swimming against the current but at least he was making his way towards the bank.

Jadee ran round to where he was heading. Seconds later she was helping him out of the water. It looked as if they were going to be all right after all.

Kaleem watched them have a short conversation and then they started shouting at him. It was no good, though. The water was thundering too much for him to be able to hear. He pointed to his communicator but he doubted that any of them would work. All three of them would be soaked through.

Miraculously his own pinged and he could see Exton speaking into his. He opened his. It crackled a lot. "You stay put and we'll get some help. You're not to put yourself into any sort of danger. Can you keep out of sight? Will you be all right?"

"I guess so." This was going to be a bore. "Can't you just use your communicator?"

"Well of course we'll try that first but we're not sure how long this signal will last. We may actually have to make our way back rather than wait for someone to rescue us."

There were a couple more crackles and then Exton's communicator died. Exton shrugged and waved. Kaleem switched his off. He should try to save the battery.

He watched Exton and Jadee set off.

There was a sudden sound of rushing water that was even louder than what he had heard before. It sounded like another flood surge coming. He had to move. Now. He started running. Could he out-run this water? He would have to try.

He ran and ran, occasionally looking behind him to see what the water was doing. It just kept on coming. He didn't know whether he would make it. Then, just as suddenly as it had started, it stopped. There was one final surge and the new wave was over. In fact, he even thought the other water was subsiding a little. It seemed less noisy now. Perhaps it was just the contrast.

He realised he had no idea how far he'd come. Surely he couldn't be too far away now from where they thought the beast was hiding? If he existed at all, of course.

Yes, this looked like the road towards the Daschia settlement where they believed he'd been living. And even if there was no beast, there was definitely something not right there. He looked at the river again. It seemed calmer but he didn't like the look of it. There might well be another sudden surge anyway. The path towards the settlement was pretty desolate. There were no signs of any vegetation and it was covered in a very black form of shingle. But it would be safer than staying near to the river.

He would do it. He would follow the path. He had his communicator. The other two would get help. What harm could it do, really?

The light was bizarre. Everything was grey and damp but there was nevertheless an eerie brightness about everything. Kaleem found himself screwing up his eyes. It was strange, though, walking along this path. His feet hardly seemed to touch the ground. It was almost as if he was floating. Was it some sort of force field?

What was he walking on, anyway? He bent down to touch the dark material. It burnt his fingers. He pulled his hand back quickly. The material that made the path was hard and brittle. He looked at the bottom of his shoes. There was not a trace of anything there.

He carried on. He would have expected the strange substance to be hard underfoot and perhaps crunch when he stepped on the finer pieces. But nothing happened and in fact walking was easy. It was as if something was pulling him along. It was deadly boring, though. Nothing but a black path, grey sky, cool damp air and his own company. The normal vibrant Zenoton colours were missing.

He felt more and more uneasy as he went on. There was something very wrong here though he didn't know exactly what it was. There was an atmosphere of heaviness. The further he went the heavier it became. It was pure evil. He knew that. He wasn't sure, however, how anyone could actually know what evil was. This was nasty, though, certainly. It seemed to suck the life out of him.

As he went on, just putting one foot in front of another, it got darker, colder and damper. He gradually became aware of a smell of rotting vegetation or perhaps even flesh. It made him gag.

He wasn't sure where he was going but he felt an urge to carry on.

Something began to become clear in his mind.

A strange orange glow surrounded him. The smell seemed even worse now. Then he could see him. The beast. Large, orange, and foul-smelling.

What the heck? Was he sleep-walking? Dreaming while he was awake? Was his imagination working overtime?

He shook his head and tried to concentrate on the path ahead.

Wait. It was a little lighter now. And it was a vaguely orange light.

There was something else amiss. It wasn't just that feeling of evil now. There was something about to happen. It was like just before a Terrestran thunder storm. Except here there weren't any birds to stop singing here, nor any domestic animals to seem disturbed. The atmosphere was charged, though. It didn't feel dead anymore. Something was waking up. There was a curious energy stirring.

The ground beneath his feet began to rumble. Vibrations passed through his whole body. Then the path began to shake. Was this an earthquake? Like they used to have on Terrestra? He remembered the landquake on Zandra. That had been frightening enough but this threatened to be more. At least there were no trees that could fall on him, not on this stretch of the path. What should he do, though?

He didn't have time to think. The path lifted up and he had difficulty keeping his balance. It subsided again, almost throwing him to the ground. Then it came up again.

The rumbling had now become loud cracks and bangs and the path snaked up and down. He had to keep his balance and didn't quite manage it all of the time. Twice he fell down as the path came back up to meet him. A few times it slapped the back of his head. The loose pebbles attacked his face and hands and pummelled his calves and thighs. He began to get the measure of it after a while. Oddly it reminded him of riding a kaartje in Terrestra's Z Zone. That made him remember Rozia. She had been so good at driving kaartjes.

There were a few more twists and turns and then the shaking began to subside and Kaleem was able to stand on firm ground. Eventually it stopped altogether. It gradually grew lighter. The sky was no longer so dark and the path that carried on forward was sandier now.

He set off again. He was covered in scratches and bruises and he was aware that he was limping but he didn't think he'd suffered any major damage.

Indications of the Final Days, my friend? Will there be a great calamity now? If there is, will you survive? Or is this melodrama? You decide.

He trudged on along the path. He was slightly stiff but he became more and more convinced that he'd suffered no real harm. In fact, even the scratches and bruises seemed to be healing up quickly now. Were they even real?

A faint sun now peeped out from behind silvery clouds, dissipating the orange glow. The feeling of evil was diminishing. Had he been imagining things? Had the earthquake been real?

It became even more mysterious, though. He began to have a real sense of where he was going. He knew, and he didn't know why or how he knew, but he most certainly did know that he was looking for a home that was in a cave. Could he have just been thinking about his own childhood home? No, it wasn't just that. This cave home was more luxurious. Or at least it had been. He could see it quite clearly now. Fading beauty, definitely.

He began to hear a whimper. Was that the beast? Was it in pain? The whimper changed to a growl and then to a roar. He sensed anger but pain as well. Disappointment, maybe. He suddenly felt sorry for the creature. But what was this? What was he thinking? Did this thing really exist? And if it did, and it was as evil as they supposed, why should he feel sorry for it? Was this just a Peace Child thing?

Suddenly the smell was overpowering. It was now like rotten flesh. This was definitely real. He gagged and tried to cover his nose and mouth. Yes this was real, whatever it was. Had something died here? Could it be death itself that he could smell? Did this mean the beast was dying? Would that be the end of all of their troubles?

He wanted to turn back, to turn away from this horror, but he knew he would have to confront it.

He took as deep a breath as he dared and quickened his pace.

He heard a faint rustling from both sides. Perhaps a wind was getting up. The rustling became louder. Something tapped his arm and then something brushed his leg. He looked down. His foot was caught in a shoot from a nearby plant. He hadn't noticed the scenery change. It happened very suddenly. At least everything was a bit greener now, a little less desolate.

He tried to shake his foot loose but then he watched in horror as another shoot wound its way around his other foot. Soon there were fronds and thin branches snaking their way towards him and threading themselves around his body.

In just a few seconds he was completely stuck.

The shoots and the branches didn't look very strong but as he tried to pull away from them, hoping that he would be able to break them, they just pulled tighter and tighter. What was he going to do?

He mustn't panic.

He realised that this vegetation would eventually die; he could see that it was no longer attached to the trees. But he might have to wait a long time for that to happen.

Then he had another thought; this couldn't be real. Trees just didn't behave like that. Something illogical was going on. And even if something more logical were happening, his Peace Child training taught him that although bad things can happen to good people, the universe is rarely fully hostile. It was always a matter of attitude.

So, these fronds and branches weren't really hurting him. They were just bits of vegetation. They were annoying and they were in the way. Eventually, and possibly sooner rather than later, he could be rid of them.

He pulled some of them off his arms. A few found their way back round him but they mainly stayed away. He bent down and started removing them from his feet and legs.

Then they were all gone.

The path led out of the woods. He arrived in what looked like a deserted village. The desolation was back.

CHAPTER SIXTY

Mist swirled all around them. There was a stale smell in the air. The ground was slippery, as if they were walking on damp leaves but when he looked down Kaleem could see nothing. He could hardly feel the ground beneath him either. "Is this place for real?" he murmured.

"Oh yes."

"Where are we then actually?"

"You may as well say we're walking though the mists of time. Excuse the cliché."

"Oh."

"Just keep walking. Concentrate. Just listen to your footsteps. Think only about your breathing."

Alright. He'd been there before. Meditation had always been good. Meditating and moving at the same time was a bit different though.

The ground did gradually become more solid. The mist cleared a little.

"So now we have it," muttered Meelak. "Now it's becoming real."

"What's becoming real?"

"Me. You. The Beast."

"What do you mean?"

"How on Zenoto do you think all of this happened? Or anywhere? Every reality is the result of a dream."

"Are you saying I dreamt you?"

"Didn't you?"

Had he? Kaleem couldn't decide. Perhaps he'd always been a bit bothered about how plain and boring he was. And yet when he was younger he'd always worried about how different he was from others. Had he tried too hard to be the same?

He glanced at Meelak. He positively sparkled. Did he want to be like that? He thought he rather did, actually. He held himself taller. The mist lifted completely. The sun was shining and steam was coming from the ground.

Meelak stopped walking. "We are almost at the sacred place," he explained.

"The sacred place?"

"The very centre. Listen to the silence."

Kaleem listened. He could hear nothing.

"Have you ever heard such silence?" Meelak asked.

Kaleem certainly hadn't. He shook his head. There was just nothing. No sound at all. He couldn't even hear his own breathing.

"Some call it the still small voice. Some find it through meditation or what the old monks used to call mindfulness. Empty your mind. If you can't, count backwards. See every single number and think only of the numbers."

Ah. That again. That was at least familiar.

"Start with a hundred."

Kaleem began to see the numbers in his head. 100, 99, 98…

Meelak disappeared. The mists dissolved. All he could see now was bright light. He was still aware of Meelak, though. He couldn't hear him or see him but he knew that he was still there.

"Just concentrate on the numbers," a voice in his head said. Was it his own voice? Meelak's? Someone else's?

He was suddenly aware of an almost overwhelming peacefulness.

"Don't think about it. Don't try to define it," the voice said. "Open your eyes and look."

He opened his eyes.

Everywhere was light. A white light, edged with gold.

He could now see Meelak again. "This is the sacred place. Remember it well."

"Is it really a physical place?" asked Kaleem.

"It's real. Which is more real? The truth or the physical world? What is the physical world?"

Kaleem began to hear soft sounds. The hint of a breeze. The rustling of leaves, perhaps. Maybe a stream running in the distance.

"Oh yes," said Meelak. "It's hard to stay in the sacred space."

"What's its purpose?"

"It'll always bring more clarity when you go back to your own world. Come to it often. But now we have to move on."

He sort of had done that, hadn't he, from time to time? This type of meditation. Perhaps he could now use it more often as a tool?

And he had the feeling that now something had changed though he couldn't quite define what.

"Look," said Meelak. "Look at me closely." He stopped walking, put his hands on Kaleem's shoulders and turned Kaleem to face him. He nodded. "Yes, look at me really carefully."

Kaleem found it hard to keep eye contact with Meelak.

Meelak shook his head. "You've got to look right into my eyes. You've got to see who I really am. There's nothing to be afraid of. I am you and you are me. At the moment we are two extremes. There is a middle way. We must find that and then we can be one. We're better together. Come on now. Look into my eyes."

Kaleem swallowed and tilted his head upwards. He felt drawn in by Meelak's eyes.

He pulled back a little and looked at Meelak's face. It was actually rather fine. His features were emphasised by the lines and shading. He was well defined. Did it give him more authority? Kaleem peeped though his eyelashes. He could still see Meelak clearly. He looked bold and confident.

"So, what is it you see, Peace Child? Is there anything abhorrent here?"

Kaleem shook his head. Meelak was only beautiful.

Meelak grinned and nodded. "Don't ever forget any of this."

Could he ever be like that though? Really? He touched his own forehead. Then he looked at his finger. There was a smudge of pink on it.

Meelak smiled. "You have to make the changes."

"How can I do that? I'm so used to being me."

"You'll figure it out."

Kaleem wondered whether he would. How could he become more like Meelak? Yet apparently he was already. He looked again at the smudge on his finger.

Meelak nodded. "You're only going at half speed at the moment. All that you do is good, very good even verging on excellent. But it lacks the final buzz."

Kaleem nodded. “Yes I get that. I really do get it. But how do we become one?”

“You need to stop thinking of us being separate. We are actually one.”

“It’s difficult.”

“Oh yes. Most certainly. Nobody said it had to be easy.” Meelak jumped and clicked his heels in the air.

Was he supposed to do that?

Meelak grinned. “Go on. What’s stopping you?”

Kaleem tried it. He landed clumsily and a pain shot through his ankle.

“Don’t worry. You’ll get used to it.”

Meelak started humming. He couldn’t do that, could he?

“It’s easy, you know. Everyone can sing. Everyone can hum. Just hear the note before you attempt to make it. Take a deep breath first.”

Kaleem took in that breath. And surprise! He found he could hum.

They carried on tramping forwards. Their footsteps were just as in tune as their humming. Kaleem didn’t know where they were going. It didn’t seem to matter. All that actually mattered was that they were together. Humming and walking together felt like working together.

Kaleem began to notice odd things. Light on a leaf. Clouds forming shapes. Faces in rocks. Were these his thoughts or were they Meelak’s? Occasionally he looked at Meelak. Meelak smiled back and nodded. “You’re getting there.”

The ground started to slope away. The path went down steeply. It was covered with leaves, just like on Terrestra. Without stopping to think, Kaleem jumped into the leaves and then slid down the incline. Out of the corner of his eye he could see Meelak doing the same.

Kaleem felt a strange jolt. Then Meelak was no longer there. Had they become one now? Did he feel any different? Kaleem couldn’t tell.

He carried on down the slope, not really sure where he was going.

He touched his face and then looked at his fingers. Yes, they were smudged again but this time the colour was darker. He'd become Meelak then? But what was left of Kaleem? Did he feel any different? Maybe. Less frustrated. More willing just to see what would happen. Perhaps that was useful.

Kaleem carried on walking. He could really sense Meelak inside him now. But then Meelak had always been there hadn't he? Or should have been? He still had to get that sense of oneness rather than that of there being some separation. He walked on, one foot in front of the other. He started to hum again. That at least felt natural now.

He would have liked to look in a mirror. Fat chance of that out here. But as he looked down to the ground he noticed something silvery and shiny. A small piece of metal. He picked it up. He held it up in front of him. It made an efficient enough mirror. Oh, yes, he was Meelak indeed. But his eyes were Kaleem's. Was he going to carry on looking like this? Would others accept him this way? Time would tell, he supposed.

He put the piece of metal into his pocket. That was a Kaleem act all right.

He still wasn't sure where he was going. He was confident, though, that he was going in the right direction. He stopped worrying. Meelak became a little more cautious. The scenery was changing. He was now walking on a path. The sky was becoming brighter, the mist now completely gone. He would soon be where he needed to be, he knew it.

He sensed he was nearing civilisation or at least a place where civilisation had once been. What looked like abandoned houses began to appear at the roadside. What were these places? What had happened? In the distance he could see there was somewhere more built up.

He sensed, too, something he thought might be to do with other people's feelings. A feeling of utter blackness. Meelak? No. They were one now, weren't they? And Meelak would never feel that desolate, would he? There was a faintly unpleasant smell as well. It gradually got stronger.

Then he was in the middle of the built-up place he'd seen in the distance. It was exactly where he'd been when everything had gone black and Meelak had appeared.

CHAPTER SIXTY-ONE

This was it then? The place where the most evil part of the Clementine Order was hanging out. What happened to all of those ideas of excellence, then? This was so poor and desolate. Even Terrestra's Z Zone had been more pleasant. It had at least functioned. But this place was squalid and deserted. The door was battered. There was a smell of decaying rubbish. It was deadly silent.

"Anyone there?" called Kaleem.

He thought he heard a groan. It didn't sound quite human. He pushed at the door. It crumbled and gave way. A cloud of dust rose into the air, making him cough and making his eyes run.

This wasn't really a proper dwelling at all. It was a cave with a door across its entrance. It was cold and damp inside. The smell of rotting rubbish grew stronger and made him gag.

"Where are you?" Kaleem called again.

Something rustled. Were there rats as well?

His eyes got used to the dark. The dim light from his communicator helped him to see a little more easily as well. Maybe it wasn't just a cave after all. The walls were certainly lined with high quality tiles though they were filthy. There were tiles underfoot as well but they were broken in places.

He could hear a low moaning, like someone in pain.

He took a deep breath. Yes, he needed to see what this was all about. It was the sort of thing he did, wasn't it? It didn't get any easier though. Confronting what might be labelled the enemy was always scary even when you knew what to do.

He followed the corridors towards the noise. As he rounded one corner he could see that he was moving towards the light. Then the cave opened out and he could see the source of the noise.

He had never seen anything quite like this. Was this some sort of intelligent being? It was an alien form, not from a colonised planet, though it had a vaguely humanoid shape. It had no hair and what passed for skin was a dusty orange. It had a head but no neck.

It appeared to have limbs; there were four of them at that. The beast was sitting in what looked like a mixture of blood and excrement. If these were bodily fluids though they were different from anything he'd seen before. The liquid was streaked green and purple. So this was the source of the putrid smell he'd noticed from the beginning of his journey into the cave. It was much stronger here.

The beast seemed to be sleeping. What might be described as a chest was heaving up and down. It breathed then. Was it taking in oxygen and expelling carbon dioxide? Or did it breathe another way? What was it exactly?

It stirred and grumbled to itself. Its eye lids opened. It probably couldn't see though; there were only milky cataracts in the sockets.

"Well, boy. What do you want?"

It knew he was there and that he was male. How? Was it some sort of telepathy?

"Tell me boy. Or go away. You're disturbing my peace."

It was sophisticated and intelligent enough to run a translator programme then. That was Terrestran English – and almost without any accent at all.

"Speak!" A dart of blue light shot out of the tip of a long protrusion at the end of one of the creature's upper limbs.

Kaleem dipped out of the way.

The creature made a deep gurgling sound and started to shake. Kaleem had the impression he was laughing. "Very clever. Tell me what you want or I will get you next time."

What did he want? Well to find out what was really behind the House of Clementine. But how did he broach that? "How do you know where I am? You can't see me surely?"

The creature wobbled again. "I can feel you. Sense you. Don't even you humans only use eyes to check? The other senses do most of the work. Surely you knew that?"

He'd heard the theory before but never really had the opportunity to test it.

The creature laughed. "Oh, and I can tell you're a snazzy boy."

"You can? Who are you? And why are you here?"

The creature wobbled again. "You haven't figured it out?"

Kaleem shook his head. Now what?

"Before you ask. Yes, I know you're shaking your head." He pulled himself up. "I am the incarnation of Oroban."

Incarnation? This thing wasn't of the universe, then? And if not, then where had it come from? Kaleem shuddered.

Oroban sighed. "I am trapped in this body. In this piece of rotting flesh. It is dying but not quickly enough."

"So where have you come from? What are you doing here?"

Oroban sighed again. "I am from a different realm. I am a demon of the first class. Some of you might call my home Hell. But you universals don't really understand the other realms so you make up all sorts of interesting stories. Very colourful sometimes." He started shaking again and now it really did sound as if he was giggling. "Fire and brimstone. Whatever next?"

"Well, what is it like? The place you would call home."

"Like nothing you could imagine. And it isn't even distasteful or unpleasant. Not as much fun as this very physical world, though. Or at least, how this world is when you have a functioning body."

"So what is a demon then?"

"We're partly made up from the imaginations of the physicals. Then we become a test for them. Each demon develops his or her own specialities."

"And yours are what?"

"Speaking the truth. Predicting the future. Commanding other demons."

"But you're connected to the House of Clementine?"

Oroban made a sound that Kaleem now recognised as a chuckle. He plucked at his leathery skin. "You'd noticed the colour?"

"So you're saying the Clementiners invented you? Do they – worship – you? The bad ones?"

Oroban chuckled again. "It's not that simple, my sweet Peace Child. They don't believe in me as such. They may have a sense of something lurking in the shadows but they don't really know I'm here. Their thoughts and actions have brought me into being. As I get stronger, so do their deeds. And as they become more competent at those things their deeds become more effective. It has gone so far this time that I am stuck in this wretched body. Yes, the Clementiners mainly invented me but the hearts of ordinary universals can also reach me. You remember the ones in brown? Yes, they come up every now and then. When everything is uncertain. When they think they're being deprived."

"So, we're talking about evil?"

"Good and evil. Two sides of the same coin. Okay, I'm one of the manifestations of evil. But the House of Clementine isn't all bad is it? You do know that it all started out with Obek Lampeter growing clementines to perfection? That isn't evil, is it?"

"No. But when the pursuit of excellence excludes and corrupts?"

Oroban nodded. "That's all part of universal nature. You universals; when you are good you are very, very good. But when you are bad you are horrid. It's all comparative isn't it? And snazziness is always so important isn't it?"

"If you could get out of this body would it make a difference?"

"Something would change. It would allow the lighter side a better chance."

"So how can you get out?"

"I can't. I can't even die. Some Clementiners are good enough that the body is decaying. But others are evil enough to keep me here."

"Are you in pain?"

Oroban nodded. "And so undignified." On cue, the demon farted loudly and purple liquid flowed out from him. The smell was overpowering and Kaleem began to retch.

"I am so sorry. I have lost all bowel and bladder control." Oroban's voice quivered as he spoke. Was the demon close to tears? He chuckled again though. "I could do with a dose of your or Clementine's snazziness."

Kaleem managed to recover. He chose to ignore the smell. "Do you even eat? Or drink? Do you need food?"

"I can enjoy a physical existence on the same terms as you

physicals when the body is fit and well. But the only food I consume now is the evil that the Clementiners and other universals send me. As you can see, it's enough to give me the runs. Oh, and that was a particularly good one. President Exton threatening to attack Lupino. Poor little isolated planet. Such a defensive little leader. So scared of the big boys that he shouts all sorts of abuse and makes empty threats. Exton should know better. You know better don't you? Oh yes, that fed into this putrid body all right."

"So, what can we do?"

"Can you kill me, Peace Child?"

"I don't know." It would be murder, wouldn't it? It would make him as bad as the evil Clementiners, if not worse, surely?

"Don't forget, I'm not real, not in your sense of the word, even though I'm manifesting really strongly. Once the body has gone, I am gone and there will be no trace of me at all."

"Well, can I kill you? How?"

"You could bash my head with a rock." He chuckled. "Oh yes, I created the torcal rocks. They couldn't form naturally here. But one of those would be superb. Go on. Pummel me to death." He nodded to the side of the cave room and there was a large rock. It looked like something that would belong to the cave but not in its present state with the lined walls and floor.

Oroban chuckled again. "As you'd expect, we can do clever tricks. But it's all illusion. You may certainly use the rock but what you think will have even more power."

"And what should I think?"

"Good thoughts. And in particular what is good about the House of Clementine. Go on." He nodded towards the rock again.

Kaleem picked it up.

"You can do this thing."

Kaleem hit at Oroban's head. The rock slipped right through it.

"Good thoughts, Peace Child. Good thoughts."

Kaleem struck him again. He thought of how well the Clementiners treated their workers. The demon gasped. With the next blow he thought about his knight's training. The demon slumped forward. Next the very high standards the Clementiners set themselves and the one he set for himself.

Oroban cried out in pain. But then he laughed. “Go on Peace Child. You can do it.”

Then Kaleem couldn’t hold back. He hit the demon over and over again. A blow for the perfection of the Zenoton non-monetary monetary system. Another for the excellent medical system on Zandra. One for the gentleness of the Z Zoners on Terrestra. One for the kindness of Saratina. One for the perfection of Rozia. One for the lovely nature of Petri, always so cheerful despite her pain. One for everyone’s sense of snazziness. One for a society without brown tunics. Now that he’d got started, he couldn’t stop.

Oroban weakened. He became unconscious. He began to fade. Kaleem gave him another blow. “That is for the goodness that is the basic nature of all universals.”

There was a loud bang. The unpleasant stench was replaced with a faint smell of orange blossom. There was no trace of Oroban. Everything seemed lighter.

Kaleem sat down, exhausted.

But then he heard a voice calling.

CHAPTER SIXTY-TWO

As far as Kaleem could tell the voice was coming from outside of this building.

"Help. Is there anyone there? Help. Can you find me?"

The voice sounded familiar. It was definitely that of a female though he couldn't quite remember whose.

"Keep on shouting. I'll find you."

"Who are you?"

Kaleem hesitated. Should he reveal who he was? "Don't you have a communicator that works?"

The woman laughed. "That stopped working a long time ago."

He was now half way along the corridor that led to the outside. The voice was getting fainter again. So, she must be in the basement of another building nearby.

"Can you find anything to make a noise with?"

There was no reply. Never mind. Perhaps he'd be able to find her anyway. He sensed that she was to the right of him.

Then the tapping started. It sounded like metal on other metal. Good. She'd found something.

The corridor now twisted and turned and gradually daylight mixed with the artificial light. The tapping was very faint but as soon as he was back at the surface and in the sunlight it became louder again. Yes, it was coming from the building next-door.

"I'm nearly there," Kaleem called.

He pushed open the door to the building and immediately found a simple staircase down to the cellar. Was this all a bit too easy? Was it some sort of trap?

"I think you're just above me now."

Now he recognised her voice. Dr Joahnsa Brooken. But it could still be a trap, couldn't it?

He crept down the stairs, looking and listening all the time. There were several doors in a hallway. One was partly open. He pushed it with his foot. It opened completely and artificial light flooded the room.

There she was. A very good holo or the real thing. Dr Joahnsa Brooken. But looking tired and a little dirty.

"I knew it," she cried. "I recognised your voice."

Kaleem nodded. "How long have you been here?"

"A long time. And it's a long story."

"Well, it'll take us quite a while to get back to civilisation. No doubt you'll be able to tell me on the way."

"I can't move just yet. I've been tied up a long time. And gagged."

Kaleem frowned. "There's no sign of any ropes or a gag now."

"No. That's the puzzling thing. The ropes and the gag just disappeared a short while ago. That's when I started shouting. The room went warmer and stopped smelling so putrid. Then every time I moved a little the light came on for a few seconds."

She started rubbing her legs and arms vigorously.

"Tell me then."

"It was actually about a week after you came to see me with Petri and Rozia." She paused and sighed. "That poor child. That's just another regrettable part of this whole business. And I just happened to be working on some ideas about how we might further help her. I was really getting somewhere. It was such a pity.

"Anyway, the door communicator sounded and two officials from the One World Community Steering Group presented themselves."

"You let them in?"

"Not straight away, no."

"What made you think they were genuine?"

"They passed all the identification tests. The dataserve didn't pick up any discrepancies. They checked out with the One World Site."

Kaleem nodded. "And what did they want?"

She bit her lip. "What a fool I was. But they were convincing. They told me they wanted me to work on some top-secret disease control with a specialised community."

"The Daschians?"

"Yes. The Daschians."

"Why them?"

"Because they live a simpler life. Lived, I should say. Disease spread more quickly but immunity also increased more easily."

"And is that what you've been doing?"

Joahnsa rolled her eyes. "Not exactly."

"When did you realise that it was a con?"

"It took a long time, actually. When I first got here, everything seemed normal. They gave me an apartment that suited my status. You know, comfortable, bordering on luxurious. If anything, it was slightly nicer than my normal one. Nice view of the woodlands from the window. State of the art dataserve. Better finishes on the furnishings."

"What about the journey?"

"Again totally luxurious." She rubbed her eyes. "But looking back there was a bit of a clue there, I suppose. I was kept totally isolated. I wasn't allowed to talk to other passengers. In fact I'm not sure there were other passengers."

A whole supercraft just for her? That didn't seem believable. "Was that uncomfortable, being so alone?"

She laughed. "They gave me plenty of work to do. Besides, I don't keep a lot of company normally. I'm usually too absorbed in my work."

"What was it like, then, working with the Daschians?"

"Fine. Absolutely fine. They're just normal people, you know. They've just always been a bit isolated."

This sounded familiar. "Just normal people". That was what he found over and over again. He'd met plenty of isolated communities. He'd even belonged to one himself once. "So, what were the particular outcomes of the isolation for them?"

"A low level of attachments so the community was gradually dying out. Fear of letting outsiders in because they might bring disease."

Oh even more familiar. But they didn't seem to suffer from the poverty he'd seen in Terrestra's former Z Zone. "But there were no problems with supplies of food or energy?"

Joahnsa shook her head. "No. All supplies were delivered by

droid. Droids maintained all life support systems as well. The Daschians had no need to contact other universals."

"So tell me more about the work that you did."

Joahnsa shook her head. "It seemed perfectly legitimate. I did find a defect in them. Every single member of the Daschian community I tested was suffering from an as yet not recognised disease that stopped their immune system functioning properly. It may be that at some point in the past they knew this but have since forgotten. That may have been why they isolated themselves."

"So it all sounds like legitimate research. So why did the One World Community want you to do it and why so secretly?"

"Because for a starter, they weren't the One World Community. They were really working for Exton."

"So, nothing to do with you helping a couple of Terrestrans?"

"I don't think they were even aware of that. No, they wanted to scare the Daschians."

"Why?"

"To help convince other Zenotons that Exton is right."

"I don't follow."

"The Daschians make only a little contribution to the Zenoton economic life. They did some outsourced work. If the Zenoton enabling system is going to be replaced by a monetarist one, they may not have survived anyway. In such a system they would not be able to get the medical aid they are almost certainly going to need in the future." Joahnsa covered her eyes. "It was my job to show them that."

"When did you realise there was something wrong?"

"It took a long time. It really did. It only started to become clear two days before the suicides."

"So what happened?"

"All three executives seemed on edge and then one started threatening me. Told me I'd better get on with reaching a conclusion to my findings."

"He was hostile?"

"Yes, he said they would have to replace me and that if they did I'd have to be held in isolation indefinitely – perhaps forever. I knew too much."

"How did you react?"

"I told them I could only go so fast. But they then said I had to present what I had found to the Daschians straight away."

"That must have been tough."

"It was. They looked devastated. When I'd finished speaking there was silence. They all left the meeting room without saying a word. And the supposed One World Executives were all but dancing for joy."

"So that's what led to the suicides?"

"It seemed so at first. I was pretty much left to my own devices after that meeting. Now that it was clear that the Executives were bogus I didn't feel inclined to work for them anymore. They didn't come near me, though. So I just went for a walk, looking for some of the people I'd got to know. I couldn't find anybody anywhere. But then I heard a vague noise from next-door – I think where you've just been. There is a huge secret meeting place down there. Did you know?"

"No. I only saw a disused, slightly decrepit building."

"How long have I been here exactly?"

"How long do you think?"

"A few days?"

Kaleem shook his head. There was a lot that didn't make sense about this. Obviously Joahnsa was a bit stiff from having been tied up but otherwise she seemed fine. She ought to be dehydrated by now. "Maybe a little bit longer. So, what happened at the meeting?"

She shook her head. "It was terrible. They were planning the mass suicide. They had it all really under control. They'd stock-piled the right sort of lethal wands. Women and children first, whilst they were heavily sedated, and then the men." She sighed. "I tried to stop them. I really did. I told them we could find a way of making them healthier. But they told me it wasn't just about this disease. They didn't want to live in this new form of society."

"So, when were you tied up?"

"Shortly after the suicides started. In some way it was a relief; I didn't have to watch it. It was eerily quiet, though. They were so calm about it all. And it was then that I found out the truth about the people who had brought me here. They admitted that they were working for Exton. They said that my work here was now done and that I wasn't needed any more. And then they went away."

"Scary. But it doesn't explain why the bands and the gag just disappeared."

"No, it doesn't. But I can still feel the effects of them." She rubbed her wrist.

"What were the executives were like?"

Joahnsa shrugged. "They looked like quite normal Zenotons. Their ordinariness completely fooled me. There was one thing, though. One of them had a small tattoo on his arm. A picture of a small orange hanging from a branch. Another had a badge with the same picture on his sleeve. These were so tiny I didn't notice them at first."

"Did the third have anything similar?"

She shook her head. "But he did often wear that orange colour that was in the tattoo and badge. Does that mean anything?"

"Have you heard of the House of Clementine?"

"No. Is that what all of that orange is to do with?"

"Most likely."

"So what is it?"

Kaleem frowned. "Apparently it causes people to commit suicide en mass."

"How do they do it?"

He sighed. "It's a long story and I can't be certain. But it's a very perfectionist organisation. It's also quite controlling and will get rid of anybody that gets in its way."

"Was I getting in its way, then?"

"They probably saw it that way." He hesitated to mention the beast. That would sound so improbable to someone as scientific as Joahnsa, though there was still the mystery of the disappearing restraints.

"So, what next?"

"Well we need to get out of here for a start. There have been massive floods so that is going to be a challenge. But I have a feeling that some good people will be on to that already. It's all beginning to turn around."

"Oh? How do you know?"

Kaleem grinned. "Peace Child instinct, I guess."

"I could do with some of that. Seriously though, how can I follow this?"

"You've done some really valuable work here. It will have another application, surely? It's terrible about the suicides but they weren't your fault."

Joahnsa grunted. "Difficult not to think that I caused them."

"Well you must stop that. And how about in the meantime you do more work on Petri's case? Perhaps we can persuade her and Rozia to come back to Zandra." If only.

Joahnsa stood up and brushed herself down. "Okay then. Let's go. I'll follow you."

Kaleem heard footsteps in the corridor.

"Kaleem are you there?" someone called. "Is everything all right?"

CHAPTER SIXTY-THREE

Kaleem and Joahnsa made their way outside. All traces of the horrible smell had disappeared. The air was now sweet and fresh. There were four people waiting for him: Jadee and three men he only vaguely recognised. Kaleem quickly introduced Joahnsa to Jadee and filled Jadee in with what had happened. The three men introduced themselves.

"We don't know exactly who these so-called One World Community executives were, except that they were undoubtedly from the House of Clementine," Kaleem explained.

One of the men stepped forward. "Did you find anything of this beast?"

Kaleem shook his head. "No. The place was empty. There were signs that somebody or something had been living there but it's not been there for a good deal of time now, I should think. There was some excrement but it doesn't smell anymore. It seems to have been some sort of animal. I'm not sure how intelligent it was. It was well housed so maybe somebody's been looking after it. Come and look for yourselves."

Jadee shook her head. "We need to get on if we're to get to the bottom of all of this."

Kaleem looked at the three men and then at Jadee. "Doesn't it feel as if something has changed?"

Jadee shrugged. "What do you mean?"

"Doesn't it all seem lighter?"

"I think I know what you mean, but it doesn't really make sense." Jadee was frowning and biting her lip.

"So what can we do?" asked one of the men.

"Maybe we should go in after all then and see if there are any clues as to who or what has been living there," said Jadee.

Should he confess what he knew? Would they believe him? Change was happening, he was sure. But when would it show up?

"All right. Let's do it." Kaleem indicated that they should follow him. He hoped that all trace of the beast really had gone.

They all started making their way towards the entrance.

One of the men's communicator's buzzed just as he was about to enter the cave. He pressed the send button and stopped walking as he watched what was happening on the small screen. "Wait," he muttered. "You've got to see this. Turn on your news channels."

They all did as he asked. Kaleem could not believe what he was seeing. Pangwit Exton was speaking. "There is actually no need for a president on Zenoto. Yes, perhaps there needs to be some sort of administrator. A chairperson, even, as they used to be called. But not one that has a casting vote. Just someone to keep order and make sure constitutional rules are followed."

"So how will the planet be governed?" asked the Zenoton reporter.

"By a group of Zenotons who will sit around a round table, like Terrestra's King Arthur and his knights. They will be the democratically elected representatives of the people who will work with the best interests of the people always in mind."

"And what of yourself, sir?"

"Naturally I shall step down. I hope, though, that I may be elected as an executive."

"And will you still push to change the monetary system?"

"No. It's not in the Zenotons' best interests. I was wrong. I was wrong about the barrier too. I have ordered it to be taken down." Exton nodded and walked back into the building behind him.

"This is an extraordinary turn of events," said the reporter. "And just as extraordinary is what is happening on the streets."

The camera panned out to show Zenotons shaking hands, hugging and patting backs.

Kaleem quickly found a Zandrian channel. The same was happening there. The brown tunics were mixing freely with the ordinary people. A Zandrian reporter's face appeared. "All of this on top of the latest poll that shows that over 97% of Zandrians wish after all to remain in the One World Community. Another referendum will be held tomorrow."

And Terrestra? It had remained quiet and mysterious during all of this upheaval. What was going on there? What was happening to Rozia and Petri?

His communicator buzzed. Then they were there. Rozia and Petri waving to him. They both seemed to glow. "It's great, isn't it?" said Rozia.

"Yes, but what's been happening on Terrestra?"

"Not a lot. Everything's been really quiet. They shut down a bit. They started to cut themselves off again, like when we were younger."

"You look well, Petri."

She giggled and waved.

Rozia smiled. "She's been spoilt by the New-Zoners. We've still been using the Zandrian wands but we've been eating a lot of the fresh vegetables grown here. It's done us both good."

"Good." Kaleem couldn't work out what to say next. He longed to know whether she would come back to Zandra. Could they take their relationship forward again? Or had that just been a one off?

In the end they both spoke at once. Petri laughed. "Honestly, you two. Just get on with it."

Kaleem nodded. "You go first."

"Well, she's doing really well. But we've been invited back to Zandra. They're going to work on a permanent cure. So, we're setting off as soon as we can get places on a supercraft. Will you be coming back soon?"

"I hope so. I really hope so."

Joahnsa grinned. "I hope I'll be able to help too."

He was interrupted by Jadee. "Well, there doesn't seem to be anything else here to do. Let's get back to civilisation."

CHAPTER SIXTY-FOUR

Rozia's Ulog

Hi everyone,

Just a quick update. I'm sorry it's been so long. I'm not sure where the time went.

We quickly got used to life back on Terrestra. It was almost as if we've never been away. Except of course Terrestra had moved on too and we've been living somewhere quite different. We took one of the refurbished former Z Zone underground apartments. They're almost unrecognisable and really luxurious now. Each has its own piece of cultivated land above ground level and we've actually managed to grow some fruit and vegetables. Being underground was better for Petri and we could go up on to the surface to deal with the garden at night. Some people thought we were a bit strange until we explained about Petri's illness.

"So why didn't you stay on Zandra?" they asked.

They couldn't grasp how difficult it had become there for outsiders like us. Surprisingly, Terrestrans have become really tolerant. Who'd have thought it? They accepted us anyway.

I managed to get work as a research assistant and rarely had to go to meets. I've been looking into super-crop growing. It's all so easy on Terrestra. Since the poison cloud went the planet has become really fertile again.

Petri enjoyed her schooling. She even managed to get to the meets and got to know the other kids. The medication isn't too bad here. They were able to give her enough to allow her a few hours in daylight without getting too uncomfortable.

At first we communicated with Kaleem quite a bit. I

always made sure he could see I was wearing the brooch. In fact I never take it off – even though it's quite annoying when Petri keeps asking when we're going to get attached. It got really awkward though. He could never say much about what he's doing. I told him a little bit about my work and how Petri's doing. I've explained about the changes on Terrestra. Then there didn't seem anything more to talk about.

I was almost afraid of saying too much. I wanted to tell him how much I missed him. I'd have come back to Zandra in a heartbeat if he'd asked me. I just didn't dare say it, though. I had no idea what he was thinking. He looked so sad all the time and he was quite quiet. Can the Peace Child ever have a permanent attachment?

It became really worrying when he was tried and then confined on Zenoto. I'm sure they were listening in to all of our conversations. Perhaps that was why he didn't say much. I suppose also as he couldn't get out often he hadn't really got a lot to talk about.

He did tell me about some of the things that were going on on Zenoto. It was changing. The Zenotons were trusting each other less. It used to be almost like paradise. Now they were ready to stab each other in the back. It was no longer the Zenoto we all knew and respected. It had become like any other planet. Worse than many, in fact.

Then of course he had to go and disappear. Typical Peace Child trick. I tried to tell myself this was a good reason why I should give up all thoughts of ever being with him again. I should try and make my life on Terrestra really work.

Petri, of course, saw through me.

"You should track him down. Find out where he's got to. Let him know what you're thinking."

I always have to do what Petri says. She is so wise.

I got in touch with Nazaret and Marijam. They hadn't

heard anything either and Marijam was clearly as worried as I was. Nazaret was more pragmatic, though. "Peace Child stuff again. You know what it's like. Anyway, no news is good news. We would have heard if anything bad had happened."

Then we did hear. He had been found. He was well. He had reconciled two opposing parties again. The threat was gone.

"You should get in touch," said Nazaret. "He'll be pleased. But he'll be shy about making the first move."

"Go on then. Do it," said Petri as soon as we finished the communication.

Well it took me a couple of days to get round to it.

He seemed shy at first, it was true. But as soon as I saw him I knew I wanted to be with him again. I think he wanted that too though he only told me in a roundabout way. It was all sorted, he said. Zenoto and Zandra would go back to the way they had been. The discontent was over. Trust would soon come back. "It would be safe again here for you and Petri," he'd said. "Will you come back?"

"I'll think about it," I said.

"There's nothing to think about," said Petri after Kaleem had disappeared from the screen. She was right, there wasn't.

Two days later I contacted him again and told him we would be back on Zandra as soon as possible.

We had to wait weeks before we could get a place on a supercraft, even with Kaleem paying. But we're off tomorrow. We're a little scared after what happened on the way here and I'm still a bit apprehensive about being with Kaleem again but it seems like the right thing to do. Yes, I'm sure it is.

My next post will be from Zandra!

CHAPTER SIXTY-FIVE

Kaleem bit his nails as he waited at the supercraft docking station. It was busy today. Trade was working well within the One World Community now. Zenotons had become frequent visitors as they came to teach the Zandrians the mechanics of the non-monetary trade system. Zandrians were eager to learn. It had taken Rozia and Petri a while to secure their place on a supercraft. Terrestrans were finding a new lust for interplanetary travel.

At least they'd been in touch. Petri was excited about coming back. And every time Kaleem had spoken to Rozia she had been wearing her brooch. A good sign perhaps. But what would it be like when they got there? Would they be awkward with each other?

A Zenoton craft had docked just a few minutes before and its passengers were making their way into the waiting area. They had that confused look that all supercraft travellers had on arrival: they were bemused by the slight change in gravitational pull and the difference in air make up. Plus these seemed not to be seasoned travellers.

An attached couple fumbled clumsily. Oh come on. Why couldn't they get this hall cleared faster?

They wouldn't let Rozia's supercraft disembark until these people were out of the building. Their supercraft had left the stand and he could see Rozia's hovering a little way away.

As the Zenotons made their way to the exit, the supercraft from Terrestra glided nearer. They always looked like huge whales as they moved gently into place. This one was moving a little too slowly, though, for his liking. It took several minutes that seemed like hours for it to finish docking, for the doors to open and the passengers to start making their way along the corridors. He watched the video hoping that they would appear any moment. What seemed like thousands of Terrestrans and a few Zandrians filed by. No sign of them. Had they changed their minds?

Of course not. He shouldn't be so silly. They'd spoken to him from the supercraft only two days ago. They'd been excited about getting here then. But what if they'd now decided to stay on the craft and return to Terrestra on her?

He bit his lip anxiously as the passengers carried on filing past.

Still no sign of them but then he spotted somebody he did know. It was so clear now why they had cast Karlo Dunston as him in the film. They did look quite alike. Especially today.

Karlo made his way over to Kaleem. He offered him a Terrestran handshake. "Howdy, alter-ego." He nodded. "Love the eye shadow."

Oh goodness. He'd almost forgotten about that. What would Rozia and Petri make of it? But they'd seen it and not commented. How strange.

Karlo rubbed Kaleem's shoulder. "I was thinking of doing something similar. Being a bit snazzier. Seeing you like this gives me permission somehow."

"So, what took you to Terrestra?"

"Family matters. Plus I fancied the trip."

"Family matters?" Kaleem had always thought he was the only Terrestran / Zandrian hybrid.

Karlo laughed. "Bro, your father wasn't the only one to sow a few wild oats."

He wasn't? "So were you…?"

"No, no. I was developed in a tube. But note my name begins with 'K'!" He tapped the side of his nose. "Terrestra wasn't as isolated as it thought it was. There were more visitors than you'd imagine."

What? Was this Hidden Information?

Then he saw them.

They walked slowly past the camera. Petri was skipping ahead and then running back to Rozia. Petri waved up at the camera. Of course she'd figured out that he would be watching them arrive. In just a few minutes they would be with him.

"You must excuse me," he murmured to Karlo. "I can see my visitors."

Karlo nodded. "Catch up some time then?"

They shook hands again and Kaleem returned to looking at the screens.

Then there they were, at the barrier. Petri rushed forward and flung her arms round him.

"You're looking good," Kaleem whispered. He looked over her head towards Rozia who was clearly holding back. She was smiling though and then she started walking slowly towards him.

Petri was now dancing around him. "We've come back for ever, you know. Rozia says if you'll have us. You will have us, won't you?"

"Of course I will. You know that, surely."

Rozia was almost there. He could see that she was wearing the brooch. She was grinning now.

"Welcome home," he said, when she was finally standing right next to him.

She nodded and pulled him into an embrace.

ABOUT THE AUTHOR

Gill James writes novels for middle grade and young adults and short fiction for everyone. As well as this science fiction series for young adults she is working on a cycle of novels set mainly in Nazi Germany, as well as occasional short stories and flash fiction series.

She is published by Chapeltown Books, Tabby Cat Press, The Red Telephone and Butterfly.

Her stories are published on *Litro, CaféLit, Alfie Dog, Ether Books* and in several anthologies.

Reviews by Gill can be found in Armadillo Magazine, IBBY, Troubador and on her own web site.

She teaches creative wring in various settings and this has included in higher education.

Member of the Society of Authors, the Society of Children's Book Writers and Illustrators and the National Society of Writers in Education, Gill has an MA in Writing for Children and PhD in Creative and Critical Writing, thesis title: *Peace Child, Towards a Global Definition of the Young Adult Novel.*

She edits for Bridge House Publishing, CaféLit, Chapeltown Books and The Red Telephone.

She also works as a volunteer reporter for the e-zine *Talking About My Generation* which was granted the Queen's Award for Voluntary Service in June 2022.

Before becoming a writer and an academic she taught modern languages for 23 years in various schools and has continued to make school visits as a writer of fiction for children and young adults.

PLEASE LEAVE A REVIEW

Reviews are so important to writers. Please take the time to review this book. A couple of lines is fine.

Reviews help the book to become more visible to buyers. Retailers will promote books with multiple reviews.

This in turn helps us to sell more books… And then we can afford to publish more books like this one.

Leaving a review is very easy.

Go to https://amzn.to/487PcWM, scroll down the left-hand side of the Amazon page and click on the "Write a customer review" button.

OTHER NOVELS BY THE RED TELEPHONE

The Prophecy

by Gill James

The Prophecy is the first part of the *Peace Child* series.

Kaleem Malkendy is different – and, on Terrestra, different is no way to be.

Everything about Kaleem marks him out from the rest: the blond hair and dark skin, the humble cave where he lives and the fact that he doesn't know his father. He's used to unwelcome attention, but even so, he'd feel better if some strange old man didn't keep following him around.

Then the man introduces himself and begins to explain the Babel Prophecy – and everything in Kaleem's life changes forever.

"It's thought-provoking and it's unique. I enjoyed it wholeheartedly, and will be looking forward to visiting Gill James' vision of the future again in the second Peace Child novel. Those who enjoy stories set in the future should definitely consider giving this out-of-the-ordinary tale a look." *(Amazon)*

Order from Amazon:

Paperback: ISBN 978-0-955791-08-6
eBook: ISBN 978-1-907335-12-9

Babel

by Gill James

Babel is the second part of the *Peace Child* series.

Kaleem has found his father and soon finds the love of his life, Rozia Laurence, but he is still not comfortable with his role as Peace Child. He also has to face some of the less palatable truths about his home planet: it is blighted by the existence of the Z Zone, a place where poorer people live outside of society, and by switch-off, compulsory euthanasia for a healthy but aging population, including his mentor, Razjosh.

The Babel Tower still haunts him, but it begins to make sense as he uncovers more of the truth about his past and how it is connected with the problems in the Z Zone.

Kaleem knows he can and must make a difference, but at what personal cost?

Order from Amazon:

Paperback: ISBN 978-1-907335-10-5
eBook: ISBN 978-1-907335-13-6

The Tower

by Gill James

The Tower is the third part of the *Peace Child* series.

Kaleem has given up the love of his life in order to protect her. He now lives and works on Zandra.

A sudden landquake, not known on the planet for many years, destroys many of the forests his father has planted to bring life back to the planet. The new relationship Kaleem has helped to establish between the Terrestrans and the Zandrians is also under threat.

A third party gets involved and Kaleem has to use all of his diplomatic skills to keep everything on track. Mistakes cost him dearly and he looks set to lose Rozia for a second time.

The Babel Tower mystery, others mysteries and sadness plague him. Can he find a way through to fulfil his role as the Peace Child?

Order from Amazon:

Paperback: ISBN 978-1-907335-29-7
eBook: ISBN 978-1-907335-30-3

Milton Keynes UK
Ingram Content Group UK Ltd.
UKHW020743190424
441445UK00013B/537

9 781914 199486